Raves for the Previous Valdemar Anthologies:

"Fans of Lackey's epic Valdemar series will devour this superb anthology. Of the thirteen stories included, there is no weak link—an attribute exceedingly rare in collections of this sort. Highly recommended."

—The Barnes and Noble Review

"This high-quality anthology mixes pieces by experienced authors and enthusiastic fans of editor Lackey's Valdemar. Valdemar fandom, especially, will revel in this sterling example of what such a mixture of fans' and pros' work can be. Engrossing even for newcomers to Valdemar." —*Booklist*

"Josepha Sherman, Tanya Huff, Mickey Zucker Reichert, and Michelle West have quite good stories, and there's another by Lackey herself. Familiarity with the series helps but is not a prerequisite to enjoying this book." —*Science Fiction Chronicle*

"Each tale adheres to the Lackey laws of the realm yet provides each author's personal stamp on the story. Well written and fun, Valdemarites will especially appreciate the magic of this book." —*The Midwest Book Review*

"The sixth collection set in Lackey's world of Valdemar presents stories of Heralds and their telepathic horse-like Companions and of Bards and Healers, and provides glimpses of the many other aspects of a setting that has a large and avid readership. The fiften original tales in this volume will appeal to series fans."

—*Library Journal*

Under the Vale

TITLES BY MERCEDES LACKEY
available from DAW Books:

THE NOVELS OF VALDEMAR:

THE HERALDS OF VALDEMAR
ARROWS OF THE QUEEN
ARROW'S FLIGHT
ARROW'S FALL

THE LAST HERALD-MAGE
MAGIC'S PAWN
MAGIC'S PROMISE
MAGIC'S PRICE

THE MAGE WINDS
WINDS OF FATE
WINDS OF CHANGE
WINDS OF FURY

THE MAGE STORMS
STORM WARNING
STORM RISING
STORM BREAKING

VOWS AND HONOR
THE OATHBOUND
OATHBREAKERS
OATHBLOOD

THE COLLEGIUM CHRONICLES
FOUNDATION
INTRIGUES
CHANGES
REDOUBT
BASTION

THE HERALD SPY
CLOSER TO HOME*

BY THE SWORD
BRIGHTLY BURNING
TAKE A THIEF

EXILE'S HONOR
EXILE'S VALOR

VALDEMAR ANTHOLOGIES
SWORD OF ICE
SUN IN GLORY
CROSSROADS
MOVING TARGETS
CHANGING THE WORLD
FINDING THE WAY
UNDER THE VALE

Written with **LARRY DIXON:**

THE MAGE WARS
THE BLACK GRYPHON
THE WHITE GRYPHON
THE SILVER GRYPHON

DARIAN'S TALE
OWLFLIGHT
OWLSIGHT
OWLKNIGHT

OTHER NOVELS:

GWENHWYFAR
THE BLACK SWAN

THE DRAGON JOUSTERS
JOUST
ALTA
SANCTUARY
AERIE

THE ELEMENTAL MASTERS
THE SERPENT'S SHADOW
THE GATES OF SLEEP
PHOENIX AND ASHES
THE WIZARD OF LONDON
RESERVED FOR THE CAT
UNNATURAL ISSUE
HOME FROM THE SEA
STEADFAST
BLOOD RED
Anthologies:
ELEMENTAL MAGIC
ELEMENTARY

*Coming soon from DAW Books
And don't miss THE VALDEMAR COMPANION
edited by John Helfers and Denise Little

Under the Vale

And Other Tales of Valdemar

Edited by
Mercedes Lackey

DAW BOOKS, INC.
DONALD A. WOLLHEIM, FOUNDER
375 Hudson Street, New York, NY 10014
ELIZABETH R. WOLLHEIM
SHEILA E. GILBERT
PUBLISHERS
http://www.dawbooks.com

Cover art by Jody Lee.

DAW Book Collectors No. 1568.

DAW Books are distributed by Penguin Group (USA).

First Printing, December 2011
5 6 7 8 9

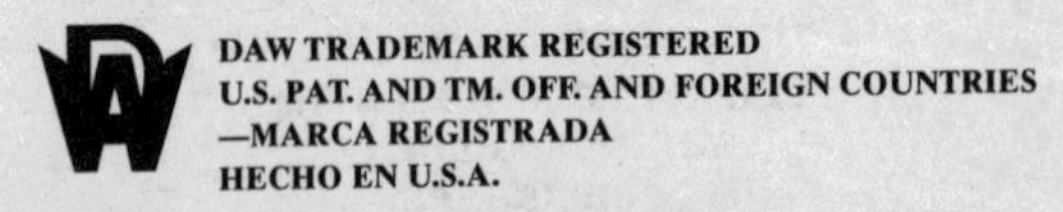

PRINTED IN THE U.S.A

Acknowledgments

Contents

The Simple Gifts

Mercedes Lackey

The last thing I expected when I woke up that morning was to find myself running for my life with my clothing in one hand and the other hand holding a sheet rather insecurely about my impressive torso.

Wait, let me back that up a bit.

First, please understand that I have no illusions about myself. I know what my talents are: charm, rugged good looks, wit, a great voice, and an instinct for how to make a lady very happy. I know what my flaws are: the desire to do as little actual *work* as possible, coupled with a taste for all the finer things in life, and a tendency to stretch the truth paper-thin. These two things make me the ideal candidate for no actual *job,* but they make me very good at being company for females (face it ladies, you really do *not* want to know that your butt looks like the rear end of a brood mare in "this dress").

Yes. Alas, I am a man-whore.

Now that we have the technicalities out of the way, let me add that I specialize in ladies of a certain . . . age. Those who (so they tell me, and so I will fervently believe as long as I am with them) are underappreciated by the husbands. Because, oh yes, I *only* specialize in married ladies. That way if anything happens, they have a husband to deal with the consequences. And most of them actually are underappreciated. In the class I deal with exclusively, those husbands will have gone out and gotten themselves one or more pretty, young mistresses, so why, I ask you, is the sauce for the gander not just as appropriate for the goose?

I had somewhat worn out my welcome in the western part of Hardorn, so I had crossed into the eastern part of Valdemar, a country with which I was just marginally familiar. Hardorn was rather more to my liking: lots of rich merchant wives, lots of rich minor nobility, lots of husbands who were always somewhere else. However, I'd temporarily run out of the former, and since I was ill-equipped to fend for myself for very long, I took the very *nice* farewell present from my last "friend" and got a ride with her cousin's trade caravan west. Her cousin was a widow, and I made an exception to my rule of wives only, and we passed the time pleasantly enough in her plush little wagon.

They left me in a little town called Winefold, which produced, strangely enough, not wine but a pungent little berry that they liked to use in Hardorn to flavor alcohol. Geniver, it was called, and collecting the harvested and dried berries there was the end of the road for the caravan. So I bid the immensely grateful (have I mentioned that ladies of a certain age are always enthusiastically grateful?) widow a fond and somewhat teary farewell, got the best room in the inn (for now, I didn't intend to be paying for it long) and set about looking over my prospects.

They seemed rosy. A lady of the correct age and more than correct income, spouse away and (supposedly) unappreciative, and charms that, while a bit on the weathered side, were still, well, charming. And besides, candlelight is always flattering. Like me. The campaign was easy enough, pity on the poor stranger with only a few halting phrases of Valdemaran in the marketplace, a meal or two together at the inn, a meal or two together at her manse, a brief overnight trial of my paces, certain key phrases exchanged and understood, and there you go. I was quite satisfied with the results of the evening and was looking forward to leaving my room at the inn and setting up in a guest room as a "cousin"—in fact, I was mulling over just those arrangements while idly tracing circles on the bare shoulder next to mine, when my musings were rudely interrupted by five men bursting into the bedroom with drawn swords and daggers. One of them was richly attired, also of a certain age (but of a dismayingly athletic build) with the outraged expression on his face that told me he was either a husband or a brother.

Now, this sort of thing happens in bardic songs all the time; the sort with seven hundred verses to them. There're about two hundred to get to the bedroom, and then comes the part where the outraged husband says, "Get up, it will never be said I slew a sleeping man," allows the subject of the song to get up (and presumably get dressed, though that never seems to be mentioned no matter how many verses there are), arm himself, and even strike the first blow—presumably so the spouse can claim self-defense. This usually takes about another hundred verses. The rest of the song describes how the subject is cut down, mangled, dismembered, eviscerated, hung up for all to see, has various bits pecked out by crows while women lament, and finally is buried beneath a willow, which weeps for him eternally.

I was not going to be around for those several hundred verses, thank you. Especially not the killing and dismembering part.

Out of careful habit and no few close calls, I keep all my clothing right at hand in an easy-to carry bundle when I go to bed with a lady. So as the outraged gentleman opened his mouth, I was already halfway out the window, clothing in one hand, sheet held around me as best I could.

The advantage of going out a window is that your pursuers, if there are more than one, always manage to get themselves jammed up trying to follow you. By the time they sort themselves out, you've got a lead on them.

Small problem being in a little town, however: They were going to know where to find me, or rather, my belongings. Which meant I had to get there before they did. Fortunately it was early enough (good lord, not even *dawn,* what kind of uncivilized barbarians were these?) that I didn't attract too much attention sprinting through the streets in nothing but a sheet. Bad idea going in through the door, but the inn building was a single, sprawling story, all at ground level. I had left my shutters unlatched but closed—I had all my money with me, and in a town this small, stealing my clothing and other gear would be pretty foolhardy, since it would be immediately recognizable. I'd nipped in, grabbed my gear, pulled on my pants and boots, and nipped out again by the time they came roaring up to the door, which the innkeeper's servant was only just opening for the day.

I saw all this from my vantage point hiding in the thatch of a roof across the street.

And that was where I stayed, figuring I would wait until the fuss died down, then get a ride out with a farmer or something.

But the fuss didn't die down. This fellow was persistent! First he made the innkeeper turn out my room to prove I wasn't in it. Then he made the innkeeper turn out all the vacant rooms to prove I wasn't hiding in them. *Then* he made the innkeeper turn out all the other guests to prove I wasn't with one of them! Then he ransacked the stable. Then he and his four bully boys began searching the rest of the town.

Fortunately none of them thought to look up in the

thatch of roofs. I suppose they figured that someone of my sort wouldn't know how to climb. Silly fellows. Windows aren't always on the ground floor.

However, this left me with a real problem. By the time they were done, the entire town would know about me, and I hadn't been here long enough to round up any allies. Which meant not only could I not find a real place to hide out, but it was going to be hard to find a way out of town.

Which was when I saw it: the army-supply wagon train.

We'd passed this thing on our way in, and my hostess had told me what it was, because I honestly had never seen anything like it in my life. The main roads here in Valdemar all had this groove running down the middle, which I had assumed (wrongly) was some sort of gutter. In fact, it was a slot for a guiding wheel for a peculiar sort of thing that she called a "wagon train"—as in, "trailing along behind." These people didn't have a lot of bandits (if any!) on their main roads, so they didn't need a lot of guards on the wagons that carried common supplies. Which meant they really only needed people to drive and care for the dray animals. And if they could hitch a lot of wagons together, they didn't need as many of them. The problem with that was that pulling a lot of wagons was difficult; they tended to stray off the road. But *not* if you had a guide-wheel in the center of each that dropped down into that groove down the middle . . .

Ingenious, really.

So there it was, pulling through town. Twenty mules at the front, a couple of drivers, fifteen wagons, each carrying two tons. The last wagon in the string carried the supplies for the men and the mules and had two spare mules tied to the back. They wouldn't stop in town; they'd stop once at midday to water the animals and again at night. Because they wouldn't stop in town, and because they belonged to the army (called the "Guard" here), no one would bother searching these wagons. Ideal!

I watched for my opportunity, and as soon as the street was clear, I was down off that roof and in under the canvas flap at the rear of one of the middle wagons. A quick survey of the tightly packed interior showed me the only way to get to the front of the wagon was over the top of the crates. I was hoping that since all the wagons looked alike (that's an army for you), there would be a space at the front with a driver's area that you couldn't actually pack goods into.

I was right—though let me tell you, it was a tight squeeze to get in there under the canvas roof, and I had to be careful and inch my way along so no one would notice a moving bulge. There was a driver's bench all right, with the canvas stretched down tight across the front of the wagon, giving me just enough room to settle. No one would look up here; if anyone did inspect this thing, they'd look at the back at most. I made myself comfortable with my pack and my stolen sheet, waited until we were well clear of town, just in case, and then resumed my interrupted sleep.

I woke again when they stopped the mules at noon for watering. When the voices were distant, I took a quick look at the crates that surrounded me and could hardly believe my luck when I saw they were all labeled "field rations." At least I wasn't going to starve! I spent the rest of the afternoon slowly and carefully prying the side off one of the crates. Sure enough, it was packed full of bars of something covered in what felt like wax. When I got a bar out, I saw that it actually *was* wax, the sort some cheeses are coated in. It peeled right off with the help of my knife, and the bar proved to be dried fruit and meat pounded together, just about as hard as ironwood. I spent the rest of the afternoon whittling slivers off and eating them. I'd had worse. I got thirsty; I made up for it by sucking on a few peppermints that I keep to make sure I have pleasant breath. I was lucky that it didn't get too hot, and I could manage to hold off thirst for a while, but I was looking forward to getting out and finally getting a drink, let me tell you. I'd have to find something to hold water, though, because the only time I'd be able to get any would be late at night when the drovers slept.

Maybe I could find something in the supply wagon.

It took a lot of patience to just sit there, getting thirstier and thirstier, and it was worse when we finally stopped for the night. But finally the voices at the fire whose glow I could see through the canvas side of the tent ebbed into silence. I got out, and to make a long story short, I did find a bucket I didn't think anyone would miss, since it was buried in the back of the supply wagon. That was when I realized that all they did was unhitch the teams and picket them; they left the wagons in the road all night. I suppose it didn't matter; it wasn't as if anyone was going to run into them in the dark.

Days went by that way, which I whiled away by getting into the wagon one-off from the front and listening to the drovers talk. I was going to need a lot of practice in understanding Valdemaran, of which I had barely a grasp. I did get better over time, and I was anticipating getting out in a larger town—until I managed to puzzle out from something that they were saying that they were about to head deep into the wilderness.

Wilderness was *not* where I wanted to go. Oh, no. I don't do well in wilderness. I'm not a wilderness sort of fellow. That was when I figured it was time for me to steal whatever I was going to need for (what I thought would be) a day or two until I found a farm and a way on to civilization. So once the drovers settled down for the night and snores told me that a tempest wouldn't wake them, I did just that. I loaded my pack with those ration bars, grabbed a wineskin off the back of the supply wagon, plus a tinderbox, and followed the road until it was dawn. Then I got off the road and hid for a while, just in case they actually realized something was missing and backtracked. By midmorning, though, I figured I was safe and got back onto the road.

I didn't want to stay on it for too long, though, because it would only take me farther into trouble. So the first time I saw another road—this one plain dirt, with some grass growing on it, and no groove—I took it. Roads always go somewhere, right? I figured this one would lead me to a farm or, better still, a village.

Only . . . it didn't.

By midafternoon, I knew I was going to have to sleep outdoors, and I knew enough to know I needed to find some water too. So I did . . . and I did . . . I've mentioned I'm not a wilderness sort of fellow, right? It was the worst night of my life. I mean, *the* worst. I tried making a sort of bed out of leaves, only the leaves were home to some sort of ants, and they got into my clothing and bit the *hell* out of me. So I gave up and tried to sleep on bare dirt, but that sucked all the heat out of my body, and I spent most of the night shivering. The fire I made smoked, and I kept hearing things out in the woods that sounded big. Really big. Bears? Wolves? Whatever it was kept prowling around and around my campsite. And I did tell you I'm not a fighting sort of fellow, right?

I finally did get to sleep around about dawn. I'm not sure what exactly woke me up, but when I did wake up, all at once, I could hardly believe my luck. Because standing right in front of me, on the other side of my fire, was a fantastic-looking white horse.

Now *there* was my way out of here! Provided I could catch it. I knew how to ride bareback; it's one of those things that's useful to know in case your lady wants to get a romantic ride along a beach or a river and maybe swim with the horses. You don't want a saddle on them if you do that--it gets wet, and you make the grooms angry at you when you bring the horses back because they are the ones that have to make sure everything dries out right.

I was still fully dressed, of course, so I got up slowly and carefully and felt in my pack for my silk rope. Yes, *silk* rope. It's something I have with me in case the lady—never mind. Let's just say it comes in useful when ladies want something to . . . ah . . . keep me from going anywhere. It fell right into my hand. I could hardly believe my luck.

The horse stared at me. I made soothing sounds at it and straightened up, rope held behind my back. It didn't move. I walked toward it, slowly and casually. Behind my back, I got the rope into a loop to throw around its neck. The closer I could get to it, the better.

It let me just walk up to it and drop the loop around its neck.

And that was when it suddenly snaked out its neck, grabbed the back of my tunic in strong, white teeth, and shook me like a dog shakes a rag.

:What the hell do you think you're doing?: said a voice in my head.

Something *else* came crunching through the underbrush, and as the horse dropped me at its feet and, with a contemptuous toss of its head, shook off the rope, *another* big white horse emerged from between two bushes.

I looked wildly around for the owner of the voice.

:He's all we've got, Destin,: said another voice. *:We missed the wagon train, we can't get her to them, and they can't backtrack. He'll have to do. I just wanted to make sure he knew we were nothing to fool about with.:*

The new horse snorted with contempt and stamped a foot. *:He looks about as useful as teats on a boar.:*

I suddenly realized that there was no one else around but the two horses, I *knew* I wasn't asleep or hallucinating, so the voices had to be coming—from them—

:Of course the voices are coming from us, you moron,: said the second voice, as the second horse put his face down to mine and let those blue eyes burn contempt at me. *:We're Companions, and unfortunately we don't have hands, but you do, so you're going to help us.:*

"I'm—wait, what now?" I was beginning to think I'd fallen and hit my head, that I'd been poisoned by something that had bitten me in the night or had come down with a fever, and I was hallucinating. I vaguely recalled something about white horses in Valdemar, but I hadn't paid much attention at the time. I never expected to be here, after all. It didn't make any sense to come here, where I didn't know the language or the laws, or, well, anything else. What was it about white horses?

:You. Up. On your feet. You're coming with us.: That was the second voice in my head, the one belonging to the horse whose face was right in mine. *:What we're doing is Mindspeaking. We're Companions. We are the equivalent of Constables. Or City Guards, except we can enforce law in the entire country.:*

All I could do was blink. "That's ridiculous," I said. "Who'd obey a horse?"

One huge silver hoof stamped the earth right between my knees. The threat was, well, obvious. *:You will, if you know what's good for you,:* the horse said ominously. *:Now get your pack and get on one of us. You're coming with us.:*

Several thoughts flitted through my mind, but—look, I was in the middle of nowhere, with limited food, limited water, and no idea what to do with myself out here. It just did not make sense to argue with the creature. Hopefully, wherever they were taking me was going to at least have shelter. With more luck it would have a nice lady I could wrap around my finger and convince her to get me away from these . . . things. Companions. Whatever those were.

So I did what I was told. At first I had a sort of death grip on the thing's mane, but within a few paces I realized that not only was I in no danger of falling off, this was probably the best ride I'd ever had in my life. I'd have really enjoyed it, except, of course, that I was being carried off into the woods by a couple of possibly-demonic creatures disguised as horses that could talk in my head. Tends to make a man a little nervous.

I was hoping at least they'd take me toward something like civilization. But no. They left the road for a trail. They left the trail for a path. They left the path for something that *might* have been a thready little track. Wherever we were headed, it was obviously not civilization.

"Uh—" I said, finally, "I should point out that I'm a city sort of fellow."

:You've got two working arms, two working legs, and something akin to a brain. Not much of one, but we don't need much of one.: That was the second voice, which was coming from the *thing* that I wasn't riding.

Great. Just great. By implication, that meant they were heading even deeper into the wilderness.

:Yes, we are heading even deeper into the wilderness,: the voice said, somehow conveying both sarcasm and a great deal of glee at my discomfort. *:There are bears.:*

I *knew* there would be bears! The thought flitted through my mind again that I could jump off . . . but I couldn't outrun these beasts, and the thick . . . stuff . . . on either side of this pitiful excuse for a trail was going to trip me up as much as it would impede them. Assuming it did, they had tough horsehide, not tender human skin.

And that was when they shouldered through some

branches that slapped me in the face (of course), and we came out into a clearing. A lovely little clearing, a meadow, really, with a pond, and a little cottage, and a well—

A cottage! I brightened immediately. At least I wouldn't be sleeping with ants tonight.

Even as I thought that, the second beast grabbed me by the belt and unceremoniously pulled me off the first one. I yelled, and something white stirred in the long grass next to the cottage door.

The beast didn't let me go; *gods,* it was strong. It carried me by the belt over to whatever was there and *then* dumped me, and I could see that the "something" was a rather pretty girl in white. She was younger than my usual sort, probably younger than me, red-haired and green-eyed, round-faced without looking dollish, and clearly in a lot of pain.

I'm no Healer, but her left leg and arm did not look at all right. She looked up at me and grimaced.

:He's the best we could do, Millissa,: said the first horse, apologetically. *:I know you need a Healer, but there isn't one close, and if you don't get things straightened up soon—:*

"I know," she said out loud. "Believe me, I know." She looked as hard at me as she could, through the pain. "All right, fancy-man. I'm Herald Millissa."

"The ladies all call me—" I stopped myself. "My name's Donnat Stains. Call me Don."

"All right, Don. What do you know about dislocations and bone setting?"

"Nothing," I said, honestly. "How bad is this?"

"Things haven't seized up yet, so—" She bit her lip. "Just do what they show you. I think we can manage."

What they—

A very clear image came into my mind. First, I needed to deal with her leg. The horses were pretty certain it was broken but that it was a clean break. Working very, very slowly, I straightened the leg under their direction, pulling on it to align the broken bone, feeling it to make sure it was aligned. That poor girl was as white as her clothing, and her hair was soaked with sweat before I was done, but she never once cried out.

The horses showed me how to bind up the leg to keep the bone in place. Then it was time to deal with her shoulder. They had me go inside the cottage and wrestle out a table. I put her on the table with her arm dangling over the edge, then held her wrist in one hand and slowly began pulling her arm downward, increasing the pull a little at a time. I gently rocked her arm at the wrist, while keeping her shoulder pushed against the table. And slowly, very slowly, I felt the shoulder slip back into the socket, until at last she gave a little cry, the first yet, that was full of pained relief, if there can be such a thing.

After that, following the horses' directions on how to tie up her arm and shoulder was easy.

They didn't have to tell me what to do next, it was pretty obvious. There were packs and a saddle lying on the ground, and I figured, smart as these *things* were, each of them had probably stripped the other before going for help. There was a bedroll right on top; I may be a city sort of fellow, but I know how to make up a bed, and before too long I had her in the cottage, in a bed made up on one of the bedboxes there. That was when she passed out. Not that I blamed her. The pain must have been incredible. Frankly, I've seen strong men who endured less pain with more complaining. *I* certainly had.

Now . . . at this point I figured that I was done. This was a stout little cottage, stone walls and floor, a real fireplace, strong shutters on the windows, which I suspected the evil beasts could close, a strong wooden roof with slate tiles, a door as thick as my thumb. She was fine for now, one of these things could go off for some help while the other stood guard. In fact, I was going to volunteer to ride off on the not-quite-as-mean one to do just that, provided that they *left* me there (which I presumed would be civilization), when the mean one planted himself across the doorway.

:You are not going anywhere. Neither are we.:

Now, I am considered an easy sort of fellow. But I was just about ready to take an ax to this thing's he—

:Do it, and you're paste, fancy-man.: The beast reared slightly, and I backed away from the door so fast I tripped over my own feet. *:We were on our way to meet something, which is still coming this way. We have to be here for it, and someone human has to be here with two good legs and two good arms. Besides that, it's a good seven days—even as fast as we can go—between us and help. And we don't have hands. You tell me how we're to feed her, get her drink, and all the rest of it.:*

All right, put that way, I could see his point. The girl might or might not get fevered. She certainly wouldn't be able to take care of herself . . .

"So is one of you going to go?" I asked. "Seriously here, I'm . . ." I gulped. "My skills are not exactly that of even a Healer apprentice."

The thing shook its head. *:I wasn't joking about the bears. Or other things. Heralds like Millissa have enemies, and we're not entirely certain that the fall we took was an accident. With three of us, you can take the day watch, and Ardred and I can take the night with one of us at the door and one out patrolling the perimeter. With only two, it's more difficult, since you aren't the fighting type.:*

Well, there was that; the best I could do would be to yell a warning.

:Once what we are waiting for is here, Millissa will be healed enough to ride, and we can all get out of here. Or else the help we've already asked for will be here.:

Wait—what?

"How did—"

:Same way we talk in your head. Only at a distance. It takes another of us, or some human who is very strong in this power.:

Oh. Well, if we were seven days from the first vestiges of civilization, then we were probably farther than that from whatever this help was. I didn't imagine that these white monsters were all that thick on the ground, even here.

:Exactly.:

I gritted my teeth for a moment. I was beginning to resent their ability to read my thoughts.

"What's a Herald?" I asked, finally.

The beast snorted, tossed his head, and walked off. Great.

The first voice sort of—murmured at me. *:Ah, I'm Ardred. Sorry about Destin. He's touchy, and right now, he's feeling very angry at himself for what happened to Millissa. I'll be happy to answer your questions.:*

The horse wasn't in sight. I sighed. This was going to take a lot of getting used to. And meanwhile, well . . . the girl was going to need food and drink eventually, and *I* needed a bed, and although there is a style I am accustomed to, I'm not altogether incapable of some basic tasks, provided that I've not been dropped nearly naked into the middle of a howling wilderness. "Fine," I said aloud, going out to fetch the packs, mine included. "Let's start with, 'What's a Herald?' "

The first thing that Millissa did when she woke up was try to knock out my brains with a dish. I could see why she and Destin were paired.

By this time there was a small fire in the cottage—excuse me, "Waystation"—fireplace, and there was food of a sort cooking over it. That was thanks to Ardred, who talked me through how to make it. My knowledge does not include cooking. There was tea brewing—that, I knew how to make myself. I had a bed in another of the boxes—Ardred had been kind enough to show me where there was some bracken that wasn't home to insects, and I did have a cloak to lay over it. All the gear was in the Waystation. I knew, more or less, what a Herald was and what a Companion was. It didn't entirely make sense, as in, I wasn't at all sure why anyone would trust the dealing out of laws to creatures as ill-tempered as Destin was, much less something that looked like a *horse* for the gods' sake, but, well, not my kingdom.

So I had put down a dish on the side of the girl's bed as I leaned over to check on her, and the next thing I knew, she'd grabbed it with her good hand and broken it over my head. Fortunately it was a very cheap dish, so it broke easily and without braining me, but I ended up on my behind on the floor, staring at her.

"Ow," I said, very much aggrieved. "What did you do that for?" I completely forgot where I was and spoke Hardornen.

She stared back at me, wild-eyed, as if she were going to find something else to hit me with. Then, as if someone had inserted a different person into her body, her expression changed, and she flushed and winced a little. "Ah . . . oh. Sorry," she said in passable Hardornen. "I forgot where I was and I thought you were attacking me."

"I was going to *feed* you," I pointed out, crossly, rubbing my head. "We're now short a dish, thank you."

"There're metal ones in my pack," she retorted.

"As if I were going to go rummaging through your pack," I scoffed. "I have standards, you know."

"Which you refuse to rise above," she murmured, then said, louder, "Well, go ahead, you have my permission. It's the one with the frying pan handle sticking out of it."

Lovely. She had a frying pan. Which she would doubtless use to brain me if she got the chance. I made a note to keep it well out of her reach. But I did go rummage and got out the dishes she mentioned. I didn't give her the . . . well whatever the mess it was I had cooked . . . in them though. I'd use the metal ones, she could use the pottery. One less thing for me to worry about.

I wondered if she would ask me what was happening, but the changing expressions on her face led me to believe that the damn horses were just talking to her directly, and I wouldn't need to say anything. I'm sure the mean one was giving her an earful. Mindful. Whatever.

Bastard.

I thought hard about glue, dog-food, and fiddle bows.

I could have sworn I heard a snicker.

She was a little apologetic later. But when I tried my signature smoldering look on her, she threatened me with another dish, so I gave up that as a bad idea. Obviously she was going to be immune to my considerable charms.

Perhaps she favored other women . . . ?

:Or maybe you aren't as charming as you think.:

I grimaced sourly, and the gall was even more bitter when she giggled. Obviously that miserable bone-rack Destin hadn't bothered to keep his thoughts "private."

Was there *no* way to keep *my* thoughts private?

A very faint "whisper," almost so unobtrusive that I didn't even "hear" it, drifted into the back of my head.

:Order him to stay out of your mind.:

I didn't wait; I just looked out the night-darkened doorway and barked, "Stay *out* of my head, dammit! A man is entitled to some privacy! Talk to me if you want, but keep your snooping out of my thoughts!"

There was a sense of shocked silence. I looked over at the other bunk, where the girl was nursing a cup of some sort of noxious medicinal tea that she'd told me how to brew. She was looking back at me. With a certain amount of approval.

"He's right, you know," she said aloud. "Just because you're Companions, that doesn't give you the right to breach Mindspeaking ethics."

Well, that was a bit of a surprise.

"Do they often do that sort of thing?" I asked tentatively. "Rummage around at will in a stranger's head, that is."

She took another difficult gulp of tea before answering. "Not usually. In fact, Companions generally don't Mindspeak to anyone but their Chosen Herald. Destin's something of a law unto himself, though, and I can't always predict what he's going to decide to do."

I rolled my eyes. "Fabulous. And this is what you have laying down the law of the land?"

"Not . . . exactly," she said, finishing the tea. "Let me see if I can explain. Or at least, better than they did."

Her explanation did make better sense, and I could see now why the gods of this kingdom would have figured out a way to properly answer the particular prayer they'd been petitioned with. And it did prevent some pretty awful abuses of power. I mean, I did know history, and for every good monarch, you generally get a nasty one and an entire herd of mediocre ones. This at least made for a stable form of government.

What? You don't think I should have an interest in politics? I promise you, you would be amazed what constitutes pillow talk for some women.

Still, I don't think I would be even remotely comfortable with something rummaging around in my head on a regular basis. A man likes to keep *some* secrets.

After that, Millissa and I started to get along a bit better. I was feeling positively brotherly toward her as we both drifted off to sleep. Or at least, I was able to feel a lot more sympathy for her. She was putting up with injuries that would have had most people incoherent with pain and was not really complaining about it. Some of that was the tea, but most was that she was either really quite brave or really quite well controlled. In either case, I admired her.

Now, I am not the sort that tends early to bed and early to rise, so the cold, wet nose shoving insistently at me at the crack of dawn came as a literal rude awakening. The kind that makes you start up out of sleep with an incoherent noise.

:Up,: said the cross voice in my head. *:We need sleep.:*

He needed sleep? *I* needed sleep! Evidently that didn't matter, and I knew better than to try to just turn over and attempt to ignore him. He was quite capable of hauling me out of the bed just as he had hauled me over to the cabin.

Now . . . I've been a little less than honest. Just because I *haven't* done the usually lowly chores you'd need to do in and around a little cottage—well, other than the farming ones—it doesn't mean that I can't or that I didn't know how. It was because as soon as I was able, I ran away to avoid those very chores, heading straight for the city, which I saw as my natural home. So my skills might have been a little rusty, but other than the cooking part, I pretty much knew what to do.

By the time that Millissa woke up, and, poor thing, needed help getting to the privy, I'd gotten things in rough order for the morning. And when I carried her back and installed her in bed again, she looked around with a raised eyebrow.

"That's—not bad," she said. "I—"

"Didn't think I knew one end of a broom from the other?" I finished for her. "Oh, I know. I just don't *like* it. I'd much rather be waited on."

"Wouldn't we all," she murmured, but this time with

a little, pained smile that let me know she intended for me to hear her.

"I perform a very valuable service for ladies who for one reason or another need a companion," I told her pointedly. Her eyebrows arched, but I was not backing down. "Their husbands generally have at least one, and often several, attractive women that they go to. Why shouldn't they have the same? I'm entertaining, I can tell a good story, I *listen,* and I mean really *listen,* rather than pretend to listen and make appropriate noises. I am absolutely faithful for as long as the lady cares to have me about. Sometimes I can even offer advice, although mostly they don't want that, they just want sympathy. When we part ways, she's the better for it, and so am I. She knows that she is still worthy of appreciation, which raises her spirits and gives her confidence, and I am heavier in the pockets." I folded my arms over my chest and looked down at her. "And it doesn't hurt that I'm a handsome devil, which makes her the envy of her friends."

Millissa sniffed a little. "But you don't love these women!"

"On the contrary, I do," I said proudly. "I love women in general, and I make a point of appreciating all there is to admire in my clients." Believe me, sometimes that was a lot of work, but it was always worth it in the end.

Millissa's look of skepticism turned to astonishment. "You sound like you're proud of what you do!"

I shrugged. "I am. Why shouldn't I be? My father taught us to take pride in our work." Though he would have seven different kinds of a fit if he knew what I was doing now.

Well, that was his fault, not mine. Maybe if he hadn't gotten taken in by that priest and his stupid "quiverfull" notion of having your wife squeeze out baby after baby like a prize pig until you had so many children you couldn't remember their names, and what would have been plenty for a reasonably size family got stretched so thin that no one ever had enough, and everyone was starved a little—

—especially for attention—

—then maybe I'd still be there. Or maybe not. Who's to say? Maybe I would have run away sooner.

"But that has very little to do with the here and now," I told her. "I'm not a Healer, but I do have some skills that will probably help you."

Now both eyebrows shot up. "I don't—"

"Like massage."

She blinked. "Oh."

"If you've no objection, I'll take you out on the grass, give you a massage, and then set you so your head is hanging just over the edge of the pond and I can wash your hair." I knew that would get her. She'd been sweating all during the ordeal of setting her leg, and by now her scalp must be a torment.

"Really?" Ha. Had her.

"It's one of the things I know how to do," I pointed out. Then ,without giving her any time to think about it, I picked her up and carried her out into the meadow. Then I very carefully massaged all the nonerotic muscles, concentrating on making it soothing rather than actively trying to get the kinks and knots out. It takes longer that way, but the last thing she needed was more pain. When she was a nice girl-puddle, I moved her to a rock ledge on the side of the pond, stripped off, and used some of the soap I'd found on her hair. Then I moved her again, combed it all out and spread it on the grass, and left her soaking up sun while her hair dried. I vaguely recalled a Healer telling me once the people got better faster when they had sun. I don't know about that, but when I moved her back to her bed, a lot of the tension and pain was gone from her face.

The next few days were pretty much the same, except for the hair washing. We talked a lot; she did most of it while I did the listening, though I did tell a few stories out of my own past. The funny thing was that all those chores that I had loathed as a child seemed far less onerous now. Well, it was probably just because there wasn't anyone around telling me how I could have done it better and pointing out all the ways I'd fallen short of perfection. Fine, if someone else wants perfection, they can have it, but there's nothing wrong with just getting the job done competently and correctly and leaving it at that. Destin might have been a sarcastic bastard, but at least he didn't nitpick me to death.

The first three days were fine; the fourth, the Companions started getting restless. Destin even forgot to insult me. I remembered that they had said that "something was coming," and I wondered if that "something" was almost here.

The fourth day they kept going off for runs, always into the north.

The fifth day brought it all to a head.

When I woke up, I could practically cut the tension. Millissa didn't say much to me over breakfast; instead she had that "listening" look she got when both Companions were talking to her.

Finally, as I brought her lunch, she broke the silence.

"I know you're not a fighter—"

"Not even close," I interrupted.

"Right, well . . ." she bit her lip. "There's someone we've been waiting for. She's close, close enough to go get. But there are likely to be complications. It might get physical . . . and we'd planned for *me* to be the one to deal with that except—"

"So I take it you want me to go with Ardred and the walking gluepot since you can't. Right?" I'd already figured something like this was coming. "I have an easy solution for things getting physical. We run."

"It might not be that easy," she said dubiously.

It was my turn to snort. "Trust me. Take it from someone who's done a lot of running. You can *always* run."

:He has a point.: That, shock of shocks, was Destin.

She sighed. "All right, then. Destin, you and Ardred take care of him and the Chosen."

Ardred raised his head suddenly. *:She's thinking ahout running.:*

"All right then. Get those saddles on and get out of here. I'll be fine, you need to get!" To underscore her words, Millissa had me bring her everything in the Waystation that could be thrown. I admired her resourcefulness. And I shuddered a little when she hefted the frying pan.

I got the saddles on both Companions and started to mount Ardred, but Destin shoved his way in between us. *:He needs to be free for his Chosen. Mount up.:*

Once I was in the saddle, we were off, and I realized at once that we were heading for the road. They were pushing it, too. Even through the thick underbrush, they were almost galloping, and when we broke out into the clear, they did. And they were faster than *any* horse I've ever been on.

:She's running!: Ardred cried, his mental voice sharp with fear. *:He's coming after her!:*

We hit the real road, the one I'd left several days ago, and in the middle distance I could see what looked like a shabby wagon loaded down with household goods. Between us and the wagon was a girl, a child, really. She had nothing on but a shift, and as we pounded toward her, I could see there was a man chasing her, cursing. We got nearer and nearer. I could see her terrified eyes. Her thin little limbs.

The bruises.

Bruises, everywhere.

Something snapped inside me, and I'll tell you right now, I have no idea how I did this. I leaned down over Destin's neck, held out one arm, and . . . I just begged that child to run for me, to jump for me. "Here!" I screamed, "Here! Jump!"

She should have been terrified. She should have turned right around and run the other way. But something came into her face, a glimmer of hope, then determination, and as we rushed down on her, she did just that. She jumped into my arms. We thundered past the man. Thundered past the wagon loaded with stuff. Which . . . looked all wrong to me in a way I couldn't put together at the time. We turned, and without a word or thought actually exchanged, I tossed her into Ardred's saddle, where she stuck like a burr. "Run!" I urged him. "Don't wait for us. Run!"

He did. The man was on his way back toward us; he was a huge bull of a man, in a towering rage, and . . .

I'm no fighter, but I knew it would be a mistake to leave him.

There was a shovel lying under the wagon seat. I leaned down and grabbed it.

:Are you thinking—: began Destin.

"Go!" I shouted, because the man was closing on us.

Destin launched straight into a gallop and was up to speed in a few paces more. I took a firm grip on the handle of the shovel, and as we charged down on the bastard that would beat a little girl black and blue, I summoned all my rage, stood up in the stirrups, and swung straight for his face.

I hit him so hard the shock nearly knocked me out of the saddle, and it broke the handle of the shovel. Out of the corner of my eye I saw him go down.

We kept going.

I didn't look back.

* * *

Adred *did* wait for us, and the little girl clinging to his back looked at me with both hope and fear. "He's never going to follow us," I told her. "He's never going to hurt you again."

I certainly hoped he wasn't, because my arms were still tingling from the shock of that hit. The little thing burst into tears,and jumped out of Ardred's saddle for me. I realized it at the last minute, fortunately, and caught her, and she clung to me and cried. Ardred's eyes rolled with alarm, but I just smiled at him. "It's all right. She just needs someone to hold her."

The gods know I'd held plenty of women in my time who'd just needed someone to hold them.

I held her safe all the way back to the Waystation. It took some coaxing to get her to let go of me, but between us, Millissa and I managed, and we—well, I—got her filthy rags stripped off her, gave her a wash, put her into one of my shirts (which was certainly big enough on her to be a dress) fed her, and put her to bed.

Over the next day, Millissa got her story out of her. The man had been some distant relative. When her parents died, he'd come and taken everything portable, and her. He'd beaten her and starved her, made her do work that was far past her strength and then beat her when she couldn't manage it. She had whatever it was that made a Herald, and Ardred had heard her crying for him, but he had known he was never going to be able to get her away on his own, so he'd recruited Millissa to help.

Her name was Rose, and she stayed glued to me like a day-old chick to its mother. I did what I always do for a female who is hurt and frightened and mourning. I soothed her, I listened to her, I held her and let her cry, I promised her that Ardred would always take care of her, and I let her cry some more.

The next day, that help finally came. Another Herald and a Healer, who would stay with Millissa until she was fit to travel while the new Herald escorted Rose and Ardred to wherever these Heralds lived.

Then came the hitch. Rose refused to leave me. She clung to me and wailed, and I couldn't persuade her to stop. Finally Ardred solved it. *:I can carry two,:* he said firmly.

So that was how I arrived in Haven, about a candlemark after sunset, with a weary little girl in my arms who, after a good two weeks of solid work from me, had finally decided that she didn't have to be afraid any more and could start to leave the terror and learn to live.

I handed her over to the Collegium people, Ardred was led away, and—

And I know what you're thinking. You're thinking I turned around, saw one of those blasted white busybodies, looked into her eyes and—

Nope. Didn't happen. No interfering know-it-all with hooves. Just a tired but cheerful fellow in green robes who had come to see to Rose and now was standing next to me.

"Well," he said. "I suppose you've figured it out?" My bewildered expression told him otherwise. He laughed. "Ah, right. You aren't used to the Mind-Gifts where you come from, are you? All right. I'll just tell you straight out. The reason the Companions could talk to you is that you're Gifted. Like a Herald, but different."

You could have knocked me over with a feather. "I am?" I said, feeling stupid.

He nodded. "I felt you at work from half a day away, and let me tell you, my lad, we are going to be right glad to have you if you care to stay and learn to use what you've got properly. You're a Mindhealer, son. That's what you've been doing all your life—using your Gift."

"I thought—" Things I'd never put together began

tumbling into place. Things Millissa had told me. The things I'd been doing. How I'd worked with little Rose . . . "Huh."

Well, it wasn't as if I had anything *better* to do. And there was nothing saying I couldn't keep, well . . .

The Healer raised an eyebrow at me. "Oh, yes. You're still going to be very popular with the women."

I found myself grinning. He grinned back and clapped me on the back.

"Come along then, Healer Trainee Don. We're just in time for supper."

Catch Fire, Draw Flame

Rosemary Edghill and Denise McCune

South of the Yvedan Hills, in the places where constant border clashes between Karse's army and Valdemar's defenders were merely worrisome news and not terrifying reality, the land softened, spreading itself into rolling hills and lush fields. North of the Jaysong Hills, the farmsteads were built more of wood than stone; the farmstead walls were built to stop wandering chickens and not armed raiders, and shutters were not barred with iron. Here no man or woman slept with a sword beneath the pillow to arm against danger that comes in the night.

North and east of the Jaysong Hills, near—but not too near—the Hardorn border, where the East Trade Road ran straight and smooth toward Haven, the tents of Summerfair sprouted each Midsummer. From full moon to full moon a city of tents and pavilions appeared in the cup of the Goldendale, a city to which all the north came to sell and to buy.

"Why are we here?" Elade grumbled.

Despite the fact that the Summerfair Peace hadn't been broken within living memory—and despite the fact that her sword had been peacebound, as had every other weapon at the fair—her gaze roved over the fairgoers as though any might rise to menace them.

"Why is anyone anywhere?" Meran answered. His teeth flashed white as he smiled at her, and he hitched his bag higher on his shoulder. Seeing the fair in Elade's company was a bit like taking a leopard for a walk. The other fairgoers gave them a wide berth, despite the knot of yellow ribbons that bound her sword to its sheath.

"You look like a—a—a—"

"Bard?" Meran asked, his eyes round with feigned innocence. "But I *am* a Bard, sweet Elade."

Elade slanted a sideways look at Meran's crimson tunic. "You don't have to look like one," she huffed.

It was true that no one would take Elade for anything but what she was. Short cloak, high boots, studded leather bracers, and chain mail tunic all proclaimed her identity as a mercenary soldier. Elade had no reason ever to conceal herself . . . unlike the rest of them. In the places they travelled—and with the work they did—it was far better he and the others not travel garbed in Bard's scarlet or Healer's green or . . . *Not that we could ever get Gaurane into Whites without knocking him unconscious first,* Meran thought.

"Why not?" he asked (it was fun to tease Elade). "It would be very wrong of me to do otherwise. Only think—I might enter all the competitions and carry off every prize."

Elade snorted. "You'd have to be better than everyone else to do that, Meran," she pointed out.

"Hey, Bard here," he protested.

"*Journeyman* Bard," Elade corrected, just as if she could tell the difference between the playing of a Journeyman and a Master. Elade insisted all music was nothing more than cat-squalling.

"Elade, it's Summerfair." Meran dropped the teasing and set out to convince her in earnest. "We have a whole fortnight where nobody's trying to kill us. You should enjoy yourself. We'll be back on the Border soon enough."

"I like the Border," Elade said. "You know who your friends are there. *And* your enemies."

Only Elade, Meran thought, *could say something like that and mean it, when our work is finding those whose minds had been warped by Karsite demons and working to save them, minds and lives alike.* The Touched hid their damage from themselves, and the demons that overshadowed them were clever at concealing themselves. Often, the only clue was in the way people or animals nearby had died. It was a pattern they'd all become adept at following in the moonturns since Gaurane had gathered them together.

"We need supplies," Meran said, changing the subject to one less likely to produce an unwinnable argument. "Bowstrings—*harp*strings—medicines." The soldiers who held the Border and the holders who farmed it were seldom willing to part with what stocks they had, not even for gold and silver. It would be different if Gaurane were willing to ask—all doors opened to a Herald—but Meran knew better than to raise the topic with him.

"Gaurane's out of brandy, you mean," Elade said, but the gibe was without real malice behind it.

"Do you really want to listen to him complain about his hangover?"

The question startled a laugh from Elade. "No. But it doesn't take two full sennights to pick up a few supplies."

"It does not," Meran agreed. "But if you can think of a better way to get Hedion to rest, I'm sure we'd all like to hear it."

"Ah, I see," Elade said. "It's a trick."

"All the best things in life are," Meran said. "But not on us, this time. So we might as well enjoy ourselves while we're here." He took Elade's arm and tugged her gently toward the merchants' street. "And that means you should come and look at the pretty things, instead of trying to terrify some poor horse trader into giving you an honest price on a new pack mule."

"We wouldn't need a new pack mule if the last one hadn't been *eviscerated*," Elade grumbled, but she came.

When Meran had been a child singing for coppers on the streets of Haven, he'd dreamed of being able to walk into the shops and purchase anything he chose. His Gift had gained him entrance to the Collegium, and there he'd dreamed of a rich patron,whose fortune he might share. Most Bards entered a noble household upon achieving Journeyman status, for it could be the work of years to produce the song or poem that elevated a Bard from Journeyman to Master. Meran had been as surprised as anyone when he found himself choosing—upon taking the Scarlet—to travel. True, a Bard could hope for a meal and a bed at any inn he stopped at, but it was hardly as certain as it would be for a Herald. Traveling Bards slept rough and cold in a hayrick or outbuilding more often than not, and they paid for their bread and beer like everyone else. Even as he chose that path, Meran castigated himself for a fool. And yet year followed year, and the store of songs he'd made grew, and still he did not turn his steps back toward Haven.

He'd never realized what he was looking for until the shaggy man in the tattered, threadbare clothes came to the inn where he was singing and told him there was a patient who needed his attention.

"Beg pardon, my good fellow," Meran said. "But as you see, I am not the one you seek. I wear the Scarlet, not the Green."

The shaggy man gave a sharp bark of laughter. "We already have a Healer," he answered. "That's why we need you."

He'd been curious, so he followed. He played the Healer to sleep that night and the next, and he played to soothe the Healer's patient on the third. And as the days passed, Meran had come to realize this was what he'd been seeking, all unknowing, all along. It was unheard of, of course. Bards sang of great deeds; they didn't do them. And the street urchin he'd been would have mocked the idea that his heart's desire was to serve anything but himself—or even his Gift, once it woke.

Were he making a song of this, it would be Healer Hedion who held them all together and gave them their purpose. But in fact it was Gaurane who was their leader—Gaurane who would not be called "Herald Gaurane," whom Meran had never seen entirely sober, who refused to acknowledge the Companion who followed him everywhere like an exceptionally large and very white dog. Gaurane's story would make such a song as would be any Bard's Master work.

Except Meran didn't know the tale and had never asked. Elade, who had joined them a moonturn later, *had* asked (Elade had a knack for asking inconvenient questions, which had gotten her turned out of her Free Company), but if she'd received an answer, Meran didn't know it. How Gaurane and Hedion had met, why Gaurane could not Hear his own Companion, why Rhoses was content to follow his Chosen along the Border rather than seeking help for him, why, if there was Healing to be done, Hedion didn't do it—all were mysteries Meran was content to leave unplumbed.

It was only at times like this, when the Summerfair merchants' bright and glittering wares lay spread for display like the fabled treasure-cave of the legendary Queen Lilyant of Bai, that Meran spared a thought for the life he'd once thought to live. Even Elade was drawn to the splendor along the street of merchants, though her eye was caught by the table of blades, while Meran lingered before the scentseller's booth. He wondered if he could persuade Elade that oil of violets was a necessity vital enough to expend some of their scant resources upon.

A woman stepped up to the table, and Meran drew back courteously. He did not truly intend to buy, after all, and it was only polite to leave room for those who did.

As the two women, buyer and seller, dickered over the price and kind and quality of the wares, Meran let his gaze and his attention wander. The street of merchants was only a very small part of Summerfair. For the truly exotic and the truly costly, one must seek out Haven's Harvestfair or the shops of her High Street. Summerfair was for the farmers and holders of the south. It sold horses and mules, pigs and chickens, cows and goats, and it was also a hiring fair, for harvest was coming, when every hand would be needed. Meran had known nothing about the farmer's year when he'd left Haven; since then he'd come to know it ran opposite to the year the townfolk kept. Spring was for planting and autumn was for harvesting. Winter was for doing all the tasks of making and mending there was no other time for. But summer was a time of near leisure.

With a practiced ear, he followed the sound of the bargaining, paying no real attention. Its cadence told him the transaction was drawing to a close when a new note was added to the song.

"Here, mistress, let me hold that for you."

Meran turned toward the speaker. Young, dressed in clothing that was plain but of good quality, with something of the look of Iftel to him--no odd thing, when Valdemar lay open to any who wished to live in peace. He smiled as he held out his hand, and the farmwife placed a plump sack of coins into it.

Meran was about to turn away again—so the woman

had a manservant; there was nothing odd in that—when he saw the young man step smoothly away from the table, tucking the money pouch into his tunic as he did. Meran would have raised the hue and cry, or even moved to stop him, were it not that the woman gave no indication anything was amiss. In a moment, the young man had disappeared into the crowd.

"My purse! Where is it?"

The indignant cry behind him summoned Meran's attention again.

"Help! Thief! I've been robbed!"

"It didn't make any sense," Meran said, a candlemark later. "I watched her hand him her purse. And a moment later, it was as though she'd forgotten she had."

They'd found Gaurane and Hedion at the aleseller's nearest their lodging. There was always someone willing to rent space to travelers who had not provided their own accommodation. On the Border, they could always find an inn or a village to lodge them in exchange for a song or two if it was not giving them lodging for Hedion's sake. Here, entertainment could be had for the asking, but beds required coin.

"Maybe they were working together," Elade said, sounding puzzled.

"Fairs are made for thieving," Gaurane said. He took a long pull from his tankard of ale and sighed appreciatively. "Thieves everywhere." He tipped it up again, draining it, and reached for Meran's cup.

"There's a whole pitcher of ale in front of you," Meran said indignantly, whisking his cup out of reach.

"Yes," Gaurane said. "And if I drink it, it will be gone."

"I'll buy you another one," Meran said. Then kicked himself when Gaurane smiled beatifically.

"Good lad. I knew I could depend on you."

"She handed him her purse. And then she said she'd been robbed?" Hedion frowned, clearly still trying to make sense of the puzzle.

Of the three at the table entitled to wear the colors of one of the schools of the Collegium, only Meran was dressed in accordance with his rank. Everyone—even Elade—had been firmly against Hedion wearing his Healer's tunic here. Summerfair was supposed to be a holiday for all of them, Hedion most of all. Even now—a full sennight after the last Mindhealing he'd performed—Hedion's face was pinched and drawn, and he clenched his hands to stop their constant trembling when he thought no one saw. Meran knew, without having to be told, that left to himself, Hedion would pit his strength against the impossible task he'd set himself until he dropped from exhaustion. No one man could stem the tide of damage the Karsite demon-callers caused. But Hedion Mindhealer would try. If not for Gaurane, Meran knew, Hedion would have broken beneath his burden already.

"She swore someone must have taken it," Meran said. "The scentseller told her she'd handed it to her servant—"

"But she swore she had no servant," Gaurane finished, in the tones of one who knows how the tale ends.

Meran nodded in agreement. "She was quite indignant about it, too," he said dryly.

"So he could hardly have been her partner," Hedion said. "She loses her coin, she doesn't buy the scentseller's wares, and the man escapes. A mystery."

"The only mystery I'm interested in solving is how long I am to stare at the bottom of my tankard before it is full again," Gaurane said.

It was certainly a mystery, but hardly one they were likely to solve. The Heralds of Valdemar were charged with keeping the peace and meting out justice, but Gaurane insisted he was no Herald, Rhoses' presence notwithstanding. Meran doubted the man still owned a traveling uniform, much less a set of formal Whites. As for Rhoses' saddle and silver-belled bridle . . .

. . . there were some things it was better not to wonder about.

No, they could hardly look to Gaurane to hunt their quarry. But Meran disliked thieves. It was one thing to steal when you had to steal or starve—he'd done that often enough, before Bard Meloree found him. It was another thing to steal for sport or out of greed. The man he'd seen with Mistress Theret's purse looked well fed (and clean, which was more to the point), and his clothes had been of good quality and in good condition.

"If you want to be a Guardsman, I'm sure they'd take you on," Elade said in a low voice.

"You didn't have to come with me," Meran answered.

"Easier than buying you out of the stocks. Gaurane would complain about the waste of coin, and Hedion would worry."

"If you can get Hedion to worry, you're doing better than Gaurane is," he said absently, his gaze never leaving the crowds around them.

"Hedion worries," Elade said. "As long as it's about somebody else. I'm sure even you notice that."

"Point," Meran said.

He didn't know what he was looking for—or rather, he *did* know, but he wasn't sure he'd see it. Anywhere there was money, there was thievery, but the style of thievery varied from city to countryside. There might be a few cutpurses working a crowd like this, but it was unlikely the experts at that craft would travel all the way to Goldendale to ply their trade. Here you were more likely to find snatch-and-grab artists, horse traders selling spavined nags as sound, or even an old-fashioned mugging or two. What he'd seen the day before didn't fit any of those categories. It was trickery, but what kind?

"There. See him? That's the man."

Meran kept his voice low—though there was no possibility of being overheard in the crowd's noise—and nodded toward a pieseller's stall. As he watched, the same man he'd seen yesterday walked up to the table and pointed toward the shelves. The pieman reached back and took down a pie. He handed it over, smiling. Though Meran watched closely, he did not see any money exchanged.

"Wait here. I'll get him." Elade took off like a hound that's suddenly seen a rabbit break cover.

The man dropped the pie and bolted. He and Elade vanished into the crowd.

Meran sighed. Not the way he would have done it, but he had no doubt Elade would catch their culprit. Then they could ask him what he'd done with Mistress Theret's purse. Since there was no chance of catching up to Elade, he settled himself to wait.

It was half a candlemark before Elade returned. She was alone.

"I can't believe he outran you," Meran said.

"What?" Elade asked blankly. "Oh, no. I caught up to him quickly enough. But he said he wasn't the man I was after, so I let him go."

For a long moment, Meran stared at her. "He said he was innocent, and you believed him?"

Elade simply stared back at him, looking cross. Then her eyes widened, and she looked utterly horrified.

"Come on," Meran said, sighing. "It's time to consult an expert."

There was no place in all of Valdemar where a Herald and a Companion would not be made welcome. In fact, there were several Heralds at Summerfair, for one of a Herald's duties was to hear disputes and give judgment, and another was to keep the peace, and those whose circuits brought them near the great fairs made sure to attend them.

The only time things became awkward was when one traveled with a Companion whose Herald flatly refused to acknowledge himself as a Herald.

They found Rhoses with three other Companions in an open space behind one of the larger pavilions. One of them was probably with a Herald Trainee on Progress, while the other two would be the Companions of the Heralds working the fair. In his time at the Collegium, Meran had become used to the sight of the dazzling white creatures who held the peace and safety of Valdemar in their charge, but no matter how much the Herald Candidates insisted they were easily distinguishable, he'd never been able to tell one Companion from another.

But it was certainly Rhoses who came walking over to them, ears pricked forward in curiosity. When he reached them, he nudged Hedion hard in the chest.

Hedion staggered backward. "Oh, not you too?" he said.

They'd had to find Hedion before coming for Rhoses. While Rhoses could hear them perfectly well, it would be a rather one-sided conversation, since no one but Hedion could hear him.

Not even Gaurane.

A pause. "I *am!*" Hedion protested. "Here I am, doing nothing at all!"

Meran had gotten used to listening to only half a conversation in the past several moonturns. It had never stopped him from being curious about the half he couldn't hear.

"You know him better than I do," Hedion said darkly. "Come on, then."

Rhoses tossed his head, and once again Meran had the sense of a conversation taking place just beyond the range of hearing. Rhoses walked forward, and Hedion fell into step beside him. Few of those the little party passed gave them a second glance. Before he'd left Haven, Meran would have thought it impossible for anyone to mistake a Companion for a horse. But many of Valdemar's citizens never saw a Companion at all—and many of those who did were woefully unobservant, at least in Meran's opinion. A Bard was trained to observe, so that the things they saw could be used to add life and heart to the songs they crafted.

"You see," Meran said—he'd quickly learned to speak to Rhoses in the same way he'd speak to Hedion, "we've run into something a bit odd. There's a man here at the fair with the power to make Elade change her mind."

Elade thumped him—hard—in the shoulder with her fist.

"Ow," Meran said ruefully, rubbing the bruise. "And that part isn't the problem. But he's a thief. And I'm not sure how he's doing it."

"'A Bard should know all the Mind Gifts.'" Hedion translated Rhoses' reply. "'Even if he *is* a mere Journeyman.'" A lifted eyebrow conveyed the irony Meran couldn't hear.

Meran bowed mockingly without breaking step. "I *did* pay attention to my teachers, you know. All I can tell you is what it isn't. Not Mindspeech, not Farspeaking, not even Overshadowing. People just . . . *believe* him."

"'Not Compulsion?'" Hedion (Rhoses) asked.

"You think I wouldn't recognize the kissing cousin of the Bardic Gift?" Meran demanded indignantly. He sighed. "I only saw him up close once," he admitted. "If he was using Influence, he did it faster and stronger than I've ever thought was possible."

"Apparently he used it on Elade directly," Hedion said, answering the silent question.

Elade scowled ferociously. "If that's what it was, I'll make sure he never does it again once I catch him. I chased him through the crowd. I caught him. He . . ." She hesitated, and her next words were spoken with obvious reluctance. "He told me I'd made a mistake—that he wasn't the man I was after."

"And?" Hedion prompted.

"And I let him go. I realized I'd grabbed the wrong man, and I let him go. I would have gone on thinking that, too, if Meran hadn't opened his big mouth."

"Would you rather not know you'd been an idiot?" Meran demanded.

"Children," Hedion said (or it might have been Rhoses; who knew?)

"So," Meran said. "If it's a Gift, I wondered if you knew what it was. And if it's that strong, why hasn't someone come for him? A Companion, I mean?"

Rhoses seemed to be thinking the matter over before answering. " 'Companions only come for future Heralds,' " Hedion finally relayed.

"But . . ." Elade said, puzzled.

"I think he means our nameless friend doesn't have the morals to be a Herald," Hedion said.

No one knew what qualities Companions looked for in their Chosen. The people they brought to the Collegium were as diverse as the people of Valdemar. But all of them had that *something* that meant they would someday don Herald's Whites and dedicate their lives to service. *I suppose that includes Gaurane*, Meran added, with the usual puzzlement the thought brought. If there was an ideal Herald, then Gaurane was sort of . . .the anti-Herald.

They'd reached their lodging.

"I suppose I'd better—" Hedion began.

Gaurane staggered through the doorway, squinting painfully at the daylight. "Oh, it's you," he said, regarding Rhoses without any sign of welcome. "I suppose it was inevitable. Come along then, if you're coming." He turned and strode away.

You had to walk quite a way before you left the outskirts of Summerfair behind, but at least Meran was used to walking. Beside him, Elade kept up an endless, nearly inaudible grumbling. But at last they'd put a good mile between themselves and the nearest fair straggler. Gaurane located a convenient rock, sat down with a grunt, and reached into his tunic for the ever-present flask.

"Maybe someone can tell me why this is our problem," he said, after he drank. "You—" he regarded Elade balefully "—hate being got round with Mind-magic, and you—" now Meran was his target "—never saw a wasp nest you didn't want to poke. *You* have a death wish—" this was for Hedion "—and *that* is a compendium of all the virtues," he finished, gesturing toward Rhoses. "And none of this has to do with Karse."

"How resistant are Heralds to Mind-magic?" Meran asked. "I'm not asking you," he added hurriedly. "I'm asking *him*."

All of them looked at Rhoses.

"'It . . .depends . . .'" Hedion finally quoted.

Gaurane snorted. "Can't fool one of the circus ponies, you know that damned well," he said harshly.

"But you can . . . *fool* . . . a Herald," Hedion said, speaking for himself now. "If Healer's Gift works on them, so do the others. Depending on the Herald. You don't need a strong Gift to be Chosen. Or even one of the Mind Gifts at all."

Rhoses tossed his head. Hedion paused, listening. "'When we are not with our Chosen, we only know what they know. Yes. It is possible.'"

"What he means is, even if you dragged your man right up to one of those idiot meddlers in their pretty white suits, it's even odds he'd convince them to let him go again sooner or later," Gaurane said irritably. "And we *still* aren't thief takers. So why is it our problem?"

"Thieves are cautious," Meran said slowly. A thought had been taking shape in his mind from the first time he'd run into their Gifted thief; even now he wasn't entirely sure of the shape of it. "You'd say it would be more cautious not to steal at all, I know, but imagine you have no choice. Or just think you can get away with it. Even so, nobody wants to be caught. So a thief—a *career* thief, a professional—doesn't take risks. But imagine there *are* no risks. Imagine you'll never be caught—or if you're caught, you'll never be punished. Once you were sure of that . . . what might you do?"

"You mean he'll do worse," Elade said flatly.

"Maybe," Meran said.

"We can't risk it," Hedion said firmly. "But if you've guessed right, Meran, how do we catch him? Or keep our hands on him once we have?"

He looked toward Gaurane, and Meran knew Rhoses must be speaking. But whatever he said, Hedion didn't repeat it.

Carjoris Lor was a happy man. Why shouldn't he be, when the whole world was his treasure sack? From the moment he'd made up his mind to come west to find his fortune, Fortune had found him.

He'd always lived by his wits. He'd grown up traveling from farm to farm, following the work, and a quick tongue and a gift of invention had saved young Carjoris from countless beatings. In his itinerant world, theft had few consequences: it would be a year and more before a laborer's caravan returned, and by then the theft would have been forgotten.

He was not clever enough to see—not then—that the things a child might steal were small and easily forgotten . . . but that the theft of clothes or boots or coin would be mourned and long remembered. He'd been shocked when, upon their return to a place he'd nearly forgotten, his family was accused of stealing—and outraged when they cast him out.

You never cared where things came from. In all the years I brought you things, you never asked. But in the end, you cared more about being welcome back in some mudhole than you did about me.

But it was an old injury now, half forgotten. He wasn't sure when it was that the lies he told as he wandered from town to town began to be taken for truth. At first he thought it was his cleverness—or their stupidity.

But later he came to realize it was *magic*. Whatever he said—whatever he *wanted*—would be taken as truth.

It was a pity it never lasted long. Once he was out of sight, his victims remembered their own truths. No matter how hard he tried to settle down, he'd always had to keep moving.

Then one day he'd heard that in Valdemar no one believed in magic.

People who didn't believe in magic would surely be ripe for the plucking.

When he reached Valdemar, he'd been careful and cautious at first, using his magic for small things, things no one could say did them any harm. But the fact it worked had made him bolder. A country fair was just the place to test his powers. And after that . . .

A fine horse and fine clothes and a pocket full of gold—and no one ever again telling me what to do.

Today Carjoris decided to visit the horse fair. He did not fear arrest—even the guardswoman who'd chased him yesterday hadn't been immune to his magic. If anyone accused him, all he had to do was say he was innocent. They'd believe him. He moved quickly past the lines of mules, the broken-down hacks, the plow horses and cart horses. There, at the end of the street, were the creatures he sought. Their coats gleamed like satin and silk, and a man who rode one of those fine mares or geldings would be seen instantly for a man of wealth and stature.

And a man who looked to buy would be feted like a prince.

He passed a shaggy unkempt fellow loitering nearby—obviously some poor fool looking to exchange a day's work for a meal and a bed. *Perhaps I shall hire a servant,* he thought as he walked toward the horse seller, his mind on a pleasant afternoon of wine and flattery.

Then something struck him, and Carjoris knew nothing more.

He did not know how long it had been when at last consciousness returned. He was lying on the ground with a sack on his head. He groaned and rolled over with a grunt. Someone had put a *sack* over his *head.* He pawed it away and sat up, wincing at the brightness of the sun.

"Hello," a voice said pleasantly.

Carjoris blinked. The voice belonged to the ruffian he'd seen near the horse seller's. The man was sitting on a rock holding a wineskin. A white horse—superior to any of the beasts Carjoris had been admiring—stood behind him, though since it had neither saddle nor bridle, it clearly didn't belong to the stranger.

The rock was in the middle of a field, and the field was in the middle of nowhere.

"What happened to me?" Carjoris asked. His mouth was dust-dry; he spat to clear it.

"I hit you over the head with a club," the stranger said. "I'm Gaurane. Who are you?"

Carjoris blinked, certain he could not have heard correctly. "I'm thirsty. Give me the wine." He held out his hand.

But instead of handing over the wineskin, Gaurane laughed. "Sorry, Thirsty. I don't share."

"It's mine," Carjoris said. "Give it to me."

Gaurane simply shook his head. "Save your breath, my son. Your tricks aren't going to work on me." He tapped the side of his head. "Deaf as a post."

Carjoris got to his feet painfully and looked around. They weren't alone here, as he'd first thought. In the distance he could see three people watching them.

"I'm leaving now," he said.

"Did you know Elade's from Sensolding?" Gaurane asked. Something in his voice made Carjoris hesitate. "Sensolding, that's Holder lands. Harsh country. Hard people. I suspect none of that means much to you, but try this: She learned to use a great bow almost before she could walk. The range on it is . . . well, from where she's standing to here. That's her over there." Gaurane waved, and one of the figures waved back. "Walk away from me, son, and she'll put an arrow into you."

"That's murder," Carjoris said.

"Only if she kills you," Gaurane said. "Now sit down. I have a few things to say to you."

Carjoris looked from the figures in the distance to Gaurane, and he sat.

"You aren't from here, are you?" Gaurane asked.

There wasn't anything to do but answer,and hope he could find a way out of this. "Iftel."

"Ah. So, likely you think you have some kind of magic power. But you see, magic doesn't work in Valdemar. We call what you can do a Gift."

"You're making a mistake," Carjoris said.

"Oh, I don't think so. Elade doesn't think so—you used your power on her, you know. Meran doesn't think so—he saw you take the purse at the scentseller's stall.

And me, I really don't care. But my friends do, so we're going to make sure you don't do things like that any more. Stealing is wrong," he added virtuously.

"I won't ever do it again—I promise!" Carjoris said desperately. If he could convince the man that he repented and get the maniac to let him go —

"Well, here's the thing," Gaurane said. "I don't believe you. And using a Gift to trick people, that's even more wrong. But it's tempting, isn't it?"

"I never took anything anybody needed!" Carjoris said. "They were rich!"

"Ah, well, that's a matter of perspective," Gaurane said. "Now me, I think you're a nasty little bully, and I wouldn't lose a moment's sleep over slitting your throat. Hedion's got standards, though. So I suppose we could just dose you up with something that shuts down your Gift—oh, don't look at me like that; this is Valdemar, they understand the mind-gifts here—and send you off to Haven. They'd put Truth Spell on you, you know. And when you'd told them what you'd been up to, why, they'd get someone to burn your Gift out of you before they sent you off to prison. Or we could just do what Elade suggested, and slit your tongue. Hard to talk people into things when you can't talk."

Carjoris looked at him for a long minute, trying to judge how serious he was. When Gaurane did not so much as blink, Carjoris knew there was no escaping this disaster. "Please," he said, covering his face with his hands. "Please."

"And then there's Meran," Gaurane said, as though Carjoris hadn't spoken. "Did you know he grew up on the streets in Haven? A beggar and a thief. But one day a Bard found him and took him off to the Collegium, and he never stole again. He didn't have to. The question is, would *you* steal if you didn't have to?"

Carjoris lifted his head and stared at Gaurane at that

ray of potential salvation. "I wouldn't! I won't!" he said desperately.

"Ah," Gaurane said sighing. "Never lie to a drunk, boy. We're good at seeing the truth. Of course, you have a third choice." He reached down into the grass beside him and picked something up. Carjoris couldn't see what it was before Gaurane tossed it at his feet.

He looked down at it, and could not believe his eyes. "You want me to wear—a collar?" The silver flashed in the sun.

"It's even got a lock," Gaurane said cheerfully, bouncing a small object in his hand. "And the thing about this collar is—oh, I don't suppose you can read, so let me tell you about it—the engraving on it says you should be handed over to the next Herald who rides by. You'll recognize them. They'll be the ones riding something that looks like that." He jerked a thumb over his shoulder at the white horse standing patiently behind him. "And those things are smart, and you can't trick them, and they aren't horses, no matter what they look like. And you'll find yourself in Valdemar before you can blink. They'll probably hire you out as a laborer there so you can pay back what you stole. After they burn out your Gift, of course."

"If— If I wear that, you'll let me go?" Carjoris stammered. Once he was away from here, he could surely find a blacksmith to strike the collar off. Only what if they read it first? What if they chained him up and gagged him and delivered him to one of these Heralds?

The white horse snorted, and Gaurane gave a sharp bark of laughter.

"Or you wear that and come with us. Do what you're told. We work hard, harder than you've ever worked a day in your life, but the reward is well worth the labor. We'll put you to work, teach you what you need to know in order to be of use. If you're a good boy, we might even get someone to teach you the *right* way to use that Gift of yours someday, once we're convinced you're done misusing it. Run, try to compel any of us, make any trouble—and you'll wish I'd let Elade put an arrow into you now."

Carjoris shook his head, trying to make some kind of sense out of all this. "Why—Why—Why—" he stuttered.

"Maybe you deserve a chance to be someone better. Maybe you were born with your Gift for a reason. Maybe all you need is somebody to show you how to be a hero. Maybe I'm tired of listening to Elade bitch about doing all the work around the camp. Or maybe I bet Hedion you'd rather take your chances in Haven than do an honest day's work. But like I said, it's your choice."

"Who . . . *Who do you think you are?*" Anger got the better of caution, of the hard-learned lesson that the only way to survive was to smile and give soft words no matter what words were said to you.

"Me?" Gaurane said. "I'm nobody. But I *was* somebody—for a while. And it's a funny thing, but if you give someone a thing worth doing, well, sometimes that's worth quite a lot." He got to his feet, grunting with the effort. "Time's up, youngster. Choose."

"I . . ." He looked down at the collar at his feet. Trapped, and trapped well, that much was certain. He could run and take his chances with the woman's aim. He could put on the collar and take his chances with finding someone to strike it from around his neck. He could give himself up to one of their Heralds and take his chances that their punishment would be lenient and easily survived.

But Gaurane was watching him, a little smile lingering at the edges of his lips. He looked like a man who held a secret. And Carjoris suddenly, desperately, wanted to know what that secret was.

A hero. He liked the sound of that.

"My name is Carjoris," he said. His hands shook as he reached for the collar. It was lined in leather, and the metal was warm from the sun. But it still felt cold and heavy as he closed it around his throat.

"A pleasure to meet you," Gaurane said, without irony.

He tossed the lock into Carjoris's lap. It clinked against the metal as Carjoris threaded it through the clasp and squeezed it shut.

"Come on." Gaurane was holding a hand down to him. Carjoris took it, and Gaurane pulled him to his feet.

"What— What happens now?" Carjoris asked. He knew he ought to feel afraid, or even angry at having been trapped so neatly. But he didn't.

He didn't know what he felt.

"Now we go back to the fair—should be there by dark—and you hand over everything you've stolen, and Meran goes and finds a Herald to give it all back. And tomorrow we buy you a horse and whatever else you need. Did I mention we spend our time living rough up on the Border? You'll get used to it."

He turned and began to walk toward the others. The white horse followed. As it passed him, it turned its head and gave Carjoris a penetrating look.

"Come on if you're coming!" Gaurane called, and Carjoris found himself running to catch up.

"You've lost me a five-mark piece, you know," Gaurane said when he reached him. "Ah, well, maybe I can get Hedion to go double or nothing. Over a moonturn, you know. To give him a sporting chance."

"You'll lose," Carjoris said with sudden confidence.

They walked on.

In an Instant

Elizabeth A. Vaughan

The thick yellow dust caught in her throat, right next to her heart.

The euphoria of their victory over Ancar of Hardorn was starting to pass, the ragged cheers starting to fade. Selenay remembered all too well what happened next. The cold harsh wind of dealing with the aftermath. She'd managed to keep herself together this long. Her officers could handle the next few minutes without her.

"I just need a moment," Selenay whispered to her guards, seeking the privacy of her tent. They nodded, taking up their positions. They probably thought she wished to thank her gods or see to her own needs. But the truth was not so simple.

Once the flap was raised, once she'd retreated into the darkness of its shelter and its relative silence, her emotions overwhelmed her. She stumbled past the table of maps into her sleeping area and collapsed on her stool. She dropped her head to her hands,and fought to hold back tears. This could not be happening, not here, not now, not ever.

He is his brother.

She gasped then, pulling in stale air, and shivered.

She was a Queen, a mother, a Herald, for the love of all the gods. She was in the middle of a war, fresh from a battle she never thought they'd win. She should be rejoicing at their victory and dealing with the consequences thereof. The dead, the injured, the damages to the land. Her people, her land, her kingdom. Instead, here she was like some silly girl weeping over— Her heart skipped a beat.

He is his brother.

The sounds outside the flimsy canvas of her tent were muted and distant. All she could hear was her heart in her ears, her ragged breath in her throat, and her thrice-damned memories.

"In that case, gracious lady, let the Prince prevail upon your noble nature and present himself!" the young man said, flinging himself at her feet in the most romantic posture possible.

She'd been so young and so stupid, dreaming of romance. So gullible. Karathanelan, Prince of Rethwellan had appeared as if in answer to her dreams and swept her off her feet. She'd fallen for him so fast, so foolishly. So blindly in love that she'd swept all opposition aside, ignoring the concerns of friends, advisers, even her own Companion, like a child with a new toy. She'd been stupid, arrogant, naive, and . .

Dearest Gods, was it happening again?

It couldn't, it just couldn't . . . no . . . this couldn't be happening. She'd slammed the doors and windows on that stupid dream the day her loving husband had smiled at her over the glint of his sword. She could still feel that lance of fear as his friends had surrounded her, and she'd faced them for long moments alone—

Never alone.:

Selenay lifted her tearful face to a beloved white head pushing its way into the tent.

"Oh, Caryo," she whispered.

Caryo stepped closer. Selenay stood and pressed her

face into that warm neck, feeling the soft silky mane of white absorb her tears.

:Whatever this is, whatever happens, we face this together.: Caryo's Mindspeech carried all of the warmth of her love with it. *:I am here for you, Chosen.:*

:I . . . I think it's a Lifebond.: Selenay held on for dear life, and let her tears flow. *:He is his brother,:* she wailed in despair, sharing her fear. *:Caryo, I can't—:*

:He is his brother.: Caryo confirmed. *:But he is also Chosen.:*

Selenay lifted her tear-streaked face and drew a sharp breath. *:He is? I didn't notice. He was in front of me, and I was so stunned, I didn't see—:*

:See again,: Caryo commanded and Selenay saw again in her mind's-eye Lord Darenthallis of Rethwellan, his helmet in one hand, stretching out his hand to kiss hers. Saw him lift his head, saw his brownish-blond hair, and gazed into those hazel eyes . . . and saw him seated on a Companion.

Her knees buckled, and she went down onto the stool. Caryo followed, lowering her head to nuzzle Selenay's face.

:Chosen,: Selenay wiped at her eyes. *:By?:*

:Jasan.: Caryo said. *:On the battlefield. As is Kerowyn. By Sayvel.:*

Selenay blinked, as a slow smile crept over her face. "Oh, Kero's going to hate whites." she hiccupped a weak chuckle.

A snort of agreement from Caryo.

"Chosen?" Selenay frowned, pushing her hair back from her face. "How will we deal with a mercenary company? For that matter, how do I explain this to King Faramentha? What will he say, to lose his Lord Marshal?"

:You are thinking like a Queen,: Caryo noted, shaking her mane in approval. *:That is well.:*

:Why do you say that?:

:Because he's standing outside your tent, hesitating, not sure what to say, or how to say it, but knowing . . .:

:The bond.: Selenay felt it too, vibrating between them.

:Rolan says that Talia says to breathe. That a lifebond is overwhelming and confusing. Go slow, and remember that you are not the girl you were.:

:He is his brother.: Selenay nodded slowly, still nervous and unsure. But the terror was ebbing away. *:But I am Queen, and Herald, and mother of a half-grown daughter. I can handle this.:* She put her hand on Caryo's neck. *:We can handle this.:*

Daren took a deep breath of heat and dust and let it out slowly. He adjusted his cape,and tried to brush dust from his uniform.

:One would think you were facing your final battle,: the voice in his head said.

"I am." Daren looked over his shoulder at the white stallion behind him.

:Companion,: Jasan reminded him. The big horse shook his white head and somehow managed to look amused.

Daren concentrated. *:This is going to take some getting used to,:* he thought. His head was still whirling from the last few days, the confusion of the battle, the victory, being Chosen. And now the Queen of Valdemar was—

The bond between them vibrated with her nervousness, echoing his.

:It will take time,: Jasan agreed. *:But you should not keep her waiting.:*

Daren looked back at the tent before him. The Queen's guards were looking at him with odd expressions. He wasn't sure why he was hesitating so much.

He'd known many women, been in and out of relationships like he changed garments, but this. . . .

His heart clenched in his chest. This mattered.

Daren pushed through the tent flap; he stood in the darkness and let his eyes adjust.

She stood opposite him, her Companion's head over her shoulder, the table of maps between them.

Dearest gods, she was lovely.

Golden hair, blue eyes that were strong and yet like a startled doe's. Her armor was a mixture of plate and white leather, and it didn't show much dust. But there were smudges on her face and the trace of tears. It hurt him to see her pain.

"Your Majesty," Daren placed his hand over his heart and bowed his head.

"Lord Darenthallis," Selenay's voice trembled.

"Daren," he blurted out. "I go by Daren."

"Daren," she repeated. Her voice trailed off and they both stood there, staring at one another.

"I didn't intend this," Daren said. "I never thought that something like this could happen. I. . . ."

:Your brother's greeting,: Jasan prompted.

Daren pulled himself up. "Your Majesty, I bring greetings from King Faramentha of Rethwellan. He bade me say that our presence here today honors the pledge that King Stefansen made to Herald-Prince Roald, preserving the honor of Rethwellan and the friendship between our lands."

"You look nothing like him," Selenay whispered, wonder and relief in her voice.

Daren stared back at her helplessly. "Faram and I favor my father," he replied. "Thanel favored our mother."

"Thanel? He went by Karath when he was here."

Daren shook his head in disgust. "Thanel was what he was known by in Rethwellan," Daren continued. "My old weaponsmistress called him a *'grek'ka'shen.'* That's an animal found on the Plains," he explained. "Scavenges anything dead, soils its own nest, and eats its young."

Selenay grimaced. "Appropriate," she murmured, dropping her eyes. "I wish I'd known that before. . . ." her words trailed off.

Daren shook his head. "Would it have made a difference?"

"I—I don't know," Selenay answered, her honesty wrung out and raw.

"He could charm the sun out of the sky, the vicious little beast." Daren took a step forward. "I am not him," he said fiercely.

Selenay lifted her head and looked at him, a faint wondering in her eyes. She nodded slowly and then frowned slightly. "I seem to remember someone telling me . . . your weaponsmistress was Shin'a'in, wasn't she?"

Daren nodded. "She wouldn't train Thanel for any price. Trained me though, and Kero," he laughed, shaking his head. "Taught us the trick we used today in fact. Worked out well." He stared at Selenay, wanting her to know everything. "We were lovers when we were young," he blurted out, then covered his face with his hand. "Oh, gods, why did I say that?"

Jasan whickered outside.

Selenay coughed, and Daren opened his fingers to see her choking back a laugh. "We are not at our best," she offered. "You traveled far to save us. To save Valdemar."

"I served my King, Your Majesty." Daren took shelter in a return to formality. "But never so joyously." He paled as he thought on his journey. "Hardorn's Ancar is another *grek'ka'shen*. What he's done to the land," Daren drew a shuddering breath. "He's not done with

Valdemar yet, Lady." He looked back into those lovely blue eyes. "With us."

He lost himself in her face again, just staring at her. Thankfully, she seemed lost in his as well.

"You have a smudge on your nose," he whispered.

Selenay blushed. His heart flipped as she lifted a hand and rubbed her nose. He took a step forward, wanting nothing more than to—but he stopped and took a conscious and deliberate step back.

Selenay's eyes were wide, questioning him.

"Your Majesty," Daren said carefully. "I need to see to my people, as do you. We both have duties here and now. But I would like to . . . explore this possibility. The possibility of us."

Selenay nodded. "As would I."

"But know this, Queen Selenay." Daren set his shoulders, trying to find the right words. "Your Majesty, I'd . . . wherever this leads—if it leads to something growing between us—I'll not be crowned."

"What?" Selenay stared at him, and her Companion also seemed taken aback. He heard the rustle of canvas behind him, and Jasan pushed his head into the tent. Daren suppressed a surge of satisfaction. He'd surprised them all.

"But if this thing between us," Selenay gestured toward Jasan. "Being Chosen, you would qualify as Co-Ruler in a way that Karath never–" she stopped herself.

Daren nodded. "Karath, Thanel, whatever you decide to call him, he left a taint, and I will not walk in his footsteps. But even more than that, I do not wish to wear a crown. Faram deals with so much as a result of that burden, and I know full well the price."

Selenay nodded her understanding.

"But if you would allow," Daren said softly., "I would stand with you. Support you in all ways, all things. Behind the throne," he smiled at her. "Not on it."

Selenay took a breath, her eyes tearing up. "Are you sure?"

"More than sure," Daren said. "Now, with your leave, Your Majesty, I'll–"

Jasan bumped him in the middle of his back. *:Kiss her.:*

Daren scowled and shook his head.

"What?" Selenay asked.

"He thinks I should kiss you," Daren looked at her ruefully, then glanced back at his Companion. "Were you born in a barn?"

Selenay's laughter burst out, like rain on his thirsty soul.

Selenay could not restrain her laughter, rising out of her relief.

Daren gave her a boyish grin. "Are they always that pushy?" he asked.

"Most times," Selenay said teasingly, then laughed again as Cayro shook her head in denial. "Daren, this is my Companion, Cayro."

"My lady," Daren bowed. "I believe you already know my Companion, Jasan."

Jasan snorted as he backed out of the tent.

"I really, really want to kiss you, Your Maj-"

"Selenay," she interrupted.

"Selenay." His smile lit his face. He drew a breath. "But there is time for that. We'll talk first. Before we explore other . . . possibilities. I'd want to really know you before . . ." Daren paused. "Do you know what I am trying to say?"

Selenay nodded, her throat tight with emotion, unable to speak, feeling the truth of his words within the bond.

"But you'll forgive me if I hope the wait is not long," Daren said. "And I'd ask one favor," he added, his eyes sparkling.

Selenay raised an eyebrow.

"Don't believe anything Kero says. I don't snore."

Selenay laughed again, and the band of pressure around her chest eased. Daren gave her a boyish grin and lifted his eyebrows. Her heart turned over at the sight.

"I'm not sure how I am going to explain this to Faram. It's going to take me a score of letters to convince him that I've been Chosen and explain what that means." Daren's eyebrows danced. "Maybe I'll tell him that Jasan is a Shin'a'in battlesteed. That might do it."

There was an offended snort from outside.

Selenay suppressed the giggle that rose in her chest.

"I'm in Valdemar to stay," Daren said. "I am not going to give up Jasan or you, Selenay of Valdemar."

"I'm glad," Selenay replied, confidence flowing through her.

Daren put on his helmet, looking satisfied. "Your Majesty." He swept a graceful courtly bow as he backed away.

Selenay stepped forward, suddenly reluctant to part. She extended her hand.

Daren took it gently in his and lightly touched his lips to it. Then he left, with a flourish of his cloak.

Selenay stood for a moment. *:He is not his brother.:*

:He is not.: Caryo agreed. *:And I am here, always.:*

:Always,: Selenay said, as the tightness in her shoulders eased even more.

Noises from without, and the flap was raised. "The Lord Marshal is here to confer with you."

Selenay rubbed her face, hopefully erasing her tears. "Let him enter," she commanded.

"A battle won, majesty." The Lord Marshal strode in with his staff.

"But there are consequences yet to be dealt with," Selenay stepped to the map table. "Let's see to it, shall we?" She bent her head to the reports he laid out for her, with a new energy. No, she smiled to herself. More like a new anticipation.

And a new determination to protect Valdemar and those she . . . loved.

A Healer's Work

Daniel Shull

The greenhouse was worse than he'd expected. The tools had gotten damp from the constant storms, and plants were either dying or running riot. Whoever had last been inside appeared to have trimmed just enough materials for their use and then run off. Several of the windows had been left open, and drains had not been cleared, resulting in a sludge that clung to everything. The mess wasn't insurmountable, just extensive; only there shouldn't have been a mess to begin with.

Healer Serril looked around the dilapidated greenhouse with more than a bit of irritation, tempered only by his fondness for the Trainee standing a few feet away from him. Jayin waved a slightly rusted trowel in the direction of the Healers' Collegium, fury radiating from her normally placid brown eyes.

"Idiots! Ham-fisted children! Delinquents! Fumble-fingered—" Serril interrupted her before someone came to investigate the furious ranting.

"Jayin." Her name, backed by all of his authority, was enough to stop the Trainee midrant. She grimaced but bowed in apology to her mentor, eyes to the ground in a show of contrition. The apology was certainly genuine; everything else was for show, Serril knew from long experience. He *also* knew that the Healers who'd require her contrition would be the ones most likely to accept a display and not probe deeper. Brone immediately came to mind.

She had good reason for her irritation, to be sure. Ever since Elspeth had returned, the Collegia and Court had been all atwitter for their suddenly strange Herald-Mage and her even stranger allies. The two Hawkbrothers alone would be enough to turn anyone's head; add the creatures called gryphons and their younglings, and it was no wonder that most of Haven occupied themselves with little else. Gossip left the court, galloped around the city and returned with three heads, seven legs, and no sense whatsoever. The Hawkbrothers were descended from the gryphons, or vice versa. Elspeth was nothing more than a chew toy for the ravening monsters that were set to take over Valdemar. Vanyel himself had been resurrected and somehow brought to the Court. And those were the tamer stories. It was enough to make a cat sneeze.

And the normally sensible Healers had mostly fallen prey to this absurdity. Essential duties had been let slide. Reports from the countryside were stacking up because the secretary was too busy loitering in the diplomatic wing, hoping for a glimpse of their exotic guests. Despite his incessant lurking, nobody quite had the heart to shoo the man away when this was probably the most excitement he'd ever had. The library was in disarray because nobody was thinking about putting books away. The greenhouse had suffered because not one Healer–until now–had come in to maintain it for at least a week. The sensible ones had simply been overwhelmed with trying to deal with everything their counterparts should have been doing.

Serril and Jayin had valid excuses though. They'd been at Briarley Crossing, attending to the results of what was best called a string of strange luck: an outbreak of the flux, several broken bones, and no fewer than five births–all within two weeks time. The local Healer and the midwife had been swamped and grateful for their help. Then, the day they were due to leave for Haven, a particularly nasty storm had blown up and made travel impractical for another two weeks.

When they had finally ridden into Haven, Jayin had muttered something about hiding from the Dean of the Healers for a few days. Serril had nodded, knowing exactly how she felt. Sadly, he wouldn't be able to dodge that worthy as easily as Jayin, even if he hadn't planned to visit the Dean to recommend that she receive her full Greens for their work in Briarley Crossing. They'd been assisting at a Healing station in the North and were on their way back to Haven when they'd arrived in Briarley Crossing just as things took a turn for the busy. So of course he had to report to the Dean to explain the whys and wherefores behind their late arrival and then give his report on Jayin.

Dean Ostel had mostly paid attention to Serril's report and his recommendation for Jayin, massaging his temples as if fighting off an oncoming headache. Serril didn't think the stocky man had a problem with his report, but several months outside of Haven politics made him more than a bit wary. He did his best not to play the games, but he knew how to watch for them and avoid the most troublesome ones. The Dean's next words took him by surprise.

"I'm afraid I can't let you rest just yet, my friend. I need you and your Trainee to deal with the greenhouse." Ostel grimaced, his blue eyes a touch dull underneath furrowed pale brows. "I'm not sure if you've heard the rumors, but the truth is a bit more strange. I've made notes for you both, but the upshot is that nobody has seen to the greenhouse in about a week, and I trust you not to get, well, distracted."

* * *

Serril snapped back to the present and watched as Jayin caught herself before she ran muddy fingers through her straight brown hair. "This is absurd, Serril. I mean, I can understand getting distracted by the Hawkbrothers and those astounding creatures, but this!" She gestured again, the trowel gripped as delicately as a scalpel might have been, slender fingers maintaining control at all times. Somehow the gesture took in the Healers' Collegium, Bardic, the Heralds, the Palace and the surrounding city–and made it clear that she found them all lacking. Jayin had grown up in a traveling performers' caravan, and the drama learned in the tents and the wagons occasionally surfaced.

"Healers are only human. And with the Heir renouncing the Crown on top of everything else–"

"Smartest thing she *could* have done," Jayin muttered.

"–it's upset the apple cart, as it were. And yes, Herald-Mage Elspeth was politically smart to do what she did, but, my goodness, Jayin, I'd expect you to keep that opinion to yourself. There's more than enough uproar throughout the capital without a soon-to-be Healer interjecting her opinions in so impolitic a manner." He chuckled as he dug his fingers into the next pot, where a plant was barely surviving. He added quietly, "Not that the rest of them haven't been, but at least *we* can attempt to present an air of neutrality." He had the Healing Gift–like Jayin, which was why they'd been paired–but greenery responded to his particular Gift quite well. Serril gently pulled the plant out of the pot and transplanted it to another, cushioning it with his Gift against the shock of the move. The new soil was better suited for the plant anyway. A faint surge of energy, and he felt the roots "wake up" and settle into the new soil with what, in a human, he'd have called a contented sigh.

Jayin snorted. "Since you yourself taught me about maintaining that neutrality, I'll presume you're teasing me, especially since there's not another Healer anywhere near here–" She stopped, about to gesture yet again with the trowel, when the hurried knock at the greenhouse door interrupted her. Serril kept himself from laughing, but only barely. Fatigue had lowered his guard too, it seemed.

"Come in!" he managed.

As the Healer walked in, Serril thought, *Thank goodness it's Tessa and not Brone.* The Healer was obviously distracted, though. As she began speaking, Tessa didn't even see the interior of the greenhouse or the two Healers painted with mud, fertilizer, and pieces of dead plants.

"I'll need a few leaves of the woundwort, no more than three, and—" She stopped dead as she refocused on her surroundings. "Blessed Haven, this place is a disaster! And look at you two!"

At that, Serril lost control completely, sagging against the workbench and wheezing laughter to Tessa's obvious surprise. Jayin very primly placed the rusted trowel next to her and then planted her hands on her hips. In the midst of his laughter, Serril managed to remember her pose for the next time he teased her about how you could take the girl from the theater, but you couldn't take the theater out of the girl.

"If it weren't you, Healer Tessa, I'd tell you there was none to be had. It's in bad shape and might not survive another few days." She steadfastly ignored her mentor's further laughter, instead giving him a polite yet disapproving look. As Jayin's left eyebrow went up, Serril turned away to keep himself from giggling further.

Tessa grinned at them both. "Back less than a day and Ostel's already put you to work. My apologies, Trainee

Jayin. I'm on an errand for the female gryphon–Hydona, her name is–and we're comparing medicinal herbs and uses. She may well be a treasure trove for all that she can't use a mortar and pestle." She paused a moment, then continued, "Fair enough, the woundwort's out of bounds. Why don't we pick a few leaves from the plants that will survive it, then?"

Jayin's eyes drooped, and Serril reflected that he probably didn't look much better. The greenhouse had been set to rights as best as they were able: floors, tables, and tools cleaned, the plants likely to survive given as much care as possible, and requests sent off for replacements for the unrecoverable ones.

When they'd arrived, it had been midmorning; they hadn't eaten all day, and they'd barely made it to dinner. The two of them had gotten what food was left, and they now slowly made their way from the refectory toward their rooms. The long day had definitely taken its toll on both of them; Jayin navigated the path more by memory than by actually looking at it.

"I don't care if my bed hasn't been aired out yet, I'm going to fall in and not get up for a week."

Serril opened his mouth to suggest she might want to change out of her dirty clothes when a sound interrupted him. It took him a moment, but for anyone who'd spent time in Haven–and at the Palace–the sound of hooves chiming on the gravel path was unmistakable.

A Companion.

It walked right up to Serril, staring at him and Jayin with impossible blue eyes, as if evaluating the two. It nudged gently at Serril's shoulder and then Jayin's. The creature looked for all the world as if it–no, she–were on the verge of tears as she took a step back, shifting her head in an unmistakable "follow me" motion.

Jayin gaped and looked on the verge of tears. Serril

swallowed and said, "Your pardon, but my Trainee and I haven't had any rest for the past day–"

:I know, and if I had any other choice, I wouldn't be asking this.: The voice–decidedly female, anxious and fearful–came from the Companion in front of them. There was really no other explanation. Jayin must have heard it as well from the strangled squeaking she made.

:I'm breaking a host of rules by doing this, of course, but it seems to me that the rules are going to get rewritten soon enough. My Herald has need of your particular talents, the both of you. And she doesn't have much time.: The Companion blew air through her nose in not quite a snort. *:I'm Layelle, and my Herald is Mellie. Please, please, please say you'll come?:* The worry came through even without the words being spoken out loud–in fact, it was even more apparent this way.

Jayin squeaked a bit more–she'd had dreams once of being a Herald–but Serril gave the Companion a slow nod. No, Layelle. "If you have need of us, Companion Layelle, then lead on. We'll do what we can."

They followed Layelle to the hospice meant for the most seriously wounded who could still be treated. Firm beds made it easier to move patients, detachable wooden railings prevented accidents such as rolling off the bed, and various pulleys allowed for broken limbs to be kept elevated. And a quarter of the beds were meant for Heralds as well, since they had wide near-doors by each bed that could allow a Companion to stick his or her head in during decent weather.

They reached Mellie's bed about the same time as Layelle nudged open the wooden panel. The evening was temperate enough that Serril didn't object–for the moment, it seemed to not be raining. As he looked down into the bed, he sucked in air through clenched teeth, shock jolting him awake. Mellie was tied to the bed frame as gently as possible but her wrists and ankles showed signs of resistance. Her sweat soaked hair flared around her head across both pillow and blankets. Already pale features looked ghastly against the sheets. The young woman, barely older than Jayin, muttered despite the depth of a slumber produced by the contents of the cup next to the bed.

Serril looked over the slate board at the foot of the bed. Convulsions and fever were the only obvious signs of illness. No bite marks from insects or snakes, no unaccounted bruising to either body or head, and no trouble breathing–in short, nothing the Healers could label and treat. Mellie was capable of taking in light broth and milk sweetened with honey, according to the notes, but alone those were not enough to sustain the Herald.

"Companion Layelle," Serril began, "since this information isn't helping me, what do you know?"

Blue eyes met his even as Jayin ran a standard round of tests. Absently Serril noted that his Trainee had woken up as well. *:It began when all the Heralds in Haven were struck with that headache. Mellie and I weren't too far from here, but her headache seemed particularly bad. She got over it, though, and I didn't think about it until she started having trouble sleeping. We were headed out on Circuit but Mellie kept insisting that we had to go back. Her Mindspeech wasn't good enough to reach the capital, and I didn't feel the same pull she did.:* The Companion paused, though Serril only noticed it because he was listening so hard. *:A few nights ago, we slept at a Waystation. Mellie had been irritable all day, as if she had a mild headache, but it wasn't anything I felt through her. The next morning, she barely woke up enough to get up on me, practically crying from the pain. I came back here as fast as I could, but nobody here seemed to know what to do.:*

Jayin must have heard something in the Companion's

mind-voice, because she asked, "You have an idea of what's going on, though, don't you?"

The brilliant white head sagged, like a child caught with a hand in the candy jar. *:The thing that caused the headache was a source of magic landing right in the middle of Haven. I think that woke something up in Mellie, maybe Mage Gift, but. . . :* Here the Companion paused obviously. *:I think the Mage channels were damaged in the process. And the two of you are my best hope of healing those channels, because each of you has worked directly on Healing channels before. Unlike the other Healers here in Haven.:*

Serril blinked. "Are Healing channels that similar, then?"

:Close enough that with the three of us, Mellie has a chance. Otherwise . . ..: The Companion trailed off, the fear once again rising in her voice.

Jayin put a hand on Serril's arm. "We have to do this. With the war still going on, Valdemar's going to need all the Herald-Mages she can field."

Serril knew this. Just as well as he knew how risky it was to go mucking about with someone's channels of energy. It wasn't a matter of strength in the Gift, patience, or delicacy–most Gifted Healers had all three. It took a Master level of talent to even touch the Healing channels. Never mind that these were Mage channels, not Healing channels. But the situation needed them. Mellie and Layelle needed them. After a moment, he nodded.

"Jayin, get the blankets and some lanterns. We'll need as much privacy as possible for this. Layelle, I don't know how, but you seem to know what we need to do, so whatever help you can give us will be appreciated."

In moments, the four of them were isolated from the rest of the room. Jayin had added a tiny bit of mint oil to the lamps' reservoirs, something Serril wouldn't have thought of, to keep the air smelling clean while they worked. Layelle leaned over to gently lip Mellie's hair then looked at the two Healers.

:Here. I'll link to you both so that I can "show" you where the channels are.: And as Serril "reached" for Jayin, to link their Healing together as they'd done so often recently, he felt a third presence join them: female, warm with hope, cool with worry, familiar in a way that told him that Layelle knew Healing in more than the abstract.

The three sank "into" Mellie, finding the obvious places they would ordinarily touch to bring Healing but knowing that those would need to wait. Layelle "pointed" in a direction that was new to the two Healers, guiding them toward a "place" that Serril immediately compared to a muscle-deep cut. It pulsed, raw and bleeding, even the faint trickle of power that he could now sense abrading the already sensitive "surfaces" of the channels. Where the channels began, the Healer could "see" that Mellie had unconsciously tried to block everything off; even that wasn't enough, her "wall" only able to contain some of the energy that wanted to flow through those channels. Some deep part of himself hummed in both excitement and satisfaction. Together, he and Jayin would teach other Healers how to look for Mage channels, spread the knowledge so it wouldn't be lost.

Now that Layelle had "shown" him–and Jayin–where the channels existed, the next step was to determine how best to Heal them. In Healer Trainees who had overextended themselves, the Healing energy itself would often help restore those channels, as long as the Trainees remembered not to use their Gifts. Here, though, the Mage energies were different enough that they couldn't just sit back and let nature take its course. The channels were already so raw that Mellie might never be able to use them even when Healed.

:How can we do this?: It was very odd, hearing Jayin by way of Layelle. The Companion must be breaking even more rules to allow the three of them to communicate as if they were all Gifted with Mindspeech. A faint flare of guilt tempered with the feeling of necessity answered his question.

He thought for a moment. *:We need to insulate the channels from the Mage energies. Layelle, is there anything you can do about that trickle of energy?:* Serril felt more than heard the snort.

:It's breaking even more rules, but yes. Odd, how easy it is to "see" everything now that both of you are working with me.:

Amazement filled him as he watched the trickle fade entirely. He couldn't tell where it was going, but what mattered was that Mellie no longer had the flow of energy rubbing raw channels. Dimly, he knew that her body had finally relaxed. It was a good step, but only a first one.

:Now,: he drew Jayin's attention to the channels themselves, *:we need to Heal those without sealing them off or creating so much scar tissue that they'll be unusable.:*

The next words out of his Trainee surprised and pleased him.

:It's like a burn, more than anything else. If we use our Healing to create a layer of "skin" over the raw places, that should allow the "walls" of the channels to recover without creating any scar tissue. It'll take more energy, but she'll recover more quickly, I think.:

Layelle's surprise echoed around the three of them, but the Companion immediately supported Jayin's idea.

:If one of you creates the "skin," the other should be able to Heal the rawness of the channels at the same time. Healer Jayin, you're brilliant! If I could, I'd *stand in front of the Board and Dean to tell them so.:*

:Jayin, then, if you would create the "skin," I'll start the Healing. Not only is it your idea, you've got a more delicate touch . You have more than twice over earned your Greens, young woman.: And the two set to work, with Jayin protecting the surface of the channels while Serril took on the simpler but more intense work of repairing the damage. The Healing went slowly as neither of them wanted to run the risk of accidentally damaging Mellie or her Mage channels. Serril couldn't be certain, but he suspected that other Healers had come and gone while they worked. Anything else simply didn't register in his awareness.

When they had finished their work with the channels, Serril was seriously drained, but they couldn't stop. There were areas around the channels that needed attention that nonGifted healing wouldn't touch. Jayin was drained nearly as much as he was, but he felt her determination through the link shared with Layelle.

:We'll finish this the right way.: Serril felt the pride welling up in him. The good Healers–whether Gifted or gifted–had that drive. He'd seen it enough in others, and in that moment Jayin stopped being a Trainee, at least in his mind.

:That we will, Healer Jayin.: Her pleasure radiated through the link, and the two of them reached out with their Gifts to Heal the remaining damage. At the end of it, as he slowly withdrew from the Healing trance, Serril heard Layelle one last time in his mind.

:Thank you both so very much. Leave the rest to the other Healers, the Companions, and the Heralds.:

The lamps had burned out. A faint light streamed through the opening where Layelle had been. The Companion slowly trudged out of sight toward Companions' Field, head held as high as it could be considering she'd been just as busy as the two Healers. Serril could barely keep his eyes open, but he knew that he needed to take

Jayin immediately to the Dean and request–no, *demand*–that she be given her Greens immediately. Investiture and graduation were formalities at this point, in his opinion. He was about to say so when the woman on the bed opened her eyes and inhaled slowly.

"Pain's goon." The Herald's voice was creaky, low, and the she swallowed carefully. "Yuz'r gud fer sommat." Before she could say any more, Jayin laid a careful hand on their patient's forehead.

"Of course we are," the soon-to-be-Healer said with a note of pride singing through her obvious fatigue. "We have to be. Our work doesn't stop with just healing." Ignoring the surprised snort, she stood and wavered a moment before catching her balance. "Let's go tell the Dean, get my Greens, and then–then maybe I can sleep."

They supported each other all the way to the Dean's office.

A Leash of Greyhounds

Elisabeth Waters

The greyhounds were upset. There was blood, which wasn't surprising because Shantell's husband, Lord Kristion, and his friend Teren had taken the dogs with them when they went out hunting, but there was something wrong . . .

"Lena," Lady Shantell said gently. "You'll never finish your embroidery if you just sit there staring at nothing. Besides, it's rude."

It's the wrong blood . . . Lena shivered. "I apologize," she said aloud. "It's very kind of you to teach me to embroider."

"Your mother would have wanted me to," Shantell said simply.

That's probably true, although I don't remember her all that well. It is *kind of Lady Shantell to invite me to stay at her home and to try to teach me the things a young lady should know. Just because she was a friend of my mother's doesn't mean that she's obliged to do anything for me. And it certainly isn't her fault that I'd rather be back in Haven at the Temple. I'm glad that I'll be going back next week; I miss the animals there—and the people.* Lena bent her head and concentrated on the embroidery. Whatever was bothering the dogs, she'd find out soon enough.

The men had still not returned when the tea tray was brought in and Shantell's son joined them. Jasper was ten, five years younger than Lena and about the age she had been when the last member of her family died. Lena was now a ward of the King, so she took classes at the Palace complex along with the Herald, Bardic, and Healer Trainees, but she lived at the Temple of Thenoth, Lord of the Beasts. She had been there for the past several years, ever since her gift—Animal Mindspeech—had started to develop.

Shantell was a devout follower of a god who had no name—or perhaps a name too holy to be spoken, Lena wasn't sure which—and she used teatime to concentrate on her son's religious education. They believed that their god was the only one that existed, another concept that Lena found strange. She had, however, quickly learned to keep quiet about her own beliefs. Lady Shantell didn't approve of a god who cared about animals, and Lena's explanation that there were plenty of other gods who cared about people had earned her a scolding for blasphemy. *I don't think my saying it is blasphemy if I don't worship her god. And the King and all of my teachers say there is no one true way. That's the law. Still, I'm not going to tell her that I have Animal Mindspeech; I don't think she would appreciate* that *at all.*

But at the moment being able to talk to the dogs wasn't helping much. They weren't making any sense. Lena knew that they were still in the woods, guarding the kill and waiting for somebody to carry it home, but why were they so sad?

When the butler appeared in the doorway as soon as Jasper had returned to the nursery, Lena hardly needed to look at his face to know that something horrible had happened.

"Lady Shantell," he began gently, "there's been an accident. Lord Kristion was shot—"

Shantelle jumped out of her chair and hurried across the room. "Where is he?" she demanded.

The butler actually turned pale. "They're bringing his body home now, Lady."

Shantell collapsed on the nearest chair and started screaming. The butler stood frozen in the doorway, gaping at his mistress, who had probably never been anything but gentle and soft-spoken in her life. Crossing the room past her so that she could talk to the butler without trying to scream over her, Lena suggested that he summon her maid and the priest. The butler bowed gratefully and left at a speed that was just a bit slower than flight. Shantell continued to scream, leaving Lena wishing that she could flee the room as well.

With the help of the housekeeper, Shantell's maid got her to drink some sort of sedative and put her to bed. The body was brought home, washed, and laid out in the chapel, where the priest said prayers over it. Apparently he considered it proper for someone to be in the chapel with the body until it could be buried, and Lena, who was in the habit of rising before dawn at the Temple, volunteered to take the predawn watch.

She found herself wide awake over an hour before she was due in the chapel, and she could still hear the greyhounds in her head, so she dressed quickly and went out to the kennels. The Kennelmaster was asleep—*I don't blame him; he must have had a* really *horrible day yesterday*— and the dogs whined quietly and crowded around her. Lena stroked heads as they were shoved into her lap and tried to calm them. But all too soon it was time for her watch in the chapel, and the dogs were unwilling to be parted from her. *At least they're quiet as long as they're with me, so I guess it's better if I just take them along.*

Lena preceded the dogs into the chapel and told

them to hang back, so that the housekeeper, who had the watch before hers, left without seeing them. Lena sat on a bench at the head of the bier, and the dogs formed a circle around the body.

The chapel was made of stone and was separate from the main house, so it was very cold inside. Lena wrapped her cloak more tightly around her, but it didn't help her shivering much. She rose to her feet and paced around the bier, envying the dogs their fur. They lay quietly, but she could feel them, a low mumble in the back of her mind, mourning for their master.

She heard heavy footsteps approaching, and she hastily returned to the bench and bowed her head as if in prayer. She wasn't sure how to pray in this situation; she didn't know enough about Shantell's god to feel comfortable addressing him, but she was pretty sure that Shantell would object to prayers addressed to any other god, especially in her god's chapel. Possibly her god would too, and Lena had no desire to anger him. So she mostly thought about the life of Lord Kristion and how much everyone was going to miss him.

The footsteps had entered the chapel, and Lena had heard a thud as their owner collapsed onto a bench near the back of the chapel. Now she could hear weeping, the choked sobs of a grown man trying unsuccessfully not to cry. Without raising her bowed head, she cast her eyes sideways. It was Lord Teren, Kristion's best friend—the man who had killed him.

Lena had heard enough of the talk when they brought the body home to know that the death had been a tragic accident. The men had become separated in the woods, and the arrow that Lord Teren loosed had not been intended to lodge in the heart of his best friend. She could understand his grief, and she sympathized slightly—*though I still think it's stupid and dangerous to loose an arrow when you are not absolutely certain of your target.*

And I don't think there's any *god that will help you if Lady Shantell finds you here . . .*

Naturally, that was exactly what happened. Shantell had awakened at dawn, as she usually did, and her first act was to come to the chapel to pray. She didn't see Lord Teren at first, so she started by scolding Lena for bringing the dogs into the chapel. "I'm sorry," Lena murmured and then stopped talking, knowing that no defense could possibly appease Shantell. *:Go outside and hide where nobody will see you,:* she directed, and the dogs slipped down the side aisle of the chapel and out though the door that Shantell had left ajar.

Shantell, turning her head as they moved, saw Lord Teren and started screaming again, but unlike yesterday her screaming had words. "You murderer! How dare you show your face here?

"Shantell," he began, "I am so sorry—"

"You killed my husband!"

"It was an accident—"

"You *enjoy* killing, you and those damned dogs!"

"If having the dogs here is distressing to you, Shantell, I can remove them to my estate so you won't have to see them again."

Shantell's voice dropped from a scream into something that Lena found much more frightening; it was cold, hard, and intense. Each syllable was precisely enunciated as she said, "I will have every single one of them killed before I allow you to profit by what you've done." She turned on her heel and stalked out of the chapel.

Lena sank back onto the bench and shivered uncontrollably. *She means it*, she realized. *She really will kill them. She thinks of them as dumb animals, and technically they're property . . .*

"Lord Teren?" she asked timidly.

He looked at her in surprise. "What is it, uh—"

"Lena," she supplied, not surprised that he'd forgotten her name with all that was going on. "What did she mean by 'profit'?"

"Greyhounds, especially trained hunting dogs, are valuable animals," he said with a sigh. "But if she thinks I'd kill anyone, let alone my best friend, just to get his dogs, she's . . ." he faltered, apparently unable to come up with any description he considered acceptable.

"—crazed with grief," Lena finished for him. It was a condition she understood. She didn't remember her mother much, but she had adored her father, and her initial reaction to his death had been very similar to Shantell's. She had screamed wordlessly for at least half an hour. *And if I'd known what life was going to be like with my brother as my guardian, I'd probably have screamed even longer.* "Can she really have the dogs killed?" she asked anxiously. "Do they belong to her now?"

"I believe that Kristion's will leaves them to Jasper."

"But Jasper's a child, so he doesn't get to make decisions." *Another subject I know about.* "Who is his guardian?"

Lord Teren looked sick. "God help us all; I am." He buried his face in his hands. Lena wasn't sure whether he was praying, crying, or both. She sat in uncomfortable silence until the steward arrived to take over the vigil and then quietly left the chapel.

She wasn't hungry, so instead of going in search of breakfast she went to the kennels. The Kennelmaster was there, but the dogs who had been in the chapel with her were not. The only dogs in the building were Minda, a female who had just given birth, and her six puppies. To Lena's surprise, Jasper knelt next to them, sobbing disconsolately.

"I'm sorry, Jasper," she said, starting to express condolences on the death of his father, but he turned at the sound of her voice and flung both arms around her legs, almost knocking her to the floor.

"Make her stop!" he begged.

"Make who stop what?"

Over Jasper's sobs, the Kennelmaster explained, looking both ill and ill-at-ease. "Lady Shantell stormed in here about half an hour ago and ordered me to kill all of Lord Kristion's dogs. Jasper had come down to look at the puppies, so he heard her."

"Oh, lord." Lena detached Jasper's arms, sat down on the floor, and put her arms around him as he crawled into her lap. She looked up at the Kennelmaster. "Are you planning to obey her right away?"

"I'm hoping she'll calm down and rescind the order."

"Even if she doesn't," Lena pointed out, "does she have the legal authority to give that order? The dogs may belong to Jasper; nobody knows until Lord Kristion's will is read. If they are Jasper's, it's pretty clear that he doesn't want them killed. Also, the dogs are valuable, aren't they?"

"Yes," the Kennelmaster said. "There are people willing to pay large sums for the puppies, and the trained dogs are worth even more."

"So even if Lady Shantell is Jasper's guardian, and we don't know that she is, killing the dogs would not be in his best interests from a financial standpoint, let alone an emotional one." *I'm glad I was paying attention during those classes on Kingdom law.* "So, if I were you, I'd keep stalling. Maybe we can get a ruling from the local Magistrate—who is that, anyway?"

"Lord Teren," Jasper mumbled into her shoulder.

"I don't think your mother is listening to him right now," Lena said ruefully. She looked around innocently. "Where are the rest of the dogs?"

The Kennelmaster frowned. "I don't know. Someone came in and let them out during the night."

"I let them out," Lena said. *No point in lying about that, even if I wanted to—Shantell saw them with me.* "They were restless, so I took them with me when I went to the chapel for my share of the vigil. Then Lady Shantell came in and yelled because they were there, so I sent them outside. But if you can't find them, you can't kill them."

"Good," the Kennelmaster said. "Just as long as they stay safe wherever they are." He sighed. "Where's a Herald when you need one?"

That's a really good question. Lena looked down at the child in her lap. "Jasper, have you had breakfast?" He shook his head. "Let's go to the kitchens and see if we can find something to eat. Things probably won't seem quite so bad when we're not facing them with an empty stomach."

After making sure that Jasper ate and escorting him back to the nursery, Lena slipped out of the house, avoiding both Shantell and the servants, and made her way unseen into the forested portion of the estate. *I should be safe enough; I'm pretty sure that nobody is going to be hunting here today.* She sat down on what passed for a comfortable boulder and cautiously opened her mind to the animals in the vicinity.

The dogs were the first to respond. In moments she was surrounded by the entire pack. *:Home?:* they asked.

:Too dangerous.: She sent an image of Shantell's raging and the Kennelmaster looking sick at the thought of killing them. *:Can you find enough food here?:*

:Lots of rabbits. And deer.: With the discipline she had learned at the Temple, Lena ignored the images that accompanied the replies. Fortunately she had never kept rabbits as pets, and Maia, a fellow Novice who also had Animal Mindspeech and had taught Lena much of what she knew, had grown up next to the Forest of Sorrows, so Lena had some experience with how animals who were not being fed by humans regarded meals. Thinking of Maia reminded her of the crows. Maia had brought a

group of them ("a storytelling of crows," she had called them) to the Temple with her—or, more accurately, they had chosen to accompany her. If they liked you, they would do you favors, like following someone and reporting back on what they did. Maia had taught Lena how to talk to them, and Lena was pretty sure that at least a few of them had followed her on her journey. She reached out with her mind . . .*There!*

The crows were not nearby, and she didn't want to consider what they were eating, so she sent a mental picture of a Herald and Companion, along with *:where?:* and the emotion of needing help. Several crows lifted up above the treetops to scan the surrounding countryside, and Lena settled down to wait, petting the dogs as they leaned against her legs.

Between using her Gift and stroking canine fur, Lena was half in a trance, so she wasn't surprised when, some unknown amount of time later, a Herald appeared in her vision. The Herald looked startled, as anyone would be when a crow flew directly toward her face, but even through the crow's eyes Lena recognized her. Samira was one of the Heralds Lena knew well, and her Companion, Clyton, even deigned to speak to Maia on rare occasions, so it was possible that he might be able to hear her. Lena tried to reach his mind, but apparently they were too far away. Samira, however, was a friend of Maia's, so it didn't take her long to realize what a crow behaving unusually in this area must mean.

"Lena? If you can hear me, you'll know that we're on our way." Then Clyton moved so fast that he was a white streak passing the crows who perched in the trees above him. Lena looked through their eyes as they rose to fly back long enough to figure out what route Samira and Clyton were taking. Then she pulled her concentration back into her body, rose to her feet, and headed through the forest toward the road so that she could intercept

Samira before she rode into the chaos of the household unprepared.

Clyton almost charged right past her despite the fact that Lena was standing alone in the middle of the road. She had persuaded the dogs to stay out of sight in the woods.

"What's going on, Lena?" Samira asked. "Are you all right?"

"Pretty much," Lena replied, "but Lord Kristion is dead, and things are not going well."

"What happened to him?" This was Samira's current Circuit, so she knew that Lord Kristion had been young and healthy.

"He went out hunting with his best friend a couple of days ago . . ." Lena took a deep breath and blurted out the rest: "Lord Teren shot him by accident, and Lady Shantell called Lord Teren a murderer, and now she's ordered the Kennelmaster to kill all of the dogs, and Jasper's really upset about that."

Samira pinched the spot where her nose met her forehead as if the muscle had gone into spasm and shook her head. "Are you sure it was an accident?"

"Lord Teren says it was, the servants who were with him say it was, and the dogs say it was. I believe them."

"What does the Magistrate say?"

"Apparently Lord Teren is the Magistrate."

"Yes, that's right; he is." Samira sighed. "Why does Lady Shantell want to kill the dogs?"

"I don't know. Maybe because she can't kill Lord Teren?" Lena shrugged. "It's too bad her religion isn't one of the ones that teaches forgiveness of one's enemies."

Samira looked at her oddly. "It does teach that."

"Are you sure? She certainly isn't acting like it, and she scolded me for worshiping Thenoth. And her own son seems to believe she'll kill the dogs; he was out in the kennels crying over them this morning."

"The dogs are still in the kennels?" Samira raised her eyebrows. "Knowing you, I'm surprised there's a dog on the estate she can still find."

"Minda just had puppies; they can't be moved. The rest aren't there. The Kennelmaster doesn't want to follow Shantell's orders, and if he can't find the dogs, he can't kill them."

"I'm sure he appreciates your help," Samira said dryly.

"He seems to, actually. I also pointed out that there may be legal questions—the dogs may belong to Jasper instead of Shantell, and her husband may have named someone else as Jasper's guardian."

"That's a good argument," Samira admitted. "How likely is it?"

"Lord Teren said that Lord Kristion had named him."

Samira groaned. "I can tell that this is going to be complicated." She and Clyton started forward at a walk that Lena could easily keep pace with. "Let's go face the noise."

:Stay in the woods,: Lena told the dogs as she accompanied Samira and Clyton toward the main entrance to the estate.

"Have they set a time for the funeral yet?" Samira asked.

"This afternoon."

"It *is* afternoon," Samira pointed out. "When this afternoon?"

Lena cast an anxious look at the angle of the sun. "The ninth hour," she said in a small voice.

"Less than an hour from now. I need to wash and change into a clean uniform, and *you* look as though you dressed in the dark and then spent the day in the kennels and the woods."

"I did."

Samira's eyes closed briefly and then opened again.

Apparently she had been Mindspeaking to Clyton, because he stopped long enough for Samira to reach down, grasp forearms with Lena, and swing her onto Clyton's back. "What's the fastest way to reach the stables without Lady Shantell seeing us?"

They left Clyton being rubbed down by the Stablemaster, and Lena turned Samira over to the housekeeper to be shown to a guest room. Then she ran for her room, washed in the now-cold water that someone had left out for her that morning, and pulled on a dress that was suitable for the funeral. She slipped quietly into the chapel, aided by the fact that most of the household was gathered there. Samira, resplendent in the dressy version of her Whites, was seated in the front next to Shantell and Jasper. Lord Teren was in the back of the chapel, trying to be invisible. Either he succeeded or Shantell didn't deign to notice him, and the funeral service and the burial that followed it went as well as could be expected.

After the funeral, it was customary to read the will. They gathered in the library: the priest, who had charge of the document; Lady Shantell; Jasper, who despite his young age was now Lord Jasper; Samira; Lena, partly because Jasper wanted her there and partly because Samira had requested her as a neutral high-born witness; and Lord Teren. Shantell protested his inclusion, but the priest told her it was needful, and her piety—at least for the moment—overcame her wrath.

The moment ended abruptly when she discovered that her husband had named Lord Teren to be Jasper's guardian. "Should my son be forced to face his father's murderer?" she demanded indignantly.

The priest said something about forgiveness; Lena couldn't make out the exact words, because Samira's voice overrode his.

"Normally we could ask the local Magistrate to hear this case," she started, but Shantell interrupted her.

"*He*'s the Magistrate!" she exclaimed passionately. "Do you think he'll rule justly on his own actions?"

"That's why Valdemar has Heralds," Samira reminded everyone. "I ride this Circuit so that I can hear cases where normal practice cannot be used, and I believe that this one qualifies. Does anyone disagree?"

Shantell fell silent.

Lord Teren spoke sadly. "I yield this case to your judgment, Herald Samira. I agree that I am not the person to rule on it, being involved myself."

"Please," Jasper added. "Everyone's so angry, and they keep yelling."

The priest nodded agreement. "Obviously this was not the situation Lord Kristion envisioned when I drew up his will."

"Very well," Samira said. "Lord Teren, are you willing to answer the accusation of murder under Truth Spell?"

"Absolutely." Lord Teren looked grim but not at all afraid.

Samira cast the Truth Spell, and Lena watched with fascination as a blue glow appeared over Lord Teren's head.

"Who went hunting with you and Lord Kristion?"

"In addition to the two of us, there were three servants and seven hunting dogs."

"Was it your arrow that shot him?"

"Yes." His voice held anguish, but the blue glow remained steady.

"Did you intend to shoot him?"

"No. Never. We became separated in the woods, and I had no idea that he had circled around so that he was opposite me. The servants were with me, so they didn't know either."

"What was he wearing?"

Teren looked blank. "I don't remember."

Lena must have made some sound, for Samira looked at her. "Do you know what he was wearing, Lena?"

"Yes." *And it was one of the most stupid things anyone could wear to go hunting.* "Brown boots, brown pants, and a deerskin jacket."

Samira looked at her incredulously. "Deerskin? Are you positive of that?"

I certainly can't blame her for not believing me.

"That's correct," the priest said. "I saw his body when it was brought home, and that's what he was wearing."

Samira managed to refrain from comment on Lord Kristion's clothing choices. "Lord Teren, do you swear that your shooting of Lord Kristion was accidental and that you had no reason or desire to kill him?"

"I do so swear."

Despite the steady glow of the Truth Spell, Shantell cried out "That's not true! He wanted the dogs! He said so, this morning in the chapel!"

"That's not what I said!" Lord Teren protested.

"Was anyone else in the chapel with you?" Samira asked.

Teren pointed at Lena. "She was."

I think he forgot my name again.

"Lena?" Samira asked. "What did they say?"

As Lena opened her mouth to answer, Samira held up a hand. "Wait. I'm going to put a Truth Spell on you before you answer."

Lena nodded her consent and sat quietly until Samira gestured her to continue. "Lady Shantell came in at dawn, near the end of my vigil. Lord Teren had come in earlier and was sitting near the back of the chapel. When she saw him, she called him a murderer. He said it was an accident, and she said that he enjoyed killing—he and the dogs. What he said then was that if having the dogs here was distressing to her, he could remove them to his estate so that she wouldn't have to see them. Then she said that she'd have every single one of them killed before she'd let him profit—and then she went to the Kennelmaster and ordered the dogs killed."

"Did you hear her give that order?"

"No, but when I went to the kennels as soon as I got out of the chapel, Jasper was there with the Kennelmaster, and they both said that she had ordered the dogs killed."

"She did," Jasper said positively. "I heard her. And I don't want the dogs killed. And the priest said that the dogs are mine now."

Samira held up a hand again. "We'll get back to that in a minute, Lord Jasper. Lord Teren, did you or do you have any plans to profit from the dogs?"

Lord Teren shook his head wearily. "No. I will never hunt again. My only thought was to give the dogs a home where they would not trouble Lady Shantell."

The blue glow of the Truth Spell remained steady. Samira took a deep breath and said, "On the charge of murder, I find Lord Teren innocent. Lord Kristion's death was accidental."

"He still killed my husband!"

"True, but he did not murder him. There is a difference."

"My husband is dead, my son is an orphan, and the man who killed his father is to be his guardian?" Shantell protested.

"That issue is still to be resolved," Samira said.

"I would be willing to cede the guardianship to Lady Shantell," Lord Teren said.

"No!" Jasper protested. "She'll kill the dogs!"

"Jasper!" Shantell's voice was somewhere between hurt and fury. "Would you favor your father's killer over your own mother?"

Lena, who was still holding the hand Jasper had slipped into hers when the reading of the will began, gave it a warning squeeze. She leaned over and murmured softly into his ear. "There's no good reply to that question; don't even try to answer it."

"I see that we had best settle the question of the dogs before the guardianship," Samira said, shuffling priorities. "What kind of dogs are we dealing with?"

"Greyhounds," Lord Teren replied. "Trained hunting dogs. Not only does Jasper not want them killed, but they are also quite valuable. It would not be in his best interests to have them killed; indeed, it would be a breach of duty for a guardian to order such a thing."

"Well, I won't have them here, and I won't let you take them!" Shantell said furiously. "And I don't want them around my child—he doesn't need anything to tempt *him* to take up hunting!"

"Lord Jasper," Samira asked. "Would you be willing to have the dogs live someplace else, as long as they would be safe and well cared for?"

Jasper chewed on his lower lip for a moment, and then nodded reluctantly. "I'll miss the puppies, but it's more important that they be safe."

"Is there anyone you would trust to care for them?"

"Yes. Lena."

"But Lena lives in Haven," Samira pointed out. "That's rather far away."

"She lives with . . . people . . . who like animals."

Thank all the gods that he didn't say "a god who likes animals."

"Lena?" Samira asked.

Lena thought quickly. "Yes, I can take them." *The Temple of Thenoth will certainly grant sanctuary to animals under the threat of death.* "The King is sending a carriage to take me home; it's due in two days. We should be able to transport Minda and her puppies in it."

"How many dogs are we talking about here?" Samira asked.

Lena ticked them off on her fingers. "Minda, six puppies, and the seven hunting dogs. Fourteen."

"You're willing to travel all the way to Haven in a carriage with fourteen dogs?"

Lena nodded. Samira shook her head. "Better you than me. Very well, if everyone agrees that this is what should be done with the dogs—" She looked around the room until she got agreement, however reluctant, from everyone involved.

"Now, with regard to the guardianship: Lord Kristion named Lord Teren. Does anyone know his thinking on this?"

The priest was the one to reply. "He felt that if he died while Lord Jasper was still a child, he would benefit by a man's guidance."

"So it was not that he considered Lady Shantell incapable of managing the estate?"

"Indeed not." The priest was definite on that point at least. "She customarily ran the estate when he was absent at court or performing military service."

"That's true," Lord Teren corroborated. "Lady Shantell is fully capable of running the estate and raising her son. That's why I'm willing to resign as Jasper's guardian in her favor." The Truth Spell showed that he believed what he said.

Samira looked skeptically at him and even more skeptically at Lady Shantell. "At the moment, I'm not particularly impressed with the soundness of her judgment." She looked from one to the other and then at the priest. "I therefore rule as follows: For the next half-year the two of you will be joint guardians, and any decisions that affect Jasper's well being or the assets of the estate must be agreed upon by both of you."

Shantell opened her mouth to protest, and Samira

glared at her. "If you are unable to work together in person, your priest may serve as a mediator." She looked at the priest and added, "If that is acceptable to him."

"I will be happy to do anything in my power to help," he replied.

"Very well." Samira dismissed the Truth Spells. "Those are my decisions."

Samira stayed at the estate for a pair of days, ostensibly using it as a base for her duties in the surrounding area. "Actually," she told Lena, "it's partly that I want to be sure that Lady Shantell is calming down enough to think rationally again and that Jasper is all right—but mostly I want to see you fit fourteen dogs into a coach with you and your luggage!"

"Luggage?" Lena grinned at her. "I'm donating some of my clothing to the housekeeper for cleaning rags—it's amazing how much of it got torn up in the woods while I was here. So I won't have much luggage, and it can go on the roof. And I like dogs."

"Will you still like them when you get back to Haven?" Samira asked teasingly.

By the time she got back to Haven, Lena's remaining dresses were covered with dog hair, and she had a close bond with all of the dogs. She had sent the crows to warn Maia of the new arrivals so that there would be a place prepared for them in the kennels, and Maia was in the temple courtyard when the carriage arrived.

"Is there one of your fancy names for the dogs?" Lena asked Maia as they carefully carried the puppies to the kennel, escorted by Minda and the rest of the pack.

"Yes," Maia replied. "You've brought us a leash of greyhounds."

Warp and Weft

Kristin Schwengel

No one could say for *certain* what had happened to Triska, but the disordered heap of robes and the unique necklace found inside the Change Circle—and the mangled remains of a rather average-sized lizard just outside that circle—spoke volumes.

The hertasi artisan had known, had heard the warnings of the Elders, and yet she had gone outside the protective shields of the Vale. The residents of k'Veyas, warned by the Alliance Mages, had known that it was coming, this final Mage Storm, had realized that it could destroy them all if the shielding failed. Triska, of course, had known. And she had still gone out.

"The silk waits for no one," she had been fond of saying, usually just before leaving the Vale in foul weather to harvest cocoons. And the Change Circle where the remains had been found, the locus of mutation formed by the overlap of two rippling waves of magical energy, was not far from her favorite trees, the ones whose silkworms always produced the strongest, finest, smoothest fibers.

When the Elders showed Stardance the broken chain and cracked amber stone retrieved from the pile, the gift she had given to the cloth artisan, she buried her grief after the first stunned moment. Fury was simpler, covering the dark, hollow loneliness that threatened. The anger warmed her, kept her from drowning in that aching emptiness, and she fed it, raging in turn at the Elders, at Triska, and at the implacable Storms themselves, then fled to the most private corner of the Vale, the secret nook she had discovered as a child running from her mother's death. This time, there would be no Triska to find her, to take her into her care and heal her hurting, bringing her back to the life of the Vale.

Back then, the Elders of k'Veyas had found it amusing, the human child following the hertasi, when usually the lizardfolk were the dutiful aides and helpers of the Tayledras. Since Triska did not seem bothered by Stardance's presence, the girl had been allowed to spend most of her time in the company of the clothworker, sometimes seeming like a daughter, sometimes an apprentice. Her father lived in his home Vale of k'Lissa, and since at the time he was unable to care for a youngster, k'Veyas agreed to keep her in their Vale. She had always been a solitary child, and with the hertasi to help her she was allowed exceptional freedom.

Even after Stardance showed signs of her father's Mage Gift, she still stayed with Triska. The Elders taught her, and she was an apt pupil, but she was more often to be found practicing her skills with the threads and fibers in Triska's cliffside den than in the heavily warded practice rooms. None of the Tayledras were quite certain what a hertasi could or couldn't do with magic, but since Triska seemed unconcerned about her adopted daughter's magical "play" the Elders permitted Stardance to remain with her.

After several years of this odd training, Stardance was just old enough for her Mage Gift to truly begin to develop into its full power and potential. Now, though, the Storms had come and gone, and magic was no longer the same. The Heartstones were weakened or empty, their accumulated power drained to maintain the last desperate shields over the Vales, to save the people within them. Outside, caught in a Change Circle, Triska had not been so fortunate.

Winternight stood, and respectful silence fell. The Storms had aged him so that his usual pallor now seemed ghostlike, his energy spent and drained from him just as the once-vibrant Heartstone was now emptied of all but the faintest flickers of magic. His staff, once used to help him direct his considerable power, now served only to provide physical support, and he leaned heavily on it.

"We do not yet know the extent of damage in our own region of the Pelagiris, much less that of the other Vales," he said, in response to several questioners. "Only the strongest Farspeakers have been able to communicate with them. Our scouts have been taking care of Change-Beasts as they have found them, but our perimeter of safety is much closer to the Vale than ever it was." He paused to emphasize the reality of the damage done and the isolation of their Vale, off on a western edge of the Pelagiris.

"I propose that we send Mages out with our border patrols and scouts, one Mage with a group of two or three trained fighters. The Mages can begin to assess the extent of the damage to the magical energy around the Vale and help guide Silverheart's efforts to Heal it. If they encounter Change-Creatures, the Mages will also recognize which might be more than physical threats."

"What of the students?" someone asked. "Even if all the magic is gone, what should they be doing? We can't send them out to the perimeters!" An immediate babble followed—some in favor of utilizing every resource the Vale had, others insisting that those who were not confirmed Mages should not even attempt to use magic until the lasting effects of the Storms were completely known.

Winternight raised his hand, and the din drifted back to quiet. "The students will not go to the outer perimeters, but every bit of help is needed." He paused again. "They will work within the areas where the scouts have already passed at least once, where they are not likely to encounter Change-Beasts. They will be searching these areas for trace magics, studying any changes in patterns, looking for subtle echoes of power." A few more questions, these from some of the instructors, and Winternight gathered those few around him for private conference.

Stardance shook her head and shifted backward, edging away from the group and drifting between the trees, headed for her too-empty ekele. She did not dare defy the direct command of the Elders that all the Mage-talented and trained of k'Veyas attend the meeting, but she had chosen to stand in a half-hidden spot on the outskirts of the assembly. *It is all folly, anyway,* she thought bitterly. Of what use were they, now that the magic had disappeared? What good was anything now that Triska was—she shut down the thought before she could complete it, returning to her anger to cover the aching void inside her. What good was magic, anyway? After all, it had been a centuries-gone excess of magic that had caused this nightmare. Maybe there was a lesson to be learned. Maybe their Shin'a'in cousins had the right of it—maybe it was time they did without magic entirely.

She was almost out of view, almost free, when a gentle but firm hand fell on her shoulder.

"You, too, will take part in the search tomorrow." Windwhisperer's voice, though quiet, was implacable.

"What would be the point? There's nothing left!" Hostile resentment lashed through her words.

"We don't know that for certain. But we need to find out."

"I can't be what you want," she muttered to the ground, unsure what the words meant even as she said them.

"What would you be, then?" That quiet voice held no anger, no demand. She turned to look at him. The Elder's face was as still as his words, giving her no impression of his thoughts.

She shifted away, her eyes dropping again. "Once, I might have known. Now, there's no point. It doesn't matter." She thought briefly of Triska's cave, of working with the richly colored fibers and fabrics, creating beauty with functionality, and sharp loneliness arced pain through her heart before she shuttered her face. "Why go out there when it won't change anything?"

"Perhaps it won't. Or perhaps it could." The silence between them lengthened. "Out there, it may be that you could find an answer to my question." She heard a faint shushing, like a breeze lifting the wide leaves outside her ekele, and she looked up once more, only to find herself alone on the sanded path.

When morning came, Stardance found herself walking beyond the borders of the Vale, one of the first group of students assigned to a small section of the "safer" areas. Just as the confirmed Mages were partnered with experienced scouts and patrols, the students, too, were accompanied by younger fighters. Stardance was the youngest student in the group traveling to the east of the Vale, and the simmering resentment in the oldest scout trainee was palpable as he paced near her. Clearly, he felt that he belonged in the unexplored places, not in the safe areas with the students.

"You don't need to babysit me," she finally snapped, knowing she sounded like a petulant child but not really caring. “If you want to go farther out, my Kir will let your bird know if I need assistance.”

The scout, barely five summers older than she, gave her an odd look, but he didn’t reply. Instead, he allowed a little more space to drift between them, no longer matching his steps to hers but lengthening his stride until he moved first beyond her view, then beyond her hearing. She shrugged. If he went too far and found something he couldn’t handle, he would deserve it. He was good enough, at least, that it had taken only moments for her to not be able to hear him. No longer distracted by his angry presence, she frowned and returned her attention to her own task.

The area she was to inspect was a rough wedge shape, curving outward from the Vale between a stand of large pines and a meadowed area and along the cliff edge that dropped down to the stream that would eventually join the Anduras. Pacing the approximate borders, using her Mage Sight to look for magical signatures or unusual tracks of anything the scouts might have missed, Stardance felt her frustration mount. *It’s just useless makework*, she thought angrily. *There’s nothing out here--they just want to keep us busy until they can figure out what to do next. I don’t know why we’re even bothering.* Even so, she continued with her task.

At first, Kir had flown overhead, helping her keep track of where her wedge overlapped with segments being examined by the other students; their bondbirds were in the air for the same purpose. After she had finished the first circuit of her area and started a closer inspection of the inside of the wedge, she gave Kir permission to land.

For several candlemarks, Stardance combed the forest, starting at the outer border of her space and spiraling inward until she reached the landmarks of the clearing that was the last, central piece of the area she was assigned to. She heard only the natural sounds of the forest, although as she neared the edges of her wedge she sometimes heard mutterings from the other students or scouts. At one point, she looked up to see the scout's goshawk bondbird lazily coasting overhead, but she neither saw nor heard any trace of the young man himself.

After another candlemark of pushing through brush and finding nothing of more concern than small rodents, Stardance stood in the small clearing that marked the "point" of her wedge. Releasing her Mage Sight with a sigh of relief, she loosened her water skin from her belt and took a drink.

:Thirsty.: Kir's MindVoice was her most plaintive. The falcon had alternated between soaring on the thermals and perching in trees near Stardance to watch her, her head cocked to the side as though she were trying to make sense of her mistress' actions.

:Come, then,: Stardance replied, lifting her hand for the falcon, who plummeted from the sky. Raising the bird from her arm brace to the leather pad on her shoulder, Stardance held up the water skin, tilting it so a careful stream poured into Kir's beak. Kir shook her head, sending droplets spattering over Stardance's face and hair. Stardance winced and pulled the water skin away, mock-glaring at her bondbird. The falcon was unchastened, her eyes glinting as she tilted her head, and Kir's teasing amusement in the back of her mind drew out the first smile Stardance had felt since the last Storm. Since Triska . . . she stopped the thought abruptly.

:I, at least, still have work to do,: she scolded the bird, but her tone was affectionate. Rather than return to the skies, Kir folded her wings back and shifted her talons on the leather pad, stabilizing her grip and rebalancing her weight so Stardance could move without disturbing her.

Stardance turned in place, her irritation with the fruitless exercise of looking for magic now returning. She studied the clearing again, glancing to the sun for her bearings. As she recalled, this place had once had a strong ley-line, which had been tapped and drawn deeper toward the Vale to power the Heartstone. Most of the sections of forest the students were searching today contained at least one former line or node. Might traces of these have survived the Storms? Was that what the Elders had hoped they would find with their closer examination?

She closed her eyes, the better to feel for any echo of the crackling energy of the magic, once so familiar to her, and expanded her Mage Sight outward. She Saw nothing—no lines, no web of energy to draw from—but she had a vague feeling, a sense that the magic was still there, somehow. She frowned in frustration. Not even sure how to go about it, she tried to change the focus of her Mage Sight, broadening and refining it at the same time. Suddenly, her mind seemed to twist, and she could See a faint tracery, limning everything around her with a subtle silver, fainter than the tiniest of ley-lines. To this odd Mage Sight, her shielded self was now surrounded by a faint haze of what she was sure was power, but she couldn't tap it or shape it. How could anyone make use of this?

"It looks like I seize the fibers, but is not so. Look deeper." Triska's voice rang in Stardance's head so clearly that the girl opened her eyes and looked around the wild forest, expecting to see the beloved snout hovering just behind an exceptionally large leaf, laughing at Stardance for believing her to be gone.

But even Kir was silent, and though the falcon liked to pretend to be aloof and regal, she would have been twittering like a magpie if anyone familiar were near.

Stardance took a deep, unsteady breath, fighting back

the crushing disappointment, the weight of loss heavy within her. Then she remembered when she had heard those words. It had been a spinning lesson, when she had been trying to use magic to help feed the fibers to the spindle faster—and had, of course, ended up with great clumps instead of smooth thread.

After those words, she had watched Triska spin, this time with her Mage Sight, sure that the hertasi was using some innate magic. How else to explain how far superior Triska's threads and weaving were? But Mage Sight had shown her nothing, just the glow of Triska's door wards, like and yet somehow unlike those used in the training rooms.

"Is in mind," Triska had finally said. "Think to make self *attractive* to fibers, no more." It hadn't made sense to Stardance at the time, so she hadn't given it further thought, but had continued to practice spinning without attempting to use magic.

Could this faint magic be spun like the loose fiber into stronger thread? Stardance looked around the clearing, trying to remember where the lines had lain before the Storms. Unable to recall, she shrugged.

"See if it works, first," she muttered. "Time enough to reshape later."

:?: sent Kir.

:Not you, silly thing. As if I'd reshape so much as a feather.:

Kir preened her plumage briefly, then resettled on Stardance's shoulder, tucking her beak behind the girl's ear in a gesture of reassurance.

Stardance closed her eyes, then opened her Mage Sight with that same twist of her mind until she could once again See the faint fog of diffuse energy around her.

Like attracts like, she thought, and fed a tiny bit of her personal power outside of her shields, letting it drift and ripple a fine radiance over her skin, inviting the nebulous energies around her to join it.

Long minutes passed, and she was about to throw up her hands and go back to the Vale in disgust, finished with this pointless task, when she again heard Triska's voice in her head.

"The silk waits for no one, but it will not be rushed."

Stardance fed a little more of her energy out to her surface, ignoring the first warnings of energy strain, imagining waggling fingers of magic waving "come, dance with us" into the energy-mist. So caught up was she by the image and the feeling she was creating that she almost missed the response of the magic-haze around her.

It was exhaustion that caught her attention—or, rather, that she no longer felt exhausted, despite using her personal energy. Slowly, she brought her Mage Sight back into sharper focus and was astonished to See faint tendrils coalescing out the mist, drawn into her shields, replenishing her.

Stunned, she thoughtlessly reached out, almost grabbed for those precious strands of power, until she practically *felt* Triska's presence beside her and remembered what had happened when she had first spun thread, how everything had tangled together when she had stopped letting the fibers flow through her fingers and had started to reach urgently for them.

Slowly, she stretched out to those tendrils with her coruscating Mage-fingers—bringing the strands together, plying one to the next and to the next with utmost care, until she had a tiny line started.

It was a mere runnel, nothing like the ley-lines that had fed the Heartstone and powered the Vale, nothing even like the line that had once flowed through this very clearing, but it was still decidedly a line.

But what to do with it? She couldn't stand here forever, a living lodestone in the magic-haze.

Now, she was unsurprised when Triska's voice again echoed in her head. "Every weaving starts with the warp thread."

With Mage Sight and normal vision layered one on the other, Stardance examined the clearing, which stood on a slight incline. Like water, magic tended to run downhill, so she shifted, trailing the tiny threads of magic down the slope, careful not to move so quickly as to break even one.

As she paced the lowest edge of the clearing, she found what she sought.

Though not of the quality of a Heartstone, the large rock at the edge of the tree line seemed to have enough quartz in it to hold the power from this tiny line she had created. It would serve well enough for her to tie off a warp thread here. Maybe, once the power had gathered and grown, weft threads could be brought in to shape it, reweaving the network of lines that had once tracked through the Pelagiris. Or it could be guided to run its path elsewhere, perhaps even back to the Vale.

With exquisite care, she reached out to the stone with her shimmering Mage-fingers, sending some of her own power to dance over the stone, to wave invitingly to the tendrils she had drawn with her. Ever so gently, she nudged the line she carried toward the stone. It wavered uncertainly, but she waited, dimming her own radiation bit by bit until the fine line quivered and with an almost audible snap fell into place, finding the stone and settling, sinking into the earth, drawing the energy-haze with it.

Now separated from the support of the tiny tendrils of power drawn from the fog, Stardance staggered as a drain-headache blossomed into full power, drumming the insides of her skull. Kir launched to a nearby tree, chittering her concern, but Stardance kept her from calling to any nearby bondbirds. Moving slowly, keeping to paths that were as out of the way as possible, she stumbled, she hoped unseen, back to the Vale, barely able to climb the stairs to collapse onto the bedroll in her ekele.

"Are you sure?" Winternight leaned forward, one hand twisting over the head of his staff. "None of the students were Healing Mage-talented, so far as we knew."

Dayspring nodded. "It was a ley-line and what resembled the beginnings of a node. I'm not sure why I scanned the safe areas we were crossing as we returned to the Vale, but I'm glad I did. It was tiny, but must have been formed by an external influence, not the natural gatherings of power in channels. There hasn't been enough time for the magic to settle so cleanly. And this was the only place where I saw such a thing."

"We need to know who was in that area. We need that student, that Gift. K'Veyas has never had many Healing Mages, and now that Silverheart is the only one left, well, she's wearing herself out."

"I never noticed signs of Mage Healing in any of the students I taught," Silverheart added, her voice soft. She was too young for the lines that had creased her face in the last few days, strained not only by the Mage Storms themselves but by the demands of attempting to restore some balance to the power around the Vale. "But neither did I work with all of the trainees."

"My apologies for my lateness," Windwhisperer said, brushing aside the curtains at the entrance to Winternight's ekele. "There was a Change-Creature in the area I was working in, which delayed our return until we had dealt with it." He shrugged off the questions. "Not magical, so the scouts will be better equipped to relate the details. My younger son had an interesting tale, too, from his work in the safe area, but we can discuss that later. First, why the summons?"

Winternight gestured to Dayspring, and the younger Mage spoke.

"You assigned the students this morning, didn't you?" Windwhisperer nodded. "We need to know who was in the area that went east toward the cliffs, between the stand of tallpines and the slope just before the meadow. There's a ley-line and a node there, and they weren't there when we went out this morning."

Only a close observer would have noticed the flicker in Windwhisperer's eyes before he leaned back, his face as calm and still as ever.

"There were three students in that approximate area, but as it happens I know who created it, for my son observed her. Stardance."

The other three Mages inhaled sharply.

"I never taught her . . ." Silverheart murmured at last.

Winternight was silent for a moment, studying Windwhisperer's face. "Is your son near?"

Windwhisperer nodded and bent his head toward his kestrel bondbird, who hopped off her perch and darted out the open window. "I thought you would want to speak with him, so I asked him to wait below and said I would send Tria when we wanted him to come up."

A moment later, the young scout tapped at the entrance, then pushed aside the curtains and entered the room.

"Welcome, Nightblade," Winternight nodded at a seat next to Windwhisperer, and the new arrival sat. "Your father tells us you were paired with Stardance in the searching of the safe areas today."

Nightblade lifted one shoulder in a slight shrug. "Not so much paired," he replied after a moment's thought. "I thought it would be best for the oldest scout to stay nearest to the youngest Mage student." His voice left a subtle shade of emphasis on the fact that he was the oldest of those assigned to work in the safe areas with the students, hinting that he felt he deserved to be out with the rest of the fully trained scouts.

Winternight chose to ignore the implication. "What did she do?"

"As we left the Vale, Stardance made it clear that she did not wish for me to be immediately near her, so I went farther into the forest and watched her from the trees, or through Miel's eyes. She was diligent, tracking back and forth so that she covered every bit of her assigned area of the forest. She finished in a clearing, and it was there that she seemed to be working magic, although I don't have enough Mage Sight to know for sure. At times she moved her fingers, very slowly, like she was working with something fragile that was held between them. A couple of times she tilted her head, as though she were listening to something or someone. Then she walked to the stone at the edge of the clearing and held her hands over it, not quite touching it, for a long time. After that, she nearly collapsed and barely managed to stagger back to her ekele. I made sure a hertasi would take care of her and found my father, to tell him."

Windwhisperer nodded confirmation, while Silverheart leaned forward. "Did she say anything? Anything at all?"

"She talked aloud to her bondbird a couple of times, and I think she said something about 'seeing if it works.' Other than that, nothing that I heard."

When there were no other questions, Windwhisperer nodded a dismissal, and his son slipped out. The Mages turned to Silverheart, waiting for her thoughts. The only Healing Mage in k'Veyas, this was her field, her expertise.

Silverheart leaned against the wall of the ekele, her eyes half-closed in thought. "Stardance. She was the one more or less adopted by the hertasi who was caught in the Change Circle, correct?"

"Yes."

"So. Hurt, angry, lonely, and, from what Windwhisperer said of her last night, stubborn. Not the ideal time for any of us to ask her what she did, and why. And how."

"She would not refuse the direct command of the Elders," Windwhisperer said thoughtfully, "but I agree that she would not respond well."

"I need to watch her do this, to see how she is working. But we can't send anyone extra out with her, or she might not do anything. I wish I could use Mage Sight through Cede's eyes!"

"But you can through mine," Windwhisperer replied. "I realized today that I'm getting a little old and weary to keep up with the scouts," he continued with a wry smile. "You can link to me, and I can watch her with Far Sight." He paused, considering. "Is it likely that she could harm herself, or anyone else, if she experiments on her own?"

Silverheart thought for a moment. "It is possible that she could become too absorbed, too focused, and forget to come back to herself. But if we are watching her, even from a distance I should be able to recognize the signs, and we can use a bondbird to shock her out before she gets lost." She shrugged. "The magic is so diffuse, so faint, that there is little risk for injury. There just isn't enough power for her to do anything significant."

The Mages all nodded in agreement. Even in these few days after the Storms, magical accidents had been fewer. And smaller.

Stardance woke, blinking and rubbing her eyes to shake the last traces of exhaustion-headache from her mind. It took a moment for her to remember how she had gotten so drained, and then the images flooded back over her. The magic-haze, the tendrils, memories of *Triska* . . . She almost murmured the hertasi's name, waiting for the ache of loss to build, to overwhelm her with emptiness as it had every time she'd thought of Triska in the days since the last Mage Storm—and was stunned when it seemed a little muted, as though she was a tiny bit less raw inside. She would have considered it further, but a hungry Kir was already protesting how late she had slept.

As morning drew on, once again she gathered with the other Mage students for Windwhisperer's instructions. Each day they were to expand their search farther away from the Vale, as the scouts and full Mages widened the range of the safe areas.

Stardance was surprised to be glad when Windwhisperer told them to take areas just beyond those where they had searched the day before. She would have the chance to see what had happened overnight to her little runnel. A tiny bubble of unexpected anticipation welled up within her, not dimmed even when the young scout (Darkmoon? Nightdark? No, Nightblade) again paced his steps to hers as they left the Vale. Today, he seemed less angry, less resentful of his assignment, but she was still relieved when he drifted away from her, farther into the forest.

When she was sure he was out of her hearing, she slipped between the trees into the clearing where she had threaded the little line together. It was easier today to make the shift in her mind to See the more diffuse energies around her.

Her little line still glowed to her Mage Sight, tracing down the slope to pool in the large rock. Was the line a little broader, a little stronger than she had left it? Stardance couldn't be sure, but she thought that maybe it was. The stone itself had retained the magic that trickled through the runnel. She paused, considering. Would it accumulate enough power that it would need an outlet? Reaching out with a gentle touch beyond her shields, she tested the energy in the stone, then released it. Unless a great deal more magic suddenly flooded down the tiny line, the quartz in the stone could hold the gathering power for days, at least. She turned and moved deeper into the forest, heading for the outer limit of the new area she would be searching.

Silverheart unlinked herself from Windwhisperer's mind, rubbing her eyes to clear the afterimages of Mage Sight layered on Far Sight.

"So, what do you think?" the Elder asked her, his eyes closed as he continued to "watch" Stardance move through the forest.

"She is very young," the Healing Mage answered slowly, "but her instinct seems good."

"Is she truly working with the earth magics on that level?"

"It seems so. As Dayspring suggested, that is a tiny runnel and rudimentary node—well, more of a locus than a node. Since she knew exactly where they were and only touched them to verify their presence, it appears that she did create them." Silverheart paused for a moment, considering. "There had been a fairly strong ley-line and node in that clearing. If the girl remembered that, and tried her experiment there because of it, I don't think we need to monitor her closely until she gets to where there used to be stronger nodes. From the old maps, I think there are two in her area today. One just beside the little waterfall and one closer in, near a stand of pines."

There was a brief silence, and Windwhisperer stood, shaking his shoulders to loosen himself as he released his Far Sight half-trance. "I've set Tria to watch her and alert me when she nears either of those areas or if she does anything unusual. No sense in using Far Sight for that long if I don't need to."

Silverheart nodded. "It may not take much energy, but there is little from which to replenish yourself. Now, we wait."

Stardance looked up, checking her position. Yes, she had completed the first arc of her wedge and was almost at the waterfall that dropped the stream down below the cliffs that had marked the edge of her area the previous day. Hadn't there been a node, here, too? The ley-lines often followed the patterns of the streams, for there was so much life in the water to supply them.

This time, she sat comfortably beneath a tree before she twisted her Mage Sight to the broad and shallow focus that allowed her to See the nebulous fog of power. The haze seemed stronger here near the water than it had been in the other clearing. Would it be easier to work with? Opening her shields, she once again cascaded a subtle ripple of magic over her surface, imagining the enticing fragments drawing the diffuse energy toward her.

Back in his ekele, Windwhisperer sat up and hissed an alert to Silverheart. "Tria says she's sitting down near the head of the waterfall." He linked to the kestrel's eyes, then shifted to his own Far Sight once he had Stardance's position fixed in his mind. With a soft touch, he felt Silverheart connect to him, and suddenly her Healing Mage Sight layered over his, so that he saw the faint life force limning the area the girl sat in, the haze of fragmented power that was slowly floating toward her.

"*That's* what you See and work with?" he murmured in amazement, and Silverheart chuckled.

"Very small, as you see. It takes patience. A lot of patience."

"But how is she working with it?"

Silverheart didn't answer for a long time as she studied the young girl, watching the fog gradually coalesce into tendrils that reached out toward the girl's glowing form. "She's making herself into something like a living lodestone, using some of her own energy to draw the bits of power to herself. Once it connects to her . . ." Her voice trailed off as Stardance raised her hands, her fingers gathering the first of those tentative strands and doing . . . something . . . to blend them.

Windwhisperer put voice to Silverheart's question. "What in the Star-Eyed's Name is she *doing?*"

Silverheart had no reply, for she had never seen anyone work with magic this way. Instead of guiding the tiny bits of power with her mind, nudging them together as Silverheart had been taught to do, Stardance used her hands, fingers twisting nimbly but carefully, to blend the fragments together, folding them over each other and weaving—Silverheart was so shocked when the word came to her that she broke her link with Windwhisperer.

"The hertasi," she said at last, "Stardance's caretaker. She worked with cloth?"

"Ye-es," Windwhisperer replied, his brow furrowed with confusion.

Silverheart slowly connected back with him, this time not using her Mage Sight, looking only at the deft movements of the girl's fingers.

"She's spinning the power like thread, weaving it together," she murmured at last, a hint of awe tinging her voice. "That's how she could attempt it, without any training in guiding the subtle magics. She's using her own power to connect with it and then treating the tiny bits of energy like the bits of fiber to be spun into thread." With a twist of her mind, she shifted into her Healing Mage Sight, again sharing what she saw with Windwhisperer, and they watched as Stardance blended the last of the tendrils that she had drawn to her with the ones that already wound together around her coruscating fingertips. Then the girl slowly shifted, drawing her hands and the fragile strand of magic to the rock that had once anchored the waterfall's node.

"How is she going to connect—oh, she's using her own power again." Silverheart answered her own question as Stardance held her hands over the stone, then rippled some of her personal energy down to it, to guide the tiny runnel down from her hands.

"This one is larger than the one she created yesterday," Silverheart murmured. "I hope she doesn't . . ." Even as the words left her, they both saw the little line "snap" into the earth, and the girl pitched forward, unconscious. Her bondbird was instantly beside her, her beak wide with distress cries, and Windwhisperer's Tria soon joined the falcon, her presence calming the larger but younger bird. In another moment, they saw Nightblade drop from one of the nearby trees, carefully turning the girl over and checking for injuries before scooping her up and heading back toward the Vale.

Windwhisperer released his Far Sight, and Silverheart broke her link with him, the two of them staring at each other in disbelief.

"Should we question her when she is restored? Will she be more open to talking? Does she even realize how very important it is, what she has done with no instruction, nothing beyond that of the other trainees?"

Windwhisperer shook his head. "I think she is still too fragile, too hurt for questions. She has lost much, this one, and the Storms especially have taken much from her. It would be good for her if something could be gained from them, as well. If she is not a danger, if she is not creating anything that she cannot handle, can she be left to make that discovery on her own?"

Silverheart frowned, thought a moment, then determination set in her eyes. "K'Veyas needs her to be trained in her new-found Gift before it becomes too strong. To do something once is accident, twice is coincidence, but a third time . . . if she goes out tomorrow, I want to follow her. If she attempts this again, I will have to interrupt, to confront her in some way. It may not be dangerous now, but if left too long, it could become so."

The last traces of exhaustion-headache were stronger this time, more difficult to shake free. Stardance frowned. She had no memory of coming back to her ekele, although she vaguely recalled being on her bedroll already when one of the hertasi had brought her the cool, refreshing drink commonly used by those who overextended their Gifts. Other than that brief exchange, her last clear recollection was of creating the second little ley-line. The thought of it made her smile—they were things of beauty in their own way, the tiny runnels of power that she had spun together. Hadn't there been another node, too, in the area she had been in, near the stand of pines? Maybe she could go back out to that one today. If she could not weave works of beauty with Triska, perhaps—she paused, then probed the thought of Triska. For the first time, the ache didn't threaten to swallow her, and she didn't feel cut open on the sharp and jagged edges of grief.

Before she could ponder further, Kir chirped from her perch, Sending a feeling of combined hunger and eagerness to stretch her wings. Stardance rose and freed her bondbird from her hood, a faint thread of anticipation to match the falcon's dawning within her.

Discordance

Jennifer Brozek

Rax wept in what was left of his ale as the Bard finished the ballad of love lost and betrayal. It wasn't like him to lose his composure outside the house, but things had been so difficult this season, and he didn't see it getting any easier with the baby on the way. As the Bard struck up the next tune, a war chant with a heavy drumbeat, Rax called out to the bar wench.

"Sarry, get me another and another after that." He felt the chant beat in time with his heart and felt his blood rise to combat the sorrow.

Come, come, come to the beat of the drum, drum, drum.
And kill, kill, kill with your sharpened sword!
To take, take, take every last crumb, crumb, crumb.
And do as you will!

Sarry, distracted by a handsome man with coin, ignored him, fussing over her target for a tip and possibly a tumble later if the stars aligned.

"Sarry!"

She glanced over her shoulder at him and smiled a tight-lipped smirk that told him all he needed to know before turning back to the man before her. "Is there anything else I can get you, Seder?"

Before Seder could answer, a clay mug sailed past Sarry's ear and crashed against the wall in a shower of shards and dregs of ale. Sarry turned to see Rax standing tall and shaking with rage. The mood of the tavern turned ugly with the beat of the drum and song of violence. Rax took a step toward the bar wench, only to be stopped by another growling man—already angry at the sound of Rax's voice.

She didn't see the first punch or who threw it. Years of experience in rough places told her this was going to be trouble and wouldn't stop until blood was shed. As she fled to the back of the tavern, the room erupted in chaos—men yelling and swearing, the pummeling of fists on flesh, the crash of furniture thrown, and the sharp sound of metal weapons being unsheathed.

Mathias grabbed her and pulled her behind the bar. She let him do it, thinking that he was trying to protect her. Instead, she found herself flattened face down on the dirt floor with him behind her—one hand holding her down, the other fumbling with her skirts. She had a brief moment of confusion. She trusted Mathias. He'd always protected her. Now, this? Sarry let the rage of being attacked flow over her, and the pounding of her furious heart beat in her head like the sound of the Bard's drum.

Sarry screamed her rage, bucking her body up as she reached for a weapon. Her hand found one: a large serving fork. As Mathias wrestled with her, trying to hold her down, she twisted her body around and stabbed the man who had been her friend, protector, and boss in the throat. Blood spurted from the wound as he reared up in pain and she yanked the fork back. They both screamed now, two more voices in the din of the total tavern melee. She plunged the fork deep into his stomach.

On the other side of the bar, Rax already lay dead with his head caved in by a chair. Seder was dying; a sword pierced his chest, and his enemy was being beaten to death by two other men using clubs and their feet. Those who were not fighting were dead.

Except for one.

No one noticed when the music stopped. Nor did they notice when the Bard picked up his pack and drum and walked with careful steps through the violence and out the door.

The only survivor of the night, Sarry, would not remember what the Bard's name was or what he looked like.

Terek frowned at the letter in his hand. Usually, letters from home were a thing of joy. Not today. There had been a brawl at a tavern, and people had died. People he knew. Mathias had been a brother to him. His death was a shock. He closed his eyes and rubbed his brow. *There is more to this*, he thought. *People don't murder each other over ale. Maybe in the slums of Haven, but not in Woodberry. Not in a tiny settlement like that.* Something within his Gift told him he was right.

"Terek?"

He opened his eyes and smiled at the always fashionable Mari. She was a Bard who knew those worth knowing in the court, and she looked the part. "Yes?" He frowned at the worry lines around her eyes. "What's wrong?"

"I'm not sure, but I was listening to a couple of Heralds talking and I think something's happening."

He gestured for her to come in and sit down. "Tell me."

"I'm not sure what's happening," she repeated. "I got a letter from home. A friend of mine died while carousing with his friends." She bit her lip, marshaling her thoughts. "Then I heard the Heralds talking. They'd just come off Circuit, and there was a bit of bad business in the North. They had to judge a murderer. The thing is, at first, I thought they were talking about the death of my friend because everything was the same—the victim had been killed in a huge tavern brawl. But they weren't. They were talking about someone else. So, I asked them more about it. Two different villages, next to each other, had the same thing happen about a sennight apart. Bar fight, unusual amount of death."

Terek nodded, his heart thumping hard in his chest. It sounded far too much like his letter from home to be coincidence. "It's been a hard season in northern Valdemar," he allowed.

She shook her head, hair flying in its vehemence. "Not that hard. Look." She pulled a rolled up piece of paper from her bag. When she spread it out on his desk, he saw that it was a map with small marks over four villages in the north.

As soon as Terek saw the map with the marks, his stomach dropped in horrified recognition and his mouth dried. He sucked air in through clenched teeth.

"These villages," Mari said, pointing to the places they both knew well, "have all had horrible events with people dying in taverns or. . . ." She stopped and took a breath before continuing. "Or have had a bunch of people kill themselves. Valdemar has had hard seasons before, but this is different. I looked into it. This is one village after another in a line."

"In a circuit," Terek corrected and tapped Woodberry. "Make that five villages. Maybe more." He drew his finger over the map from village to village in an oval circle. "What aren't you telling me?"

Mari paused to brush invisible lint from her ruffled crimson sleeve, reluctant to speak. "There's a Bard involved. Only, no one can remember him after the carnage. They just know he was there the night of the deaths, but no one can find his body, and he isn't in town the next day."

"One of ours is doing this on my old circuit." He looked up at his former protégé, his eyes bleak. "One of ours. And it has something to do with me."

He listened to his lord's voice as it instructed him where to bury the shard. Eyes closed, he stepped forward or to the side as it commanded. He could feel the power flowing through him as he dropped to his knees and dug a small hole. As he placed the shard, chanting the words that had become his mantra, his prayer, his obsession, he knew his revenge was nigh. Either the object of his hate would come to him, or everyone who used to laud the old Bard would suffer for ages to come.

Poisoned stone planted on the edge of the village, he stood and brushed the dirt from his hands. He hefted his pack with its evil secret, put on a real smile in anticipation of the carnage that would happen that night, and sauntered down the road into the village where kindly folk smiled at him, pointing him toward the nearest tavern.

It was a modest thing with only one story and small windows, but it was one of the nicer buildings in the square, with uncracked walls and a freshly painted sign of a mug frothing over with ale. He nodded to himself and entered. Empty at this time of day, the proprietor sat at one of the tables, eating from a bowl of steaming porridge. He didn't get up, only nodded and gestured the stranger forward with his wooden spoon.

"Good day, I'm Sorrel. I'm looking for a room and a place to show my skill." Sorrel tapped his drum for emphasis.

"Daven, here." The proprietor gave Sorrel a critical once-over. "Bard, eh?"

"No, good sir. Merely a wandering minstrel. I wear not the red of an esteemed Bard." He watched Daven calculate in his head for a moment.

"Then I can't pay you Bard wages, but I can make sure you have a warm bed and a full belly and maybe a coin or two to rub together as you leave."

Sorrel smiled, "Excellent. For that, I will give you an evening of entertainment you won't forget for a long time to come."

"May I sit with you?"

The old man looked up at Sorrel's smiling face, glanced at the mostly full tables around him and nodded with a grunt.

"I'm Sorrel," he said as he sat, arranging his pack and drum next to him on the floor.

"Aaron." He gave Sorrel another look and then returned his gaze to his ale.

"You local?"

"Nah. Traveling through."

"Where to?"

Aaron looked up again, "Why?"

Sorrel pulled back and raised a hand, "Just curious. I'm a traveler, too. Thought I'd make conversation. Sorry."

The old man gave a long, gusty sigh. "Nah, I'm sorry. Heading to Woodberry. Got grandkids to look in on. Their Da died."

"Woodberry. Bad bit of business there."

"You know?" Aaron paused in his mug in midair.

Sorrel nodded.

"What've you heard?"

"Big brawl. Lots of people died. It was a mess."

"You were there?"

"Nah. Just picked up the word on the road. Avoided it."

Aaron drank deep from the mug and clonked it on the table. "Yeah. That's what I've heard, too."

"It's why I travel." Sorrel saw Aaron's questioning look. "To spread joy and leave a place a bit lighter than when I arrived. He tapped the drum on the ground.

"A Bard?"

"Just a minstrel."

Aaron nodded. "Playing tonight?"

"Aye."

"Good. I could use some music. It lightens the soul."

Sorrel gave him a smile with too many teeth. "This will be a night to remember. Speaking of which, it's time for me to earn my supper."

Word of the minstrel had spread throughout the small village. Music was always welcome, and the tavern was almost full. The sounds of wooden mugs clopping to the table mixed with the smacking of satisfied lips and the laughter of good conversation. However, when Sorrel took his place in the corner where the singers and dancers performed, the place quieted with an anticipatory buzz of people whispering to each other what they knew of the stranger. Two beats of a drum later and the tavern was almost silent.

"Tonight, a dream of mine is about to come true and all of you here will witness it unfolding." Sorrel reached down into his pack and pulled out something small and black. "Terek, this is for you." With that, he tossed the black thing toward Aaron.

It is the most natural thing in the world to catch something tossed to you in a casual manner. Terek's hands were already wrapping themselves around the cursed item as Sorrel's drum sounded out a slow beat and Terek realized that his real name had been used. By then it was much too late.

He rocked back as the power of the thing, a statue with large blank eyes and a larger mouth filled with sharp teeth, caught him in a spell. Staring into the statue's eyes, Terek knew that Sorrel had captured the rest of the audience in a spell, and they would be no help. He felt his own power draining from him as he fell into the statue's trance.

* * *

"Before me stand three promising youngsters, but not every dream can come true." Terek recognized himself from years before while riding his last circuit. He had been asked to judge the children in the village for potential. And judge he did. "You, young Sorrel, you have some skill but lack both the creativity and the Gift of a true Bard. You will be welcome at campfires, but not in the halls of the Collegium." With a shake of his head and a turn of his shoulder, he dismissed the boy. Terek saw the boy's anguish as he fled the square, but that was no longer his concern. These other two children were.

"Aric, you have proven yourself to be both skilled and creative. I have spoken to your parents, and they have agreed to send you to the Collegium. You won't go alone. You will take with you my personal recommendation. You will be welcomed in courts and merchant houses around Valdemar after your skills have been honed." Terek gave Aric a scroll tied with a crimson ribbon while the villagers applauded. He patted the boy's shoulder and gave him a gentle push toward his beaming parents.

Terek smiled and allowed the power of his trained voice to carry his pleasure as he made his final announcement. "Mari, my dear child, you have proven that you have the skill, the creativity, and the Gift to become a Master Bard. I have spoken to your parents, and you will travel with me, finish out my circuit, and then enter the Collegium as the most esteemed of students. You are what every Bard strives to become and the kind of apprentice every Master Bard seeks. You end my quest."

Locked in a vision of the past, Terek could feel his power, his Gift, being torn from him bit by bit. He struggled to bring his considerable will to bear, but this trap was too well laid and too long in coming. He had fallen for it, and this knowledge settled heavy on his heart. All around him, he was vaguely aware that even his hidden companions, Kolan and Pala, Gifted bards both, were locked in Sorrel's spell. He wondered how the unGifted peasant boy could have become so powerful. As if in answer to his query, a new vision clouded his mind.

Fleeing through the trees, Sorrel sobbed as his heart broke. His one dream in life, to become a Bard, to show the village he was good enough, was gone. There was nothing left for him now. It was the end. He tripped over a tree root and fell headlong into the dirt. He stayed there, trying to choke off the sobs that threatened to overwhelm him again. He wished he would die.

No, little master, no. Don't die. I can help you.

Sorrel lifted his head, looking through wet lashes into the forest around him, tears smudging his dirty face but the sobs had halted in surprise at the voice in his head. He shuddered as he took in a breath and wondered if he had gone mad.

Not mad, little master. Far from it. You have found me and I can make all of your dreams come true. Would you like that?

As he looked around, he felt something smooth and cold under his hand. Sticking up from under a tree root was a glossy black stone. He dug until he could pull it out of dirt. It was a statue, a squat thing just longer than his hand and as thick as his fist. Carved on the front of it was a frowning creature with large eyes and a large mouth with thick lips. On the back, the same hideous creature was smiling, open-mouthed, showing off rows of sharp teeth.

"Make my dreams come true?" Sorrel marveled at the thing in his hand as it spoke in his head.

All I need is a sacrifice of blood. Feed me and I will be your slave.

"Sorrel?"

It was Aric. Most likely come to tell him of his failure, too. "Here," he called as he stood up, statue in hand. He waited for Aric to appear. He'd show him the statue, and the two of them would figure out what to do—just as they always did.

Aric burst into view. He was smiling. Before Sorrel could say anything, Aric grabbed him by the hand, "I did it! I'm going to the Collegium with Master Terek's recommendation! I did it."

Sorrel stared as his friend broke his heart all over again.

"I'm sorry you didn't make it, but I was thinking after my training, you could travel with me, anyway. You're really good on the drum. You could be part of my entourage. I'm going to have one of those I'm sure after I'm done. We'll still be together and making music!"

Hot roses bloomed on Sorrel's cheeks as Aric added insult to injury. Come be part of Aric's entourage? Become one of Aric's lackeys? An unfamiliar emotion rose out of the shards of Sorrel's dream. Hate. Hate for his friend and his good fortune.

Heedless of Sorrel's clenching fists and flushed face, Aric had continued on, dancing around his friend, "Maybe they'll let you come to the Collegium with me anyway. Maybe I can say I won't do it without you. Or maybe I should just take you with me, and we'll just see what happens. We're going to get out of here! Isn't that great?"

I need just one blood sacrifice and all your dreams come true. Will you sacrifice him to me?

"Yes," Sorrel said and stepped close to the boy lost in his own dreams.

Aric grinned at Sorrel, not realizing that his friend had not answered him until the first blow came. By then, it was much too late.

* * *

Terek groaned aloud as he watched Sorrel beat Aric to death with the statue. As each blow landed, he felt as if he were being beaten himself. His vision clearing, he saw blood on his hands. Where it was from, he did not know. All around him, he saw people fighting with each other. The heavy drumbeat dominated the sounds of chaos. Sorrel's voice was strong and overwhelming. Terek could feel the power of it. It was as if Sorrel had a corrupted Gift.

As if sensing his thoughts, Sorrel looked through the melee of bodies when Terek raised his head, and their eyes met. That one look told Terek everything. This *was* his fault. He was the reason so many people had died. He had been callous, careless, and mean to a boy who had not deserved it. As the thoughts slammed into his head, Terek realized that they weren't true thoughts, but the thoughts forced into him by foul magic. Be that as it may, he also knew he was going to die. Still, Terek fought will against will, praying that Kolan or Pala would be able to break the spell.

Then the tinkling of finger chimes cut through the drowning drumbeat, and a high soprano voice powered by the Gift brought forth a light. The sounds of love and laughter on the music gave Terek the strength he needed to push back against the draining force of the cursed thing in his hands. Sorrel's beat faltered and Terek, saw why. Mari stood in the doorway of the tavern, and Sorrel stared at her as she sang familiar words of their past.

You and I together,
Far from all that ails.
Young and loved forever,
And forever we will sail.

She strengthened her song, singing of childhood days and the innocent love the two of them had once had long ago. Terek could breathe again, and now he brought forth his own voice in harmony with Mari's. Sorrel's face hardened once more, and he turned his focus back on Terek, willing the statue to finish its task, but Terek met him, voice to voice, will to will, while Mari sang her own attack.

The village folk, who had stilled at the first sounds of Mari's song, now stirred as if waking from a bad dream. Those who could, fled the tavern, limping, bruised, beaten, and bleeding. Mari stepped into the tavern and went over to Kolan and Pala, who had regained their senses. Mari's finger chimes urged the village folk on as the other two Gifted bards raised their voices to Mari's, allowing her to lead them in the fight against Sorrel and the evil artifact.

Terek stood, statue clenched in one fist. He stepped toward Sorrel, whose wide, hate-filled eyes refused to give in. The Bard raised his shaking fist and forced it open to reveal the small statue, a twin to the original one that Sorrel had found in his grief. He showed it to Mari and the others, who turned their voices on it, and all at once the statue vibrated and then shattered.

As black stone shards flew in all directions, cutting unprotected flesh, Sorrel's head snapped back, and all the music stopped. His, Mari's, Terek's. Sorrel staggered backward, hit the wall behind him, and slumped to the ground. It was only then that the Bards could see that the largest of the black stone shards had taken one last bloody sacrifice by embedding itself in one of Sorrel's eyes.

Terek rushed forward and went to his knees, but it was too late. Sorrel was dead, leaving the old Bard with questions and an apology unspoken on his lips.

Terek sat in his office, staring at the one shard of black stone he had kept.

"We found the rest of the shards and buried statues at the affected villages. They've all been taken care of—except that one," Mari said from the doorway to his office as she gestured to the one in his hand.

"I feel I should keep it to remind myself of what my hubris had wrought."

"You can't blame yourself. Not all dreams come true. Sorrel chose his path."

"But . . ."

"But nothing." Mari stepped forward and held out her hand.

Terek hesitated before handing it over. "Why did you follow us?"

She shrugged. "I always wondered why Aric didn't make it to the Collegium, and I always wondered what had happened to Sorrel. Once you decided this was happening because of you and your past, I realized that I was part of that past and that, perhaps, I could help."

"You were right."

She smiled. "Sometimes." She turned, paused, and turned back. "The Herald-Mages are about to do a seeking to find the statue you described from your vision. We know it's still out there. Want to help?"

Terek did not say anything for a long moment before he nodded and stood. "Yes. I started this, I should help end it. One last circuit to complete."

Slow and Steady

Brenda Cooper

Shay leaned down and filled her fist with fresh earth. It felt cold, and damp, and absolutely awful. She almost opened her fist, almost let the earth drop again. It wasn't real that she needed it, wasn't real that she stood in front of her whole village by her mother's grave with a fistful of dirt. She was going to wake up any minute and hear her mom searching through the shelves in her apothecary for moonflower or homemade tinctures or bandages.

"No, now. Go on." The voice belonged to the innkeeper, who had gotten her in trouble for climbing in his barn rafters to watch the horses from Haven just yesterday. Only now his voice was soft and sweet, almost wheedling. "You can do it."

She shook her head. She needed to think. It was so hard to think.

"Shay. Throw the dirt." the innkeeper repeated, a little more firmly this time.

She took a close look at her surroundings, the cold hole in the ground just big enough for the slender wooden coffin, the winter-bare trees, and the shivering townspeople.

She raised her fist above her head, gripping so hard the dirt became a wet, hard ball, bits of it falling through her fingers like everything she knew about life. She threw the mud onto the coffin, watching it smear across the top and stain the clean white pine of the lid.

She backed up, slowly, one foot at a time, trying not to be noticed, letting others come in and throw their own dirt on her mother. A few adults hugged her as she went. She stiffened, their touches feeling more like fire than help. The children and teenagers ignored her, which was better than usual.

As she finally got behind everybody and could turn and walk away, the first strains of a funeral song began to fill the air. The song seemed to be for her as well as for her mom. After all, she had to leave. No one would want her here.

At their house, Shay stopped outside and gazed at the dark windows. Shay wasn't smart enough to manage all the things her mom did. She could have been her mom's helper until her mom died, years from now. But there was nobody else in town who would be patient with her.

She didn't go in.

She pulled the kitchen knife she'd hidden from the woodpile and tucked it in her belt, the blade long enough she felt it with the top of her thigh. The water jugs swung easily over her head, but when she shouldered her pack, she had to work to get the whole assemblage adjusted. The water pouches hung on a leather strap sized for her mom, and Shay had to tie a knot in them.

At fourteen, Shay was nearly her mom's height, but she was all bones while her mom was soft. Had been soft. She couldn't remember what she'd thrown into the old pack, but surely it had been the right things. She'd been filling packs for her mom since she was seven, and for the last two years she'd even been allowed to go along when the farm or homestead a call for healing came from was close enough for the trip to be safe.

Surely even this new empty person she had become knew what to do.

Shay turned away from Little's Town. She didn't look back, couldn't bear to look back. No one would notice her missing until after the funeral or even, with luck, after the funeral feast. By then it would be dark.

Little's Town sprawled across a meadow, surrounded by more meadow and low hills in three directions. Cold, harvested hayfields alternated with sheep pens, full now since the sheep wintered near town. They were quiet today, huddled together for warmth, heads down as they tried to find fodder in between feedings. Shay went in the fourth direction. Up. The same way her mom had gone, toward a homestead on the top of the cliff that looked down on the town from the north. She wound up a forested path that wasn't straight up but rather a series of nasty switchbacks with a few good breaks of flat trail. They'd found her mom on one of those trails.

Cold wind drove at her back, helping her up.

The sounds of the town faded, replaced by birdsong and the rill of water running thinly down cold streambeds, just fast enough that only the very edges froze. Her thighs started to hurt, but she drove them up and up anyway. If she could do this climb in summer, she could do it now.

Her mom would have liked to meet the women from Haven, especially the one in green. The Healer. Healers came through about once a year, sometimes more often, sometimes less. Her mom and the Healers would usually take tea together and talk, maybe sit by the fire if it was winter. Too bad there was no fire here. Shay was getting cold.

Shay never talked to the Healers, or anyone from Haven. By definition they were the best Valdemar had to offer, and Shay had nothing to offer them. She was always scared she would say the wrong thing. But there had been no tea this time. Her mom had been off getting killed by bandits, and the women had been gone before anyone knew that. No reason to call a Healer for the dead.

She stopped at the first flat place, looking for signs of struggle. She spotted a few broken twigs by the side of the path and the footprints of the townsmen who had gone looking for her mother, both going up and coming back. Here and there, the mark of a horse's hoof going toward town.

The fresh human tracks kept going, so Shay took a long drink of water and followed them. She should eat, she knew she should eat, but she couldn't remember if she'd brought food. She didn't want to stop long enough to dip into her pack.

Night had started lying cold along the trail when she stopped at the next flat place. The signs she'd been looking for were here, even bigger than she'd expected. Bushes lay flat. Footprints went every which way. It seemed tainted by people and hurt. She found a few spots of what looked like black liquid on sticks and rocks. Her mother's blood. Cold now, gone back to the forest already.

She'd overheard one of the men say her mom hadn't been given a chance to fight, but had been killed from behind, and quick. There was nothing for bandits except a pack full of herbs and bandages. They should have left her alive and asked her to help them heal their hurts. It would have been better for them, and her mother would be alive.

Shay's pack did yield food: Bread that had been fresh the day before lay squished in the bottom on the pack beside five apples. Shay ate the bread and one of the apples. She should have taken more. Her mom would have patiently helped her lay out what she needed, but no one would talk her through plans any more, help her survive in a world that demanded more ideas than it had given to Shay.

She felt sure it wasn't smart to stay here, where she could see her mother's blood and the tracks and everything, but it couldn't be smart to keep walking either. Shay looked around for a place to build a bed, careful not to step on any healing plants and careful not to step into anything with thorns, settling for a flat place made soft with old pine needles. She pulled down blue-pine branches thick with cold needles until she had enough to make an even softer spot to lie on, and then twice as many more branches to put over her and hold in some of her body heat.

She did all of this slowly and steadily, careful to focus on her task.

She climbed carefully in as the dark took the last of the light away, and she lay still under the boughs, her knife right in front of her in case any night animals came sniffing around. She tucked her pack under her head so nothing could steal it. Tomorrow she'd have to keep going as fast as she could manage and still be steady. More snow could come before winter was over.

She was going to need something to do. She had tried to help the innkeeper clear dishes, but he had yelled at when she was too slow for him. He'd told her no when she asked to work in the stable, mumbling something about not wanting the horses let out. Her mom had refused to let her try to herd sheep with the other children after they threw rocks at her one day. She knew all of her mom's herbs, and how to count them, and how to hold a crying child while a bandage went on a knee or a splint on an ankle. Maybe she could pick plants for people and trade them for food. She wondered how far the next town was down the track. Too far for common visiting in winter. She wasn't too dumb to know that much.

It took a long time to fall asleep, and then she didn't

stay that way very well. Branches poked her, and the cold found its way through her blanket of needles and poked her in the ankle, and her fingers grew so cold she finally fell asleep with them tucked up between thighs.

She woke up in time to see the last stars fade. After an apple and some water, she stood and looked at the place her mom had died. For just a moment, the idea of going back down to town seemed better than going up, but there was nothing left in town that loved her except a few of the animals.

After two candlemarks spent trekking uphill, Shay came to the top of the ridge. If she went right, she'd end up at the homestead, but she didn't know very much about it. Just that Mr. Crestwell, who owned it, didn't pay enough for the long trek up. At least that was what her mom had said. So she didn't turn that way. The path kept going straight along a ridge for a long while, thinner now since it wasn't used as much as the one between Mr. Chrestwell's homestead and Little's Town. She surprised a few deer and a wild pig, but they were all afraid of her, and she was afraid of the pig. She dug roots for lunch, using a hard stick and a rock just as her mom had taught her. She ate an apple, but she was still hungry. Well, there were two more apples, and she could make it the rest of the day on those.

The trail wound back down the far side of the ridge for a while, almost as steep as the path up had been. Shay was careful where she put her feet, so it took a long time to get down. Slow and steady, her mom always told her. Take care of yourself, and don't worry about what other people think. Besides, there was no one but the birds to care if she was slow and a little clumsy out here.

Clouds bunched above her, but they didn't rain or snow. She stopped a few times to look at animal tracks. The horses of course. Deer and something bigger with cloven hooves. Not many, though, and mostly not completely fresh. But animals had passed over this path many times since the last time humans had walked it; the only boot tracks she saw were old ones with hard edges that had been frozen by earlier snowfalls and not yet crumbled by other steps on the path.

She refilled her water jugs from a tiny waterfall at the bottom of the hill. The water was colder than the water in the insulated jugs, and when she took a few sips, it made her cold inside.

The cold jolted her. Her right foot slipped on a wet rock as she stood up, and she fell down hard, knees and feet in the cold water. She pushed herself too quickly out of the water and fell in again, this time twisting her ankle.

Now she stopped, even though one foot was still in the water and the other hurt. Slow and steady. She needed to be slow and steady. She couldn't put weight on the foot, and her shoes were wet, and her teeth clattered against each other. So she crawled on her sore knees and her cold hands, the pack making it harder, the water jugs trailing behind her.

Shay sat on the path gasping and shivering and cold for so long that the sun fell behind the tall trees that lined both river and path. She knew better than to stay on the path. That's where the animals were, and her mom had told her they came to blood. This was also the path the bandits who killed her mother had come down on. She hadn't really thought about that. She'd only thought about not being in the town by herself, without her mother to stop the other children from taunting her. If bandits came, she didn't have anything worth stealing except for the kitchen knife, but she was a girl, and her mom had warned her about strange men.

When she stopped thinking so hard and decided to move, her body felt stiff. She crawled to the side of the trail until she found a grouping of young pines that would shelter her from the sky. After she stopped, Shay reached her fingers down to feel her ankle. It had grown bigger. While it didn't hurt much to touch it, if she touched it hard enough to move her foot, pain shot up her calf.

She was a village healer's daughter, and she knew to stay still.

It would be light enough to see for a few candlemarks. Everything was winter-cold and winter-bare except for the evergreen trees. Maybe it was better to live on the apples. She pulled down the few branches she could reach, apologizing to the small trees that would probably need them. She got enough to cover her legs and feet, and then she couldn't reach any more. Shay dug her knife out of her backpack, being as careful as she could. She felt a little better with the shaft in her fist. She watched the water, letting it mesmerize her into a cold, shivery nap where she dreamed of horses and dogs and of her mother tucking her in at night.

Something in her dreaming must have caused her to move her foot. Pain woke her up to cold. Snow had started to fall, the flakes a bit golden in the late afternoon air. She felt stuck in place, cold and hurt and alone and empty.

She was hungry, but she didn't want to move enough to dig out an apple.

A horse whinnied.

Shay stiffened and stilled.

Voices. Women's voices. One of them saying, "The snow will hide tracks."

The other responding. "We need to stop for the night soon."

The first woman said, "I'd rather keep going." Then silence fell except for the soft sounds of the horses hooves in the slight blanket of snow that had fallen while Shay dozed.

Shay shivered. Were they looking for her? On horseback? Most bandits were men. She held her breath and waited to see who rode up on her.

The figures of horses emerged from the snow on the path between her and the stream. Snow spangled their saddles and stuck to their manes and tails. Their riders were the two women who had gone through town, the Healer and the Bard. She recognized them even though they were closely bundled against the cold, bits of red hair escaping from woven hats.

Maybe she was still asleep and dreaming. She clutched the knife hilt tighter, or at least she tried. Her hand was stuck curled tightly around the wood. "Hello?" she rasped, her voice slight.

The first horse was past her, the second right across. They hadn't heard her! She wasn't directly on the path, and they'd have to look her way. She took a deep breath and tried to let go of the knife, croaking a disappointed sound when her bare, cold fingers still refused to move.

The woman turned and the horse stopped, and the next thing Shay knew, a cloak was thrown across her shoulders, and a face was close to her, saying her name, "Shay? Shay, is that you? Are you Shay?"

Then she was lying on a blanket by a fire, the warmth and light both slowly seeping into her. Night had finished falling, so all that seemed to exist was the fire and the women and blanket around her. The Healer held a cup and poured a bit of something warm between Shay's cracked lips. The Bard sang to the fire, something soft and meant to help babies sleep. It was a song Shay had known once, because her mother used to sing it to her. She fell back asleep.

When Shay opened her eyes again, the fire was just as high, but the quality of darkness had turned toward the gray of dawn, although it was still dark enough that the fire lit the falling snowflakes so they looked briefly like sparks. She was lying on her back with her foot on a log, a saddle blanket under her head that smelled like clean horse sweat and snow, and a heavy cloak over her. The Healer was sitting and staring at the fire, and no one was singing except the storm itself, soft and thick and windless, the snow falling in a whisper and sometimes sizzling a tiny bit when it hit a coal just right.

Shay tried to say something, but what came out was more like a squeak.

The Healer turned toward her. "I'm Dionne. I'm glad we found you."

Shay managed a "M-me t-too."

"Are you still cold?"

"Only a little"

Dionne reached for a cup that sat on a little bank of coals away from the hottest part of the fire and held it up. "Will you drink some more tea?"

Shay tried to sit up, and then Dionne was beside her lifting her up and whispering. "Rhi?"

"Mmhhmmmm . . . .not morning yet." The protest emerged muffled from a pile of blankets.

"She's awake," Dionne said as she lifted the cup so Shay could drink.

"Mmmmmhhhhh. It's snowing. Leave me alone." But the blankets moved, and the woman sat up and smiled at Shay. "Hello. I think we just found you in time."

"Tha . . . thank you." Shay said, and took another sip of the bitter tea ,which seemed to warm her blood so her whole body got a little warmer. She took two more sips before she asked, "Why did you come?"

The Bard answered. "You needed to be found." She pulled on boots that had been left close enough to the fire to be warm. "Master Johaness sent us after you."

The innkeeper? "He doesn't like me."

Dionne took the cup for her and set it back on the coals, letting Shay lie back down all the way. "He sure seemed worried when he caught up to us on that great big beast of his."

The idea of the innkeeper riding after her refused to sit in her head. "Why didn't he come himself?" At least her words were coming out better.

"Maybe he thought you needed Healing." Dionne said.

"Or a song," the other woman answered.

She hadn't been close enough to see how much the women looked alike. "Are you twins?"

"The twin with no manners is my sister, Rhiannon." Dionne said it gently, almost teasing. "And now that you can talk, your ankle is swollen. Is there anything else wrong?"

Shay shook her head.

Dionne bent down over Shay's foot and took the swollen ankle in both of her hands. At first nothing happened, then it felt a little warmer, and then it felt a lot warmer. When Dionne took her hands away she cocked her head and asked, "Is that better?"

Shay could move her ankle. "Much better. Thank you."

"Can you sit up?" Dionne asked.

For answer, Shay sat up and held her hands out to the fire. "Are you going to take me home?"

The two women exchanged glances full of meaning Shay couldn't read. "Do you want to go there?"

"No."

They answered with silence for a bit. Then the Bard, Rhiannon, said, "I heard your mom died. I'm sorry."

Shay swallowed. "Me, too."

"What did you plan to do?" Dionne asked, her voice gentle.

So they must have talked to people in town, knew she didn't have any family. It sounded as though no one had been willing to take care of her. That stung.

She threw a stick into the fire, marveling again that her ankle didn't hurt when she shifted her weight. She watched the stick burn, thinking. Slow and steady. "Do you need someone to help you?" she asked. "I don't have a horse."

"Where were you going?" Dionne asked.

Shay kept her head down. "I don't know."

"Do you have family anywhere?"

Shay felt like Dionne's questions punched her. Adults did this a lot. Avoided answering her questions by asking questions of their own. The small hope that they had really been looking for her felt even smaller now. They'd been doing their jobs. Saving people stupid enough to get into trouble. The thought made Shay laugh, the unfamiliar taste of bitterness burning the back of her throat. She was used to avoiding people, used to being laughed at and yelled at, but since so much of what people teased her about was true, she deserved those things. They seemed fair. But she had wanted these smart women on the beautiful horses to want her.

At least they didn't ask her again when she didn't answer, but just let her sit and watch the flames.

After a while she noticed that Rhiannon had started singing again. Both women were moving around camp. Shay should help. She stood up, but Dionne said, "Sit down a bit longer. I've got something for you to do there." Sure enough, she showed up with two metal sticks, each with a sausage on the end. "Hold these over the fire. They're cooked, so they just need to be warmed."

Shay kept one stick in each hand, turning them slowly, her belly waking up at the rich fat dripping onto the coals.

They stopped feeding the fire while they ate, and then the women were careful that it was all the way out. Shay approved. They might not be slow and careful, but it was the careful part that mattered. She liked these women a lot even if they didn't need her to help them.

Snow fell off and on all the next day, although thankfully no winter wind came with it. Shay couldn't sleep in the saddle behind Rhiannon--the horse was too tall and swayed too much. But she had wanted to ride for all her life, and she might not ever ride again. So by the time they made camp, she fell exhausted and cold and pleased onto the ground. Dionne took one look at her and covered her up with the damp cloak. It was still dry inside even if was heavy and smelled of wet horse.

Shay drifted, listening to the murmur of the women's voices and the sounds of wood being gathered, thwacked together to knock off snow, and piled. She should be up helping them since gathering wood was something she did well, but her body didn't want to move. So she lay still, warm enough under the blanket to think, and thought about how to be helpful. If only she could prove that she could be a good helper, maybe Dionne and Rhiannon would want her.

A candlemark later there was more warm tea to drink and some dried meat and slightly stale bread to share out. Dionne mentioned that they'd be out of the snow the next day and would be close to a town, High Meadow. Shay had never been so far from home, but she said, "Sometimes people come from there to buy our sheep."

"Do you know how to herd sheep?" Rhiannon asked.

"No." She didn't want to tell them about the kids throwing rocks at her.

Dionne frowned. "What did you do?"

"I helped my mom pick the plants she used and helped her dry them."

Dionne stood up and rummaged in her packs, which had been hung on a nearby tree. She drew out three bags of dried plants and handed one to Shay. "Do you know what this is?"

She opened the bag and smelled it. Then she touched the dried plants. "Sweet rose."

"What did your mom use sweet rose for?"

"She made tea when people had headaches and used it in one of the salves that makes cuts stop hurting."

Dionne nodded and handed her the second bag. "Don't touch this one with your bare hands."

"Nettle. She made soup with it, but she never let me touch it until it cooked. She also mixed it with other plants to make things for swelling."

After Shay identified the third bag as fleawort, Dionne sat back on her haunches and looked at Rhiannon instead of at Shay. "It might work."

Rhiannon was still for a moment, and then she looked at Shay and smiled. "Let's try it."

Shay was so busy thinking about her mom and plants, she didn't think about what they meant for a long time. Besides, they hadn't been talking to her. She would be patient.

They stopped in High Meadow and stayed at an inn, all three of them sharing one room. Rhiannon sang for the people in the inn while Shay and Dionne sat on a nearby bench and ate a thin stew that tasted like heaven even if it was only root vegetables and spices and water.

When she fell asleep that night, Shay told herself not to want anything, that what Dionne and Rhiannon had done so far was enough. Surely they would leave her here, and she could find something to do or someone to take her in. She should find a way to thank them in the morning.

After breakfast and some bargaining with the innkeeper (a woman here, fat and round and a little grumpy) Shay helped them gather up the tack and their bags from the room and stood out of the way while they got the horses ready.

The stable boy brought around a sturdy little red pony with a saddle and bridle already on it, and Dionne and Rhiannon grinned widely when he helped Shay up onto it. She had never been so surprised by anything good in her life. "His name is Apple," the boy said.

"Is that because he's red?" Shay asked.

The boy laughed. "He's not that red, but he loves apples, and he'll come all the way across the pasture for a little bit of one. Sometimes it's the only way to catch him."

Shay was afraid to ask if the pony was hers, but they rode away from town with Shay on its back and a long lead line between her and Rhiannon to keep them together. Maybe the women were going to let her stay with them after all.

The roads were clear now, and the going was still cold but dry. Apple's hooves made a pleasant sound on the frozen trail, and Shay focused on that and talked to him, trying to ignore the way her legs and butt hurt from riding.

By the time they had been riding three more days, her legs didn't hurt anymore, and she'd fallen in love with the pony and wanted her life to stay like this forever. She couldn't bring herself to ask, so she did everything she could to help and was very careful not to do anything wrong.

They started going through bigger towns with places that made metal and fields of horses instead of sheep and guildhalls for people who built houses.

The roads became busier. And then they came up to the biggest place Shay had ever seen, one with wide cobbled streets and walls.

Haven.

It felt like seeing a story come alive. She gaped when she saw two Heralds ride out on Companions, and she understood for the first time what her mother had meant when she said Companions were nothing like horses. They were not; they were so beautiful she thought she might die of happiness for just seeing them.

As they wound farther into the city, Shay felt the good feelings shrinking inside her. A sadness filled her, completely against her will. She had nothing to offer here. If she couldn't wash dishes in Little's Town, what could she possibly do in Haven?

She patted Apple on the side of his neck, focusing on the mixed brown and white and red of his coat that looked simply reddish-brown from a distance. Focusing didn't help, because she couldn't possibly keep Apple. No one had ever said he was hers, and it made sense that they procured the pony so she didn't tire out the other horses.

They pulled up outside a great big building that looked like the school from Little's Town only bigger and grander and grown up. Students in gray and pale green streamed in and out of the building, everyone moving fast and looking smart and neat. Rhiannon still used a long lead attached to Apple's bridle, and she came up and held Apple by the head, whispering sweet nothings to him. Dionne came around to help Shay dismount. She managed to get off without any more than the steady form of Dionne nearby, staying slow and careful in her movements so she wouldn't embarrass the women by falling here, or herself by needing help with simple things.

Shay noticed that she was wearing the same clothes she'd started out in, and while they'd been washed once, that had been two days ago. Her pants had tears in the knees where she'd fallen. Her shirt had been mended in three places and smelled like horse and cold and the road, not right for Haven at all.

"This is the Healer's Collegium." Dionne took Shay's chin in one hand and guided Shay's face so that she looked Dionne in the eyes. "Are you all right?" she asked. "You look scared. There's nothing to be afraid of here."

Shay nodded, not willing to try to talk in case it made her lose control and loosed the tears she felt in the corners of her eye.

"We want you to come with us to meet someone."

"Okay." Her own voice sounded small, so she straightened her back and said it again. "I will."

Dionne took Shay's hand, and they followed Rhiannon down a twisty cobbled path worn smooth by many feet. They turned onto a thinner path and went through a wooden gate into a garden. Stone benches sat in each corner of a lovely little garden full of raised beds. Only a few were full now, since it was winter even in Haven. The bare beds lay fallow and ready for the spring, neatly raked and cleaned out. Shay's mom had kept a few pots to grow herbs she couldn't gather, but this was richness beyond imagining. Shay let go of Dionne's hand and started walking through the beds that still had plants, smelling each one. Half were familiar.

When she turned around, Dionne had gone. Rhiannon stood by one the benches, looking like she was waiting for something or someone. Shay went and sat by her, and Rhiannon put a hand on her shoulder. Then she started singing one of the tunes she'd sung for Shay almost every night, the lullaby her mother had known. It calmed Shay and reminded her to stop her racing thoughts and fears and take things slowly. They waited a long time, but the longer they waited, the more Rhiannon's song calmed her and chased away her worries about what people here would think of her. So she felt easy when Dionne brought out an older woman with a thin, sharp face and bright eyes. "This is the herb mistress for Healers. She likes to be called Janelle."

Shay held her hand out. "I'm Shay."

The woman's handshake was warm, and neither soft nor too hard. "Dionne told me quite a lot about you. I'm sorry about your mother."

"Me too." The easiest shortest response she could make.

"Can you tell me what the plants out here are?"

Shay licked her lips, suddenly afraid she'd forget all the names. But she took is slow and easy, and managed to remember the names and how her mother used and cared for all of the plants she had seen before.

Janelle nodded at Dionne, then looked at Shay. "Would you like to stay and help me the rest of the winter?" She paused. "I could use a hand soon, getting the spring plants started."

Shay didn't react. Slow and steady.

Janelle gestured toward Dionne and Rhiannon. "They need to go on."

Dionne spoke up. "But we'll check on you next time we're in Haven. Then if you want to go back home, I'll take you."

Shay shook her head. "I don't have a home."

The herb woman whispered, "Maybe you do now."

Shay looked at Janelle and thought, and then she said, "Thank you."

They went to get her pack, which had been tied behind Apple's saddle. Shay hugged the pony tight. When she let go, she was crying. They were going to go without her. She had a place, but she didn't want to leave the twins. "Can I ride somewhere else with you sometime?"

Rhiannon smiled. "Maybe. If Janelle gives us good reports. And you can ride yourself if you have someone to go with you."

Shay blinked, confused.

"We're going to put Apple in the common herd and give you rights to draw him out if you want and to visit him and bring him apples."

She couldn't believe that her mom dying was luck, but coming here was good. She was in Haven, and someone wanted her help. She'd have Janelle and Apple, and her new friends would visit. "The only thing better would be if I could go with you all the time," she said, leaning over and giving Rhiannon a hug.

"I'm sorry," Rhiannon said.

"Don't be sorry. Mom always told me to take things slow and steady."

Dionne had come up behind them. "Maybe Rhiannon could learn that from you."

Rhiannon swatted at her, but it was playful, and the mingled laughter of the women made Haven look beautiful again.

Sight and Sound

Stephanie D. Shaver

"Wil?"

:Chosen?:

The Herald snapped out of his reverie, sitting up with a snort on the hard wooden chair. "Sorry," he said to Kyril. "Must've been woolgathering. You were saying?"

"I was *asking*," Kyril said, "about the circumstances that led to Herald Elene's death." His pen tip gleamed with ink, poised over the parchment.

"Right." Wil rubbed his eyes. The burden of being awake put a strain on his ability to be tactful and thorough. *She died*, he wanted to say. *I'm sorry. She went into a river and drowned and died.*

But Kyril would pick every bone of the story until he got his damn details. No easy way out of this one.

"She went into the river at Callcreek to save a boy who'd been caught in a flash flood," Wil said. "Bad situation, all around."

"The boy—did she . . . ?"

"Yes," Wil said softly. "She Fetched him to shore."

Kyril nodded. "She is . . .was . . .terribly Gifted. Continue."

"They started to pull her back in, and apparently a log—"

Blue flash of Foresight—

—in the water out of nowhere so dark and cold and ah gods mother so sorry Elene so sorry Alrek no Alrek—

It wasn't a Foresight Vision—just the memory of one. It hit like an aftershock: not as bad as the original, but with enough intensity to stall his narrative.

Wil envied Heralds who only knew who had died when the Death Bell rang. He always knew who and where. Sometimes, for people like Elene, his Foresight showed him firsthand details leading up to the death. People he'd been close to—internees, instructors, yearmates . . .

Not that there are many of those left . . . dammit, focus! He grabbed hold of the disparate threads of his thoughts and forced himself to rattle off details, devoid of the panicked terror that his Foresight made him privy to.

According to the shore crew that had been on the other end of Herald Elene's lead rope, a log had tangled in her lifeline and dragged her under. Some of the men swore the rope snapped, others suspected someone panicked and cut it. Elene's Companion, Alrek, had berserked, run in mad circles, and then galloped off, the frayed bit of filthy rope trailing behind him.

"Did you question the locals about who might have cut the rope?" Kyril asked.

"I did, sir. Under Truth Spell," Wil said. "No guilty parties. It sounds like the whole situation was a big, confused mess."

"And Alrek?"

Wil shook his head. "Hasn't been seen since the incident."

Kyril nodded and picked up a clean page. "We'll find his body. Sometimes they just show up in Companion's Field. Was Elene recovered?"

"Yes, but . . . she'd been in the water awhile." The villagers had done their best, given what time and the muddy waters had done to Elene. She'd been carefully wrapped in sackcloth and transported on a bed of sweet grasses and flowers.

"Her grave is by the Temple of Astera near Callcreek," Wil finished.

Kyril made a note. "Anything else?"

Wil mulled the question. The Vision had been useful in caulking the gaps, giving him questions to ask the denizens of Callcreek. Wil felt that he'd gleaned all he could from it for Kyril's report.

And yet . . .

"Sir, something *is* nagging at me," he said at last.

"Oh?"

"But I *can't* tell you."

Kyril raised a brow.

"I mean I can't tell you," Wil clarified. "It's my Gift, sir. My gut says there's something, but not what."

"Ah. The famously unreliable Foresight."

"Sorry, sir."

"Quite all right. I know better than to try to pry it from you. Just be sure to tell me when it surfaces."

Wil nodded.

"Excellent. One last thing, then." For the first time since they'd begun their dialogue, Kyril set his pen down, then sat straight up and folded his hands onto the desk. "Elene had a family," he said.

Wil felt his stomach twist.

"We have an obligation to them," Kyril continued. "When possible we prefer to deliver the news in person. I understand you knew her personally."

Wil nodded.

"What I'm about to ask of you isn't for everyone," Kyril said. "Honestly, it's not for anyone. It's a hard task, telling a mother her daughter is never coming home. Can you do this, Herald?"

:Wil, you're exhausted,: Vehs said. *:If you don't want—:*

"Yes," Wil said. "I can."

:Or you could ignore me completely.:

Kyril gave a small sigh. "The Queen and the Circle thank you. Come back tomorrow—we'll talk about protocol for notifying the family." He cocked his head. "Meanwhile, you look like you need sleep."

"In buckets," Wil admitted, laughing a little. "Thank you, sir."

"Thank *you*, Herald," Kyril replied.

Wil departed the Records Room to the rhythmic scratching of Kyril's pen.

:. . .nightmares are getting worse. You need a Healer. Are you even listening?:

:*No,*: Wil replied honestly.

As usual, unseen someones had prepared his apartment for his return to Haven. There was fresh water in the ewers and seasoned firewood by the hearth.

He'd been focused on building the fire, not Vehs. Wil's hands were callused and leathery from years on Circuit. He didn't bother with gloves or pokers anymore, just shoved the lit wood around until the configuration pleased him, ignoring the sparks and splinters.

:*Healers —*: Vehs started.

:*The Healers want me to drink sleep tinctures,*: Wil shot back. :*And not the cute stuff made with hops and shamile. The mean stuff you give to a bull when you need to geld him.*:

:*No one is gelding you, Chosen.*:

Wil snorted.

But Vehs wouldn't let it die. :*If it's what you need to sleep . . .*:

What Vehs was nattering on about was that the Vision didn't just intrude on his waking thoughts. It had become a recurring nightmare, one he couldn't seem to shake. Wil hadn't slept—*really* slept—in a week.

His sleep-debt had been growing even before Elene's death, thanks to nights on the Karse Border. Now that debt was coming due, with interest. Hallucinations, jittery nerves, the acute, fleeting sense that he was being watched (when he wasn't).

It was nothing he hadn't dealt with before. The Vision would fade eventually. He'd endure until then.

:*I'd rather deal with the nightmare.*: Wil rolled his right shoulder, wincing. Spring had been damp and chilly, and his joints protested the chill. He shucked off his Whites, the cold air making his skin and scars prickle. Under the bedcovers it felt even colder.

Not for long, he thought, his eyes drifting shut. *Warm . . . no time.*

He slept. And in his dreams, Elene died again.

—in the water—

Freezing, all the way up to her neck. A hard shock of cold as she allowed the current and rope tied to Alrek carry her to the child clinging to an outcropping of rock. She practically blanketed him with her body, getting a good hold.

She turned to look back at the shore, Alrek's white form blazing like a guiding star.

Then she reached, her Gift struggling with the child's weight and mass, struggling with the distance, struggling as she struggled against the current.

The boy vanished beneath her. She saw a dark figure appear near Alrek, heard the shore crew cheer. For a moment, her heart soared—

The log came—

—out of nowhere—

—and dragged her down, her body pinned beneath the wooden anchor and the tangled lead rope. Everything became a confusion of sound and sensation, *so dark and cold*, and all she could think was, *Ah, gods—mother, I'm so sorry.*

:*Elene!*: Her Companion's voice, pleading in her mind.

:*So sorry, Alrek.*:

She felt him and the villagers straining to drag her in. The rope jerked, and her chest blazed with pain as ribs cracked. Her Companion's mindless panic threatened to overwhelm her.

:*No! Alrek—*:

She fumbled with something at her belt—

Wil shot up out of bed, fighting his own blankets, spilling out onto the floor with a scream in his throat. He sat, panting, until his heartbeat settled.

Am I missing something? he thought. *When will I stop dreaming about you, Elene?* She had been a yearmate, an infrequent lover, a fellow Circuit rider. She could be in his head another day, week, month . . .

:Year,: Vehs said adamantly. :*And in the meantime, you aren't* sleeping. *Go do something about it already!*:

Wil pushed a hand through his close-cropped hair, smearing sweat across his scalp. :*I'd rather you sang me a lullaby.*:

:*Chosen—*:

:*No tinctures, Vehs.*:

:*Stubborn—bull-headed—*:

But Wil's annoyance at his Companion's meddling had reached its breaking point—he snapped down his shields, cutting off Vehs's rant. Not that he could block him completely. Just enough to muffle the chatter.

He curled up on his side in his bed, and sometime around midnight he finally eased into a half-waking doze that lasted until dawn.

Food and a bath briefly revitalized him, but by the time he took the stairs back to his quarters, he found his steps dragging. He flopped onto his bed and settled his eyes shut.

In the water—

Knock! Knock! Knock!

Wil jolted up and for a moment sensed something nearby, watching—

The feeling vanished. Someone was knocking on his door, but he was alone in his bedroom.

Wil lurched over to the door, yanking it open. A red-haired girl in the orange-red of a Bard Trainee waited in the hall.

"Hi!" she said brightly. "I'm Amelie!"

"Hello," he replied, fighting the instinct to close the door again. Bard Trainees were, in his experience, never a good omen.

"Milady Lelia would like to see you." Amelie smiled brightly. "Is now a good time?"

Wil raised a brow. "'Milady' Lelia?"

Amelie maintained her blazing smile and nodded.

Wil glanced back at the bed, then back to her. He forced himself to smile. "Now's a fine time," he said.

They didn't have far to go. Wil hadn't seen Lelia in years, so he didn't know how the Bard had managed to win a Palace wing apartment from one of Selenay's distant relatives, but she'd done it.

What surprised Wil was not that she had finagled it but that she had *chosen* to settle down. Lelia seemed the type of Bard who would wander Valdemar until her shoes wore away and her toes fell off.

Amelie led him in, and if the woman waiting for him was barefoot, he couldn't tell because she was bundled up in a red velvet blanket.

"Wil," Lelia said, with enough warmth to make his heart swell. She remained unvarnished loveliness, albeit with an air of fragility he did not remember seeing before.

Aging, just like me, he thought. *Only with a little more grace and flair.*

"Milady." He bowed.

She rolled her eyes at his airs, pushing out of the chair to hug him. The sudden, friendly movement pushed away the melancholy he'd felt a moment before. He returned the gesture, smiling.

"I'd have given you a full day to rest and recuperate, but the last two times I did that you were gone before I could gain an audience." She sat back down. "You just love to go, don't you?"

I could say the same about you, he thought. He took a seat on a couch as Amelie plied him with tea, cream cakes, and other snacks. He waved them off politely.

"My protégé," Lelia said, nodding toward Amelie as she swept out of the room. "She's all sorts of mischief."

"You seem to be doing well."

She stretched her smile so wide he thought her face would crack. "You've no idea. How've you been? Stopped any assassination plots lately?"

He shrugged. "It's been a slow year or two. Mostly citizens irate over taxation, property lines, and who owes whom for what."

"Assassination plots sound more fun."

"Same amount of paperwork, too." His lips twisted in a grim smile.

She sipped tea as they talked. He gradually grew at ease with the sumptuous setting. No one disturbed them, though judging by the number of chairs, settles, and low tables, Lelia was accustomed to entertaining groups.

"When do you head out next?" she asked, topping off her cup from a nearby pot.

"Tomorrow," Wil said. "Probably. Maybe the day after."

"Another Circuit? So soon?"

"No," Wil replied. "I have to go deliver bad news to Herald Elene's family."

Lelia tilted her head to one side. "She died a fortnight ago, near Callcreek, yes?"

"Yes." He gave her a curious look. "You knew her?"

"No, but I make a practice of knowing for whom the Death Bell tolls."

"Ah." He lifted his brows sympathetically. "Right. Lyle."

Lelia smiled. Her twin brother was a Herald; he had, in fact, been Wil's internee.

Every time it rings, she has to wonder, he thought. *Even if sometimes it's a little more than I want, at least I* know.

"I was near Callcreek when she died," he said. "On my way back from the Border, actually. I did the footwork of finding out where, when, why, and how."

"No 'who'?"

"She drowned on a rescue mission. No one's fault." His chest twinged as he said it though, and he remembered the crushing pain from his Vision. "Her family needs to know. So I'll be heading to Boarsden shortly."

Her eyes lit up. "Boarsden, eh? That's near Winefold."

Wil knew the map of Valdemar the way parents knew the faces of their children. "Correct."

"Would you like me to go with you?"

He blinked. "What?"

"Me. Go with you. I admit in advance I have ulterior motives."

He swallowed around a suddenly dry throat. "Such as?"

"My family travels to Winefold around this time of year. There's a festival to bless the fields—it's at least a week long. Good work for traveling entertainers. I'd love to see them, and once you're done at Elene's you could view it as—" She cocked head again. "Brace yourself, Wil. I'm going to use a strange word on you." She shaped it slowly. "Hol-i-day."

:*The Bard is wise.*:

Vehs's interjection startled Wil. It was the first thing

the Companion had said since Wil had awakened and eased his shields.

Lelia took his silence for disapproval. "No?"

"Let me think about it."

"Oh. Well. Do." She drained her cup and set it next to the pot. "You'd be doing me a favor. I'm a frail little Bard, getting on in her years." She draped her arm across her forehead and slumped. "And I surely would love the company." She straightened and winked. "My destrier and I can be ready to go either day."

After leaving her, he headed to the Collegium common room for supper. Trainees chattered earnestly around him as he ate and contemplated the bitter work ahead.

:*You know,*: Vehs said, somewhat unexpectedly, :*she's unattached. Unbridled.* Available.:

Wil furrowed his brow, wiping up the last of his stew with a crust of bread. :*Who?*:

:*Lelia.*:

:*What does that have to do with anything? And how do* you *know that?*:

Vehs ignored the second question. :*You liked her once.*:

Wil wiped his mouth and collected his empty plates. :*It's been a while, Vehs.*:

:*Oh, yes, it's* been a while, *Wil.*:

:*Ha ha.*:

:*She wouldn't have invited you to her quarters, or herself along on your journey, if she didn't still like you on* some *level.*: Vehs hesitated. :*I think there's a very real chance she'd like to play Stefen to your Vanyel.*:

If Wil had been drinking, he'd have choked. :*Thanks for waiting until I was done with dinner before planting that on me,*: he thought.

:*Just pointing out the blindingly obvious to the obviously blind.*:

* * *

Wil looked around. "Where's your destrier?"

Lelia patted the neck of the slender-legged chestnut palfrey waiting beside her. "Right here. Wil and Vehs, meet my horse. Destrier."

Wil and Vehs exchanged a look.

:*Forget what I said,*: Vehs said. :*This one's crazy.*:

"You named a *palfrey* 'Destrier'?"

Lelia grinned. "I always said I wanted one." She cocked her head. "Exit through the Haymarket Gate?"

"Haymarket Gate," he agreed, and helped her mount her . . .Destrier.

He'd left the question of bringing her along to Kyril. The Seneschal's Herald had spent the better part of the evening explaining the art of breaking bad news to good people, and he had provided a small box of Elene's personal items. According to Kyril, Elene had no living family except for her mother, Kaylene.

When Wil had asked about letting Lelia accompany him, Kyril gave him a thoughtful look and then said, "Having a Master Bard along might not be a bad idea."

"Assuming she's discreet," Wil had said.

"Oh, she is," Kyril said knowingly. "But I'll want a full report on how it works out when you get back. Perhaps it'll be an improvement on the process."

Perhaps, Wil thought, taking a sidelong glance at Lelia as they rode. She sat straight in the saddle, eyes ahead, reins loose in her hands.

Finally, he cleared his throat and said, "You pack light."

"I used to do this on foot," she replied, smiling. "I learned to get by with very little."

"No gittern?" he asked.

She shrugged from within her voluminous scarlet cloak. "Takes up space."

Wil frowned. "Won't your family want to hear your music?"

"I don't need a gittern to sing, Herald."

You've plenty of room, he thought, but he let it slide. Lelia seemed focused elsewhere, as if listening to something Wil could not hear. Even when they finally got free of Haven's crowds and the open road spread before them, she remained silent, her gaze soft.

The silence gave Wil time to mull over what he was going to say to Kaylene. Kyril had given suggestions, but they all sounded so . . . formal. But then, what could one say that was "right" in this situation?

Nothing. But "nothing" wasn't an option, either. He would have to say *something*.

They stopped for the night at an inn where the owner greeted Lelia personally. People, Wil reflected, remembered a good Bard. After making sure his things (and Elene's) were secure in his room, he joined Lelia in the common area for a simple but tasty meal. They capped the evening with hot drinks—he with wine, she with her personal tea blend, which she had packed much of for the journey. They nursed their drinks in companionable silence, stretched out on comfortable chairs and settles near a hearth. Despite the heat, Lelia remained wrapped in her cloak, nothing emerging from it but her head and hands.

"You must be sweltering," Wil said.

She smiled drowsily at him. "I'm quite comfortable, thank you."

The wood in the hearth popped loudly, showering sparks. A moment later, it resumed its gentle murmur of crackles and pops.

"Such a lovely ditty," Lelia murmured. "Practically singing me to sleep."

Wil started to nod, but the phrasing caught his fancy. "Can you do that?"

Alertness crept into her gaze. "Do what?"

"Sing someone to sleep. With your Gift."

"I have, on occasion. Why?"

Because I haven't slept in over a week, and I'm going mad drowning in a cold river every night, he thought, but as usual, the actual words became stuck in his throat. "Just curious," he said.

She studied him, then drained her mug and set it aside. "Goodnight, Herald." She patted him on the shoulder before disappearing up the stairs.

Wil could feel Vehs in his head. His Companion *wanted* to say something . . . but, ultimately, did not.

In that, they were similar.

He drank two more cups of wine before he finally went to his room.

Wil clawed his way back to waking.

And again that sense of being watched—

He blinked. It vanished.

It wasn't far past midnight, and the thing that had woken him had not been the Vision—though he'd been up to his neck in cold water—but his bladder. He threw on clothes and trundled out into the night, toward the outhouse.

He turned the stable's corner—

Something was out there.

Wil had never feared the dark. But the yawning space between the stable and the outhouse filled him with sudden, unspeakable dread.

Something was there.

His eyes scanned the uneven shadows of the forest hemming the inn. Did he see a shape there? A blot of movement in the darkness?

Cold dread filled him. The *presence* felt true—not just a hallucination. His mind flitted back to his time on the Karse Border . . . was it possible he'd raised a Sunpriest's ire? Was something following him, waiting for a chance to strike?

The presence evaporated. The darkness became just that, the movement in the trees nothing more than wind and woodland beasts about on mundane business.

Wil crept back to his room, hunkered down in his bed, and waited out the night.

When he emerged from the inn the next morning, Lelia stood next to Vehs, one hand on his withers.

"Good morning," Wil said, faintly suspicious about them together. Something in their posture suggested . . . conspiracy.

"You look like hell," Lelia replied cheerfully as a groom emerged with Destrier and helped her up into her saddle.

:*She's worried about you,*: Vehs murmured.

:I'm *worried about me.*:

:*Well,* finally.:

Wil swung into the saddle, ignoring the jab. :*Last night—something was out there.*:

:*Something?*:

Wil toyed with the reins. :*Alberich . . . he mentioned night-demons once —*:

Vehs snorted. :*This far into Valdemar? Not possible.*: More gently, he added, :*Chosen, you're* exhausted. *Your mind is playing tricks on you.*:

:*I felt something, Vehs.*:

Vehs said nothing.

:*You don't believe me—*:

:*No!*: Vehs said sharply. :*I believe that you* think *you saw something.*:

Wil took a deep breath. :*Fine. But let's stay in a Way-station tonight. Just in case.*:

:*This close to Traderest?*:

:*Yes.*:

:*With the Bard?*:

Wil frowned. Now he wished he hadn't brought her

along. They were potentially in danger, but he was sure if he told her to turn back, she'd only want to know why, and no matter what he told her, she'd still want to come along.

But better one overcurious Bard than a village full of innocents . . .

"Lelia," he said, "we're going to stay at a waystation tonight."

He braced for the inevitable questions.

"All right," she replied.

He gave her an odd look. She smiled back congenially.

"Whatever you say, Herald," she said.

The Waystation outside Traderest was typical of its kind—small, with a water pump and trough, and secluded among the trees. Wil slid out of the saddle, and Lelia tethered Destrier as he hauled their packs into the Waystation. They had a fire and a pot of porridge going within a candlemark.

She still hadn't asked why they were here. He watched as she finished smoothing one of her cloaks over her boxbed—they hadn't brought bedrolls—and then left again to tend to her horse.

He sat on the edge of his own boxbed. All he wanted was sleep without dreams. He wanted . . .

One minute he was alone, the next Lelia was leaning over him. When he'd fallen back on the bed, he wasn't sure. Just that his eyelids felt so, so heavy. He could barely meet her gaze.

"You know," she said, "Heralds don't just die in fights, fires, and floods. Keighvin, the Queen's Own before Talamir, worked himself into a brainstorm and an early grave."

"Knew that," Wil mumbled.

"They throw themselves into their work," she continued, "until they're so exhausted they wind up doing something foolish." She smiled a little. "Lyle once told me . . . I was his balance. I keep him from flogging himself to death." The smile softened with sadness. "I don't know how good a job I've done with that, honestly."

Even talking, her voice had a melodic quality. His eyes slid shut, his thoughts growing muzzy. He could feel the Vision unfurling, tugging at him like the waters of the river that had killed Elene, and then—

Something stepped between him and it. A soft susurration, like the drowsy chirr of insects at twilight.

And instead of plunging into deadly waters, he found himself at the edge of a clearing, though not one he knew. It could have been the heart of Companion's Grove. It could have been any number of places in Valdemar. A faintly blue light, soft as moonlight, lit the world, but it was not *of* the world he knew.

Some distance from him was a woman in luminous Whites. She stood at the center of the clearing, and despite the unearthly light, her face remained obscured. Even so, he got the sense she was . . . watching him.

"Tell him I'm waiting," she said.

Wil sat up in near darkness. Coals gleamed in the hearth, and someone was breathing lightly in the boxbed to his right. He crawled awkwardly out of bed and emerged into the chilly night air.

Vehs walked over and nuzzled his hair.

:Sleep well?: he asked. *:We had hoped it would last through the night.:*

Wil frowned. *"It? We?"* he asked, and remembered the day before. "Have you two been conspiring behind my back?"

Vehs lowered his lashes and gave him a coy look.

Wil started to speak—

Something moved in the dark.

Wil snapped his head around, scanning the forest. He felt Vehs stiffen.

:That,: Vehs said, *:is not your imagination.:*

The Waystation door creaked, and the presence vanished. From behind him, Lelia said, "Something's out there."

Both he and Vehs turned to look at her. "You feel it, too?" Wil asked.

She nodded. "Something . . . big. Familiar, but not." She shook her head. "Whatever it was, it's gone, now." She hugged herself tightly. "It's freezing. I'll be inside."

Wil and Vehs stared into the darkness together.

:*Any idea* what *it is?*: Wil ventured.

:*Something . . . but not night-demons.*: Vehs shook his mane. :*Chosen, go back inside. Rest. I'll stand watch.*:

Wil could tell Vehs was being evasive . . . but he knew better than to try and press a Companion when he or she didn't want to give details.

Lelia had added wood to the fire. She waited by his bedside, wrapped in her spare cloak.

"You sang me to sleep," Wil said.

She nodded. "Did it work?"

Wil stretched out in the bedbox. "I think so." The fire popped and crackled. "Can you do it again?"

"Of course."

He closed his eyes. "Will you tuck me in, too?"

She laughed. "And ruin our professional relationship?"

Then she started singing, and the music stepped between him and the Vision, granting him peace.

Several nights of solid sleep did much to restore Wil's spirits. A fog had lifted from his thoughts. He found himself picking out details in the Vision that he hadn't noticed before.

Things Kyril would want to know.

So long as Lelia sang him to rest, Wil no longer dreamed of Elene's death. The only dream he had—that he *remembered* having—was of the shadow-Herald and the clearing.

Tell him I'm waiting.

Tell who?

Vehs reported no disturbances from the invisible "it." But that didn't mean it was gone, and as soon as Lelia was delivered safely in Winefold, Wil would have to figure out what "it" was.

They reached the inn at Boarsden before dusk and enjoyed a leisurely dinner. Lelia, as usual, found the biggest chair in the house, curled up on it with her special blend of tea, and regaled him with tales of the Court.

"The clothing is the best," she said. "Some of those women layer so much junk over the bodies the gods gave 'em, they can hardly walk a straight line!" Her eyes gleamed mischievously. "Sometimes I want to go cow-tipping . . . if you know what I mean."

As Wil wiped tears of laughter from his eyes, she signaled a server to bring more hot water for steeping tea.

He took the opportunity to change subjects. There was something he'd been cogitating.

"Lelia, tell me—have you ever heard of anyone having a Gift *like* Foresight but . . ." He grasped for words. "More like Hindsight?"

She frowned. "Not sure what you mean?"

"Visions of the past instead of the future."

"Uh. Hm." She pondered. "Well, as you know, I *am* the realm's preeminent Vanyel expert."

Vehs snorted mentally.

"I recall stories where he *did* that. But it wasn't a Gift. It was just something a Herald-Mage of his caliber could *do*." She cocked her head. "Why?"

Wil shook his head. "Just—"

"Curious?" She raised a brow. "I've heard *that* before."

He smiled despite himself. "Maybe later."

She grunted. "Better."

They talked until well into the night. When it came time to sing to him, she looked so sweet at his bedside that he felt a momentary wild urge to sit up and drag her into his arms.

Sleep always came before he could act on that urge.

The squat house was built into the hillside, a bit apart from the grain fields. Flowers and aromatics flourished in boxes and neat plots around the tidy stone structure. Laundry hung from a line, faded blue and green garments fluttering in the breeze.

Wil stood on the rutted path leading up to the front door, Elene's carved box clenched in his hands.

Such a miserable recompense for a daughter.

"She's alone in there," Lelia said.

Wil glanced at her. She had a distant look on her face, a slight crease to her brow.

"How *are* you doing that?" he asked.

Lelia smiled. "It's a Bard thing."

"Oh?"

Lelia hugged her cloak around her. "You should go, Herald, before she notices us."

Wil couldn't argue with that logic. He started up the path, Vehs following.

Too soon the door was before him, and he knocked.

"One moment!" a cheerful voice called. He heard glass clink and then the thump of footfalls. The door swung open, and a rosy-cheeked dark-haired woman looked up at him.

"Yes?" she asked.

Wil cleared his throat. "Kaylene Baernfield?"

"Yes?" Her expression turned to perplexity.

"Elene's mother?"

Her face froze, and suddenly Wil didn't know how, or even what to say. Everything Kyril had told him, all the things he'd thought up along the way—they all scattered. With the cessation of the Vision, with all the rest, he'd thought he was prepared.

He knew now that he never would be.

"Elene?" her mother whispered.

"She died." He swallowed, extending the box to her and thinking again: *So small. So paltry.* "I'm sorry."

Kaylene took the box. She looked up at him, tears growing in her eyes. He reached out and touched her shoulder.

And then she was not looking at him at all but at something *past* him.

A good day to be alive.

Lelia sat at the base of the hill, leaning against a spreading oak. The ride had been long and draining, and the nightly lullabies weren't as easy on her as she let on. It felt good to sit, and rest, and breathe.

The sorrow unfolded in miniature on the hill. Kaylene clutched the box. Wil touched her shoulder, and Vehs bent his head. Lelia dashed tears from her own eyes.

Something stirred in the brush to her right. Something *big.*

Her heart skipped a beat.

She extended her Gift, as she'd done that first night she'd sung Wil to sleep, and she *felt* it—that oddly *familiar* presence—

Familiar, because it was a *Companion* that stepped silently from the trees. Odd, because this Companion should not be. His tack was heavily worn and stained with mud. A bit of frayed rope trailed behind him, one end still secured to his saddle.

The saddle . . .

Lelia's eyes traced the name worked into the leather, and her mouth formed a silent "oh." She used the tree to clamber to her feet and put a hand out to the Companion.

Up on the hill, a voice called, "Alrek?"

Kaylene pushed past Wil, shoving Elene's box back into his hands. Wil turned to see the Bard slowly making her way up the hill, a Companion beside her.

:Vehs?:

:It's him.:

"Alrek," Kaylene said again, hoarsely. She stumbled forward and wrapped her arms around the Companion's neck, weeping.

:*I am sorry,*: an unfamiliar mind-voice said, and by the startled look on Lelia's face, Wil guessed that they all heard it. :*I did not protect her. I did not bring her home.*: Lelia looked down and away, tears on her cheeks. :*I am so sorry.*:

"You brought her home plenty of times." Kaylene stepped back. "And you brought yourself home." She stroked his cheek. "That's more'n I had before."

The Companion sank to his knees, Kaylene kneeling beside him. "It's all right," she whispered, over and over. "Oh, dearie, I know you did your best."

:*I did not protect her.*:

:*Alrek,*: Wil Mindspoke to him.

The Companion looked up, agony in his eyes.

:*Why have you been following me?*: Wil asked.

:She—: Alrek bent his head. :*I don't know why, but she . . . is* near *you, somehow. I* feel *my Chosen watching over you! She—:* The Companion keened, a low, soft sound that broke Wil's heart. :*I* killed *her!*:

Wil glanced at Kaylene. Alrek had not projected their conversation to her, for which Wil was grateful. As much as anyone could, he understood the why of it all now. But Kaylene did not need that burden.

Reaching out with his mind, Wil showed the grief-crazed Companion what he himself had Seen, night after night—what only a strange twist of Foresight could know. Threads of time not as they *would be* woven, but as they *had been.*

Elene in the water—fumbling for her belt knife—the weight of the log—sawing at the lead line until it broke—

The water carrying her away . . .

The Companion shuddered, then sighed. His head came to rest on the grass, his eyes closing.

"Go on," Wil said, softly. "She's waiting."

With Vehs and Wil's permission, Kaylene took a lock of Alrek's white hair. She tucked it into the carved box, alongside Elene's things.

All of Boarsden came to bury the Companion. The sun was heading for the west by the time Wil and Lelia left, the Bard riding behind him, thin arms circling his waist.

:*Chosen,*: Vehs said.

:*Hm?*:

:*You should really visit your father sometime.*:

Wil stiffened. :*Maybe someday.*:

"What's wrong?" Lelia asked.

"Nothing," Wil replied, making a conscious effort to relax his shoulders. "What are they feeding you in the Palace? Water and moonbeams? You're practically all bones."

"Moonbeams? Bright Lady, no. Too fattening." But the jest sounded faltering at best, and he wondered.

They spent the night at the inn. Lelia was departing early. There was no talk of singing tonight; Wil had a feeling he wouldn't need it anymore.

:*How often does this sort of thing happen, Vehs?*: Wil asked.

:*A Companion surviving his Herald? Not often. The shock alone . . . I don't know how Alrek endured it.*:

:*Promise me you wouldn't do something like this. Please.*:

Vehs went quiet. Then, :*Do you jest? After putting up with a Chosen like you, I'll be* galloping *for the Bright Havens when my time comes!*:

Wil snorted, set his empty cup aside and headed for the stairs.

:*That's truly morbid.*:

:*Be glad I don't take a head start!*:

:*Yes, yes,*: Wil thought, smirking as he opened the door to his room. :*I'm such a burden on—*:

Lelia was curled up on his bed. She opened an eye as he entered and smiled.

Wil stood very still, finding it suddenly hard to breathe.

:*Good night, "Vanyel,"*: Vehs murmured.

"So. I was thinking," Lelia said.

"Yes?" Wil managed.

Lelia pushed back the covers. "To the hells with our professional relationship."

He groped for words and finally said, "This wasn't what I meant by tucking me in."

She laughed, and she was still laughing as he kicked the door shut behind him and went to her.

The Bride's Task

Michael Z. Williamson and Gail L. Sanders

Keth're'son shena Tale'sedrin was learning weapons work: the sword. This would have been useful to know for his journey to Valdemar, but his people were warriors from horseback and with the bow–not with the sword and dagger and on foot. He stepped aside from a sweep, blocked and countered, but his teacher parried that and beat back at him.

:But no knowledge is ever wasted, Chosen. You won't always have a horse to hand. What if I were injured? Just because your people haven't done something before, it doesn't mean that it's not a valid way to do things.:

Keth' replied, *:I know, "There is no one true way." But it's taking some getting used to. Traditions have always played a strong role in the life of a Shin'a'in; they had to.:*

:Right now, you need to pay attention to your role here, or the weaponsmaster is going to give you the "traditional" bruises.:

:You know, I would probably be doing something like this at home as well. I wonder how Nerea is doing with her lessons; she was always better with the bow than me.:

:You miss her.:

:Did you really expect that to change? We are pledged.

She's why I work so hard at these lessons. I only hope that she'll wait until I can return. I'm not sure she understood why I had to come up here when I wasn't sure myself.:

Yssanda was silent.

"There's a herd of horses in the Palace courtyard," one guard said.

"Why is there a herd of horses in the courtyard?" asked the other.

"I don't know, but isn't that a Shin'a'in on the back of one of them?"

"Sure looks like it. Heya, it's a girl! And look, she's getting down."

"Do you think we should tell somebody?"

Sergeant of the Guard Selwin spoke loudly behind them, "Yes, you halfwits, I think you should tell somebody! You, Rolin, go get Herald Captain Kerowyn. *At a run!* You, Vark, suggest to the young lady that she should stay outside the Palace door."

"Yes, sir!" the two guards saluted in unison and moved with a sense of purpose.

Shaking his head, the young guard sergeant moved toward what seemed to be an escalating argument. The burly guard was having an increasingly difficult time with the slim Shin'a'in, who seemed determined to simply get through that door. He'd managed so far without actually laying a hand on her, but it didn't appear that was going to last very much longer. She wasn't so much aggressive as persistent.

Moving past the string of exceptionally quiet and serene horses, Selwin came within range of a contrastingly loud and agitated Shin'a'in girl.

"She doesn't speak Valdemaran, sir!"

"I'm gathering that impression. Let's see what I can do." He strained to remember a bit of the language.

In very slow and careful Shin'a'in he said, "Please hold, coming someone who speaks language."

The young girl nodded briskly and moved back to reassure her riding horse. Selwin wasn't sure who needed the reassurance more, the horse or her.

Herald Captain Kerowyn didn't take long to arrive, which was all to the better as far as Sergeant Selwin was concerned. He wasn't a diplomat and very much preferred going back to his post near the main gates. He simply briefed Kerowyn on what had happened so far, saluted, and then gestured the guards to head back to the gate.

Striding forward, Herald Captain Kerowyn gave the impression of impatience. She didn't hide it. It might help speed this encounter.

:What happened to Shin'a'in staying on the Plains, where they belonged?:

:What happened? The Mage Storms happened and erased the tasks the Shin'a'in had been given by their Star-eyed.:

Kerowyn really hadn't needed the rejoinder to what had been a rhetorical question, but trust Sayvil to make sure her opinion was heard–needed or not.

"Welcome to Haven. I'm Herald Captain Kerowyn. What brings you here so far from the Plains?"

"My name is Nerea shena Tale'sedrin. I'm here looking for my pledged, Keth're'son shena Tale'sedrin. The Clan Elders said that he had come up here for training in his 'Gifts.' " Her skepticism in the need for such training was obvious. "They gave me permission to bring his Clan share up here to him when the Tale'sedrin came up for the Bolton Fair. Where is he?"

"Ah." Suddenly Kerowyn understood both her animosity and her vulnerability. By giving her permission to bring Keth's Clan share up here to him, the Clan Elders were both telling him that they weren't expecting him to come back to the Plains and giving him permission to stay where he was. They were also putting the responsibility of telling his pledged this, off their shoulders and onto his.

:Practical but not very kind of them. This Nerea must have been quite a nuisance.:

:Yes,: Kerowyn sighed to herself, *:And now she's our nuisance. Sayvil, please tell Dean Teren about the situation out here and ask him to bring the Shin'a'in envoy with him if possible. Have them meet us at the stables.:*

To the girl, she replied, "He is here at the Collegium. But first, we need to get these horses settled and out of the way. If you'll follow me, I'll lead you around to the stables. There should be room for them there." Kerowyn knew better than to offer her any help with this. After all she'd gotten them here from Bolton. It would also keep the girl busy while Kerowyn figured out what to do. The girl followed agreeably enough, since the horses were something she cared for. She did not seem to care for local rules.

The Companion-relayed message brought Dean Teren down from his office in a rush. From another direction, the Shin'a'in Envoy, Shaman Lo'isha shena Pretara'sedrin, was only a minute behind. The Dean arrived at the stable entrance panting. The Shaman heaved one sigh and had his breath back under control.

The Dean said, "A Shin'a'in invasion? That wasn't quite the message, but I gather this matter is important?"

"Not quite," Kerowyn said, hiding a smile. "However, we do have a Shin'a'in girl, far out of her area, seeking her pledged, who is one of your students." She indicated the stables.

"I see," the Dean said, and he seemed to grasp the import. He followed her gesture, to where the girl was taking proper care of the horses, including a quick brushing, with an economy born of lifelong experience.

When Nerea finished watering them at the trough and ensured they had a panful of oats and plenty of hay each, she turned and walked back. She seemed fully aware of the Dean and Shaman, but she waited for Kerowyn to make the introductions. She greeted the Dean with a bow, and spoke formally to the Shaman.

"Nerea, there are things I must attend to, but the Dean and Shaman will aid you."

"Thank you for the introduction, Cousin."

"You are welcome."

With that, Kerowyn turned and left, intending to find out just who in Bolton let Nerea off her leash with fifteen horses and who there might be missing her.

Lo'isha shena Pretara'sedrin, Shaman and Shin'a'in Envoy, found himself left with the problem. With Kerowyn gone, he was both translator for the Dean, speaker for his own, and the only possible authority figure the girl might acknowledge.

Neutrally, he said, "Nerea, you are far from our lands."

"As are you, Elder. We both have our reasons," she replied, with not quite a smile.

"Yes. You are here for your pledged, I'm told."

"I am. If he is to be here, I am to be with him."

He recognized her expression now—determination, with a slight challenge.

Lo'isha translated for Teren. Teren raised his eyebrows.

"Well, first I suppose I need you to help explain about the training."

Lo'isha nodded and translated for Teren.

Dean Teren twisted his mouth for a moment, apparently in thought, then spoke. "Nerea," he said, "Mind-magic is much more than empathy for animals. I know you can work with these creatures—" he gestured toward the stables "—better than most people, and it's a natural talent for you. However, Keth' is able to do the same to people and objects, whether they want it or not, whether he wants it or not. He and his traveling companions were attacked not far from the city on their way here. His reaction caused unconsciousness for the brigands, and two never recovered properly, being mind-lame since then." He waited while Lo'isha caught up.

"Well, good," she said. "I approve of retribution to such *grek'ka'shen*."

Teren winced slightly at that.

"Perhaps, but it wasn't an intentional response. He panicked, they collapsed. This could happen to innocent people, too. Nerea, I understand pledging is something that has been planned for some time. You must understand that his Mind-magic changes things. He needs to learn to control it, for his own safety, and yours, and that of others." Lo'isha translated.

She stared right back at Teren, then spoke to Lo'isha. "I understand that. You must understand that our pledge doesn't change due to side matters. He is alive, he is very much himself, and he is very much mine. I remain with him and he with me. Explain that to him, please." She gave a single, firm nod. With a raised eyebrow at her firmness, Lo'isha turned and translated for Teren.

Teren said, "That is not possible." The flat tone in his voice almost did not need translation.

"For you, perhaps not. I assure you it is quite possible for me." She sounded almost haughty, certainly confident and stubborn, and yet calm. She was like a mountain in storm, while the trees swayed in distress.

The Dean looked at Lo'isha in controlled exasperation. It wasn't that she didn't understand. She understood fully and was unswayed.

The Shaman placed a calming hand on Teren's wrist and tried a different tack.

"It is obvious this is true. Things have not changed for you, and you are on your course. However, have they remained the same for him?" Lo'isha spoke with the authority of a Shaman and brought up exactly what Nerea did not want to hear.

She flushed slightly.

"I don't know," she said. "I haven't seen him since he left our lands. That is why I am here now. This must be resolved between us." She almost stamped her foot in emphasis.

"I don't disagree. This training, though, is for safety. Consider a fire on the Plains. There's a reason children are taught to tend a fire carefully. They must know how to judge fuel, to avoid a flare of flames and disaster."

Her expression was most put upon.

"I don't seek to hinder that. Only to be near him."

Inwardly Lo'isha sighed; the girl wasn't being unreasonable, just stubborn, and adamant, and unswerving in her intent. The Shaman said, "Well, then please let me start by offering a place to stay and clean up from the journey, in the embassy in the Hawkbrother *ekele*."

She widened her eyes slightly.

"Thank you," she said. "I will be comfortable with our cousins."

"If you wait, I will show you the way. I and the Dean need to discuss how we can arrange this meeting for you."

With a frown and flick of her eyes, she said, "You have only to tell me where he is, but clearly that is too simple for this city, with its costumes and rules and gates and castes." She paused briefly, as if only then aware of her bad manners. "Forgive me. Thank you for your hospitality. I will leave you to your discussion, and I will await your direction, for now."

For now, Lo'isha thought. This wasn't over by far.

He watched her move a discreet distance away, enough to be in another tent, were there any tents here. She paid attention to some detail of the bricks and moss, and, while not relaxed, she was not intruding.

He turned to the Dean.

Teren asked, "How do we get her out of here?" in a whisper. He glanced over suspiciously at her.

"I don't know that we can. It would be up to her and her pledged."

"The distance should have made this impossible, especially for one so young."

"For our people, they are man and woman grown. You mustn't mistake her for a child."

"I'm not mistaking her for a problem." The Dean clutched his hands together.

"No, but you are mistaking her for your problem. I will show her to the *ekele*. Then we can talk."

"Very well, and thank you. Then we can have Keth' deal with the issue."

Teren seemed quite exasperated, and Lo'isha surmised that by "issue" he meant "sending her home."

He didn't think it would be that easy.

"I will meet with you shortly," he said. Then he turned, and to Nerea said, "Come then, and I will show you to the *ekele*."

Teren was in his office when Lo'isha returned. He gratefully put aside his writing and said, "Please, have a seat." Lo'isha sat in the one available chair in the cluttered and paper–filled office.

"Always one chair not used for storage, I see," the Shaman offered with a chuckle.

Teren shrugged and nodded and chuckled back. "It's my way. If anyone were to straighten my clutter, I'd never find anything again. But as to the other . . . Thank you for your aid in this matter. This is most awkward. Students are unaccompanied, and if they are not single when they commence training, they are by the time they graduate. This is how it is done, and most arrive knowing it. If he's to be a Herald . . ."

"You are assuming he will complete the training and follow your chosen path. There are at least two people assuming his fate for him. It seems to me that is a question for him to answer."

Teren looked startled at that. "How could he refuse to be a Herald?"

"Quite easily. Are you asking, 'Will he be the first to refuse?' "

Teren had no response. He never considered that possibility. There were traditions and cultural assumptions at the Collegium. Those weren't necessarily the traditions and assumptions of the boy, and they most definitely weren't those of the girl.

By choosing him, Yssanda had thrown things into a fine tempest. Perhaps it was an amusement for her. Or, it might be a necessity. What would have possessed a Companion to go all the way to the Dhorisha Plains to choose a Shin'a'in child? What would Valdemar need him for, or was it that the Shin'a'in would need him more?

Regardless of the cause, this situation needed resolution.

"I suppose we should arrange for them to meet," he said, leaning back and stroking his chin. "After that, we'll see."

"Are you going to warn the young man?"

"I'm not sure we should. He'll want to meet at once, and it will distract him. I'll arrange some time, and we'll let them meet. He can explain to her better than we."

"I'm not sure it will be that simple."

"Oh, of course he'll have second thoughts and some

homesickness. However, he's a fine pupil. He's learned a lot of fundamentals quickly, and he's even accepted the separation. It was long in his mind. They've both grown and changed, and this will make it clear."

The next morning, Lo'isha met Nerea at the ekele entrance. She was staring wide-eyed at the lush and fragrant growth. It was very different from the Plains. and being surrounded by the local terrain only emphasized the differences. Hearing his footfalls on the graveled path, Nerea turned and greeted the Shaman.

"Bright the day, Elder," she said cheerfully.

"Did you sleep well?"

"I did, thank you."

"How are the younger-sibs?"

"They are comfortable and getting refreshed. How much is stabling? I have little money, but I can offer work."

"Nothing is required for now. You are a guest at our invitation."

"That's gracious of you."

Quite a few youths would have assumed hospitality without even thinking. They expected adults to manage things for them. The locals had trouble grasping that, by Shin'a'in tradition, she was a woman grown. Of course she asked about debts.

"Actually, it's gracious of the Dean and of the Queen," he smiled. "But it's something they plan for, so you need not mention it."

"I will do so, at least once, but I understand," she said.

He sighed, slightly. Yes, the ways here were strange, but as a guest, one should learn and abide by the local rules. She was a headstrong and inexperienced youth, well-intentioned but fiery.

"If you are ready, then please come with me."

They walked out into a damp spring morning. It had

rained during the night. It might be warm and muggy later, but was clear and fresh now.

He led her through Companion's Field, along Palace garden paths, and to the Collegium main hall. At a side entrance, Teren awaited, and with him Keth're'son shena Tale'sedrin.

Nerea was not so formal with Keth'. She charged forward and threw her arms around him in a tackling hug, feet off the ground and looking melted in place. Lo'isha stood back and let them resolve that. Their embrace was one of innocent companionship, not of long-parted lovers, but it still held that same intensity.

Keth's mind whirled. How did Nerea get here? But she was so warm, and her grip so tight. He could smell her hair and the scent of her leathers. He closed his eyes and hugged her closely.

When he finally bent to put her down and her feet touched the ground, she stepped back and grinned hugely at him, her dark eyes glowing.

She said, "It is so good to see you, my pledged. I have traveled far to keep our bond." Her voice, that language, was music to him, after months of the strange tongue and stiffer rules it used. Shin'a'in flowed from the lips as was proper, Valdemaran seemed to march backward instead.

He remembered there were others here, and they were being watched. He kept hold of one of her hands and said, "I am so thrilled to have you here. But I must introduce you to someone."

He tugged and she followed him, smiling, into Companion's Field and away from prying eyes.

"Who did you need me to meet?" Nerea asked.

They had been walking away from the Palace and the Collegium for some minutes now, while he enjoyed her company. She'd come so far. He had so many questions and so much to say, but first he had to introduce her to his Companion.

There she came, from a shady copse of trees, toward them. He pointed as she came close, then laid a hand on her shoulder.

He said, "This is Yssanda. She is, in part, the reason why I came here."

"She's beautiful. Good lines, broader head. How did they get the silver hooves, and does she suffer any eyesight problems with those blue eyes? Do the hooves breed true?"

:I can see as well as you do, dear, and sometimes clearer. And don't you even think about breeding me—I can pick my own mates, thank you very much!: Yssandra let him hear her comment, even though she spoke to Nerea.

Well, that certainly moved things along.

Nerea stood very still. The sensation of having someone speaking inside one's mind was disconcerting to say the least, he recalled. Having that sensation come from a horse made it even more so. While the Shin'a'in consider horses to be their younger-sibs, they didn't expect them to talk back.

"Nerea, she's not a horse," Keth' said gently. "She's a Companion, a person in her own right. She's been my friend, teacher, and ally while I've been in this foreign place. Even after I'm done here, she's going to have to be a part of any of our plans."

"What are those plans going to be? You've already been gone so long, am I still a part of any plan?"

Keth's heart went out to her. She seemed to shrink inside herself a little, both wanting to hear the answer and not wanting to hear. Nerea deserved his honesty, but he wasn't sure himself.

"We need to talk about that. I think that's why you're here."

* * *

Dean Teren sat in his office, yet again considering the problem that Nerea and Keth' presented him. Neither one of the youngsters was taking into account what the Collegium might have to say in the matter—they just assumed that they could order the world according to what they wanted. After all, they were young and together—who could stand against them . . .

That was exactly the reason Herald Trainees were expected to be unaccompanied.

It occurred to the Dean that while it was certainly possible to stand against them, it might be very problematic to do so—sufficiently so to give the Bards song fodder for a long time.

Keth' wasn't precisely a disappointment. He learned very well. However, he hadn't internalized the right attitude and didn't see a problem with Nerea remaining here. She stayed at the *ekele* and had worked out a labor exchange for lodging. She was quite competent.

Teren realized he'd underestimated them. A Valdemaran youth of that age could be swayed through reason, emotion, or social suggestion. Not only were these two from another culture, they'd grown up much faster. They were a strange mix of adult minds in juvenile spirits and bodies. He needed to talk to the envoy again.

Keth' walked with Lo'isha, near Companion's Field, with his own concerns. There were few people he could even begin to discuss this with.

"It's aggravating," Keth' said. "All this past year, I've been told I must continue alone. I had accepted that—well, somewhat—but now she shows up here. *Here.* Halfway across the continent."

The Shaman paused to study a flower. Keth' was not interested in flowers.

"It should be flattering," the Elder said.

"It is," Keth' agreed, quickly. "It's also very inconvenient."

"Not just for you."

"I understand. But I want her to stay. I want to go home with her. So does she. I also do want to continue my studies. There's so much to learn, and I'm improving." He paused, unsure what to add.

"You are improving," the Shaman assured him. "You also can't control this situation. Unlike Mind-magic, this involves people's intent. Even if you had that power, it would be unwise and unfair to use it."

He nodded. That such might be possible was disturbing.

As to the matter at hand, he asked, "So who does control it? And what should I do?"

"We each control our own part, or we think we do. Eventually, each of us will find a path that fits the events."

"That makes sense," he agreed, and he did feel better. "I just wish it would hurry up." He realized he was pacing back and forth as the Shaman strolled.

The Shaman said, "It is better that it take time. As to other things, I understand Nerea is taking language lessons?" He smiled with a twinkle.

"Yes, Clan k'Leshya also have given her lodging and some small allowance in exchange for stable work. I let her have a little of my own funds," he admitted, blushing. "I do care for her." She was so stubborn. Or not stubborn, but simply unswayable.

"There is no reason you shouldn't," the Shaman said.

"But they want me to become a Herald, and Heralds—"

"You are not yet a Herald, and you remain Keth're'son shena Tale'sedrin. Those are two more things that must be reconciled."

"This doesn't sound possible," he said. He'd wanted reassurance. This was making him feel more depressed.

He didn't feel Shin'a'in, nor Valdemaran, nor even himself now.

"It is all possible, and we need not know how at this point. It will all resolve in time."

"Thank you, Elder, I suppose." He tried to smile. "Can you give me something more immediate and practical?"

"You are free for the day. Why not take your pledged into Haven? I'm sure she'd like to see more than stables."

Lo'isha found himself quite busy. While he couldn't fault Kerowyn for handing the problem off, and it did involve his people, it was quite an interesting one, with all that entailed.

"So, Teren, what are we to discuss today?" He took the empty chair and noticed it was a different one. The piles of parchment had moved.

"The same as we've discussed every day for the last two weeks. Nerea."

"Yes, she's quite the item."

"A pest. Sweet, pretty, too clever for her own good, and a pest." Teren twiddled a quill in his fingers.

"The language lessons?" he guessed.

"That, and still being here, and loitering around. I suggested she stay in Bolton. I offered to pay for quarters across town, to make some distance."

"She would refuse, of course."

"She did." Yes, Teren was most agitated, and on such a fine day.

"Is she affecting his studies?"

"Not that I've noticed, and I've been watching. It is disruptive to others, though, on top of his existing differences as a foreigner."

Lo'isha kept calm and reassuring. "Well, I should think that would be good for the other trainees. They'll have to deal with such matters in the field, after all."

"Indeed. I would just prefer their practice problems be more organized."

"You can't send her away," he pointed out.

"I know." Teren stood and looked out the window. "I'd hoped she'd get bored and leave, or he'd realize he'd grown apart from her. Something. If anything, they are reconnecting and throwing sand in everyone's shoes."

"Then perhaps now is a time to walk barefoot and enjoy the sensation."

Teren said, "Walking barefoot also involves thorns."

"Then walk carefully," Lo'isha offered his friend with a smile. "I have a feeling these thorns will be trodden down by many feet."

"Let me show you the city," Keth' said. While it wasn't home, it was a fascinating place, and he was eager to introduce her to some of the more interesting foods.

"Whatever you like," she said with a smile. It caught him off guard.

He offered an arm and led the way toward the horse and animal market, figuring to stop at the Compass Rose just beyond it. It wasn't the cheapest, but it didn't attract lowlifes, and the usual clientele wouldn't be surprised to see a pair of Shin'a'in.

They were almost to the market when he realized why her smile had concerned him.

There was a glint.

They'd both grown in a year, and she felt like a part of him. Then he realized he felt the same way. Even if he did agree with the Collegium's rules, and he'd only admitted to understanding them, this was something he wanted more.

"The Ashkevrons do have some fine horses," Nerea said. "We have better, but not by much, and no others I've seen come close."

"Well, they do buy ours and breed them."

"Certainly, but it takes more than stock. It takes care and raising." Her energy never faded. He'd always liked that.

There were a lot of horses here today. It must be some market day. There were wagons, carts, horses with pannier saddles, mounts for nobles and the wealthy, and draft horses for farmers. Some of the wagons contained oats, nuts, apples, and other fare meant for the animals, and several stores had displays of combs and brushes. There were also saddles, tack and clothes for riders, and even a carpenter's display of stable making. The place smelled of fine horseflesh, and he enjoyed it.

"Some very fine creatures," she said, smiling. She was relaxed, he realized, and comfortable for now. With food and fine weather, there was nowhere he'd rather be.

Which was odd; this place was not home. He could speak the language well enough to get by, but it still felt foreign.

Rather than ponder it, he decided to just enjoy the day. Her hand was warm as she clutched his. Her shoulder brushed him every couple of steps. He was comfortably fed and had no pressing worries for the day.

It was at that moment that the Star-eyed saw fit to give him pressing worries.

A cart-hitched horse suddenly stepped sideways, reared up, and came down in a limping gallop. His cart knocked a stall askew, spilled some contents—bags of feed—and rode over the collapsed legs of the vendor's display.

The horse was clearly hurt, right rear leg tipping the ground as the rest clattered on the cobbles. People dove from its path, shouting and screaming. Other animals shied and whinnied, backed and sidled, until carts crashed and tangled in a huge mess. It would take hours to sort out. It had happened in moments.

The chaos spread as other horses and even smaller animals caught the whiff of panic. Their instincts fought their restraints, and the din of it all was astounding.

Then Nerea stepped into the street.

Keth' knew what she intended and took a half step to grab her, then decided he would only make it worse. He had no doubt she knew what she was doing, but he wasn't sure the horse did.

Three people buffeted him as they darted past, urgently clearing the street and seeking somewhere out of reach of rearing hooves and twisting wagons.

Then the horse, a very handsome dapple, reached Nerea at a near-gallop still dragging the remains of the cart. She stood calmly, stepped aside just enough to avoid it, and stroked his flank with her fingers.

He slowed haltingly and stumbled two steps forward as the tilting cart's momentum shoved at him.

Nerea walked around him, fingers tracing his muscles. After the dapple was calmed, she stepped over to a dun mare. Nerea held a hand to her muzzle, and she quieted. Then a roan stallion dropped, relaxed and stepped out of the wreckage of a pushcart yoke. The waves of calm rippled out, where waves of panic had flowed only breaths before.

Nerea turned back to the dapple, walked around, and touched his injured leg. He raised it at once, and she studied his hoof. Taking out her belt knife, she pried something long and sharp out of the frog. Releasing the foot, she patted the dapple's flank.

And Keth' smiled, because he knew what could keep her here, near him and near the horses.

He would stay here and finish his studies, because Mind-magic, and Animal Speaking, ran through his people. It was inevitable others would show their talents, and possibly more of them. He'd be needed to teach those children of the Shin'a'in who had Mind-magic and who could not or would not leave the Plains. Nerea would stay here until then and teach the Valdemarans about horses, for wisdom ran both ways.

He also understood why the day had been so sweet, even though Valdemar wasn't his home. Nor, anymore, were the Plains.

Home was where Nerea was.

"So, how are our lovebirds doing? More importantly, has Nerea started home yet?" Teren asked Lo'isha hopefully, after serving the Shaman some tea.

Lo'isha smiled at him.

"I think that is a vain hope, my friend. She does not look as if she is leaving anytime soon. If she were easy to dissuade, she would have never left the Plains in the first place."

Teren sighed and leaned against his desk. "What am I going to do with them?"

"Why do anything? They will solve their own problems and have indeed begun to do so." Lo'isha calmly sipped his tea.

"What do you mean?" asked Teren suspiciously. He had the feeling that he wasn't going to like this.

"After that incident at the horse market, Nerea has received more offers for work and horse training than she knows what to do with. She isn't going anywhere," he repeated.

"What about Keth'? Has he spoken to you at all?"

Lo'isha sat back and steepled his fingers.

"Yes, he has asked me about becoming a teacher on the Plains. He believes his talents lie not with Valdemar but with his—our—people. He's not entirely wrong. Her talent, of course, is a latent power manifesting itself. There will be others. He can hardly be the only one needing to be trained in Mind-magic. Since the Storms there is now no reason not to. My people would learn better from one who has the proper attitude; magic is not to be meddled with but controlled and tempered."

"But he is supposed to be a Herald! Anyone a Companion chooses has to be a Herald!" Teren was agitated. He'd thought Lo'isha concurred with him.

"Why? 'There is no one true way.' It's time to change. Not every Shin'a'in with power can trek to Valdemar, and certainly they can't remain here. At some point, we must have our own schools. In the meantime, he will be an intermediary, learning here, then mentoring others. Perhaps one day he will return to the Plains."

Teren said, "That's not what he wants."

Lo'isha replied, "Nor is it what you want. Nor even what I'd want, if I had a choice. None of us do, though. The Storms have blown the slate clean for us down on the Plains."

He took a final sip of tea and placed the cup down on a clear spot amid the clutter.

"I believe they have for Valdemar as well."

Fog of War

Ben Ohlander

Gonwyn pressed the bloody, filthy rag down onto where his teeth had been broken by the arrow hit. The helmet's cheek-piece had saved his life, but pain from the splintered molars flared as he tried to stanch the bleeding. He spat more blood and fragments onto the leafy ground. Distant fighting flared up, the rattle of combat carried across the torn ground. His part of the field might have gone quiet, but fighting still raged in the center and on the left.

He nudged Rath with his heels, and they moved together up the draw,and through the trees. The Companion, fastidious about her hooves, stepped around the windrows of fallen bodies. Tedrel and Valdemaran lay commingled, embraced in death.

He crossed into the rally point, well behind the lines . . . at least until the lines had moved and brought heavy fighting. The low mounded hill and its sparse trees stank of blood and loosened bowels, thick with the stench of death. Nearby wounded had been gathered here, at least until the Tedrels had swept the Valdemaran forces back. Now, the injured felt no pain.

He thought Adreal lay dead, propped against a tree with a bloody blanket pressed to his middle. The Herald Master opened his eyes and reached for his notched sword, bringing it up in defense before he recognized Gonwyn.

Gonwyn slid out of the saddle and moved closer. Claris, Adreal's Companion, came into sight, lamed by a gashing wound in her left rear leg. The skin lay open, exposing the muscle beneath. Blood slicked the Companion's side, running from haunch to hock.

"Where the hell was our support?" Gonwyn asked. "It was raining anvils on us over there."

Adreal half-smiled at him. "You sound like you have a mouth full of marbles."

Gonwyn made an apologetic gesture toward his blood-crusted face. "Got hit by a spent arrow. Lost most of the afternoon asleep in a warm pile of dead other people. Was missed by the Tedrel looters."

"There's your answer." Adreal shook his head. "Tedrel happened. Their cavalry never showed. The Lord Marshal took all the reserves and our horse to go deal with something clever the Tedrels thought up. They took all the Heralds who were controlling movement on this side. They went out of play just as they would have been useful."

Adreal coughed as he shifted his weight against the tree. "You do know that King Sendar was killed?'

Gonwyn winced as he brushed his tongue over the damage. "Yes." It came out as "yeth." "I heard he was down but was back up. Rath told me he was killed when I came to. What happened?"

Adreal shrugged and coughed again. A thin spittle line of blood leaked from the corner of his mouth. His tone remained dry and normal. "Don't know the full of it. He took what body of troops was near and charged into the center. Cracked it. Most of the Tedrel forces fell on that wedge. Just about everyone in that charge was killed, but it took the pressure off the flanks."

"What about the Heir?" Gonwyn asked.

"Alive." Adreal wiped his hand across his face. Gonwyn could see the sweat even in the cool air. "Selenay is alive. I heard Alberich got her out before that part of the line got swamped. There was some kind of assault or raid. He got her out."

Gonwyn spat again and reached into Rath's saddlebags for sour field wine. He rinsed his mouth, winced at the astringent bite, then offered the bladder to Adreal. The Herald refused with a shake of his head.

"He didn't turn on us?" Gonwyn asked. "I always thought he was too good to be true."

"Nope. Mr. 'Hide in Haven' was all over the map today, bad cess to the Tedrels. He got Selenay out after Sendar died, kept the attack going in the face of the King's fall, and led the regrouping in the absence of the Lord Marshal."

"Where's Talamir, then? Where's the King's Own?"

"He was near Sendar when he went down. They got Tavar." Both men shared a glance, first at Adreal's Claris, then at Gonwyn's Rath. The ultimate horror for a Herald, the loss of bond and blood, of a Companion's fall. Gonwyn knew both that he would take his own life if Rath fell, and that they talked about a dead man.

They both glanced as the fighting on the left side of the Valdemaran line grew more intense. Distant horns followed by a giant crash as two forces came together.

That took Gonwyn by surprise. "Lord Maybe got off his ass?"

Adreal laughed without mirth. "No. Once Sendar fell, the center went mad with fury, and most of the inner parts of the line bent inward. Commanders farther out on the flanks held back. Either they had farther to go, or there were local problems." He didn't say what Gonwyn had heard again and again through camp rumor . . . that the less reliable commanders were to be put the farthest on the flanks.

Adreal ignored his expression and continued. "Sorcha went to Lord Maybe to press home on that side and avenge the King. The rage was on them, too. Sorcha was arguing with him, and Maybe was saying "maybe," when something the size of a crow came and took his head off." He smiled grimly. "Sorcha's Elissa was impressed, and Companions don't impress easy." Adreal coughed again. "That Eastholder Sergeant . . . Split-Face . . . took over, and two candlemarks later rolled up their right side like a carpet. This was midafternoon. You can still hear that part of the fight."

Gonwyn was surprised. "Not one of Maybe's officers? They brought enough."

Adreal smiled. "Have you seen that bastard? Looks like he got his mug cut in half with an ax? Would you tell him no?"

Gonwyn shook his head. "I saw him once, when I was running messages for Colonel Perfect Boots. You'd need stones the size of catapult shot to go up against him. "

Adreal shrugged then, though it cost him. "I think the Lord Marshal put him there deliberately. You should have heard Maybe squawking about command interference. Threatened to take the matter to the King."

"Anyway . . ." Adreal picked up a broken arrow and drew in the dirt. "Split-Face broke through their right side and is driving into their center and rear. Their entire right side collapsed, with many routing into the center. Most of that was thrown over by Sendar's charge. What's left of the Tedrel right wing folded back like a gate, but Split-Face ripped right through that. He's now somewhere back in there, cheerfully tearing their rear echelons to shreds."

Gonwyn tried to whistle and settled for a wince. "He's that good?"

Adreal shrugged. "Seems so. They're outnumbered, but I've never met an Eastholder yet with enough brains to do basic math. It probably hasn't occurred to him yet that they should be getting swamped. They're all still in a blood fury, so that helps."

He made more marks to show the original Valdemaran lines, then scratched them out. "If we could hold, then we might be the anvil to their hammer, but as it stands, he's pushing them all into us."

A wounded Guardsman approached with a water bottle and a loaf. Gonwyn took the bottle and gratefully swigged from it. He sluiced out a mouthful of pink-tinged water before he drank. He considered the bread, the state of his mouth, and passed on the loaf. It was not a hard choice.

"Can Sorcha hold him up, give us time to reknit?" he asked.

Adreal stabbed the arrow into the dirt map. "No. She went down a little after midafternoon. With Eiven dead, she was our last link to the far flank on that side of the line."

Gonwyn winced. "Eiven and Selim. Sorcha and Elissa. That's seven pairs today."

"Eight" Adreal corrected. "Morevon got hit with one of those floating, flaming bastards. Pinned him and Elath to the ground."

Gonwyn made no response for a long moment. "It's been a rough day for the Companions Field."

Adreal laughed again, a dry humorless laugh. "It's been a rough day for us all." He stabbed the arrow into the ground. "There, I've shown you mine, you show me yours."

Gonwyn wiped Adreal's marks with his boot. He absently noted that blood had already stained the leather. He flexed his stiffening hand.

"Not much to tell", he said, "I was on the ass-end of the line supporting Captain Arland's Guards Regiment,and a herd of Orthallen's militia. This morning I was all the way past where the oak grove burned, watching for Tedrel cavalry trying to push our flanks. We were still holding in our original deployments. The militia gave a good account of themselves. They broke the shock troops well enough. There was no serious effort to turn our flank . . . they were just keeping us in play at first."

Gonwyn made more marks to show the evolving fight. "We'd started to give ground after we got intelligence that the Tedrel cavalry was missing and to watch our flanks. Arland had just refused his line to double spears on the right, when every damned Tedrel ever born washed over us. I saw the Terilee in flood once, rising up a dike. That's how it felt. Arland called me and his scouts in at that point."

He laughed. "Ormona was Mindspeaking for Arland and called for reinforcements. She got, 'Sorry, they're busy. Good luck.' " He stabbed the dirt with the arrow.

"The line bent, but we were doing okay. Then we got word that Sendar was down, and Orthallen . . . he commanded the bulk of the militia . . . ordered everyone back to the second rally line. Disengaging in the middle of a fight is damned hard, and while the militia was doing well, they weren't up to this. Arland's regiment got sorted out, but the militia shattered like a dropped pot."

He shrugged. "They would have had us, except that a whole horde of Tedrels took off and started running for the center. There were enough left to make us pay, but it thinned them enough to give us a chance."

Gonwyn flexed his hand and stared at the trickle of blood that ran down between his middle and ring fingers. The wound in his shoulder had broken open again. "Most everyone got back into the trees," he continued. "We were scattered from hell to breakfast in those woods. Once those black-hearted bastards sort out Split-Face and figure out we're broken, they'll turn the position. Then, we're done."

Adreal paused, assessing Gonwyn's report. "It's not that easy. Looks like most of the Tedrel leadership went down in Sendar's charge. There are a whacking great lot of them still out there, but their army is breaking up. Nonetheless, I take your point. This fight may be won, but it isn't over."

Gonwyn nodded, feeling the need to explain his own presence away from the fighting. "We'd just gotten word that the King wasn't down . . . the message got garbled somehow. Rath thinks we picked up a piece of the local chatter—that the King had gone down into the valley . . . but who knows?"

He continued to draw with the arrow. "We heard from Horvis, who was up closer to the center, that King Sendar had charged down into main body, and we were to press forward in support. Orthallen was nowhere to be found. Ormona was supposed to be Mindspeaking for Arland, but Orthallen took her with him, so we got word from a very confused Guardsman riding his captain's horse. He was looking for a Captain Elesarn, who was supposed to have a cavalry troop, when he found us. He was about a quarter compass off the mark, looking for a horse unit that were gods' only knew where at that point. We policed him up."

"Arland ordered us forward, but it took a few minutes to Mindspeak with Horvis and Ormona and get everyone singing the same hymn. Orthallen was supposed to join back up, but Arland didn't wait. He did a half-left with what he had and started sweeping in toward the center. I think our linear distance would have been about two miles at that point."

"Most of the Tedrel shock troops scattered when we came back out of the tree line. I was with about a half-company . . . a mixed bag of Guardsmen and militia. We'd hit what was left of the Tedrel shield wall and were doing okay until I got hit with this . . ." he made a gesture at his marred face, . . . "and I went down. When I came to, anything that wasn't dead was scattered. Arland and the regiment were long gone. I worked my way back to the rally point . . ." He dismissed an hour's terror, sharp fighting, and the shoulder wound with a shrug.

He looked around at the piles of dead and dying,and the evidence of heavy battle. ". . . Such as it is."

A shared glance with Adreal told him that the history lessons were over.

"I'm staying here to redirect whoever tries to make the rally point back to the assembly areas below the village. That's where Her Majesty is trying to spin dung into diamonds."

"You want me to go there?" Gonwyn asked.

"No," Adreal replied, "What I want is for you to get to Split-Face and get him to back off . . . but you'd never make it." He looked at the battered chainmail on the bloodstained Herald. "You were a Guards officer before you were Chosen. I need you to get into those woods and start rounding up the stragglers. There are parts of units all over these hills, and we have to get the strays moving back toward the village . . . that way Her Majesty can knit something together that buys us time. If I can break through the Companion babble, I'll get word to someone on what you're about."

Gonwyn reached down and gripped his friend's arm. "Be careful. I saw something in the woods that made a Karse demon look like a kitten."

Adreal returned the grip. "Probably was Karse. The Tedrels raped and burned their way across the country, even if they were in the Sunlord's pay. This battle is the best thing that ever happened to them. If Tedrel wins, they get a weakened and defeated Valdemar with a Tedrel client for a buffer. If they lose, then they get rid of an annoying and expensive problem. If it calls a draw, then they bleed us. Three throws, and they win each one. So Karse'll be watching this all very closely."

Gonwyn looked at the bloodstained blanket and knew the answer beforehand. "Can I help you?"

Adreal lifted the blanket. Gonwyn saw the poniard rammed to the hilt through the chainmail and between Adreal's ribs. A bright bubble of blood leaked out as he exhaled. "Healer Janse took the pain when they first brought me here, so it doesn't hurt. I passed out." He pointed with his chin to where the wounded had been slain as they lay. "When I awoke, this was over."

He shifted the blanket to cover himself. Gonwyn bent to offer his hand in farewell. Adreal grabbed it with a fierce strength, his expression direct and forceful. "Gonwyn, do you remember what the King said before he left Haven? You like handstrokes too much, and if we're going get out of this we need brains. Leave the sword in the scabbard. Promise me you'll steer clear of fights."

Gonwyn dipped his head, acknowledging without promising. He raised his hand in salute. "See you on the other side."

Adreal raised his hand in reply, then let it drop. He turned his attention to obliterating every vestige of their quick maps. That was Adreal, careful beyond careful. "Get something to eat and wash your face." he said, as Gonwyn turned away. "You look like you've been wading in an abattoir."

Gonwyn returned to where Rath stood. The Companion had all but demolished a pile of oats poured from a bag and onto the leafy ground. He could feel the hunger in the big mare, and the bone-deep fatigue.

:No rest for the wicked.: With Rath, there were never questions. Just statements. It used to annoy Gonwyn, but he'd had twenty-five years to get over it.

"Is there ever?" he replied.

The wounded Guardsman stood nearby. He held a soot-stained, steaming pail of water, the handle wrapped in rags. Blood seeped through the bandage on his head and ran down the side of his face. Gonwyn looked at him . . . one pupil the size of an olive, the other a pin-point.

"Just put it down, son," he said gently.

The Guardsman looked at him, confused and still.

Gonwyn took the bucket from him. He watched as the young soldier drifted back to where a larger pot of water boiled over a fire.

The Companion answered his unasked question. *:His brains were dashed about. Severe, but not fatal if he is well cared for. There will be damage.:*

Gonwyn poured most of the warm water into a pail, mixed a double handful of oats into it, and squatted on his heels to use the rest of the hot water to wash off some of the blood and filth. He took a rag and gingerly swabbed the contusion on his temple from when he'd been knocked off Rath. The mare had nearly done a backflip to avoid stepping on him but had still clipped his head and put him out.

:You done making yourself pretty?: Rath was still nose down in the pail, lipping out the last of the steaming oats.

"Yeah," Gonwyn replied. "You ready?"

:Yes. We should go. Too many oats will make me fat.:

Gonwyn looked at her. With Rath, you could never tell. She might even be serious.

He tightened the bellyband and mounted, settling in the worn saddle.

Herald and Companion moved back down the hill and across the narrow draw at a ground-eating canter. They avoided the lines of dead by unspoken agreement, angling away from the road and down through the leafy drifts to the stream that had been the control feature for the Valdemaran reserve line. They followed it some quarter of a mile, to where it bent sharply to the right. The stream went straight ahead on their crude map.

That had been the beginning of a very bad day. Turned out the map they'd copied was wrong. There were two streams, about a quarter of a mile apart, which meant some of the troops had withdrawn to the wrong stream when Orthallen called retreat. Then, when they'd tried to turn it around, the units were hopelessly scattered, and the reserves were gone. Everything else about this campaign had been a dog's dinner, so why not the maps?

:Enough.: Rath's mental voice cut through his internal monologue. The mare stopped suddenly and tensed.

"Adreal?" Gonwyn asked.

:He has passed. Claris has gone mad.: The very matter-of-factness of the mare's tone told him how deeply she felt the loss. All Companions shared a bond deeper than mortals could understand, but Rath and Claris had been exceptionally close.

Gonwyn forced himself still, pushed down the grief at Adreal's death and Claris' loss. He buried it alongside the crushing fatigue, the pain from mouth and shoulder, and the belly-deep fear . . . all the things that were normal to feel,but which he just couldn't afford.

Rath, sensing his resolve, pressed onward, picking up the pace to move through where the Tedrels had pressed forward, been stopped, and then driven back. The combat here had been brutal, with quarter neither asked nor given. The dead lay thickest where the lines had struggled longest. They rode around a few fragments of Tedrel units, none of which looked much like fighting. Gonwyn and Rath moved together with an abundance of caution, alert to Adreal's order to avoid trouble. From such came the Karse stories of "ghost horses."

They slowed after a mile or so, to pick their way carefully through a narrow draw where a small fight had taken place. A dozen dead Valdemarans and rather more Tedrels lay in little heaps and piles. He and Rath had passed this way less than two candlemarks earlier, so this fight had taken place recently. Tedrels were still bleeding through the original Valdemaran lines and into the border hills. This was bad news that needed reporting.

He slid out of the saddle to walk ahead of the mare, scuffing his feet in the leaves as they went. The Tedrels liked caltrops, and having Rath take one through the hoof would be a death-sentence.

He searched the dead Tedrels, rifling through equipment and pockets and looking at shoes. The journey bread was fresh-baked, so they had both ovens and wheat. The shoes were mostly old, but well tended and stuffed with fresh hay to pad the feet. The equipment tended to be simple and poor but well maintained . . . the standard tools of a sell-sword. There were a few small coins but no significant booty or loot. That suggested a couple of things, but none definitive. No writing material, orders, or maps. The mix told him that they were decently supplied and had resources close by. Bakers and cobblers did not strap their kit on a field pack. This was no Tedrel advance guard. This was the Tedrel nation.

In some ways the Tedrels were better supplied than the Valdemarans they faced. King Sendar had to cajole and command to force the Council to put aside its spats and march as one country. The delay gave the army a thrown-together feel, and it was larger than the commissary could support for any length of time. Sendar . . . no, Selenay now, would have little choice but to begin disbanding the army very soon, before it started eating itself to death. They had to do for Tedrel here and now.

He took some buttons, small coins, and other trinkets that might show where the Tedrels had been. He also gathered up a brace of fat rabbits they had snared along the way.

:What are you going to do with those?: Asked Rath. *:It's not like you can chew right now.:*

"I'm not going to leave two patriotic Valdemaran rabbits in the clutches of the Tedrels. It's only right I find a good Valdemaran stomach for them. Even if it's not mine."

:Whatever.:

He took the journey bread as well. He wasn't sure when he would eat, and while food hadn't been an issue, it was just a matter of time before it was.

He felt Rath touch his mind, sort his conclusions, and make his report.

:It's still too hard to get through. I've passed word to Kantor directly, but he's preoccupied with Alberich's problems. I'm trying to get to Eigen, but he and Rimlee are almost out of range. They're mopping up some Tedrel cavalry. Anlina is up in the center. She's tied up with sorting out something about the King, and Adreal is dead. Otherwise, there's still too much confusion.:

Gonwyn shook his head. "The Mindspeaking is an advantage, but we rely on it too much. Once the plan fell apart, so did the way we'd planned to Mindspeak. The Queen might be able to get orders down, my friend, but no way are we going to get word back up."

:These militia did well. They held their own, then withdrew in good order in about company strength. Should we follow and make our report in person?:

Gonwyn considered it, and the attendant benefits of Healer, wench, bottle, and bed . . . in exactly that order. He judged the direction and likely time and frowned. The sun was well past afternoon and into evening. Adreal knew what he was about. Damned duty.

"No," he said, reluctantly. "They're headed toward the roadstead. They'll be halfway to the village by now.

Someone will police them up. We'll press along the main line of resistance."

:Thy will be done,: replied the mare.

He turned to mount and felt Rath stiffen.

:Be still, now. There's a Herald nearby, back up that side wash. Up among the trees.:

Gonwyn turned to look. "There where the big oak is slanted and thicket is close in where the stream tumbles?"

:Yes. It is Herald Danilla. She panicked in the fight. Her Companion is very young and was . . . overcome.:

"What the hell does that mean? Overcome."

:It means that we are not perfect, Chosen. The girl is frightened, and both are ashamed. Be gentle, Herald Gonwyn.:

"When am I not?" he replied.

Rath flickered about a hundred quick mental images between them.

"All right, but that last one wasn't my fault. She said the pig was tame."

He slid his sword out of its scabbard and laid it across the saddle-bow. "Better safe."

Rath did not respond. The Companion started down the washed-out creek bank and splashed across. Her steps were dainty and careful, feeling for a caltrop even in the water before she put her hoof all the way down.

Gonwyn, in no mood for a fast arrow from a frightened girl, stopped just inside calling distance to the stand of oaks.

"Herald Danilla," he called. "Come down. It is Herald Gonwyn." He used a note of command, broadened with inflections of concern and wary friendship.

He could feel the edges of Rath's Mindppeaking to Danilla's Companion. Many Heralds could actually hear the great pool of minds that the Companions shared. The skill, not shared by Gonwyn, had been alternately described it as a great joy and great annoyance.

Some few moments passed before he saw movement, then a quick flash as a young Herald in new chainmail and White surcoat led her Companion down from the copse of trees. He waited, letting her come to him, while he scanned the surrounding trees. They had been in this draw too long and were too exposed.

He assessed her condition as she approached, her head down. Her surcoat was streaked with blood, and the left shoulder was spattered with gray lumps that his experienced eye told him were someone else's brains. Her coat was still a damned sight cleaner than his, though. Her hauberk was tight-laced in the school style, rather than field-laced, telling him she was fresh from the Collegium. First mission, first fight, and it was this butchery?

The Companion was injured, favoring the rear left hoof. The girl looked up at him as she approached. There was a shallow wound high on the haunch, toward the back. It had been well-tended and dressed.

Tear marks traced clean streaks across the Herald's filthy face. Her hair was matted with blood, probably a cut in her head. He didn't see any fresh blood, and in any event, he'd lost his healing kit. It would have to keep.

"Equipment?" he asked.

"Sword. Bow," she replied softly, her voice muffled as she studied her feet.

"Can you ride?"

A pause while she conferred with her Companion. "Yes. Can walk. Can't run." Almost a whisper this time.

:I don't have time for this,: he thought to Rath.

:Make time,: the Companion replied. *:They're Herald and Companion. Leaving them is not an option.:*

"Mount up. We need to move."

She mounted lightly, moving with a grace that Gonwyn lacked, even when not wearing chainmail and two week's worth of grime.

She settled in her saddle and looked at him, her eyes haunted. He knew what was coming and hated it, hated her for it. He didn't like being involved, didn't want to be involved, and she was going to involve him.

"I ran," she confessed, bringing the monster in the room out in the open.

Now he had to deal with it.

"When they broke through, I helped in the fight . . . I did. I killed two with my sword. Then everything fell apart. There were so many. They killed Captain Elagen and Herald Valean and smashed Companion Saneel's head wide open. The pikemen started to run. That's when I panicked." She began to weep, tracking more clean across a landscape of caked mud, dirt, and blood. "I'm so sorry."

Gonwyn hated weeping. Anger he could deal with, drunken stupidity (his and others') a specialty, and the myriad petty squabbles and cases of two decades of riding Circuit proved a cinch. Give him a few tears, and he was utterly at a loss.

:You and half the population ever born,: commented Rath drily. *:Say something encouraging, and move out. We need to go.:*

"You broke. It's not part of the job description, but it happens. It also happens to be history. We need to round up whatever troops we can find and send them back to the village. And we have to do it sometime before I have a birthday." He stopped, feeling himself starting to run on.

:Nice,: said Rath. *:Why don't you kick her puppy while you're at it?:*

He snarled a curse by way of reply. The Companion turned downstream. The map showed this draw feeding into the creek that marked the border, but that was wrong too.

:Don't take it out on me.: Rath replied. *:It's not my*

fault you have the emotional range of a sling bullet.: The Companion's mental voice carried a tired good humor, but there was an edge. The last time he'd heard that edge, she'd dumped him in a well.

:Of course, the caterwauling when you were drunk may have helped.:

"I was singing."

:Oh, is that what that was? It sounded like a cat hung by its tail. The maid's father wasn't impressed either. He chased you for nearly a mile. And having him present the foundling's bill to Haven for the babe was what got you busted back to Circuit. That was what . . . second promotion, second bust. You know what they say about you in Haven? That's our Gonwyn . . . stand up guy in a fight or for a girl, stands up for every fight and every girl.:

Gonwyn felt stung. "Anything else?"

:You've got your own issues, Chosen. So lighten up on the kid.:

He looked back to where Danilla followed. She had mounted. Her Companion moved slowly on the injured leg. The young mare wasn't likely to pull up lame, but she wasn't going to run any races either. He furrowed his brow. Same leg, same injury as Adreal's Claris. He lodged that one away.

"Look," he tried again. "We're in a fix, and I need you in the here and now." He softened his voice, adding firm but fair compassion. Anything she interpreted as pity would only make the situation worse. "What is done is done. We can't change what happened. But we can learn from it and move on, try to do better. We won today, but it may not be over. We've got units all over these hills . . . along with many Tedrels. Our job is to find as many of the good guys . . . and as few of the bad guys as possible . . . so that we can reknit the army in case we have to fight tomorrow. Understand?"

She nodded. "Yes." A little firmer.

"Now, time to ride."

They pressed farther into the hills, calling several Valdemaran units, a half-company here, a few scattered squads, a platoon of mismatched parts, and a string of individual men lost from their units. They skipped around Tedrels, some of whom remained bent on violence, but most were as lost and confused as the Valdemarans. Gonwyn got the further sense that while the great center of the battle may have retained some organization, out here in the boonie-flanks command had all but collapsed on both sides.

He noted as they rode that the girl had firmed up. She'd stopped looking at the dirt in front of her. Once it became plain that there were others there who'd broken in that first confusion, she felt less alone. They weren't Heralds, of course, but they were all human. By the time they stopped for the evening, she was watching for traps and ambushes, and had some of her confidence back.

It wasn't in him to go tale-telling, so the girl would not have to face the Heralds' version of censure . . . where everyone understood, of course we understand. When what they meant was, we understand you failed, and then the duties got easier after that. You were still a Herald, but not quite in the same league as those hadn't let down the side. He'd sipped from that bitter cup himself and saw no reason to pass it to another.

It was better in the Guards, where the senior Sergeant took you behind the woodshed and just beat the dung out of you when you screwed up. The thrashing fixed all and let you back in the platoon's good graces.

He pulled up as the sun was eaten by the hills to the west. Full dark would be here soon, with some hours before moonrise. Rath found a good campsite, well back in a valley, with close overhead trees, a steep rill that would provide a way out in an emergency, and good water. Gonwyn's camp-picking ability remained a running joke between them, at least since the flashflood and the beehive.

He turned in the saddle back to where she followed.

"It's getting too dark to continue," he said, "with all of these Tedrels in the hills. We'll rest here until the moon comes up. Until then, it'll be too dark to be blundering about. We should have a couple of candlemarks to eat and sleep, then we'll press on."

He dismounted with a grunt and loosened Rath's bellyband.

He could see her in the failing sunlight, copying him, her brow puzzled.

"Why do you do that?" she asked.

"Do what? Ever tried to put a saddle on in the dark, when arrows are flying?"

"No. I got that. I don't understand why you usually talk to your Companion, to your Rath. Why don't you just Mindspeak, as I do with my Enara?"

He looked at her as he leaned into Rath, crossing his elbows on the saddle-bow. "I'm almost totally head-blind. I can hear Rath, and she can read me, but I can't send worth a damn. If I buckle down and really focus, I can just about get a whisper out. It's just easier to do it this way."

Her expression appeared no more than half-believing. "What's your Talent?"

:Drinking?: Interjected Rath. *:Wenching?:*

Gonwyn ignored the Companion. "I don't really have one. I was already a Guards officer, nearly twenty-one when I was Chosen. The masters said I was too old to learn Mindspeech, which is why almost everyone who is Chosen is a child." Alberich hadn't been the first adult chosen, though clearly the oldest. He wasn't comfortable with this topic or its memories and wanted to change the subject. "What's your Talent, then?"

"Oh, me?" she replied. She looked around and found

a stick as long as her forearm, and as thick as her finger. She snapped it, green wood splintering along the ends of the break. She held the stick between her hands and stared at it in intense concentration. Gonwyn was just convinced she was having him on when a thin wisp of smoke emerged, and the splintered ends burst into flame.

Gonwyn thought she looked a little relieved.

"You're a Firestarter," he said.

"I'm not very good. I can just about manage this stick, and it doesn't always work."

"Well, I'd bet it beats my flint, steel, and profanity when I can't get my tinder to light."

She smiled then, showing dimples.

:Uh oh.:

The girl had turned back to her saddlebags and had pulled out a bedroll when she abruptly laughed. She looked back over her shoulder at him. "Enara tells me I am in the presence of a notorious womanizer and flirt. She is worried you're going to seduce me."

Gonwyn turned his head and gave Rath a long stare. Rath contrived to look innocent, a dead giveaway.

"Are you?"

"Am I what?"

"Seducing me."

Gonwyn gave her a disgusted look.

"All right, all right" she said taking her bedroll, and heading toward their campsite. "How about now? Are you seducing me now?" She smiled again. "If you were, I wouldn't want to miss it."

Gonwyn managed to convey his response in a single snort that encompassed Rath, Enara, and Danilla.

"I mean, at your age, you probably would want to give it a good running start."

Gonwyn took his blanket out of his rather thin field pack and followed. "Did you have to?" he asked Rath as he passed.

:You do have a certain reputation.:

He gathered such small wood as he could find as he crossed to where the stream burbled down underneath a widespread oak. She had already dug a narrow, deep hole in the dirt and had started the side vent to let in air. The fire would burn hot and small within its deep pit, cook well, and throw out little light. Her campcraft seemed good enough, even if it looked more like a final exam than a field rig.

She still smiled in good humor but kept her attention on her work. He moved to one side and gutted the rabbits, using the skins to lay the carcasses on while he jointed them. He dug a second pit for the offal and trash, deep enough for scavengers to be put off the scent, at least until what they left began to rot.

Their camp preparations went quickly, both moving with an efficiency driven by the quickly fading light. He took a small leather bucket from his bags and soaked it in the creek water to thoroughly wet it, then set it on a small tripod to boil. He began cutting small pieces of meat from the rabbit and dropping them in the water.

She made a face at his filthy hands, then frowned as a drop of blood fell from between his fingers and onto the rabbit pelt.

"Damn," he said, seeing the blood. He reached up under his surcoat and adjusted the rag he had stuffed under the hauberk to try to contain the bleeding.

"You're hurt," she said. Not a question.

"Took an ax in the fight this morning. It split the mail."

She crossed to where he knelt to work and knelt in front of him. She pulled back the surcoat and pulled the dirty rag out of the cut in the chain where Gonwyn had pressed it back in. Blood streaked the chainmail links and stained the linen undertunic.

Her expression told him what she thought of his efforts. “No, no no” she said. “This just won’t do. That wound may need to be stitched.”

Gonwyn felt his stomach drop. “Stitched? Don’t I need a Healer for that?”

She glanced around. “Do you see any Healers? My dad raised cattle, and I’ve stitched lots of bulls after they’d gored each other.”

Gonwyn did not find this reassuring. Nonetheless, he slid out of the dirty remains of his White surcoat, then winced as he moved his arm back to unlace the hauberk. She moved to help him.

“Oh, that’s interesting. The footloops here allow the laces to be drawn with one hand and tied off. One person can do it one handed, and while the metal doesn’t overlap, it does let you loosen it to let in some air if you have to.”

She took the weight of the hauberk as he slid out of it, then felt the heavy weight drop onto his blanket. The armor was already dirty and would need a good scouring in the sand barrel, but more grime wouldn’t do it any favors.

Gonwyn was surprised and more than a little concerned at the amount of blood that soaked his undertunic. The wound had not seemed that bad.

She looked at the blood on his side, then at his face, which he kept carefully expressionless.

“I need to see it.”

He started to unlace the tunic, then gave it up as his arm wouldn’t reach.

“I’ll need your help.”

She smiled at him. “Don’t get any ideas.”

They both laughed at the joke, however thin.

She helped him out the tunic when he couldn’t raise his arm above his shoulder. Now that they’d stopped moving, the shoulder was stiffening quickly, and the movements threatened to cause the pain he’d banked away to break through.

"Gods, Gonwyn," she said, as the undertunic came away.

His entire right shoulder was a single massive black bruise, where the chain had taken the force and spread it across the links. Broken links had scored the skin when they had been driven through the undertunic. The ax wound itself was about two inches long and looked deep enough to have cut into muscle. A large, black, crusted scab covered the entire wound and oozed blood. He moved his left hand to press on the skin, and she smacked it away. He did not tell her that while he'd been hurt before, he'd badly underestimated this one.

"Bastard knew what he was about. Got me longwise instead of chopping down, just where the mail splices together. He cut right through."

"Those hands are filthy. Keep them away from the wound."

She moved to the stream and, with that innate facility that women have, produced a cake of soap. She washed her hands thoroughly and returned to him with her healing kit.

She carefully cleaned the wound, while Gonwyn pretended this was all routine. He did swear when she doused it with the astringent wine, but just the once. The sun was nearly down before she finished probing the wound, extracting a small sliver of metal that had entered, stitched it . . . bigger stitches than the Healers used, as cattle call for different threads . . . and dressed it in linen. She set his undertunic to soak in the stream for a time and hung it to dry, as he had no other. For his part, he tested the arm and made several practice swings with his sword. It hurt like blazes, but he thought he could still fight if it came to it.

"Don't do that. You'll pick them free."

She came over to him as he moved the chainmail and settled the blanket around his shoulders.

"Let's see that mouth."

He leaned away and spat out a gob of bloody phlegm.

"Nice," she said. "Now turn into the light so I can see."

They were nearly of a height. He angled his head this way and that and opened his mouth.

"I can't see much, but it looks like you you're going to have to get those back two extracted before they get infected and abscess."

Gonwyn nodded. That was about what he thought.

She looked at him, perplexed. "Why didn't you go to the Healers?"

He shrugged, embarrassed. "My friend was dying from a stab wound and was still doing his duty, right up to the last seconds of his life. I couldn't go the Healers for a toothache, not after that." He did not admit that he'd thought about doing exactly that. "I didn't know the shoulder was that bad."

She gave him a very long look, then swallowed whatever she was about to say. "Well, I don't want your dirty fingers in my dinner, so you sit over there." She looked down at where he had been cutting the rabbit. "How were you figuring on eating?"

"Boiling the meat into a broth. See if I could boil the meat soft enough to chew, and sip down the broth."

She nodded one time, an economical gesture. "We'll do that."

She set to finishing the task he had started, cutting the rabbit into bits to boil and then spitting hers to roast. The cook fire brought the heat directly under the pot and spit, so the food cooked quickly and evenly. There was little enough left for them, but this fire was about eating, not comfort.

The sun faded before the rabbits cooked, leaving them sitting ravenous underneath a purple-black darkness decorated with a skyful of bright-blazing stars. The evening brought a chill, enough that he sought his one not-as-dirty shirt from his field pack. He managed some cupfuls of soup, along with a few bits of rabbit. He shared the jouney bread he'd taken from the Tedrels, his well-soaked with broth to soften.

By unspoken agreement, the mission had ended.

Tomorrow they would abandon the search and return to the assembly area.

Gonwyn felt a voice in his head, from a Mindspeaker powerful enough to punch through his head-blindness. Danilla and Enara's heads came up. *:Any units still fighting are to cease operations and return to start lines. All regiments' and militia are to do a muster count and report by the numbers. All Heralds not assigned to military Mindspeaking duties are to report to command tent in fighting kit for briefing.:*

"Who the hell was that?" asked Gonwyn.

"I think that's Myste," Danilla replied.

"What's a Myste?" asked Gonwyn, still impressed by the strength. His head-blindness had been described as a wall fifty feet high and a hundred wide.

"Herald Chronicler." She replied.

"Herald Chronicler?" Gonwyn realized he was starting to sound rather dumb.

"Don't you ever get to Haven?" she asked him in turn.

"No," he replied, relieved to be on the granting end of the conversation, "it gives me hives. I try to avoid any kind of headquarters."

"Myste was in my year at the Collegium and an utter despair. No real friends. No one would partner with her for Trials, and we dreaded having to train with her. Couldn't see, needs um . . . spectacles. Can't fight to save her life. Nearly cut off her Companion's ear the first time she tried it mounted. Can't run Circuit."

"She can Mindspeak, though," replied Gonwyn.

"So, it would seem," answered Danilla, just a little primly. He was ready to ask her what that meant, when Myste's voice broke through again. *:Pending instruction from the Queen, all actions against the Tedrels, except in strictest self-defense, are to cease. By Order of the Lord Marshal.:*

"What? Why?" asked Danilla.

Gonwyn turned toward her. "I'm guessing it's because the commissary is running out. We don't have the time or rations to scour these hills, and the Queen has to think about the harvest. We took a lot of farmers out of fields to fill out this army, and she needs them there, or we don't eat next year. I'd wager she'll leave just enough down here to keep the Tedrels in check, and only in numbers that she can easily feed."

Rath broke in. *:Something is up . . . I'm hearing that there's going to be a raid into Karse to get some prisoners, so everyone is tied up with that.:* She paused. *:Daners made contact. Our report has been "noted." We're to pull back, and bring out Lady Danilla, and stop hunting Tedrels. I've explained what Adreal sent us on, but he died before his message could get passed through, so they're going off of your reputation.:*

"Lady Danilla?" he asked the Herald. "You said your father herded cattle."

Even in the dark, he could feel her embarrassment.

"It was a lot of cattle," she replied.

He exhaled loudly. "All right, we'll stay on plan. Once the moon comes up and gives us some light, we'll backtrack to where that big valley runs north and south. We should pick up the roadstead there and be back in the camp before moonset. The creeks are more direct, but they'll all look the same at night, and the map is worthless."

He slipped his damp hauberk back on, then the chainmail. The pain flared when it settled over the wound, as did the spots where the second-hand mail had galled his shoulders. He made no effort to put the surcoat back on. It was too torn and dirty for even his low standards. He and Danilla then packed the camp in the dark, loading the saddlebags and field packs. Both pits were carefully covered. They could not conceal that they had been there, but they didn't have to make it easy.

Once they were done and ready to ride, there was nothing for it but to wait for moonrise. The Companions stood watch, trading guard while he and Danilla dozed. Sleeping in armor proved nearly impossible, as it just wasn't possible to get comfortable. Gonwyn had done it enough to have a leg up, but his multiple hurts kept him from doing more than dozing fitfully. The time passed in short naps, measured by stiffness and metal digging into tender places.

The moon had just risen when Gonwyn snapped awake.

:How many, Rath?: He sent, struggling to make the sending.

:Some thirty, Chosen. They are close and coming this way.:

"Danilla?" he whispered.

"I've heard from Enara," she replied. "Can we get out?"

:They're astride our path out,: Rath answered to him. *:There is another body moving east of us, where I think the draw comes up.:*

"Damn," said Gonwyn. "Good water, good campsite, escape route . . . we might be camping on one of their rally points."

"What do we do?" Danilla asked.

He ran the options, all bad. "We hide. Wait them out. Rath, show us the draw."

They quickly mounted and made for the narrow watercourse. It looked intermittent and fell in a sharp vee, barely wide enough for the two Companions. The vee fell out of the moonlight, and while there was no concealment, they might just be safe in the shadow. They had just settled in and froze as the first group of Tedrels poured in.

Gonwyn quickly assessed them. They looked whipped. Many bore light wounds, but they were still armed. In the moonlight he saw Tedrels with crossbows, spears, and some better equipped with swords, shields, and some armor. A second group followed in better order, their leader haranguing them in the pidgin tongue that passed for the Tedrel language.

Few carried more than their war gear. They took out what food they had, some better provisioned than others. The stronger took from the weaker where they could, and the main body split into fragments as they moved to camp in mutual distrust.

One largish group made directly for the draw where Gonwyn and the others hid. He heard the soft creak, as Danilla drew her light bow from its case and strung it. There was a soft tap as she nocked an arrow.

He drew his sword from its saddle scabbard. The weapon slid free in his hand, a shorter blade than most, thicker and double edged. The sword was an infantry weapon, honed for killing, with none of the daintiness of the cavalry saber. He held it back against his leg, where it was least likely to reflect some stray bit of moonlight.

"If it comes to it," he whispered, "stay in the draw. I will draw them away, and we will link up later."

"I will NOT," she whispered back. "I am a Herald, and I will fight."

There was no point to an argument, and the Tedrels were too close.

The group stopped to camp, barely thirty feet from the draw. There was some argument, then one began to desultorily make a pile for a fire. The others spread out to gnaw on what food they had. One made directly for the draw. Gonwyn heard the soft, collective inhalation from the group in the draw as the Tedrel came to the mouth of the vee, adjusted his crude cloth armor, and began to relieve himself.

Gonwyn held himself ready, a bare dozen feet from the Tedrel. He could visualize the Tedrel standing there, staring into the darkness, seeing white shapes begin to resolve against the deeper black until . . .

The man's mouth opened in a soundless O.

:NOW!:

Rath launched herself, powerful withers throwing them a body's length forward. Gonwyn whipped the sword across the man's face, slashing brutally as he passed. The Tedrel screamed as Rath exploded into the moonlight.

Rath broke left, staying in the well-spread trees, in order to make a harder crossbow shot. The Companion took the distance to the sprawled Tedrels in a couple of strides, riding a second down and whirling between two thick oaks. Gonwyn pressed low against her flank, more for protection from low branches than from the Tedrel. He held the blade flat back against his boot, his left hand wrapped around the saddle-bow.

Rath whipped around the larger oak, changing direction to throw off the crossbowman who stumbled toward them. Gonwyn needed no force, only aim to slash the blade outward, taking the crossbowman in the throat. Rath took another, shattering his spine with a single kick as the man tried to flee back. Four dead in as many seconds. As Rath dodged back between the pair of trees, Gonwyn killed another with a stab backed by half a ton of charging equine. Five, quickly now.

Time slowed for Gonwyn. He felt the simple fierce joy, the power that coursed through him as his enemies seemed to slow and his senses sped. He felt the man to his right grasp the claw from his belt to load his crossbow. Gonwyn killed him with a leaning slash that took his throat. Another Tedrel bent to grab his spear, and Rath, in the same parlous state, smashed his chest with a kick that stove in his ribs. Other Tedrels, armed with spears and crossbows, emerged from behind trees as the Companion stormed among them. Gonwyn slipped from Rath's back, and in perfect dance passed under her legs to stab a spearman as she lashed out with her rear hooves to dash out another's brains.

He rushed two on foot. The rightmost raised a battered sword. Gonwyn lopped his sword hand at the wrist, whirled to stab the left-side Tedrel, who was still raising his short spear, and disabled the first with single backhanded slash to the face. He sprang back up and remounted, in perfect choreography as Rath turned again to strike out with forehooves.

A single odd image stood out afterward to Gonwyn . . . the dropped-pot sound as the Companion's iron-hard hooves shattered a skull and destroyed a life.

The moment frozen flashed into action again. Another crossbowman emerged ahead, fumbling to bring the weapon to bear. Gonwyn hurled his sword. It struck hilt first, smashing the man's nose and knocking him backward. Gonwyn drew his saddle-ax, a wicked single blade with a reverse spike.

He chopped down on another Tedrel, killing the last standing in this group with the spike, driven deep into his shoulder along the neck. Rath charged forward to where the man lay screaming as he clutched his face. Rath trampled him. Gonwyn leaned down, both palms brushing the dirt as he recovered his sword and rolled back into his saddle.

He turned the blowing mare toward the next group, dropping the bloody ax back into its sheath. A second quick grab, this time at a small shield leaning against a tree. He pulled it free and armed himself with it as Rath danced back, using the trees as cover against crossbows. Rath gathered herself to charge again as Gonwyn finished his arming.

He glanced quickly to the right and saw Danilla just emerging from the draw, with bow in hand. A string of dead or dying Tedrals lay behind him. One he had missed scrambled from between two trees and fled across the open area of the valley floor.

Danilla whipped her bow up, tracked him, and coolly released. The arrow glowed red and burst into flame as it crossed halfway to the Tedrel. It caught the man in the back as he fled. He fell to his knees, the fire spreading across him as he burned and screamed. Danilla's second arrow took him as he writhed on the ground, ending his life.

There was a moment's perfect silence, then Danilla's shout of exultation.

And Rath charged. Together, they slew, as Danilla rode about the fringes burning down those who escaped iron hoof and wicked blade.

It was done when the last Tedrel lay dead. Gonwyn, spattered with blood and exhausted, slumped as he waited for Danilla to join him. Rath stood, her legs splayed out, blowing heavily. Somewhere in the fight the stitches had broken open, but that was of little concern.

Dannila and Enara rode slowly to them. She looked around the carnage. Over thirty Tedrals had entered the campsite. None survived.

"I think you do have a Talent, Gonwyn," she said in voice that shook only a little, "and may the gods have mercy on you."

Heart's Peril

Kate Paulk

Ree stretched and sighed, feeling comfortable and lazy on the roof of the barn belonging to the farm where he'd lived for the last ten years. His family farm, in a way. Certainly the place where his family lived.

With the summer sun warm against his back, the warm roof shingles beneath him and the air full of the scent of growing things and farm animals, it was difficult to concentrate on something as painstaking as checking the barn roof for rotting shingles, much less the careful effort needed for replacing them.

His rattail twitched in his breeches, and his claws wanted to relax all the way out. But he must work. It had to be done before winter came, and Ree was the best person to do it—a hobgoblin who was part rat and part cat as well as part human, he had better balance than humans, and keener eyesight. That the wild part of him longed to take a nap right here or to head out, exploring the cool shade of the forest, was something he'd grown used to over the years.

The forest was dangerous, a place where the animal hobgoblins had taken over from more normal predators. It was also as familiar to Ree as the farm he called home. In the years since he'd come here, he'd watched the forest slowly return to a kind of balance after the hellish

Change-winter and the magic circles: the same magic circles that had changed him from a human street rat to the hobgoblin he was.

His mind wandered into times long past, from the desperate days when he'd saved Jem's life on the streets of Jacona and Jem, in turn, had saved Ree's humanity and perhaps his life. If Ree had gone on the way he'd been, he'd soon have stopped knowing how to talk, and from there to forgetting he was human at all was but a step. When all you can do is run and hide, you start forgetting you're not a small, hunted animal. And then . . . And then you start attacking humans, as animals do.

His meeting with Jem had led them to leave Jacona and head out to the countryside in which they imagined they'd be safer. Which just went to show how young they'd been.

As it turned out, it had been safer, but never in the way he expected. Jem had almost died of the coughing illness that winter, as they stayed out of towns where people would kill them. It was Jem's illness that had forced Ree to come to the farm, to look for help. By blind luck, or perhaps blind destiny, they'd blundered into a farm that belonged to Jem's grandfather. And here they'd been since. Ree and Jem and Jem's grandfather, and later Amelie and Meren, Jem's and Ree's adopted children.

No one asked embarrassing questions about Jem's and Ree's relationship. Or rather, the only one who asked was Garrad, Jem's grandfather, and only to tease them. And got a great deal of laughter out of their embarrassment. And if the children called Jem Da and Ree Papa, no one thought there was anything wrong with that either.

Anywhere else, their odd little family might be remarked, but the people of Three Rivers Valley had gotten to know the people at the farm for who they were–for their bravery and kindness and courage. Ree and Jem had helped the village too many times for anyone to remark two young men, much less a man and a hobgoblin, shouldn't be raising children together, even if one of those children was also a hobgoblin. The village saw that they clearly could and were raising happy, sweet children out of waifs no one else wanted.

Ree sighed again. Sometimes he thought the only reason they'd taken the children on was that they had no idea how hard it could be. They were good children, and Ree would miss them when they left for houses of their own, but it was like living with your heart in someone else's body. He worried every time Amelie went to the village and was late returning. And his heart about stopped when Meren took a fall from a tree.

With an effort, he focused on the work in front of him. *That one looks like it's starting to go*. Ree bent closer to the shingle, close enough to sniff the wood. The scent of decay was faint, but there. It might not be obvious now, but in a month that shingle would be starting to crumble, and by the time winter set in, it would no longer be weatherproof.

He sat beside the shingle and started prying the nails loose, taking care not to bend them too much. Good nails were expensive; it was better to reuse them if you could. Getting them straightened by the smith down in Three Rivers village cost less than new nails, but it was still a cost Ree preferred not to pay.

He chuckled to himself. Like Jem, he'd learned farmer thrift from old Garrad, the owner of this farm and Jem's grandfather. If he was going to be honest with himself, Ree had learned a lot more than thrift from the old man: Garrad had taught him the value of work, and to see himself as a man, not a street child and not a Change Circle freak.

Everywhere he looked, Ree could see the result of his

work and Jem's. The ever-growing herd of cattle, goats, and donkeys, the fields they hired men to plough and harvest, the walls of the home fields, and even the prolific damncats. Oh, they were ordinary cats, but somehow the name had stuck for cats raised on this farm.

Mostly, Ree suspected, because the Three Rivers folk were convinced he could talk to them and trained them. The things people would believe. Grown men and women, talking of training cats! It was the other way around: He observed them, recognized their calls and body language, and they knew he'd respond to something urgent.

Well, except for Damncat, the gray-and-white troublemaker with a fondness for Ree's shoulder. That cat was smarter than most and knew it, too.

"Can I help, Papa?"

Ree about jumped out of his fur. Meren might be all of four years old and part cat, but he could creep up on a body like nothing else on earth. Not that he meant to, it was just . . . Meren walked softly, especially when he discarded his shoes—which was most of the time—and he seemed to instinctively know to stay downwind.

The boy giggled, his greeny-hazel eyes lit with mischief. He was an odd sight, with his white-blond curls and sparse tabby fur. Without the fur and the pointed ears, Meren could have been taken for human, but as it was he was as much a hobgoblin as Ree, although Meren had been born that way. The child of two hobgoblins who'd been killed by the villagers, he'd been taken in by Ree and Jem as a baby and raised to be more human than animal—unlike his parents, who'd gone to the animal.

"Bored, are you?" Ree asked. Like Ree, Meren didn't like being confined to the house. At least since the dire wolf had got through the fences two years back, he'd stopped trying to explore the forest on his own. Or—

and Ree wasn't entirely sure this wasn't the case—stopped getting caught at it.

Meren nodded. "Da and Melie are cooking, an' Granddad said to get out from underfoot." His thumb hovered near his mouth, ready to go in.

Ree eased a nail out and set it beside the others. If Meren was upset, he sucked his thumb. It happened less as the little boy got older, but if something really bothered him . . .

"Granddad got mad, didn't he?" Ree collected the nails and handed them to his son—maybe not the son of his body, but Meren was his son, just as Amelie, an all-human orphan he and Jem had taken in, was his daughter. "Hold these for me, please? They're valuable, and I don't want to lose them."

That diverted the threatened thumb and gave Meren something to feel important about while Ree eased the shingle free.

"Granddad gets mad lots." Meren didn't sound entirely sure of himself.

Ree nodded. With his claws digging into the shingle, it was a lot easier to pull it loose without disturbing any of the others.

"Can you keep a secret, a proper secret?"

He had his suspicions about what Garrad had said to upset the little boy, but more to the point, he knew why. This last winter had been hard on the old man; he didn't walk much now, and when he did, he truly needed the walking stick Jem had made him years ago.

Meren sat straighter, trying to look taller and older than he was. "Yes, Papa."

"It hurts Granddad to move," Ree said quietly.

The shingle came free; he set it aside and reached into the pack on his back for a fresh one, started to ease it into place. "When Granddad is hurting, he gets grouchy."

Meren tilted his head to one side, chewing his bottom lip. "Then he wasn't really mad at me?"

"Nope. Granddad yells at everyone." As Ree well knew, having been the recipient of Garrad's temper more than a few times. "You know that."

The thumb—complete with nails clutched in that hand—threatened to enter Meren's mouth again. "But . . . Granddad said I was . . ."

Ree chuckled. "He told you to go play with the damncats because you're just like them? He tells me that too, when he's grouchy. He tells Jem just about the same, too." It was an exaggeration, but not much of one.

"Not Melie, though."

"No, but Melie is never wild, is she?"

"No," Meren said, then paused and wrinkled his forehead. "On count of being a girl."

"Probably," Ree conceded amiably, though it was more likely on account of Amelie having seen her whole family massacred when she was very young. "Could you pass me a nail, please?"

Meren stared for a moment, then carefully took a nail and handed it to Ree. "Oh."

Ree wasn't sure when it had become a weekly event to have Lenar and his family to dinner at the farm, but sometime between the time they'd adopted Meren and the time he'd saved Amelie from a dire wolf, it had started. And then by the time Meren was on his feet again after the dire wolf attack, it was simply accepted as something that happened like clockwork.

Lenar might be the Lord here, but he was also Garrad's son and Jem's father. True, he'd lost track of Jem when Jem was just a baby, leaving poor Jem to grow up as a street urchin. But he'd not done it with intent, and he loved Jem in his own gruff way. Besides, the two were so alike in temper and look that they might rub wrong but couldn't avoid loving each other. The three of them treasured their time together, even if it almost always–at least until this last year and Garrad's illness–had ended in all of them shouting at each other at the top of their voices.

On the first few visits Lenar's wife, Loylla, had been uncomfortable, but now she either hid it or mostly forgot that this was a plain farm and not the kind of manor she'd spent her whole life in. She was a cheerful daughter-in-law to Garrad, and though she wasn't so crass as to try to mother Jem, who was little younger than her, she behaved to Jem and Ree as an older sister might. Their little boy, a sturdy two-year-old, played happily with Meren whenever the family visited, and Lenar sometimes grumbled that the boy asked every day if he could go play "wif Mewen."

Ree thought that Lenar didn't really understand why little Garrad couldn't come over every day, either, because it wasn't Lenar who had to haul the little imps out of—among other things—the chicken coop, the water trough, the barn feeding trough, and every mud puddle they could find. That enviable task fell to Ree. There wasn't a fence, tree, or building on the farm that Meren couldn't climb, and if he could help or carry little Garrad with him, he would.

Which was why this warm summer night, while Amelie and Jem laid out the table and Garrad talked with Lenar and Loylla, Ree watched Meren play-wrestle with little Garrad, and made sure he was between the two little boys and the fence. At least today the worst they'd suffer was grass stains on their oldest clothes—worn, patched clothing that was kept just so the two of them could get themselves dirty without ruining good clothing.

A blur of movement at the edge of his vision caught

his eye, and he reached out, catching Damncat before the gray-and-white menace could join the fun. "Oh, no you don't." He held the cat close and made eye contact. "You want to play with them, I get to trim your claws."

The cat might not understand the words, but he understood tone and scrambled for Ree's shoulder instead. One of the other damncats—another gray and white, with the lanky build of an animal partway between kitten and adult—took great care to groom itself. As if, Ree thought with a wry smile, it hadn't been considering joining in the play fight a little before. One of Damncat's siring, of course—Damncat sired most of the kittens at the farm these days. He sired smart, troublesome kittens, the best hunters and mousers in the region.

Ree suspected some of them had thumbs, although he'd never quite figured out which ones. There were just too many damncats.

The warm weight of Damncat leaned against his head, and the cat started to purr. Ree reached up to scratch the animal without looking away from the rolling, squealing little boys. *I make a terrible wild beast, standing here petting a cat while minding two little boys.* Not that anyone from outside the valley would realize that was what he was doing. *They'd think I was watching my dinner and playing with my snack.*

"Ree!" Jem called from the back door. "Dinner's about ready."

"I'll get the boys in," he shouted back.

He and Jem shared all the farm chores between them these days, what with Amelie spending each morning at the manor, learning how to be a lady, and Meren too young to help much. But when it came to herding small boys, Ree had the advantage over Jem, lacking the family's quick temper.

Moving carefully so he didn't throw Damncat's balance off, Ree bent and grabbed the straps of a small pair of overalls, and hauled the wearer out. Little Garrad, halfway through a pretend "wild animal" growl.

Meren started to protest but stopped when he saw where his playmate was, safely held in Meren's Papa's arms. "Time to wash up and get into your good clothes, boys. Come along now." Shepherding two little boys was a lot more difficult than dealing with the goats or the cows, Ree had learned. It got worse the older the boys got; he hoped they'd start getting more sense before he couldn't keep up with them. Having to climb to the farm roof once or twice a day was one thing. Having to do that and save the goats from boys who wanted to ride them and race them was something else again.

Still, he got them washed and into their good clothes—pants and shirts, although they both went barefoot. It wasn't worth trying to keep Meren in his shoes in summer, and trying to get little Garrad to do something Meren wouldn't . . . Well, that one had the full measure of his father's stubborn streak.

He even managed to get the two sets of blond curls tamed and turn the pair of them over to Jem with time to get himself changed.

Everyone else was at the table when Ree entered. They'd set it up with the best tablecloth and the best plates and all, and Melie had arranged some flowers from the garden in a bright blue vase she'd bought at the Three Rivers fair.

It might not be a proper feast, but it looked right homey to Ree. He smiled and took his seat, nodding to Lenar and Loylla. "Did anything come of that last message you sent back east? About being confirmed as a Lord?"

Lenar chuckled. "Either I'm not that important, or some clerk is having fits." He shrugged. "It doesn't matter that much, so long as the taxes go in. I've got the records and the receipts from Karelshill, so any investigation is going to look someplace else." He covered his wife's hand with his much larger one. "The Empire's pretty flexible, Ree. If it works and the taxes keep coming, no one's going to argue with my position."

Ree nodded and didn't argue. Lenar had been a soldier before coming back to his old home with enough gold to build himself a manor, and he knew how the nobles and all did things. It would be nice to know Lenar was properly the local Lord, but if he didn't think it mattered, it wasn't Ree's part to argue.

Conversation ebbed and flowed while they ate, Loylla mentioning how fast Amelie learned and how eager she was to know everything she needed to know, and Ree giving Jem a look that said he knew Amelie was learning as fast as she could so she didn't have to be at the manor house. Not that she disliked Lenar or Loylla but she loved being at the farm, looking after her flower garden, feeding the animals, and milking the goats.

Lenar lamented how fast little Garrad was growing—he'd learned to feed himself well enough that he didn't need someone to help him, and he didn't even get too much on his face, although the food on his plate was mostly cut small enough for little fingers and didn't have any gravy or sauces a child could smear himself with—and Jem agreed, complaining that they'd had to let down the legs of Meren's overalls again so they were long enough to be decent, and he didn't think they'd last until the tailor came through to take orders for the next year's clothes.

"Oh, there's been some bad hobgoblin problems in Karelshill," Lenar said after Ree had taken both boys upstairs to sleep; it might still be full light outside, but small boys needed a lot of sleep.

Jem raised an eyebrow. He was looking more and

more like his father: a bit less weathered, and without the beard, but still. "Attacks or just sightings?"

There weren't as many hobgoblins these days, but the ones that could breed did, and some of them were vicious. Ree still needed to patrol the forest, although since he'd had to start patrolling on his own, he never went out without a weapon. The snow bears and dire wolves were the worst.

Lenar sighed. "Attacks, son, bad ones." He nodded in Ree's direction and got the frown that said that he was worried about Ree. His voice boomed, too, which is how you knew that Lenar cared. He cared enough to yell at you. "You be careful out there, you hear. Don't want anyone getting the wrong idea about you being like them. What I hear is that something's organizing them, using them to attack. Maybe softening them up for something else."

Ree winced. "That would take magic, wouldn't it?" His tail twitched and whipped against his leg. Most of the time his tail was just fine down one pants leg, but when he was worried, it tried to lash and made it look as though he had a snake trapped in there.

Lenar scratched his beard. "That's what I hear. I'm not so sure . . . I mean . . . no offense, Ree, but say someone like you, only with bad intentions, got hold of some cubs. You could raise yourself a hobgoblin army that way."

Jem made a sound of protest but stopped at Garrad's soft, "He's right, Jem. Ain't nothing that says being mostly human means being good."

Ree nodded. "Yeah, I know." There had been too many nights when he'd lain awake wondering whether he was human and what part of him made him fit to be with full humans. And some nights he was sure he wasn't. Sure he wasn't good enough to deserve someone like Jem, who could have had anyone he wanted.

"It wouldn't even have to be a hobgoblin," Garrad said. "It could be someone who didn't have any reason to care about other people . . . You wouldn't even need to be a hobgoblin to do that, although it would be harder. Humans can stop being human too, you know? I think I might have, a bit, before you and Jem came," he added, quietly.

Ree's claws unsheathed, and he tapped the tablecloth with them. "How much damage was done?"

"No one dead yet," Lenar said. "There's been some stock taken and a few injuries." He didn't look happy. "The problem is, there are plenty of people who remember a 'Hobgoblin King' who came from up this way."

Damn. That ruse, a trick Ree had used to frighten soldiers away, had come back to bite more than once. It didn't matter that he hadn't been able to think of any other way to get the soldiers to leave and not come back—and they hadn't come back, so Ree supposed he'd scared them good. It had worked. But he'd still left himself with a nasty mess that didn't ever go away.

The warmth of Jem's hand on his didn't help. Sometimes he had to remember there were other people and other places outside their special, protected relationship. "I don't suppose you could tell them the Hobgoblin King isn't happy about this but these creatures aren't his or in his territory." It wasn't a question—Ree knew very well Lenar wouldn't be able to convince anyone of that.

"I've tried," Lenar said, making Ree blink with surprise. Lenar had tried?

Lenar laughed a little at Ree's expression. "Of course, I tried, son. I want to keep you from trouble if I can, and Jem too, of course. Only I'm not a diplomat. I'm just an old soldier who got into more than he planned for."

Ree nodded. Well. Life, like raising children, was trouble, wasn't it? But it had his compensations. He squeezed Jem's hand, gently, making sure his claws weren't unsheathed.

The sun was setting when Jem climbed up to the attic bedroom to fetch little Garrad. He returned soon after, grim-faced. "They're not there."

"How . . . They never came through here!"

"No," Jem said, his mouth set. "They opened the roof hatch and got out through it. You know Meren did that last week. Down the rain pipe to the shed roof."

And down the shed roof to the chicken house, where he'd tried to collect the eggs, only got the wrong ones. The poor broody hen would never recover from the shock.

Ree swallowed. He half stood before he even thought of the words. His mouth was dry. the trouble those two could get into . . . It didn't bear thinking. If he was lucky he'd just find them trying to ride one of the goats or driving the cow to distraction.

If he wasn't lucky . . . "I'll check the outhouse. Maybe one of them had to go." And at this time of year neither of them would use the chamberpot. Not that Ree blamed them. He preferred the outhouse even in the cold of winter. He wouldn't blame them for not coming through here, either, because Garrad was as likely to yell at them as not, in the mood he'd been.

He doubted he'd find either child in the outhouse, truth be told. There were much more interesting things to do and places to go than the outhouse. But they might have gone there first, and there was a good chance of catching a scent. Besides, he didn't want to see Lenar's expression or hear anything Lenar said. His face had clouded when Jem said that Meren had got out that way before. Ree didn't want to know if he was mad at them for not telling him or mad at Meren. And he didn't want anyone to be mad at Meren.

Meren was no more mischievous than any other four-year-old, but taking little Garrad with him . . . that was new. Normally when they were in bed, they stayed in bed, talking and giggling in half-intelligible baby-language, until they fell asleep.

Ree snatched the belt with his hunting knife and the slingshot on his way out the lean-to, then paused to scan the ground. There wasn't anything obvious, but he hadn't expected anything. Neither child was heavy enough to leave much of an impression on thick grass.

The outhouse was empty, with no trace of either child's scent—or at least none that Ree could determine under the overpowering outhouse smell. From there, he circled the house, to where the air hatch on the roof was propped open. They'd open that in summer, to let breezes through and keep the house from getting too hot during the day, but it was closed at night to keep insects out.

Ree had closed both the hatches when he'd put the boys to bed. His throat tightened, threatening to choke him. And realized Lenar was keeping pace with him.

"I'll tan that boy's hide so hard he won't sit down for a week," Lenar growled. "He knows he's to stay in bed once he's put there. And following that damn hobg—" He stopped, but his glare said everything his voice didn't.

Ree didn't say anything. How could he? Lenar had to be as worried as Ree. Maybe more: sometimes Ree caught Lenar looking at Jem as though he'd never really forgiven himself for losing Jem. Rather than worry at Lenar's anger, Ree traced the line of the roof with his eyes, to the lean-to and the stone wall butting against it. Oh, yes, an agile little boy could get to that wall without any difficulty. And walk along it, too, until he got to one of the trees with branches hanging over the walls, where he could climb to the ground. The question was, which one?

Ree hurried over to the wall,and jumped up. He bent to the stone to sniff. "They came this way." Neither boy had been wearing shoes—for once Ree blessed their dislike of footwear. Once, Ree wouldn't have hesitated to drop to all fours to scurry along that wall, but he wasn't agile enough for that any more, and besides, he tried to set the right example for Meren. He tried not to think about proving to Lenar that he was more human than animal. If he said anything now, he wouldn't like the answer.

Lenar walked beside the wall, cursing in language fit to raise the dead. It certainly made Ree's fur want to stand on end.

Jem joined his father, quiet but just as grim-faced.

Ree walked so he wouldn't miss seeing anything, even though he wanted to run. If he ran like he wanted to, he could take the wrong fence, because he didn't know which way the children had gone.

A cat screamed in the forest.

Ree didn't make any conscious decisions. In the time it took for the sound to fade, he was running along the wall, aware of Jem and Lenar sprinting alongside him on the ground and damncats converging from every direction.

The cats moved ahead of them in a multicolored furry tide, responding to the distress of one of their own. Where the wall ended, Ree jumped off and followed the cats into the forest. Jem and Lenar didn't take long to catch up with him.

They didn't say anything, not that they'd be heard over the caterwauling that echoed up ahead. And under it . . . growls. Not Meren's growl. And no human screams. Did that mean the boys were already . . . Ree's stomach lurched, and he wrenched his mind away from the thought.

The damn boy knew the forest was dangerous! Why had he come out here?

A cat's death scream, then Meren's growl, shrill and childish, but dangerous too. He'd growled like that when he'd saved Amelie from a dire wolf.

Ree raced around a massive oak and all but ran into two snow bears, one batting ineffectually at the snarling cats attacking it. The other . . . It was covered with cats as well, as though every damncat on the farm had come after the bears. Meren clung to the tree, his weight held by the claws of one hand and both feet. Little Garrad was wedged into the space between Meren and tree, while Meren clawed and snarled at the attacking bear. The bear that seemed to be fighting its own body as it reached for the child.

Ree caught the first bear's fur and used that to swing himself between the other bear and the children. If the bear hadn't been injured—or if the other one hadn't been trying to fight off the damncats the way this one should have been—both boys would be dead.

Lenar pushed him out of the way, practically crushing him against the tree. "Get the boys out of here." Ree didn't argue. He scrambled up the tree trunk to the first branching, far enough above the bear's reach to be safe, then leaned down, extended one hand. "Garrad! Come to Uncle Ree." It took an effort of will to keep his claws in, with the bears and the cats and the smell of blood.

"Come on." Neither child seemed to notice. A bear screamed, dying. Ree dug his toe claws and the claws of his other hand in and leaned lower, and lower, until he could get hold of Garrad's shirt. "Come on, little man, hold onto me."

He pulled, praying that the shirt wouldn't tear, that he wouldn't lose his grip. Another bear roar and hot breath against his arm. Ree didn't dare try to look.

He wasn't entirely sure how he managed it, but a flurry of small limbs and some needle-sharp little claws later, Ree sat on the branch with his back against the bole of the old oak and Meren and little Garrad trembling in his arms.

He didn't try to move or look, just held the boys close. There was a meaty sound, then something hit the ground, hard, and Ree heard scurrying and distressed meowing. The lament in the cats cries made Ree's eyes burn.

"Well." Lenar sounded grim. "Now we know something is using magic."

Meren whimpered and tried to bury himself in Ree's shirt.

It took a while to get the boys calm enough that Ree could hand them down to Lenar and Jem. By then, Lenar had dragged the dead bears far enough away that they wouldn't attract any unwanted attention, and Jem had lined up the sad little bodies of three of the damncats.

More than a few of the other cats were hurt, but they weren't letting Jem get close. Getting back to the farm just gave Ree more reasons to worry: Little Garrad was acting like any small boy who'd just had the fright of his life, but Meren didn't seem to be . . . well, there.

He wasn't crying, wasn't screaming, he just lay limply in Jem's arms and stared at something no one else could see.

It was full dark by the time they got in, and Loylla was pacing the kitchen looking pale and frightened, but she'd boiled up water and had bandages out in case they were needed, and she didn't hesitate when she saw Lenar and little Garrad, just ran to them and embraced them both without a care for the blood spattered over Lenar's shirt.

"No one's hurt." Jem hastened to reassure her. "Is Granddad all right?"

"I'm perfectly well, and you needn't treat me like an

invalid." Garrad's voice was strong enough, coming from the main room.

"It was the damndest thing, Father." Lenar shook his head. He strode into the main room and let everyone else trail after him. "All of them headed for the forest, straight for the boys, and they all attacked two bears."

The old man paled. "Two . . . They never come this close in summer."

"Something was controlling them." Jem said.

Ree didn't want to hear this discussion. And he was worried about Meren. He pulled the boy from Jem's arms and said, "I'll be outside with Meren."

No one argued. Ree spoke softly as he carried Meren outside. "We're just glad you're safe, Meren. That's all. You two scared us, running off like that."

Meren's hands clenched tight into Ree's shirt, and he shuddered. The damncats—it looked like all of them—waited outside.

Ree found himself needing to sit and was cross-legged on the grass before he realized that he hadn't decided to sit down. Cats were nuzzling Meren, making the little chirp-comfort sounds mother cats made with their kittens. Meren's sounds were sadder, remorseful.

Ree would have sworn the cats were reassuring the boy, telling him somehow that dying happens, and the cats who'd died had died well. Whatever it was, it seemed to help, because Meren shuddered again, then started to cry. With words.

"Ree?" The sound came from behind Ree, and for once Lenar sounded uncertain. "I guess I owe Meren an apology. It was little Garrad who opened the air hatch and climbed out. Meren followed him but didn't catch up until he'd gotten to the oak . . . and then the bears came." He made a sound Ree couldn't interpret. "He's too scared to say more, but . . . I'm sorry. I said harsh things I didn't mean. It's just . . . you know, I lost Jem for all of his childhood, and so many bad things happened to him. Losing little Garrad might kill me. I can't watch him all the time."

Meren's body relaxed a little but not all the way. He couldn't understand all the words, Ree was sure, but he'd understand Lenar's tone, and he almost for sure would understand the hand on his head and Lenar's voice saying softly, "Thank you for saving my boy."

Ree waited till Lenar left. He was thinking of the cats, running like a furry tide, attacking deadly foes to save the boys. He didn't know much, but he knew that Meren didn't have the woodcraft to follow anyone. Yeah, he could follow a scent, but he didn't have enough experience to do it like that, in the woods. If he'd been that far behind little Garrad . . .

"The cats told you Garrad was going to the forest, didn't they?" he asked.

"No," Meren whispered, but it was a wavering no, lacking conviction. "They can't talk to me. I'm not an animal."

Ree held him tighter. "You're not an animal," he said "Some humans can talk to . . . creatures." Ree had read something about it, once. "The cats told you?"

There was a long shuddering sigh and then, "Yes. I was asleep. Damncat told me. In my mind." A long silence. "I didn't want to . . . but . . ."

"You're scared we won't want you because of it?" Ree knew that feeling too well—and if Meren could understand the damncats that way without words, then . . . he could understand Ree, and that . . . that wasn't something Ree wanted to really think about. If he knew how scared Ree was, all the time, it would be hard for Ree to appear calmly confident.

Another nod, a bit shakier this time. Ree pulled Meren closer, hugged him tightly. "It's just something you do. Not something you are. Being human is here—" He touched Meren's chest over the heart and tried to believe that, as hard as he could, to believe that Meren having this strange Gift was just . . . well, it was like Mages had their Gift, that was all. Maybe it was an odd kind of magic, but it didn't make Meren less human for having it.

"Having Gifts is all on how you use it. This one saved you and Garrad tonight. That makes it good."

Finally, Meren relaxed. "Fank you, Papa." The words were mumbled around a fiercely sucked thumb.

Damncat strutted over. He gave Meren a headbutt, then rubbed against Ree's leg.

"Yes, you and yours did well, too." Ree scratched the cat behind the ears, and smiled. Everything would be all right. These vessels he'd put his heart into would break it again and again and again, but somehow, it would emerge stronger from each break.

Human hearts did.

Heart's Place

Sarah A. Hoyt

Ree watched, and tried to keep his stomach from knotting up, while Lenar's Mage examined Meren.

The Mage was a decent enough fellow, and he wasn't going to do anything like denounce the boy, not here. It was just . . . after the magic circles, Ree had never really trusted magic.

Magic had made him a hobgoblin, after all, complete with a coat of sleek brown fur and claws that retracted like a cat's. And a ratlike tail, which was wrapped around one leg inside his pants.

That same magic had given Meren a coat of sparse tabby fur in addition to his white-blond curls, and who knew what else. And that, Ree reminded himself forcefully, was why the Mage was here.

You couldn't pretend that something like being able to broadcast what you were feeling to all the damncats was just a coincidence, and with the controlled hobgoblins attacking more often . . .

It was better to have Lenar's Mage make sure that his Lord's adopted grandson couldn't possibly be controlling the hobgoblins, and never mind that those same controlled hobgoblins had attacked the child last summer.

Scared people didn't think about things like that.

They got themselves worked up and went after anything that was different. That was one of the reasons Ree didn't go down to Three Rivers village much—while people respected him, and knew he'd help them whenever they needed, and get hurt for them, too, it was better not to remind them just how different he was.

The Mage leaned back with a sigh, and his eyes focused again.

Meren drooped; whatever the Mage had been doing had tired him out.

"I'll just get Meren to bed, then I'll be with you," Ree said. With Jem walking Amelie to the manor to spend the night there—ostensibly to keep little Garrad company, but more because Lenar's wife was near to term and not really able to keep up with her son—and old Garrad barely able to move, Ree was the only able-bodied person on the farm right now.

The Mage nodded. "Thank you."

A little later, with Meren not even protesting about being put to bed for a daytime nap, and asleep before Ree had pulled the covers over, Ree returned to the kitchen and filled a bowl with the stew that was always warming on the stove.

"Here." He handed the bowl to the Mage. "I heard tell you get hungry after magic."

"Thank you again." The Mage—Ree could never remember his name—was one of those people who looked so ordinary you forgot them as soon as you met them.

Not that Ree would have been surprised to find that the Mage "helped" that impression a bit with magic; it had to be a powerful advantage to a Mage to be overlooked and even forgotten.

"Well," the Mage said after he'd eaten some. "Your son isn't a Mage, nor will he be. He does have an unusual Gift, something I've seen only once before."

If the man had seen it before, that was better than

completely weird. Ree told his stomach to untie itself, and he made himself ask, "When was that?"

The Mage smiled faintly. "Oh, that was long ago, in the army. I was posted down south a way, and the tribes there had these people they called 'beastmasters' who they claimed could speak with any animal without words." He shrugged. "The way our horses behaved around them, I got to thinking it wasn't just one of those myths that grow up when someone knows animals really well."

Ree nodded. He knew about those, since he was at the center of a fair few of them, him and the damncats—who maybe weren't quite as ordinary as he'd thought.

"After I'd got friendly with one of their beastmasters, we each looked at the other with our Gifts—it's a sort of compliment, to actually open yourself to someone else's probing that way—and . . . well. What he had was just like what your son has."

"So it's a human Gift, just very rare?" Now Ree had to throttle hope. Something human, something a Mage had seen before . . . that meant that Meren was human enough to maybe be accepted that way, even if he didn't look it.

The Mage finished eating before he nodded. "Exactly. It's probably not fully developed yet; these things usually don't start showing up until puberty, although they can manifest early under enough stress."

Meren had seen enough stress in his short life for something like that to happen, what with being born to parents who couldn't keep themselves fed much less their baby—and had gotten desperate and raided the village fields, getting themselves killed in the process—not to mention two near-death encounters with hobgoblins.

"Is there any way to teach him how to . . . well, not get caught in it?" Teaching a little boy to use something he couldn't feel wasn't exactly Ree's idea of fun, but it had to be done. Meren needed to be able to tell what was inside his head and what wasn't.

Even if Meren didn't want to learn.

The Mage smiled. "Oh, that's part of why he's so tired. I took the liberty of giving him some basic shielding and showing him how to use it. It's close enough to the way magic works that it should keep him out of trouble—well, out of too much trouble—for a while."

Ree couldn't help smiling. You couldn't keep a child Meren's age completely out of trouble. At that age, they attracted it like flies to honey. "Thank you. I appreciate that." What the Mage had left unsaid—that Meren would need to learn more about his strange Gift when he got older—was something Ree figured could wait for a while. There was no point borrowing trouble when trouble came to visit regularly anyhow.

"Oh, it's my pleasure." The Mage stood, and extended his right hand. "I'll be happy to testify for you or your son, if there's ever a need."

That offer was enough to make Ree blink so his eyes wouldn't blur. Hobgoblins were killed on sight, unless they had a license and were properly controlled—which usually meant a cage or a leash. Here, he and Meren were exceptions, but that was mostly because of Lenar. Lenar being old Garrad's son, the local Lord, and Jem's father meant that Ree was family, and he'd made it clear he considered Ree and Meren equal members of that family.

What would happen without that in the future . . . Ree didn't want to think about it. "I really appreciate that," he said softly. "Thank you."

If it came to a court, him not being human meant he couldn't say anything to defend himself. Meren, too. It was something Ree mostly pushed to a dark corner of his mind, even forgot about for a while, but sometimes, especially with Garrad the way he was . . . His and Meren's situation was so precarious, so different from anything else, anywhere in the world, that any major change in the arrangement of their life could be a disaster.

No one dared defy Garrad, and Garrad had Lenar's ear. But if that were to change . . .

This farm, and the valley, were home now. Ree didn't think he could bear it if he had to leave.

With the shorter days of winter, Lenar had taken to making his weekly visit around the middle of the day, so he need not ride home in the dark. That suited Ree just fine; the chores were mostly morning and evening work this time of year, with the days he wasn't patrolling the forest spent either repairing things that had been set aside to be fixed when there was time, or helping Garrad move from bed to chair or chair to pot.

The outhouse wasn't an option for the old man anymore, not when it hurt him so much to take the few steps between his bed and the chair in the main room.

He only came into the kitchen for meals, but if anyone but Ree tried to help him, they'd get their head bitten off for being "damn busybodies." Ree suspected it was because he didn't offer sympathy, and he didn't make a fuss of the old man. He just . . . did what had to be done.

Garrad might be sick and his body failing him, but that didn't mean he didn't still have his pride.

That pride was very much evident when he received his son this morning. Garrad was sitting in his chair in the main room, combed and shaved and wearing clean clothes and keeping the pain out of his face as much as he could. And doing his best to pretend Jem wasn't hovering anxiously around the room, pretending to straighten things that didn't need straightening and looking anxiously at Garrad, out the corner of his eye.

Garrad would not acknowledge his grandson's anxiety. He would keep his dignity till the end. "Good to see you, boy," he told Lenar. Then he turned to Ree and said, "Ree, there's a rolled paper in the drawer beside my bed. I'll be wanting that now."

Ree just nodded. "I'll be right back."

The paper was where Garrad had said, new paper carefully rolled and tied with a scrap of bright yellow fabric Ree recognized as the stuff they'd used for Amelie's best apron this year. He closed the drawer, and returned to the main room.

At the door, Ree paused, struck by the resemblance between Garrad, Lenar and Jem. They were grandfather, father, and son, but they could have been the same man at different ages, looking at them like this.

You had to look closely at Jem to notice his eyes were rounder in shape and his mouth slightly softer—at least, when he wasn't in full family stubborn. Lenar's hair was darker than Jem's, but not much, and Garrad's was all white, and thinner now.

Ree's heart tightened when he looked at Garrad like this and saw something else shadowed on the old man, something you couldn't fight and couldn't beat. One day, Jem too would be like this. And the only longing in Ree's heart, unbearable and demanding, was to still be allowed to be near then. To spend his life with Jem. He didn't think he could stand to leave, to lose Jem.

Garrad nodded when Ree gave him the paper. "Lenar, you'll be wanting to keep this safe. I reckon you'll be needing it afore spring."

Lenar blinked, looking blank, as though he had no notion what had gotten into his father this time. He untied the fabric, and unrolled the paper. His face went slack for a moment, then–when he looked up–he looked much younger. Younger than Jem, even. "Oh, no, Dad. You're too damn stubborn to die."

Ree didn't want to look at him, to see the hurt, the realization that his father was human, and fading. That Garrad, and Lenar, and Jem too, weren't going to go on forever.

Garrad chuckled. "Don't you pull that with me, boy. I ain't some fool woman to be soothed by pretty words."

"Granddad —" Jem didn't get any further. His voice broke in a way that said he was fighting tears. "There are Healers that—"

"Father, I . . . Is there anything that can help? Is there any . . ." Now Lenar sounded lost, that big booming voice faint and almost childlike.

"None of that, now." Garrad wagged a bony finger. "I'm old. Ain't no Healer can fix that, nor no Mage, neither." His expression softened, the fierce light in his eyes fading a little. He looked back at Lenar. "I'd have been ten years gone if not for Jem and Ree. They've been good years, I ain't denying that. But I can feel them as went before calling for me, telling me it's my time."

Ree nodded slowly. He'd tried to pretend otherwise, but he'd known for a while now, somewhere deep down, that Garrad didn't have long. He hadn't wanted to believe it, either. Lenar's stricken look cut Ree deep. He might have been a soldier for the Empire, led his men in more than one battle, and seen enough death to make Ree cringe, but it was obvious that Lenar had never once thought his own father might be dying.

"Just read it, son. Read it, then keep it safe until it's needed." Garrad got that odd light in his face, and chuckled. "I figure you can argue better once you know what I've got there."

Beside Ree, Jem's hand clenched tight into a fist, and his face went stony. "It's a will, isn't it? Why didn't you say anything to us? To me? Why didn't you tell us you were doing this? Why?"

It wasn't—quite—an accusation, but Ree could hear

the hurt under it. He set his hand on Jem's, but he didn't say anything. This wasn't his argument. What Garrad wanted to do with his property was Garrad's business. He supposed it would go to Lenar and, in the fullness of time, to Jem. Meanwhile . . . Ree didn't want to consider that. He wondered if he and Meren could claim a corner of the forest and build a willow shelter.

Garrad all but crowed. "That's one for me, lad. I ain't said anything cause it's got to be done proper, and I wasn't going to get anyone's hopes up."

So . . . no hopes up. Which meant Ree and Jem . . . He wouldn't, couldn't finish the thought. He wouldn't resent Garrad, either. After all, the man had given him shelter and home and family. More than anyone had ever done for Ree.

Garrad nodded in Lenar's direction. "That's why it's got to go through your father first."

Lenar set the paper down again. He looked troubled. There were vertical lines between his eyes. "It can't," he said in a strained voice. "Imperial law . . . you can't leave anything to Ree. Or Meren."

"What?" Jem about exploded across the room, glaring at his father. "Imperial law can go hang itself. If Granddad wants to leave this whole place to Ree, he can."

Ree was too shocked to think. He stared, unmoving, waiting for Lenar's roar.

It didn't come. Lenar made an odd, distressed sound and hunched into himself like a child caught with his hand in the honey. "I'm sorry, Jem. I don't like it either, but . . . I've been confirmed here—the message came yesterday—and I have to follow Imperial laws."

"Even when they're wrong?" Jem demanded.

Lenar only nodded, looking miserable and . . . lost, even.

Ree cleared his throat. "Look, you . . . no one needs

to. Why . . . why can't you leave the place to Jem, and Jem . . ."

"Jem is my heir," Lenar said, booming the last word. His gaze told his son that he wasn't going to hear any argument on that, and Jem, though his lip curled as if to make a scathing remark, kept quiet. "The farm . . . He can inherit the farm, but he'll have a lot more to look after. He'll have to do his army duty or go to court, or—"

He stopped, but Jem didn't say anything, nor did Ree. They'd both assumed for a while it would be that way. If Jem was the son of a Lord, he'd need to get known as such in the outer world. Ree understood what wasn't being said. Ree could not go with Jem when he went–not unless he was willing to go on a leash or in a cage–and lots of things could happen when people were separated. Even as-good-as-married people. Hell, even married people, like what had happened with Lenar and Jem's mother.

As though to underscore it, Lenar said, softly, "You're both so young . . ."

Which Ree took to mean that they couldn't possibly know what they wanted for the rest of their lives.

Garrad made a clucking sound that usually meant he'd just heard something nonsensical, which Ree took a little comfort in, but not too much, because Garrad said, "Life is unpredictable and things happen. Look at me, with two boys and a wife, and then left all alone, all those years. If anything happens, I want Ree to be safe. And Meren. They can't go to the army or to court. They can't find their own ways. They have to know there will always be this."

"But, Father—"

"No buts," Garrad said with more than a hint of his old strength—and all of his stubbornness. "This way, no one can argue about Jem and Ree living in the same house." His eyes gleamed, warning Ree he was going to tease someone. "Ain't anyone else's business whether they're sleeping in separate beds or not."

Jem groaned and blushed fiery red, and Ree tried not to wince.

Lenar didn't react at all—which was so unlike him he had to be really worried. "Father, the law says I can't—"

"I could be wrong here, but . . .aren't you allowed to make extra laws, for things that affect just your lands?" Ree tried not to look appalled at himself. He'd just blurted out something he'd half thought about, and now . . .

It wasn't just Lenar who stared at him. Garrad and Jem were both looking as if Ree had had a litter of kittens or grown an extra head.

His face heated, and he fought the urge to curl up and hide. It was just as well his face fur hid his blushes. He fell silent.

"Go on, Ree," Lenar said, in the kind of grave voice that could give way to an explosion at the drop of a hat.

Ree tried to collect his thoughts. What was the saying? But he'd heard something about what was called Particular Laws. The Empire was so big no one person could know what was needed in every little pocket of it at any given time. And Lenar might think Ree was daring too much, and taking his inheritance and Jem's too. But Lenar didn't look upset and . . .

Might as well hang for a cow as a chicken? Ree figured he was headed for the whole herd. "I thought the Lord gets to make extra laws, so long as they don't break the Empire's laws. So . . .you can't make a law that says Meren and me don't have to be listed as safe hobgoblins. But, you can make one that says if we—or any other hobgoblin—pass some kind of test, we're human in your lands and get to be treated that way."

Ree couldn't remember where he'd learned all of that, but he thought it was maybe bits and pieces he'd heard over the years. Lenar and Jem talked sometimes—and Garrad too—when Ree was clearing the kitchen or putting the children to bed. And given the family's tendency to shout, he'd heard just about everything. He was pretty sure Lenar was the one who'd mentioned the Particular Laws, though, although he hadn't been talking about anything to do with hobgoblins then.

Lenar looked as though he'd been hit and hadn't got to falling over yet. "You know," he said slowly, "That just might be possible. I'd have to speak to a few people about it, but . . . it could work."

"You do that." Garrad wasn't making suggestions. They were orders. "I ain't changing a thing."

Lenar sighed and shook his head. "Wait and see, Father. I don't know if this will work, yet." He turned to Jem and Ree. "This damn fool old man wants to leave you two the farm—both of you."

"But . . ." Jem frowned. "Shouldn't it be going to you? I mean, you're Granddad's heir and all that." Ree squeezed Jem's hand. It was so like him, to argue for Lenar and against himself. Ree felt tears prickle in his eyes.

"Your father's got more than he needs," Garrad said with a chuckle. "Besides, he can take his pick of anything he wants that was here before you two arrived, so long as he can carry it out."

In other words, the things that might mean something to Lenar, like the portrait of the family, painted back when Lenar had been young. That made sense to Ree.

Jem stopped bristling quite so much, although the set of his jaw said there'd better not be anything else upsetting in Garrad's will.

"I'm glad the farm is going to you two, actually," Lenar said. "It might have been home once, but . . . it's your work that's made it what it is now. And Dad's right: I do have more than I need."

He chuckled softly. "Besides, I think it's a good idea, what he wants."

Which meant there was more in the paper than Lenar had revealed so far.

"It seems to me that a place where the folks as haven't got anyplace else can be welcome is a good thing," Garrad said into the silence. He gestured to Jem with a bony hand. "You and Ree took a hell of a risk, coming into the farm when you did. Ain't no doubt if I'd been well, I'd have met you with a pitchfork."

His expression softened, and he smiled. "You two showed me there's more to good than being human. Seems to me there's others out there as could use the same chance."

Ree swallowed and ducked his head to hide the way his eyes burned. He'd wondered more times than he wanted to count if Meren's parents could have been saved, could have learned to be human again. After all, Meren was as human as Ree, or more. Maybe all they'd needed was somewhere that gave them a chance to be human. And maybe not, too. That was the hardest thing: Ree didn't know.

"After you two, it goes to Meren," Lenar said softly. "If he doesn't have any children—adopted or otherwise—the farm comes back to my family, but it's got to stay a sanctuary."

He smiled, and Ree realized that Lenar's eyes were too bright, too shiny. "If I can get the two of you able to own property, I'm all for it."

Ree didn't go to the manor often—he kept himself to the farm and the forest, mostly, so he didn't unnerve people. Today was different.

Today was the ceremony Lenar had concocted to make him human. Not that Ree had any illusions about it: He'd still be killed on sight anyplace outside this valley, but here he'd be officially human and able to do all the things any other man could do, at least unless Lenar's Lord, or his, or further up all the way to Emperor Melles himself said otherwise.

To hear Lenar tell it, that didn't happen unless a Lord started abusing his people.

The important thing was, once something like this started, it was hard to take it away. People would get used to the idea that hobgoblins could take a test and become officially human—although Ree didn't have any idea what was in the test. Lenar had said it was better that way, and for official things, it was better to trust that Lenar was right.

Which was why Ree walked up to the manor in his best clothes with his tail wrapped tight around his left leg and his stomach wrapped even tighter into knots that made him wish he hadn't eaten before he left the farm.

The thick wooden gates stood open, with two men watching the stream of people coming in. It looked to Ree as if everyone in the valley had taken advantage of a fine winter's day to come see what would happen. That was a good thing. It was just that Ree's stomach didn't agree.

He recognized both the guards; they'd been village boys once, among the one's he'd helped free from rogue soldiers years ago. Now they looked every inch the real soldier, but they both waved to Ree and smiled.

Inside, the manor's Great Hall—a big, low-ceilinged room that could fit everyone in Three Rivers with space to spare—was filling up fast.

Ree couldn't help wondering how many had come to see "Garrad's hobgoblin" perform and how many actually cared about him. He didn't let any of that show; he just walked through the crowd to the front of the room, where Lenar had a solid chair, a chest to hold important documents, and a guard watching the people.

The guard nodded to Ree—he was another of the young men Ree had helped save—and gestured to a spot to the right of Lenar's official chair; it was far too plain to be called a throne. Ree took his place there and tried not to let his nervousness show. This was all he'd been told, to come to the hall and stand where he was told.

He should have worn a hat; at least then he'd have something to do with his hands. He couldn't have said whether it was better that he couldn't hear the words in the buzz of whispered conversation, but at least this way he didn't hear anything he didn't like.

Ree hadn't tried to find out what Lenar was telling people about today's ceremony. He figured it would be enough to get people to come to see without letting them know too much. The more people who saw this, the better, according to Lenar. That way they'd be talking about it as a good thing before the official documents started their long trail through Imperial bureaucracy.

Fortunately he didn't have to wait long. Lenar must have been watching for his arrival, because he walked out from a side door. He'd obviously chosen to make a point: He was wearing a red silk shirt and a cloak of snow-bear fur. His cloak pin was the Imperial crest, and it glittered as though it was worked in gemstones and precious metal. People fell silent, the hush cascading through the hall as people who'd noticed him elbowed their neighbors and pointed.

The ceremony itself went by in a kind of blur for Ree. He read a passage from a book he'd never seen before, then swore an oath of loyalty to the Empire and its local representative—namely Lenar. The rest of the test was to explain what the oath meant. Ree thought he managed that well enough.

After that, Lenar's Mage came forward, and Lenar

announced that the Mage would examine "the applicant."

That made sure no one's attention went wandering. Three Rivers had never been big enough for a Mage even before the magic storms, and most people had never seen a Mage actually do magic. The thought didn't make his stomach rest any easier.

The Mage smiled and whispered, "Relax. This is going to make you feel strange, but it won't hurt."

That wasn't what Ree was worried about. What if he didn't . . . if he wasn't . . . No. He'd deal with whatever the Mage found when he found it. He took a deep breath and nodded. "I'm ready." He spoke loudly enough for his voice to carry, and if it shook a bit, well, that was to be expected for something as important as this.

The Mage must have been waiting for him to speak, because he made a complicated gesture, and everything went . . . odd. The hall and everyone in it seemed to be a long way away, or maybe it was Ree who was a long way away, and there was a pressure on his mind, not really doing anything there, just looking. He fought down the instinctive desire to push that pressure away and make it leave him alone. It had to be the Mage, doing . . . whatever it was he was supposed to be doing.

The pressure moved, and Ree found himself remembering things he'd thought long forgotten. The smell of Jacona in the summer, clutching his mother's skirt at a fair and watching a Mage make lights spark from people's fingers, the cold and hunger and fear that never went away when he'd lived on the streets of Jacona, running from larger boys, hiding and hoping they wouldn't find him, hating that they were bigger and stronger than him . . .

The magic circle, with its blur of pain and the screams that had started as two animals and him and became just him. And the fur that kept him warm after that, the claws that made it so much easier to catch food and escape gangs, at least until the searches started and the street rats got rounded up and taken away. Losing what it was to be human, bit by bit, until he found Jem, and Jem brought him back to life, made him human again.

Then the weird distance went away and the pressure was gone, and he was back in the hall, with the Mage saying something to Lenar that Ree's ears rang too much to hear. His face fur was damp.

Whatever the Mage said, it must have been good because Lenar smiled and came over to shake Ree's hand. "Welcome to the Empire." He gave Ree a parchment certificate that had to have been done up before the ceremony.

The certificate didn't say anything about whether Ree was human or not; instead, it said that Lenar had examined him and made him a "citizen of the Empire," There was other legal-type wording there that, as Ree understood it, gave him the same rights—and responsibilities—as someone born and still human. "Thank you, my Lord." That wasn't a title Ree usually used, but here, now, it felt right.

He heard a soft harumph of approval from behind him and, turning around, saw that Garrad was there. He'd had two sturdy lads carry him up on a litter, and he was sitting straight on the chair in the litter, holding his stick. His eyes glittered.

When Ree went to him, he found himself pulled into an embrace by the elderly man's frail arm. "Welcome to the family, heir," the old man said, softly.

They buried Garrad on a bright day when the snow crunched underfoot and the wind was quiet. Ree, Jem, and Lenar had spent the day before digging beside Garrad's long-dead wife's grave, sharing memories and being grateful that in the end he'd gone peacefully, in his sleep.

Ree didn't say, but he figured the old man had held on until he knew his home would pass on the way he wanted it to, then stopped fighting the call of all those who'd passed before.

When you'd outlived most of the folk you'd known, it must get lonely. He wanted to find a quiet corner to grieve, but with Jem and Lenar both barely holding together—oh, they were being strong, and family-stubborn about it, but Ree could see how brittle their control was—it fell to Ree to arrange everything and make sure Jem was too busy to let go until after the burial, when they'd have a bit of time to themselves to sort out life without the old man.

He suspected Loylla would have helped, only she wasn't able to get about and wouldn't be for a while yet.

It was the people that surprised him. People he'd once told off for ignoring that an irritable old man's chimney had been smokeless for days, people Garrad had once had no use for . . .

Men stopped by the farm with wrapped pots of stew or haunches of beef, and helped with the chores without anyone saying anything, then wouldn't let Ree or Jem thank them. And now, they trudged up the path to the farm, men, women, and children, all of them in their best clothes, even the mayor, and they seemed to Ree to be . . . well . . . to mean it.

Lenar's priest gave a short speech, mostly asking any gods that might be listening to help Garrad's soul get where it was supposed to be. Ree supposed that was the way the army priests did it because there were so many different religions and gods in the army that you couldn't pick any one set of them without offending most of the men you were ministering to.

After, they lowered Garrad's body—wrapped in an old sheet Ree and Jem had sewn into a shroud—into the ground, then all the men helped fill the grave. Ree tried not to look at the soil falling, tried not to think about Garrad down there. It felt as though they must be hurting Garrad, as though they were suffocating him in the black loamy dirt, but it wasn't true. Wherever the old man was, he wasn't there. That was just . . . a shell, like summer scritch-bugs left when they grew. Garrad had grown and gone elsewhere, with his wife and his brother. And there, hopefully, all the hard binding of the old shell was gone, and he was free and young again.

The men packed the soil tight, tamping it down with the backs of their shovels, then everyone helped to clean up before they left, and that was that. It was quiet, and simple, and there wasn't any fuss, but somehow Ree was comforted by all those people coming to help.

The house seemed terribly empty after everyone had left, with just him and Jem and Amelie—sniffling a bit, but not actually crying—and Meren.

No one said anything, just . . .they all wanted comfort, and they all held each other, standing in front of the fireplace.

"Don't think I don't know what this is doing to you," Jem said roughly. "Don't you ever think I don't appreciate you."

Ree hadn't even considered that. He'd just been doing what had to be done. That Jem wanted him, preferred him over any of the village girls, that was a daily miracle.

Meren tugged at his pants; Ree bent to lift the boy and set him against his hip. Meren's face fur was so wet it lay flat against his skin. Amelie tried to wipe her eyes with a soaked handkerchief, then gave up and rubbed her arm against her face.

Ree held them all as tight as he could, feeling the weight of his family even more now. Not that Jem didn't do as much as he, but right now . . . Well, that was how it was. If he wasn't fit for something, Jem carried the weight.

Shared between them, it wasn't that much."Come on," he said in a voice that only shook a little bit. "We should get dinner. There's enough left from what folks brought that we needn't cook."

They'd get better. After a while it wouldn't hurt so much to look at the spot where Garrad wasn't, and maybe they'd even be able to laugh again and smile when they remembered him.

Later, in a month or two, he and Jem would move into Garrad's room and give Amelie their old room. She was getting too old and too much of a lady to sleep in the attic, separated by only a thin partition from Meren's room.

Later, there would be other challenges. The children would grow. And perhaps there would be other children who didn't have any place to go. Later, Jem would go away to do his duty by his Emperor, in one way or another, and he would come back. Ree looked between his lashes at Jem. Yes, he would come back, one way or another, because this was his heart's place. Maybe his affections would change, who could tell that, but he would never deny Ree this place they'd built together. And if he did, Ree would make him see he was wrong. And if someone, enemy soldier or courtier, tried to keep Jem away from home, Ree would go and get him, no matter what the peril or the suffering.

Garrad would want that. He'd want them to be his family, stubborn beyond reason and too damn pigheaded to give up when they were beat, and loving and caring for those who needed it, too.

It was a good legacy to leave.

Family Matters

Tanya Huff

"As there's no need to wait for a reply from Verain, you'll have time to stop by and visit your grandmother before you head back to Haven."

Ryal Verain's holding wasn't far from the forest settlement where Jors had been raised and where most of his extended family still lived, but the Dean of the Herald's Collegium did not assign Heralds the task of visiting their grandmothers. "Sir?"

"She's not likely to live forever, you know." The Dean's lips twitched, the movement nearly, but not quite, hidden by his beard. "And at her age, she'd rather not go another two years without seeing you."

"Sir?"

"She was quite insistent I do something about that in the letter. Also, your cousin . . ." He pulled a much folded and ragged-edged piece of vellum off a pile on his desk, held it at arm's length, and frowned. ". . .your cousin's daughter at any rate, Annamarin, could benefit from your experience. What particular experience, she doesn't say."

"My grandmother . . ." Jors shook his head, trying to get the words to settle into an order that made actual sense. "My grandmother wrote you a letter?"

"Herald Jennet picked it up when she stopped by on

her last Circuit." The vellum flopped limply as the Dean waved it, and Jors thought he saw the faded lines of old accounts on the back. "From the sound of it, *quite insistent* is a fairly good general description of your grandmother." Sitting back in his chair, the Dean looked measuringly up at Jors, his dark eyes narrowed. "Is there a reason you haven't been to see your family in almost two years, Herald Jors?"

"It isn't . . .I mean, I don't . . .I've just . . ." Jors ran a hand back through his hair. "I've been busy?"

"Are you asking me? No? Good. Because I'm aware of how busy you've been and while the country certainly couldn't survive without you . . ."

Jors could feel his cheeks flush. He hadn't meant to imply he'd been busier than any other Herald but, in all fairness, he hadn't just been hanging around the Collegium. Since he'd last been on Circuit, he'd taken every courier run he could get, and on those days he'd been stuck in Haven, he'd helped the Weaponsmaster teach the archery classes, run the Grays through a few basic tracking exercises, and had his butt handed to him consistently in the practice ring.

". . .but you have a responsibility to your family as well. Things are quiet right now, and we can find you if we need you. I think seven days should be long enough to sooth your grandmother's justifiable irritation." A raised hand cut off Jors' barely formed protest. "And I'm sure she'll inform me if you cut the visit short."

:But you don't like Haven,: Gervais reminded him as they made their way through the city toward the gate. Head up, neck arched, he pranced a little as a group of children called enthusiastic greetings. *:I thought you'd be happy to stay away for a while.:*

:That's not the point.: Jors forced a smile and waved at the children. *:The point is, my grandmother wrote Dean*

Carlech complaining about how long it had been since I'd been home.:

:Perhaps she misses you..:

:Also not the point. My grandmother wrote the Dean!:

:And because she did, we don't have to return immediately to Haven.: Gervais turned his head just far enough that he could fix Jors with one sapphire eye. *:If you had been to see your family, she wouldn't have had to write.:*

:We were busy!: It was a weak defense, and Jors knew it. *:You have no idea how embarrassing this is, do you?:*

:Nerial didn't believe her Herald was angry with you. She said he seemed amused.:

Jors gave serious thought to standing in the stirrups and beating his head against the sign they were passing under. The Dean's Companion thought the Dean was amused. The legendary, mystical protectors of Valdemar gossiped like a flock of crows, and, given the isolating nature of the job, there was nothing Heralds like to talk about as much as other Heralds. He was never going to hear the end of this.

Ryal Verain's expression matched that of the small, black sheep jostling about in the pen behind him–not distrustful but definitely wary. The scent was similar as well, but Jors was careful not to let that thought show as he handed over the oilskin packet.

Pale eyes narrowed, Verain cracked the seal. "Well, that's that then," he grunted as he finished reading. The wariness had vanished, replaced with satisfaction, so Jors assumed the news was good. "I can't deny the news takes a load off, but I admit I'm surprised they sent it out with a Herald."

My grandmother wrote the Collegium.

When it became clear Jors was not going to explain, Verain nodded. "I've no reply needs sending, Herald, but if you can give us time to finish this pen, we'd be pleased to have you share a midday meal with us before you go. Where *are* you going?"

"Forest settlement, out from Greenhaven."

Verain's eyes narrowed again. "You're Trey Haden's nephew."

Jors fought the urge to remind Verain he was a Herald–his instinctive response to being his uncle's nephew, his father's son, his grandmother's grandchild–and said only, "Yes." Verain had, after all, only made a statement, not the first move on an emotional battlefield. Lagenfield, the village closest to Verain's land, was close enough to Greenhaven that his family might have supplied wood had a closer forester not had what was needed.

"Well, then, you'll have time to reach the Greenhaven Waystation after you eat and no time to get much farther if you don't."

He was still speaking to a Herald, not to Trey Haden's nephew. No one with sense rode into the forest after dark. "I'd be happy to stay and share your meal." Jors shrugged out of his jacket. "If you'll let me share in your labor."

The half dozen men mixed in with the sheep, every one of whom had stopped working when Gervais trotted into the compound, shared a reaction Jors couldn't hear above the bleating, but, given the laughter, he assumed it was at his expense. Speculative laughter, though, not dismissive.

Heavy brows rose until they disappeared under the thick gray curls. "Thank you for the offer, Herald, but we're nearly done. Just this lot to send out to join the rest."

The rest were dotted over the hillside behind the compound, like a spatter of ink against the new green, surprisingly sleek without their fleece. He had had no idea that lambs actually gamboled.

"You settle your Companion, Herald Jors." The oilskin crinkled as Verain's grip tightened around it. "You've done what you do."

:You knew he was almost finished, didn't you?: Gervais asked as they headed over toward the stables.

:Hillside covered in shorn sheep, only a few left in the pen—it wasn't hard to work out.:

:So it was an offer without meaning,: Gervais snorted.

:Nothing of the kind. I made it to acknowledge the value of his work; in turn, he acknowledged the value of mine.:

:Your family values you.:

Hand up under Gervais mane, Jors paused mid-scratch. *:We weren't talking about my family.:*

Gervais snorted again.

:I think that could be arranged.:

"No, they're tougher than those sheep of the Holderkin. They're hardy, ours. Can forage on their own all over these hills, even though the land's rougher than a . . ." Cheeks flushing, suddenly becoming aware of who he was talking to, Raymond, Verain's eldest son, cleared his throat and continued without the profanity he'd been about to add. "They don't need supplemental feeding and they may be small, but I saw a ram take down a wolf once. Well, a young wolf. They're not much for goring, not with their horns turned back so . . ." Grinning, he sketched the ram's horn's curl over his own ears. ". . .but they've heads like rock, and if they charge you, you'll know it. We don't have a lot of trouble with wolves; they tend to stay clear where there's people about, and these sheep, they're smart enough to stay out from under the trees for the most part, though they head for the highest ground about if they can. Expect to be chasing them down from the High Hills some season. You saw how they didn't have wool on their faces or legs, Herald?

That's to help them move through brush," he continued before Jors could answer. "They don't get caught up so easily. And their fleece . . .ah, the fibers are fine and soft, not so long and coarse as those of the Holderkin. We shear them twice a year, spring and fall. Give us a few years to get this flock well established, and the finest woolens at Court will be from our sheep."

"Are they all black?" Jors wondered.

"You're thinking it's wool that won't take dye much." Rodney nodded. "True enough, but they throw gray on occasion, and I've a mind to breed to white. Still, nothing wrong with black woolens is there, Herald?" He waved a hand at Jors' Whites, then back at his own dark clothing. "Black's slimming, they say."

"Husband! Did you just say Herald Jors looks fat?"

Rodney turned to look up at his wife, opened his mouth, closed it, and opened it again, although no words came out. Just as Jors was about to protest for him, her lips twitched. Rodney roared with laughter, caught her around the waist, and dragged her down onto his lap, where he kissed her soundly. "I said nothing of the kind, and well you know it," he declared when they parted long enough for speech. "Now, did you actually have something to say, or are you just interrupting our talk to cause trouble?"

Twitching her tunic back into place as she slid off his lap, she nodded across the great room to where Verain stood talking to a younger version of himself. "Ryan came in to say that ewe you're so fond of has led another revolt. If you want to keep her out of the stew pot, you'd best get over there and mount a spirited defense." When Rodney–who'd surged up onto his feet at the news–glanced down at Jors, she tugged him back to her lips by his beard and murmured, "Go. I'll entertain the Herald."

For a big man, Rodney could move quickly when he had too. He was almost across the room, already gesturing at his father and brother, by the time his wife dropped into his chair. She shook her head at the crusts left behind by his empty bowl, then turned to Jors and said, "Elane. I imagine you were introduced to a dozen people all at once, shoved into a chair, and told to eat up, so I don't expect you to remember."

He didn't actually. "Your husband is the younger son?"

"Middle. Ryan is older and Ricard . . ." Elane pointed to where a young man walked up and down by the windows, a squalling infant on one shoulder. ". . .Ricard is two years younger. The family runs to boys, but I've five sisters so I'm hoping . . ." Her hand dropped to her belly. ". . . to even the odds."

There was only one thing that could mean. "Congratulations."

"What?" Her gaze dropped to her hand. "Oh. Thank you. I haven't known long; it's still so new. We haven't been married a year yet." She half-turned in the chair to smile at her husband, and when she turned back, she frowned. "Are you all right, Herald Jors?"

He schooled his expression before she could define it, hurriedly raising his mug. No one would ever smile across a room that way at him.

:My lips do not move in such a way, Heartbrother.:

A moment later, ignoring the smug, self-satisfied reaction from his Companion, Jors accepted the cloth Elane offered and coughed out an apology.

She waved it off. "Please, you got very little on me. And besides, we were almost relatives, you and I. My father is Dominic Heerin . . ."

Jors nodded in the pause. Heerin owned the mill his uncle brought their logs to.

". . . and your cousin Hamin was courting my sister Tara. Came to nothing, though. I remember when we heard you'd been Chosen. It was all anyone could talk about. I'd just turned twelve, and I spent all that summer out by the track with flowers braided into my hair hoping another Companion would come by and Choose me. Eventually, my eldest sister dragged me home by the ear and told me Companions preferred useful people over those who shirked their chores."

Elane shared her husband's fondness for monologing, Jors noted, and he wondered what their conversations with each other must be like. "This must have been different for you," he said. "From a house full of sisters and lumber to so many men and sheep."

"A little different, yes. But not so hard to get used to. Rodney loves this land, for all its rock and hills and the dangers of the forest so close. At first I loved it for his sake, but I'm growing to love it for its own. And the sheep, well, you've already noticed their main failing, but he's determined to breed to white–that ewe he's defending threw gray twins this season–and he admires them for their toughness as much as the fine wool of their fleece. My sisters say when they see me now, I've nothing to talk of but sheep and Rodney. Well, Rodney and sheep." Her laugh drew her husband's head around, and he paused in his argument long enough to toss a smile in her direction. "It's always the way, though, isn't it, as you move between birth family and found family. This is what made me . . ." She held out one hand palm up and then the other. ". . . and this is what I am. And I'll tell you this much, Herald Jors . . ." She winked and stood as her father-in-law approached. ". . . shepherds have much softer hands than men who toss lumber about all day."

The waystation was empty and quiet–although Jors supposed that, given the former, the later went without saying. Hands cupped around a mug, he sat in the doorway and watched Gervais grazing, his coat gleaming silver in the twilight.

Beyond the Companion, in under the trees, it was already night. At the settlement, the gates would be closed, animals and people penned in safely; the youngest and the eldest would be preparing for bed, and everyone else would soon follow. Lamplight might extend the day in Haven, but out here sunrise and sunset still defined people's lives.

Not so different from where he'd just come. Barring the differences between trees and sheep. And the difference between *Herald Jors* and *Jors with a Companion.*

:There is no difference between Herald Jors and Jors with a Companion. They are both you.:

"My grandmother would agree. Although she'd think they both mean Jors with a Companion."

Gervais lifted his head and turned to stare. Jors wished, not for the first time, he could pick up his Companion's thoughts as easily as Gervais picked up his. Finally, the young stallion snorted and bent back to the grass. *:If you are still annoyed with her about the letter, tomorrow you many tell her it was inappropriate.:*

"Yeah." Jors drained the mug and set it to one side. "Like that'll happen."

He didn't recognize the girl running down the track toward him until she skidded to a stop, bowed elaborately–one plait surrendering, spilling her dark blonde hair down over her face–looked up, and grinned. "Herald Jors. Wonderous One."

:I like her.:

Jors returned the grin and swung out of the saddle. "Annamarin."

In the time he'd been gone, she'd crossed from child to girl. She'd be eleven now, almost twelve, the same age Elane had been when she'd spent the summer with flowers in her hair waiting for a Companion. Instead of flowers, Annamarin's hair held a trio of feathers stuffed into the top of the remaining braid.

"You weren't waiting out here hoping to be Chosen, were you?" Grandmother's letter *had* said Annamarin could benefit from his experience.

"No! No offense," she added quickly to Gervais, dipping into another elaborate bow. "Companions Choose as Companions will, and Companions will as Companions please."

:I really like her.: Gervais said as Jors worked that through.

"May I give you greetings, cousin?"

"May you what?"

She sighed, a simple exhalation defining her as the most put-upon creature in these woods. "Can I hug you?"

"Why couldn't you?"

"You're a Herald! In Whites! And I'm tragically soiled, though tis naught but good clean dirt."

"Tis naught?"

Annamarin rolled her eyes. "It means it isn't. Sort of. Wait . . . my pipes!" She pulled a set of reed pipes out from behind her waistband. "I don't want them to be tragically crushed! I made them myself," she continued after an emphatic hug that rocked Jors back onto his heels. "Well, Lyral–she got stuck here for almost a week during fall storms, when the mud was up over her boots–she showed me how. But I made them. Mostly."

"Lyral?" As they walked toward the settlement, Jors ran through the names of the Bards he knew and came up short.

"She's a minstrel. She travels. She sings. She's the best. I wanted to go with her when she left, but Mama said no. Papa said good riddance." Annamarin blew across the top of the pipes and back. The rise and fall of the twelve notes sounded like a giggle. "He was kidding."

"What did Lyral say when you said you wanted to go with her?" It wouldn't be the first time a "minstrel" had discovered a talent in a child and made promises in order to lure that child away. If Lyral was one of those predators–however unsuccessful this time—Jors needed to find her. He'd be in and out of the settlement so quickly his grandmother would no doubt feel herself justified writing another letter to the Dean. Beside him, Gervais had both ears flicked forward.

"Oh, then." This time, the twelve notes sounded resigned. And a bit annoyed. "She said she didn't travel with children, but she'd be back this way in a year or two, and if I still wanted to go, we'd talk."

"About what?"

"About me going with her, I guess. I dunno." She shrugged a skinny shoulder, then bent back to the pipes and blew out a string of birdsong that drew answers from the surrounding trees.

"Did Lyra teach you to do that?"

The look Annamarin shot him reminded him chillingly of their grandmother. "It's a calling bird song, Jors. You spend way too much time in the city. It's tragic."

"Can't argue with that." So, since she couldn't have known they'd be arriving today . . . "Shirking chores?"

"No." When he glanced down at her, she grinned. "Maybe a little. Sometimes . . ." She turned in place and walked backward, staring down the track. "I just want to know what's out there. You know what I mean?"

He'd never given the world beyond the forest and the settlement any thought before he'd been Chosen. On his first trip to Greenhaven and the mill, he'd found himself falling into sapphire eyes and hearing an emphatic *:Finally:* in his head. Now he thought about it, Gervais had sounded a lot like Annamarin.

:I was tired of waiting for you. Most *of those who are to be Chosen find their way to Haven.:*

:If I'd known you were out there, I'd have met you halfway.:

"Jors?"

He smiled down at her. "Yeah, I know what you mean."

As they came out of the trees and into the clearing in front of the palisade, Jors found himself studying the area with a professional eye. The settlement's grant allowed a certain area cleared for living space, and it looked as though his uncle had recently expanded out as far as he was legally allowed. The edges still looked rough and there were two new buildings inside the palisade.

His mother's geese saw them first. Heads low, necks extended, the current flock charged out through the open gate, hissing, wings beating at the air. When Gervais lowered his own head and struck the ground with his right hoof, they wheeled neatly to the left, circling the willow fencing around the vegetable garden as though that had been their destination all along. A familiar voice shouted from the garden. As Jors and Annamarin drew even with the opening, their grandmother emerged, threw her cane at the geese, spotted Gervais, and rocked to a stop.

"As I live and breathe! The boy is back!" Less considerate of his Whites than Annamarin, she stumped forward and dragged him up against her generous bosom, leaving a smear of rich black earth across his tunic and down one leg. Given the amount of dirt on her hands, he didn't want think about the places she'd gripped him.

It was the same possessively affectionate hug he'd always had from her, and it made him feel seven, ten, fourteen . . .

"You've filled out," she clucked as she pushed him back out to arm's length and looked him up and down. "Well, you couldn't have stayed all arms and legs forever, I suppose, could you? Never mind," she cut him off as he opened his mouth. "How long can you stay?"

"Seven days, unless I'm needed."

"Needed." Gran rolled her eyes. "I think they can manage without out you for so short a time. Annamarin, get my cane would you, sweetheart. Had her head turned by a minstrel," she added as the girl cautiously approached the geese. Either his grandmother had gotten a little deaf or she didn't care if she was overheard. Jors leaned toward the later. "Fool woman put foolish ideas into the girl's head. I want you to tell her that it's one thing to have a Companion suddenly appear and declare you special . . ." She nodded to Gervais, who nodded back. ". . . and another thing entirely to declare it yourself. Now, come on." Hand tucked in the crook of his elbow, she tugged him toward the gate. "It's bread day. Your mother can't leave the kneading."

His mother dusted him with flour and clucked at the length of his hair, then spun him around in time to have his brother's wife, Tora, catch him up in a hug redolent with the scent of the first wild strawberries.

"Oh, stop making such a fuss over him," Gran snorted. "He's just come home; he hasn't saved the country single-handed."

Seven, ten, fourteen . . .

When he tried to step away, he discovered he had a toddler wrapped around each leg. They held him in place long enough for Annamarin's mother to appear, and while she was exclaiming over his appearance, Jor's cousin Tomlin, Uncle Trey's youngest . . .

"Took an ax to the thigh last fall, poor thing."

. . . limped into the summer kitchen followed by the rest of the settlement's children, four dogs, and a goat.

He only managed to free himself from their welcome by reminding them he had a Companion to tend to.

Jors set the saddle aside and let his forehead fall to thump against Gervais' withers.

:They're glad to see you.:

:I know. And I'm glad to see them.:

:But?:

:But I'm Jors with a Companion.:

:You are my Chosen.: Gervais' mental voice was matter-of-fact. *:Why do you need to be anyone else?:*

:I don't . . . That isn't . . . .: He turned to rest his cheek against the warmth and ran a hand up under Gervais' mane. *:Am I a terrible person?:*

:No. You are a Herald. You cannot be a Herald and a terrible person. Therefore you are not a terrible person.: Responding to a nonverbal prompt, Jors scratched along the arc of his neck. *:It is not terrible for you to want your family to see you as you are, not as you were.:*

"See lo, where yonder Herald stands!"

Jors turned to see Ammamarin just inside the lean-to, barely visible over an armload of hay.

"I know it's tragic," she said, "but this is the best of what's left. There's not a lot of grazing yet, but Mika's been taking the goats to the south clearing if the Wonderous One doesn't mind sharing."

"His name is Gervais. Have you forgotten?"

"He's too beautiful for a name." She spread her arms, the hay dropping into the manger. "He is a song walking above the mud we less lovely creatures tread upon."

:Have I mentioned that I like her?:

:You have.: Jors pulled his brushes from the saddlebag. "Trust me, he walks in plenty of mud."

"Can I help?

"You could play something for me."

"I only know three real songs." But she perched on the edge of the manger and pulled out her pipes. "Mostly, I just twiddle, you know, make stuff up."

Jors draped his jacket beside her, then bent to brush the dirt from Gervais rear leg. "So make stuff up."

He didn't know what he'd expected, but her twiddles

were just that; random notes strung together. Not unpleasant but not exactly music either.

:You know what you expected.: One hoof up on Jors' knee, Gervais rested his weight against Jors' shoulder. Jors grunted and pushed back.

"Annamarin!"

The twiddling stopped. Jors dropped the hoof and straightened. Their grandmother looked between the two of them and snorted. "That woodbox won't fill itself, child. And no one will be pleased if the bread is baked only half through. Don't look to him!"

"He's a Herald!" Annamarin declared as she jumped down.

"Am I blind now? Woodbox!"

"If this labor ruins my hands and I can tragically no longer play, you'll weep with sorrow at the loss!"

"If that woodbox doesn't get filled, you'll be sorrier. And you," Gran added as Annamarin ran off. "Did you think I wanted you to encourage such nonsense? I will smack that minstrel if she returns. Filling the child's head with clouds. You need to tell her what comes of running off, away from one's family in search of adventure."

"Gran, I . . ."

"You didn't run off, did you? You rode. It'd be different for that one, wouldn't it? There'd be no pretty white clothes and a sense of self-importance for her. She needs to know what's out there, doesn't she? And she needs to know what's here. Safety, security, no one goes to bed hungry–your grandfather and I created this from nothing, I'll thank you to remember. You missed a spot, there on the left leg above the hock." Shaking her head, she met Gervais' eyes. "I'm sure he does his best. He never was much for chores either, always off in the woods with a bow. Still, I'm pleased to see you don't look like he's been neglecting you. He missed another spot there . . ."

His Uncle Trey, his father, and his older cousins came home at twilight. They'd spent the day marking trees to be cut when the ground dried, those that had been winter-killed and those topped off in spring storms. Jors was astounded to see that Uncle Trey, a mountain of a man with more energy than any other three combined, was now almost entirely gray and his broad shoulders had begun to stoop.

"We'll put you to work tomorrow, lad!" Cheeks flushed, his uncle clapped him on one shoulder; he looked a little surprised when Jors didn't so much as sway and added, "I'm sure you've forgotten what hard work's like."

Breakfast the next morning was porridge and berries–the berries offered slightly squashed from his nephew's fingers. The boy shrieked with laughter as Jors pretended to eat the fingers too. When his mother ruffled his hair as she bustled past the long table, he realized too late he was becoming the Jors that was. The Jors they all still believed him to be.

"You'll work with your father and me," Uncle Trey declared on the way out of the common dining hall..

Jors paused, half into a borrowed jacket. "With both of you?"

"Is that a problem?" Gran demanded.

"I imagine you've forgotten most of your forest craft," his uncle said.

The day would be a test.

Jors didn't tell them he'd tracked harder quarry than pheasant and deer over the last few years–mostly because he couldn't figure out a way to do it that wouldn't sound like bragging. And while he'd done plenty of hard work as a Herald, he'd forgotten how hard *this* work was, so, as the day went on, he kept his mouth shut.

"Let it go, Trey," his father laughed at last. "My boy's still the best tracker in the family for all he spends most of his time with his ass in a saddle."

"Wasted skills," Uncle Trey sighed.

When they stopped at midday, they'd nearly reached the western edge of the grant. Sitting together on a rock shelf, they divided up the food they'd been carrying and, when they were settled, Jor's uncle smacked his arm with the side of his fist and nodded toward a stand of beech, four good-sized trees that had all been topped off. "What do you think, lad?"

"No point saving them," Jors noted, accepting a biscuit. "Best to take them down and open a hole for new growth. It's beech. The mill will take them for short boards if you stack them now and come back when the ground is dry enough for the sled and the oxen. And there's enough limb wood there to keep the ovens going."

"Well done," his father crowed. "Couldn't expect a better answer than that, Trey."

The other man snorted, straightened, and stared into the distance. "Pity we can't see if you've remembered how to shoot," he said. "Look at the size of that stag."

Jors stood up on the rock to give himself a better angle. Frowned. The distant silhouette was off slightly. "I don't think that's a stag. I think it's a dyheli."

"Don't be daft. We're too far north. Puts on a pair of white trousers and suddenly everything's got to be all mystical. You need to keep your head in the real world. Off you go and track it then."

Jors raised a hand as the dyheli disappeared into the trees and turned to see both men watching him expectantly. "No," he said.

Uncle Trey began a protest but stopped when Jors met his gaze.

His father suddenly directed all his attention to the packs.

"Well . . ." His uncle sounded as uncertain as Jors had ever heard him. ". . . we'd best be starting back then . . ."

Hands wrapped around his empty mug, Jors watched his brother and his sister-in-law carry the sleeping twins out of the large family room in the settlement's first building, his brother more than willing to leave their conversation when Tara beckoned him home.

"Why are you sad?"

He made room for Annamarin on the bench. "I'm not sad."

"You don't look sad," she said frowning up at him, "but under how you look, you're sad." Head cocked, she studied his face. "Is it a tragic love story?"

A dying bandit girl and the knowledge that he was hers and always would be. He started to say it was more complicated than that. Started to say their time had been too short for a story. Watched the door close behind his brother and his brother's family and said only, "Yes."

Annamarin nodded with all the wisdom of nearly twelve. "I thought so." Reaching into her pocket, she pulled out a honey candy, picked off a bit of lint and held it out to him. "My mama makes these. When I had my heart tragically broken by Ternin at the mill, they helped."

"Thank you."

She dropped it in his hand, although it stuck for a moment to her fingers, and ran to join the children being herded off to bed.

The candy melted on his tongue, so sweet it nearly made his eyes water. If it didn't help, it didn't hurt.

Although, he realized, other parts of him did. Jors grunted as he stood, stretched out his back, and tried to work the knots from his right arm. Hard to believe he'd only been walking and using a hatchet. He hadn't hurt like this since he'd first learned to ride.

"Used muscles you haven't for a while, lad!" Uncle Trey laughed. "Not so easy keeping up with an old man, is it?"

"Leave him be, Trey; there's a trick to walking on uneven ground," Jors' father called out. "I expect he's lost the knack of it."

"He needs to come home more often," one of his cousins called.

"A few more days of honest labor, and he'll be his old self again," laughed another.

:There's someone coming.:

A moment later, the geese sounded the alarm.

"He went out yesterday looking for that damned ewe he's so fond of. She'd slipped the dogs, late afternoon, and headed for the hills with her lambs." One of Verain's men sagged against the hands that held him as his horse, sides wet with sweat, stumbled and nearly went to her knees just inside the gate. "When the sun went down, he didn't come in. Nearly had to tie Elane to the chair to keep her from heading out to find him. But he's smart, Rodney is, and he'd have found a safe place for the night, yeah, and then he'd be back by day we told her, back with that damned ewe."

"But he wasn't." Jors stepped aside as Annamarin's father pushed past, heading for the horse.

"No. We looked, Herald, but we couldn't find him, not even a body or sign of a struggle or the damned sheep, and Elane sent me to find you, and I damned near killed the mare but Elane . . ." He closed his eyes for a heartbeat, and when he opened them again, they shone with reflected pain, obvious even in the light of half a dozen flickering lamps. "She's taking it terrible hard."

Jors closed his hand around the man's shoulder, felt the fine tremble of exhaustion through shirt and jacket, felt the tension relax as he squeezed. Pivotting on one heel, he headed for the Herald's Corner, not needing a lamp to find the way to where Gervais waited.

"Jors!"

Habit stopped his feet at the sound of his grandmother's voice.

"Where are you going, then?" She stood in the door they'd left open when they'd rushed outside, her hair, unplaited for the night spilling around her shoulders.

"I'm going where I'm needed: to find Rodney."

Heads pivoted as the men and women in the courtyard turned their attention back to the old woman.

"I understand you want to help, Jors, but it's forest trail all the way. Wait till day and go then if you must. There're men already searching for young Rodney who know the ground. What can you bring to the search that they can't?"

"Hope." Bare feet sticking out from under her nightshirt, Annamarin moved to Jors' side and swept a steady gaze over her family. "When a Herald of Valdemar rides, hope rides with him. Yes, they have men who know the ground, but with one of theirs lost in the forest for going on two nights now, what they need is hope." She paused, then, just before the silence stretched to the breaking point, she spread her hands and added, "And they need the best tracker this family has ever had."

A further heartbeat's silence, then a cheer.

Jors bent and kissed the top of her head. *:Heartbrother . . .:*

:I am well rested. We can be there before dawn.:

"Oh, it's so horribly tragic that one of the lambs died!"

Jors sighed. "I tell you a story of a gallant ride through the night, beset on all sides by terrible dangers, finishing, with the sun barely up, in the kind of tracking that one person in thousands could do in order to save a man's life, and you're upset about a lamb?"

"It died." Annamarin released her grip on his sleeve to fold her arms. "And it was *tragic.*"

Rodney had been returned to Elane from the bottom of a crevasse with a broken leg, the ewe and her remaining lamb had been returned to the flock, and Jors had returned to Trey Hadden's settlement.

Annamarin had met him on the track.

:It seems that you want your family to behave in ways you do not wish to behave yourself.:

:I don't know what you . . . :

Gervais gave a little buck. *:The girl has Talent. Speak to your grandmother on her behalf.:*

"A Bard?" Their grandmother swept a narrow–eyed gaze from Jors to Annamarin and back. "Are you certain?"

"A certain as I can be, not being a Bard myself." Jors watched her expression change, her hand begin to rise, and knew she had just asked herself, *What would Jors know about Bards?* "Gervais," he added quickly, "is certain."

"Well . . ." She nodded slowly. ". . .that's different then, isn't it?" Reaching out, she took Annamarin's hand and tugged her close. "Are you sure you want to be a Bard, child?"

Annamarin rolled her eyes. "It's not something you *do*, Gran, it's something you *are.*"

The old woman snorted. "It's not something *I* am."

"Well, no," Annamarin admitted. "But it's like what Jors is."

"Please, child, he was Chosen. That has nothing to do with what he is and everything to do with his Companion."

"With his Companion finding him worthy."

"What?"

Sighing, Annamarin tugged her hand free so she

could gesture expansively. "There isn't a Jors before and a Jors after, Gran, there's just Jors. And Jors is a Herald."

:From the mouths of babes.:

"My point exactly." Gran grinned triumphantly and whacked Jors on the shins with her cane.

When Annamarin frowned, Jors shook his head.

"Try again when you're older." he told her later when they were walking away from the settlement, down the track toward Greenhaven.

"It's *tragic* she doesn't understand!"

"It's a little annoying," he admitted. "But, in the end, I know who I am."

:Outside the palisades.: Jors jumped as Gervais tail slapped against the back of his legs. *:And staying away solves nothing,:* the Companion added.

:Not every problem can be solved. Or needs to be.: Out loud he said, "There'll be Bards visiting this summer."

"How do you know?"

"I'm a Herald." He grinned. "I know things. And, in a couple of years, I'll see you in Haven."

:You hate staying in Haven.:

:I didn't say I was going to stay. I just said I'd see her there.:

:And then tragically abandon her?:

:Stop it.:

"You don't look so sad when you talk to him in your head." She planted her feet and struck a dramatic pose. "This is as far as I'm allowed to go. Can I hug you? I'm clean."

"You could hug me if you were dirty," he told her.

She shook her head, one plait falling loose. "That would be so tragically wrong."

Hugging Annamarin had nothing to do with being

seven or ten or fourteen. When he hugged her, as her cousin and a Herald, he hugged the future, not the past.

:You didn't tell your grandmother she shouldn't write to the Dean,: Gervais pointed out when Jors was in the saddle and there was nothing but open road before them.

:I know. I was afraid it would only encourage her.:

Gervais snorted. *:You were* afraid*.:*

:That too. But the last thing I need is Gran and the Dean starting up a correspondence.: Jors twisted and looked back toward the settlement. Annamarin must have reached the end of the track because he could just hear the geese protesting her return. *This is what made me.* He settled back in the saddle. *This is what I am.*

Birth family. Found family.

:Come on, let's go home.:

The Watchman's Ball

Fiona Patton

Although the winter solstice wasn't for another fortnight, the nights had already turned cold, laying a tracery of frost over the streets of the capital like a veil of croqueted lace. Leaning against the counter of Ismy Browne's saddlery shop, Sergeant Hektor Dann of the Haven City Watch sipped a mug of hot tea, noting the extra touch of honey with a smile.

"S'good," he said. "Sweet."

Ismy cast him a shrewd glance. "You looked as if you could use it," she noted. "Late night?"

He nodded. "Stood the first watch. Would've stood the second, but Aiden made me go home."

"Your brother's a wise man," she replied in a stern tone. "You can't do a proper day's work if you're also tryin' to do a proper night's work."

"They needed extra hands. It was the first night of the Watchman's Ball." When Ismy looked confused, he smiled apologetically. "Sorry. I forgot, only the Watch calls it that. It's the first new moon's eve before winter, an' every year 'round this time things . . .well, things happen."

"What kind of things?"

"People runnin' naked through the streets kind of things."

"You mean like the Lightning?" she asked in an exaggerated tone.

"Like him, yeah."

"Oh, please, Hektor, don't tell me he's actually real."

"He's real, all right. He's been doin' it for decades, but no one's ever caught him. No one's even got a good enough look at him to identify him, but every year we get dozens of reports of him all across Haven. The bettin's four to one we'll never catch him, an' the Watchhouses bet each other on how many sightings we get every year, even every night. We had more'n seven on our patch this night last year alone. He's a wily one, that's for sure."

"My granther used to say that he was as fast as a streak of lightning; that's how he got his name," Ismy noted. "He said he even saw him once at the bottom of Anvil's Close. I used to peer through my bedroom shutters when I was a little trying to catch a glimpse of him, but of course I never did."

"I did."

Her eyes widened. "You did not? Really?"

He nodded, enjoying her reaction. "Once when I was first promoted up from runner to night watch constable. Uncle Daz an' me saw him turnin' the corner south of the Watchhouse, but by the time we got there, he'd vanished."

"Anyway," he continued, setting the mug down on the counter. "Da named these three nights the Watchman's Ball on account of the Lightning leading us a merry chase all night long, you see?"

She nodded.

"Problem is," he continued, "just the thought of seein' him sends folk out into the streets, an' some of 'em carry on and pull all kinds of antics an' pranks in his name. It's never been too much, but it's getting a bit more every year, and the new Captain wants him caught."

"Well, I should hope so," Ismy agreed primly. "On a cold night like last night, he'd catch his death.

"And don't you laugh at me, Hektor Dann," she admonished as he gave her an amused look. "If he's been doin' it for decades like you say, he must be an old man by now." She took up the mug, wiping the ring away with a flick of her cloth before pushing him toward the door. "Now, off you go to work. And no standing any night watch tonight either. You just leave that up to your younger brothers; that's their job, not yours, *Sergeant Dann*."

"Yeah, yeah, all right, I'm goin'." He paused on the threshold. "Can I come by an' see you after all this new moon's nonsense is over?" he asked, suddenly hesitant.

She nodded, equally shyly. "Do you want to come for supper?"

"I'd like that."

"It's just stew."

"I like stew."

"And biscuits, you know."

"I like biscuits too."

"Good, well . . ."

They stood in awkward silence until the city bells began to toll the hour, then Hektor shook himself. "Good, well . . . supper. After. Yeah."

He turned and headed quickly up the street, ignoring the older merchants leaning from their doors and windows. A few called out greetings, a few asked if he'd caught the Lightning yet, but most just smiled knowingly as Ismy watched until he'd turned the corner and disappeared from view.

There was a crowd of watchmen, both on duty and off, gathered about the night sergeant's desk when he arrived at the Iron Street Watchhouse a few moments later. It parted for him eagerly, but Sergeant Jons took his time collecting his reports and putting them into two neat piles before glancing over at the much younger Day Sergeant.

"Sergeant Dann," he said formally.

"Sergeant Jons."

"The night's incident reports are as follows. Four counts of fighting. One outside the King's Arms. You'll know all about that one yourself, I expect, what with you and Aiden bringing 'em in yourselves. They're still here, and the report's are still to be filed. I figured since the Day Watch Sergeant made the arrest, the Day Watch Sergeant could do up the paperwork."

He glanced over the report at Hektor much as a schoolmaster might, but when Hektor gave him an even look in response, he retidied his papers. A ripple of annoyance passed through the crowd of watchmen, which he pointedly ignored. "Where was I? Oh, yes, fighting," he continued. "Two domestic disturbances. No charges laid and no one taken into custody although Holly Poll did throw a chamber pot at Constables Jakon and Raik Dann." He waited until the general laughter and ribbing at Hektor's younger brothers died down before continuing. "But since it turned out that she was actually aiming at her husband, they let her off with a warning."

"Decent of 'em," someone at the back shouted.

"Only 'cause it was empty," Jakon groused.

"Only 'cause you're scared of Holly Poll."

The laughter erupted again.

"One count of burglary at the Hillman Mill," Sergeant Jons continued in a louder voice. "Caught in the act. Silly fool was trying to lead out two donkeys at once with predictable results. Apparently he'll be in hospital for another day or two." He gave an unsympathetic sniff before continuing.

"Five counts of public drunkenness. Two of the combatants became . . ." He lifted his head, lips pursed as if to find just the right word, "belligerent, so the charges were raised to resisting arrest.

"Three counts of public urination, one of which led to an altercation with Corporal Wright when the suspect made his opinion of the arrest clear by attempting to urinate on him . . ."

Again he paused to allow the laughter to die down. "One count of sleeping on public property. That would be old Ivar," he said in a quiet aside to Hektor. "He's in the back having a good breakfast. Turn him loose whenever you like. After lunch maybe."

Hektor nodded, and Sergeant Jons set the first pile of reports down with great ceremony. All eyes followed his movements as he lifted the second. "So . . ." he began, settling comfortably against his chair back. "Let's us see now, the Watchman's Ball reports. What to get to first, eh? Ah, yes . . ." He glanced up as the gathered leaned forward, waiting with a stern expression until they fell back into a sort of loose parade rest. "Clay Marcher's gran and granther were at it again this year."

"Runnin' amok were they?" the same person from the back shouted as Constable Marcher's face flushed red.

"Running amok, no, not at all," Sergeant Jons answered. "Dancing amok, yes. Without benefit of clothing, again, yes. But they came quietly after the dance was done and were escorted home without incident. Clay, you might want to head over there on your break and retrieve Constable Farane's cloak."

"Yes, Sarge."

"Right, where was I?" the sergeant continued before he could be interrupted by more laughter. "Fourteen sets of undergarments retrieved from various trees and fences, some of which were quite . . ." Again he lifted his head and pursed his lips as if to find just the right word. "Finely made. That's up from ten sets last year in case anyone's keepin' score." He pointedly ignored a number of watchmen exchanging money. "As no one ever comes forward to claim their property, they will be donated as has become tradition. I'm not sure to which temple this year." He glanced up with a rare smile. "I think we'd best leave that up to the Captain."

His words were greeted with a ripple of snickering and a number of surreptitious glances toward the Captain's closed office door.

"Seven people apprehended runnin' through the streets without benefit of clothing," he continued.

The gathered leaned forward again.

"Students, the lot of them," he finished to general disappointment. "Two of 'em Bardic Trainees from the Collegium." Again, more money changed hands. "All reclothed, lectured, and escorted home again. These incidents are also up this year by . . ."

"Two, Sarge," Watchhouse Runner Padreic, Hektor's youngest brother, supplied.

"Two."

"An' it took some doin' to get the last one," Raik noted sourly. "He climbed right up atop the statue of King Valdemar and got his stupid self stuck. Had to go up and fetch him down. Took the better part of an hour."

"Just about froze his manhood right off him, the silly bugger," Jakon muttered.

"Just about froze mine," Raik added. "Had half a mind to leave him up there."

"If I might continue before the Captain returns from his morning meeting with the Breakneedle Street Watch Captain?" Sergeant Jons said loudly enough to quiet them. "Sightings of the Lightning . . ."

All eyes turned expectantly.

"None."

There was stunned silence.

"What? None at all?" Corporal Wright asked.

"None at all."

The gathered slumped as if the air had been let out of them.

The entire capital passed the day in an air of dejection and speculation. Even those who had declared their disdain for the Lightning in the past were seen standing about with glum expressions. Much of the talk was of his past antics, and most agreed that nothing—not storms, not fog, and certainly not the Watch—could have stopped him. He must have been "topped."

As Hektor and Aiden headed for a local pie shop at noon, the older of the two Danns shook his head.

"I s'pose that's it then," he noted.

"Two rabbit, thanks, Jess. What's it, then?" Hektor asked, handing a pie over.

Aiden accepted it with a grimace. "The Lightning." he declared, shaking his fingers to cool them. "He's been showin' up on the first night every year for . . . years, and suddenly nothing. He's topped, like they say."

"Makes sense." Hektor blew on his own pie with a reflective expression. "Ismy says if he's been doin' it for that long, he must be really old. He probably is topped."

Aiden grinned at him. "Ismy huh? So that's where you snuck off to so early this mornin'. Ma was wonderin'."

Hektor shot him a dark look. "Liar. I told Ma where I was goin'."

"All right, I was wonderin," Aiden admitted still grinning.

"I just wanted to see her before my shift, is all."

"And?"

"And what?"

Aiden shook his head in disgust. "If you have to ask me, you didn't ask her. I told Suli you didn't have the bollocks. She owes me a pennybit. Do you two even have a proper understandin' yet?"

Hektor frowned at him. "I don't know," he answered

slowly. "I think so. She asked me to supper after all this was all done."

"Well, that's a start. Maybe she'll ask for you."

"Jerk."

"Coward."

"Eat your pie."

"You gonna stand night watch?"

Hektor shrugged. "Probably. Some of it anyway."

"Waste of time. He's topped."

"The Captain still has the extra hands on just in case."

"Waste of money."

"Maybe, but it's not like we couldn't use it. Beside, there's all the other idiots runnin' *amok* out there to deal with."

Aiden finished his pie with a grimace. "Well, they better get it outta their systems early then," he growled, a martial light growing in his eyes. "'Cause come midnight tomorrow, most of us are gonna be damned ugly."

The rest of the day passed quietly, as if the entire capital were holding it's breath, waiting for nightfall. Waiting to see if the Lightning would make an appearance or if he really was topped as most people believed.

Hektor arrived at the tenement house where he shared an upstairs flat with four generations of his family as the city bells tolled six. He figured he had just enough time to eat and catch a couple hours' sleep before he was due back at the Watchhouse. Jakon and Raik, on regular night duty, should be up and out of the small bedroom they shared with him and Padreic by now. He took the three flights of stairs two at a time, already anticipating the bowl of his mother's soup and his own warm blankets.

He met the local herbalist coming down.

"Sergeant."

"Sir."

"I've just been to see Thomar."

Hektor felt himself grow still. "Oh?" he managed.

"Your granther needs to see a Healer," the man said bluntly. "An actual Healer."

"Why? What's happened?"

The herbalist ran a hand through his hair in an impatient gesture. "He had a dizzy spell and a bit of a fall. Nothing too serious. A bump on the head," he added as Hektor's expression went from worried to alarmed. "Years of breathing in the droppings from those messenger birds of his has compromised his lungs, and a packet of herbs once a week isn't going to be enough to set things right at his age. He needs to see a Healer, but he's resisting."

"He'll say it's too dear," Hektor ventured.

"Rubbish. He's just being a stubborn old fool. I say this in all respect, Hektor. I've known Thomar for forty years. He was friends with my own father as I was with yours, and I'll tell you what I told him. He needs to see a Healer soon or he'll die." His voice dropped. "It may even be too late."

He straightened. "I was sorry about Egan," he added as he headed down the stairs. "I miss your Da, as I'm sure you all do."

"Thanks."

The flat was in an uproar when he arrived. Padreic was pacing the front room, squeezing the pig's bladder ball he was forever mending in his hands, while their only sister, Kasiath, was sitting by the coal stove, her eyes red from trying not to cry. Jakon and Raik were standing beside her, clearly unsure of how to comfort her beyond their physical presence. Everyone looked up with relief when Hektor entered.

"Where're the others?" he asked, casting a swift glance across the kitchen to the small pantry they'd converted for their grandfather's use.

"Suli took the littles off to visit her mother," Padreic answered. "Aiden's not home yet, an' Ma's gone to the Healers to get someone to come by and see to Granther."

"Granther don't need no one seein' to him!" Thomar's weak but determined voice carried easily across the flat. "He just needs some blasted quiet!"

Padreic chewed at his bottom lip. "I thought I might go down to Rosie's, Hek," he said in a hushed voice. "If that's all right. I can stay though," he added quickly. "If you need things fetched, or somethin' . . ."

Hektor shook his head. "No, you go. Just stay indoors so I know where to find you." Both of them tried hard not to glance over at the pantry again.

"We'll head out too now that you're home," Raik said.

"Where will you be?"

The two younger brothers shared a look. "Watchman's Arms if you need us."

Hektor nodded. "Kas?"

She looked up. "I'll stay."

"All right then." Hektor made a show of screwing up his courage. "So, let's go see if we can talk some sense into a cantankerous old man."

The pantry was just big enough to house a narrow pallet down the center. Thomar lay propped up on a pile of pillows, wrapped in shawls and blankets, and looking as birdlike as one of his own messenger pigeons. He gave Hektor a narrow-eyed look as his grandson pushed the curtain aside. "Don't start," he wheezed. "It's too dear, and it's not necessary."

"The herbalist says otherwise, Granther."

"The herbalist is a . . ." Thomar paused as Kasiath pushed past her brother and tucked herself on the bottom corner of the pallet. ". . . nagging little fart," he finished. "I know what's what; he don't. So . . ." He turned to Kasiath. "D'you tell him your news, girl?"

She shook her head. "There hasn't been time, Granther."

"So tell him now. It's good news. News to celebrate."

Hektor glanced down at his little sister. "I could use some good news," he prompted with a smile.

She nodded gravely. "The Watchhouse Messenger Bird Master came by today," she said. "An' he offered me an apprenticeship."

"That's great Kassie. Another Dann in the Watch, sort of. Um . . . how much is it gonna cost?"

"That's all taken care of," Thomar snapped. "Me an' Logan have an understandin'. About that, an' about other things too. So, go on, tell him the rest."

"That's not for certain, Granther."

"Nonsense."

"An' it's too dear."

"You let us decide on what's too dear, you just tell your brother what Logan said."

"He thinks he might be able to get me into some classes at the Collegium," Kasiath relented. "He says he thinks I might have Animal Mindspeech, well, Bird-speech anyway. Maybe."

"Of course you do," Thomar interjected again. "Any-one with half a brain coulda seen that years ago." He began to cough, waving off his two grandchildren as they leaned forward. "Now you get downstairs and tell Paddy to go chase your Ma down afore she wastes time and money on some high and mighty Healer what'll charge more'n a month's rent just to tell me to stay in bed.

"I won't die afore you get back, I promise," he added as she hesitated. "I wanna talk to Hektor alone. Go on now, there's a good girl.

"An' you don't be frettin' about any cost of Kassie's apprenticeship," he said, once he and Hektor were alone. "I've been puttin' money aside with Logan ever since she were three years old. Like I said, it was obvious to anyone with half a brain that she had a gift with birds. An' when I'm gone, I want what little money I've saved up to pay for those classes of hers. You understand?"

"Sure but . . ."

"Don't you sure but me, boy. My time's soon; I know it an' so should you. I won't have anyone's hard-earned pay going to some Healer just to be told it. It's a waste of money."

Hektor smiled. "It's funny. That's just what Aiden said today about working a double shift on account of the Lightning."

"Oh? Why?"

"Well, he never showed up last night."

Thomar gave a disdainful sniff. "I'm not surprised," he stated.

"Why?"

The sound of the door opening and Aiden's feet clumping through the front room interrupted them. "Get your brother in here," Thomar ordered. "I got somethin' to tell you both."

The night shift passed with the usual number of students running amok and sets of undergarments being laid out for the Lightning's approval. Clay Marcher's grandparents made another brief appearance, this time in their nightclothes as a concession to the cold, but once again there was no sign of the famous nude runner himself. After the Night Sergeant had made his reports, the four oldest Danns met in Hektor's small office with the door firmly shut behind them.

Both Jakon and Raik stared at their older brothers with their mouths open.

"Granther was the Lightning?" Raik stammered. "You're not serious."

Hektor raised his hands. "Him an' Great Uncle Daz, that's what he says."

"He's pullin' your leg," Jakon declared flatly. "There's no possible way. They were Watchmen."

"He says they got a bet on one new moon's eve walking the night beat when they were about your age," Aiden said. "Uncle Daz dared Granther to run past the Watchhouse naked. That's how it started."

"He says eventually six other Watchmen from all across the city, all the same age . . ." Hektor started.

"Young an' stupid," Aiden supplied.

"Came on board. All sworn to secrecy. Granther says he's the last. The two before him died last spring."

Jakon scratched his chin. "I guess that would be why there were always so many sightin's of him," he noted.

"An' why the Lightning never showed up this year," Raik continued.

"An' why he won't never show up again," Hektor finished for them. "Granther's too old an' too sick to carry on like that any more."

The two younger brothers cast each other an equally speculative glance, and Aiden shot them both a sharp look.

"Don't even think about it," he ordered.

"Think about what?"

The looks turned to expressions of aggrieved innocence, and Aiden just scowled at them.

"You know what. Don't. I mean it, both of you."

"'Course not," Raik protested. "After all, Granther an' Uncle Daz were the two *oldest* Danns in their generation. It's hardly *our* place to take their place, now is it? It's just a pity it's over, is all."

"A real shame," Jakon agreed. "Folks looked forward to the Lightning all year. He was like a market fair all rolled into one man."

"Eight men."

"Yeah, eight men. It would take a lot to fill those shoes."

"Yep, he was a city tradition."

"A family tradition as it turns out."

"So, let him be someone else's family tradition," Hektor replied. "An' I don't want this getting out, neither," he continued. "Not to anyone, an' that means the family too. The last thing we need is Paddy runnin' naked through the streets in some fool quest to honor Granther. What with him bein' so sick an' all," he added pensively. "Yeah, I guess it is kind of a shame, it's over. Granther's just not up to it, the silly old fool."

Jakon cocked an eyebrow at Raik. "'Course we won't tell anyone," he replied. "It's Dann business, isn't it? An' Paddy's far too young, anyway. No one'd ever believe it if they caught a glimpse of him."

"He'd just get his stupid self caught," Raik agreed.

"So, that's it, then," Jakon declared. "We're sworn to secrecy."

"All of us. Right Hek?"

"Right."

"Aiden?"

The oldest Dann brother looked from them to Hektor with a deepening scowl. "I know what you're tryin' to do," he growled. "But yeah, we're sworn to secrecy."

Satisfied, the two younger Danns sauntered through the door, leaving the two older Danns to stare silently at each other.

"So that's it then," Aiden repeated.

Hektor nodded. "That's it."

"Right. That's it."

Two nights later, Hektor sat in Ismy Browne's small kitchen, wiping up the last of the stew in his bowl with a generous piece of biscuit. Ismy set a pie down in the center of the table before joining him.

"I was sorry to hear about Thomar," she said solemnly. "It was just last night wasn't it?"

"Early this morning."

"How are the family doin'?"

He sat back. "Kassie's takin' it the hardest. And Paddy too, I guess. It's only been a couple of months since Da died. But he had a chance to talk to us all, to pass things on afore he went, you know. It was a comfort."

"Yes, I was pleased to hear about Kassie's apprenticeship. Your Ma must be very proud." She smiled at his confused expression. "There're no secrets in Haven, Hektor," she said. "Especially in the Watch. You lot gossip more'n a gaggle of laundrywomen."

"I suppose that's so. Sometimes anyway." He stared into space for a moment, then shook himself. "The funeral's tomorrow morning with a get-together afterwards at the watchhouse. Do you think you might be able to come?"

"Yes, I think so. Jen can watch the shop. It's time she took on more responsibility." Ismy busied herself cutting the pie into wedges. "She an' Shea've come to an understandin'," she said in a conversational tone. "You remember Shea? My late husband's brother? He took over the saddlery workshop after Quinn died." When he nodded, she continued. "They're gettin' married this spring. I'm thinkin' they should move into the main room. It's more appropriate for two. An' of course they'll want the whole flat when they start havin' littles. It's not really big enough for them an' me."

"Oh? Do you, um, think that might be soon?" Hektor asked, suddenly feeling too enclosed in the warm kitchen.

"Oh, yes. Like I said, they've come to an understandin'. Of course, she knew it long afore he did, but that's often the way."

She collected the bowls and took them over to the sink. "Suli tells me she an' Aiden have taken the flat below yours," she mentioned.

"Yeah. They move down in a couple of weeks." He took a deep breath. "That'll leave our main room free as well. You know, if there were maybe another understandin' to come to. You know. Maybe."

"Do you think there might be?" she asked without turning around.

"I think maybe, yeah. That is, if you do. Do you?"

She finally turned with an exasperated smile. "Like I said, it's often the way." When he continued to look uncertain, she shook her head. "That means yes, I do think there might be an understandin' to come to. Honestly. Did you want a bit of cheese?"

"What?"

"Cheese. With your pie?"

"Oh, yeah, sure, thanks."

She cut a large piece off a round in the pantry.

"That's a bit?" he asked, bemused when she set it down in front of him with an equally large piece of pie.

"You look as if you could use it. You look tired. Again."

"Yeah, well, it's been a rough few days."

"So I hear. They say the Lightning finally made an appearance last night."

He started. "You heard . . . ?"

"I did. You didn't see him?" she asked pointedly.

"Uh . . . why would I?"

She turned, hands on hips. "I know you stood night watch last night, Hektor Dann, so don't try to deny it. I told you, there are no secrets in Haven especially in the Watch. So." She folded her arms in a businesslike gesture. "Are you all through with this Watchman's Ball foolishness for another year?"

Lifting a piece of pie to his mouth, he stared at it for a long time before looking up.

"Yeah," he said. "For another year."

Judgment Day

Nancy Asire

"So, Levron, are you looking forward to returning home?"

Levron glanced at the man who rode at his side. Perran was a traveling judge, representative of the justiciary of Karse, its eyes, ears, and judgment passed by one who rightfully upheld the laws of the Son of the Sun and, more importantly, the laws of Vkandis Sun Lord. Perran was all that Levron was not: tall, with dark, hawkish features molded from the classic Karsite version of male beauty that would stand out in any crowd, even if he did not wear the dark robes of a judge. Levron could only contrast his own looks with that of his companion. At best, he would become lost in the same crowd. He had no memorable features, though he was hardly ill to look upon. And this was his strength. He could move among people and leave no lasting impression.

He was, he freely admitted, a friend of sorts to Perran, and he had served the judge many times by riding ahead to the scene of a trial and losing himself in the town or village. From this vantage point, he had been able to gather information about the accusers and accused that might have become lost in a formal trial. The insights he gathered he passed to Perran, and, in many cases, that knowledge had swayed a decision that otherwise might have been erroneous.

"It's been a while," he admitted, flicking his reins at a fly determined to light on his horse's neck. "But this time, I'll be of no use to you at the trial. There's a good chance some people in Streamwood will remember me."

"Ah, well," Perran said. "This case doesn't seem, on its face, to need your talents. You might, however, know the litigants involved."

Levron snorted. "I *used* to know them. Everyone's aware how time can change people."

"Time deals differently with us all. I'll still need your observations, Levron. You know, or *knew*, these people at one time. Maybe they haven't changed as much as you think."

"Possibly. The two men involved were acquaintances years back. The woman . . . she and I also knew each other. Her reputation was well-acknowledged around town."

"A bit of a flirt, if I have my facts straight."

"Oh, yes." Levron nodded his head. "From her earliest days."

"So the two of you weren't close, then."

"At one time I fancied I could become more than merely a passing friend." He laughed, though the laughter sounded a bit hollow to his own ears. "She came from a family far more important than mine. And she never let me, or anyone else, forget her status."

"Well," Perran said, "we'll find out exactly how she fits into this case. I still think you might be of more use to me than you imagine. You say people in town will remember you, though, by your own admission, it's been quite some time since you've returned home"

Levron briefly bowed his head. "As you know, both my parents have been dead for years, and I had no brothers or sisters, no extended family in Streamwood. That's one of the reasons I left for Sunhame, thinking I could make something of myself in the capital."

"And so you have. Assistant to a circuit judge is a respected position."

The two guards following behind, fully armed and appearing quite able to handle any situation that grew out of control, laughed at some joke passed between them. Levron closed his eyes briefly. The road hadn't changed since the last time he passed over it, only then riding in the opposite direction. The scents of the fields on either side were the same, the fall of the sunlight on those fields. A fleeting memory surfaced, taking him back to the days he lived in this region of Karse, of a childhood and young adulthood spent coming and going in the area. Despite his effort to remain unaffected, he admitted this would be no easy homecoming. His parents lay buried on the hill behind the chapel. The friends he left behind would not be the same. And he had changed as well.

Someone long ago said you could never go home again. Less than a candlemark's ride ahead lay possible confirmation of that saying. He wasn't certain what he would find, or even what he expected. If nothing else, his return to Streamwood would prove interesting, to say the least.

Perran stood in the center of the room he and Levron had been granted at the inn. It was obviously one of the best, reserved for those who could afford the price. Naturally, he would not be charged during his stay, which he hoped would not be lengthy. His two guards occupied the room next door, smaller but still more than accommodating. The citizens of Streamwood had gone out of the way to make his visit a pleasant one.

He settled in one of the chairs by the open windows, watching Levron unpack their belongings. Levron was trying his best to appear unconcerned, but Perran knew better. This journey wore on him more than he would admit. Not that Perran could ignore the significance of Levron's return. Though he thought he would be of no help since he was known in town, Perran considered the benefits of having him as a companion.

"So," he said, leaning back in his chair. "Did you see anyone you know?"

Levron paused, shaking the folds from Perran's formal robes. "A few," he admitted.

"I thought so. I noticed several people look twice in your direction as we rode by."

"When is the trial to begin?"

"Tomorrow, midmorning. Here is what I want you to do."

Levron's face went blank. "But I won't be able to disappear into the woodwork; too many people know me."

"That's my hope. We have the rest of the afternoon and evening. Since it would only seem natural, I'd like you to go out and wander around a while. See what you can find. Surely, there are a few people you might want to contact since some time has passed since you left Streamwood. I don't think anyone would find that out of place."

An uncomfortable expression tightened Levron's eyes. "I suppose. But they'll all be aware I ride with you. That fact alone won't loosen their tongues."

Perran laughed quietly. "On the contrary. I think they'll be interested in asking what you've been doing since you left and how you ended up in my company. Once you start talking, I'll wager they'll lower whatever guard they've erected out of sheer curiosity."

And so it was that Levron entered a tavern he'd frequented before he left Streamwood. True to Perran's supposition, several people nodded to him as he took his place at a table situated toward the rear of the room. He requested a cup of ale and sat quietly, nursing his drink. A few former associates stopped by, exchanged brief greetings, and questioned him as to his new station in life. But for the most part, he was left alone. It was apparent no one was overly interested in a former resident of the town, though he was certain word of his arrival with Perran had begun to spread.

"Levron!"

The familiar but strangely unfamiliar voice interrupted his thoughts. He looked up from his cup into the face of a tall man who stood by the table, a smile on his narrow face. For a moment, the features of the newcomer wavered between that of years past and that of the present; the man's name, however, was all too familiar.

"Barro." Levron indicated an empty chair. Memories flashed through his mind, not all of which were particularly pleasant.

"I couldn't believe it when I saw you," Barro said, waving to the barmaid for a cup of ale. "You've come up in the world."

Levron made a dismissing gesture. "Perhaps. Assistant to a traveling judge is hardly an exalted position."

"So you say." Barro took a long sip of his drink. "You know I'm to go to trial tomorrow?"

"Yes."

"And do you know why?"

"Not really. Only in the broadest sense."

"Well, let me give you the details. Perhaps you can offer some advice."

"That," Levron said, keeping his voice expressionless, "is the last thing I can do. I'm only a judge's assistant. I don't know the law."

Barro's eyes narrowed. "Not even for an old friend?"

"Not even for an old friend. As I said, I don't know the law. I'd hate to give you advice that wouldn't help and might harm."

"Then hear me out and maybe you'll change your mind. You know Trika?"

Know Trika? Levron managed a shrug. "Of course."

"Here's what happened. I've been half in love with her for years."

"You and the rest of Streamwood," Levron observed, uncomfortably aware he could count himself in that crowd.

"Hunh. I own a fabric shop and haven't done badly for myself. I thought I might be of standing enough to court Trika." His face darkened. "But she was already being courted."

"Let me guess," Levron interrupted, unable to stay disinterested. "Haivel."

"Haivel. That coddled papa's boy!" Barro swallowed the rest of his ale, his eyes gone hard. "He was always around her, pestering her father for more and more access to her company."

"And you?"

"I kept my distance, making it obvious I was interested as well. In fact, I went out of my way to give her father discounts on any fabric his wife wanted to purchase. I was never overt in my actions and, as they say, patience pays off. After spending most of her time with Haivel, Trika decided she preferred to see me."

Levron could tell where this was going. He knew all three individuals involved: Barro, the man who worked tirelessly to better himself; Haivel, whose parents had given him a small shop where he had set himself up as a scribe; and, of course, Trika, the beauty of Streamwood. Trika the Tease. Trika, the woman who, adhering to the customs of Karse, had been allowed to be courted by men her father deemed worthy.

"You know Haivel," Barro continued, lifting his empty cup in the barmaid's direction. "He didn't take this well at all. The more time Trika spent with me, the more upset Haivel grew. I think he was eaten up with jealousy. And finally, he couldn't accept the way things were and damaged my latest shipment of cloth."

"Oh? And you saw this?"

"I did. He came around just before dark. I was finishing the last of my orders. I'd gone to the rear of the shop when I heard the door open. I came back to the front in time to see Haivel throw a bucket of paint over the latest bolt of fine cloth I'd ordered from Sunhame! You have no idea how much that cloth cost. It was ruined. Haivel laughed at me—*laughed at me*—and ran out of the shop."

Levron leaned back in his chair. "I'm surprised. I didn't think Haivel was that sort."

"Well, he is. You haven't been in town for years and haven't seen the change in him. I immediately went to the authorities and made my report."

"Did they arrest Haivel?"

Barro's face darkened. "They talked to him. He denied everything. He said he had a witness who would swear he was nowhere near my shop that night."

"And his father took his side?"

"Of course. Dear Haivel, beloved only son, who couldn't have done anything so dishonest."

"So you're taking the case to court."

Barro squared his shoulders. "I am. Now, old friend, any advice?"

Old friend? Levron all but laughed. Barro had never been a friend . . . an off-and-on comrade, but never a friend. In fact, when he and Barro had been young boys, Barro had been somewhat of a bully, with Levron taking most of the abuse when the two of them were together.

"No advice other than to tell the truth. Judge Perran is quite adept at knowing who's lying and who's not. As I've told you, I'm not a legalist. I *do* know a person who lies before him is in worse trouble than if he had not."

"Some help you are," Barro muttered. "I guess that's all I can expect. After all, *you* aren't the judge, your master is."

Levron smiled, despite the veiled insult. "I wish you the best, Barro. Destruction of property is a crime and should be punished."

"You're damned right!" Barro shoved his chair away from the table, tossed down a copper coin, and stood. "I suppose I'll see you again." And with that, he turned and made his way toward the tavern's door.

Levron's shoulders slumped, and he relaxed somewhat, amazed that this meeting had made him so tense. Once again, he felt the pressure of memories from the past. Barro, Haivel, and Trika. He knew, or *thought* he knew, them all. And, he admitted, he was growing more than relieved he no longer lived in Streamwood.

Perran looked up when Levron entered the room they shared. From the expression on his assistant's face, he had not spent a pleasant time out in the town.

"Well, did you see anyone you know?"

Levron frowned. "A few. No one I considered close. I did see one of the people you're to judge tomorrow."

"Oh?"

"Barro."

"Ah, the fellow whose cloth was ruined, who reported it was done by Haivel."

"Yes."

"That's interesting. A man by the name of Haivel came here looking for you. I can't believe you didn't pass him on your way in." Perran watched Levron closely. "You might want to go out and see if he's still around. What did Barro have to say?"

"What didn't he have to say! He told me the whole story, how Haivel ruined a bolt of expensive cloth by dumping a bucket of paint on it. All out of jealousy . . .

over, of course, Trika. The two of them are trying to court her. She'd spent all her time with Haivel and then started seeing Barro. He wanted advice, which I refused to give him. We didn't part on the best of terms."

Perran nodded. What Levron told him matched information he'd received before he had agreed to judge this case. However, a new twist had arisen when Levron had gone out earlier and Haivel had come looking for him, information Perran wasn't yet ready to share. Let Levron find out himself, unprepared for what he would hear. Not being forewarned, his reaction would be unlikely to arouse suspicion of prior knowledge. This, in itself, could aid his observations later. *If* he could find Haivel.

And the way events had transpired so far, Perran was certain Levron would do just that.

It didn't take long for Levron to locate Haivel. The inn sported a few tables and chairs to the side of the building where, when weather permitted, people could sit and drink or share a dinner. Agreeing with Perran, Levron was surprised Haivel had missed his recent arrival. He drew a calming breath as he approached another person from his past.

"Levron!" Haivel smiled and nodded his greeting. "Sit, sit. It's been a long time."

"That it has," Levron acknowledged. "So how has life been treating you?"

"I've done well. You know I'm a scribe. There's a good life to be made writing for folk who don't have the skill."

"I can only imagine."

"So you're assistant to Judge Perran, are you? You obviously made something of yourself when you left Streamwood for Sunhame."

"I did, and I've never regretted it."

"You know I'm going to trial tomorrow." Once the

polite pleasantries had passed, Haivel jumped straight to the point.

Levron briefly closed his eyes. "And I won't give you any advice if you ask for it. I can't."

Haivel drew back slightly in his chair, his handsome face darkened. "And why is that?"

Fresh memories of his conversation with Barro surfaced, but he refused to let Haivel know the two of them had spoken a short time before.

"I'm slightly aware of the case, but," Levron repeated, "I don't know the law, and I can't offer any advice save to tell the truth."

Haivel snorted. "Well, let me tell you, if Barro thinks he's going to have a judgment entered against me, I'm countering him with my own accusation."

"Oh?" Levron blinked in surprise. "And what did Barro do that you're going after him in court?"

"He came into my shop one afternoon, in broad daylight mind you, and took a knife to an entire shipment of paper sitting on the counter before I could stop him. Cut it into pieces! Do you have any idea how much paper costs?"

Or what the going price is for a bolt of fine cloth? Levron shook his head in disbelief. "I couldn't guess, but it probably wouldn't be cheap."

"It's not! I don't have any idea what possessed him! He's been acting strange ever since . . ."

Levron waited, refusing to lead Haivel to further explanation.

"Here's the problem," Haivel said, spreading his hands. "You know Trika?"

"I *knew* her," Levron admitted. "Years ago."

"I was courting her, seriously courting her. Her father evidently thought well of me. And then, for some reason, she dropped me like a hot rock and started seeing Barro."

"And?"

"Someone vandalized cloth in Barro's shop. He swears it was me and reported the crime to the authorities. But I have a witness I wasn't near his shop. And, days later, he came into *my* shop and destroyed my paper."

"That's odd. In broad daylight, too. Do you have a witness?"

"Only my own two eyes. I can't let him get away with this." Haivel drew a deep breath. "Are you certain you can't—"

"I can't offer any advice except what I've already told you," Levron said. "Speak the truth. Judge Perran will be able to tell who's lying and who's not."

Haivel shrugged. "I understand, though I hoped you might be able to help a friend, for old time's sake."

Old friend again. Do the two of them truly believe we were friends?

"I've explained why I can't. All I can do is wish you the best of luck. One word of caution, however . . . don't dismiss Judge Perran as just another traveling judge. What I can tell you is this: he's one of the best, and anyone who thinks otherwise makes a huge mistake."

The transformation that turned Perran from traveling companion to circuit judge never ceased to amaze Levron, though he'd witnessed it many times. Seated a few paces away from the table Perran sat behind, Levron could see why people could become awed. Clad in his dark robes, the heavy gold chain of his office glittering on his chest, Perran exemplified the authority of the justiciary and, as every citizen of Karse knew, stood as the legal hand of the Son of the Sun.

After speaking with Haivel, Levron had related their conversation to Perran in exacting detail, his expected duty as Perran's assistant. He had watched Perran's face go still as all the legal ramifications of the two stories swirled about in his mind. And now, today, those thoughts would be turned into action.

Barro and Haivel had taken chairs before the judge's table, neither meeting the other man's eyes. From his vantage point at the front of the room, Levron had a good view of the people who had come to watch the trial. A few latecomers had arrived and, much to Levron's dismay, Trika had entered the room accompanied by her father.

The years had been kind to her. She still possessed a breathtaking beauty, but Levron sensed something else immediately. The hint of coldness lurked in her eyes, a calculating expression she tried to hide by keeping her gaze modestly lowered. Ah, yes . . . Trika the Tease. Levron could imagine what had driven Barro and Haivel to their crimes. Trika was the source of those misdeeds. He was certain of it.

Perran rapped the table three times, and the room grew silent.

"This court is now in session," Perran said, his face solemn. "What is said before me is seen and heard by myself as representative of the Son of the Sun *and* Vkandis Sun Lord. Every word spoken to me is given under oath. State falsehood at your peril."

Unwillingly, Levron turned his attention to Trika again. Though she maintained her modest demeanor, she looked first to Haivel and then to Barro. In a flash, he knew what motivated her and felt a little sickened by the knowledge. His faith in Perran's abilities as a judge was absolute: the truth behind Barro and Haivel's quarrel would be brought to light.

And not a moment too soon, for the sake of everyone involved.

Perran studied the two men seated before him. Neither looked away, both seemingly assured their testimony would win the day. That, in itself, spoke volumes. He cleared his throat.

"I'll question you first, Barro, since you brought the original accusation against Haivel. From what you've told the authorities of Streamwood, Haivel ruined a bolt of expensive cloth by dumping a bucket of paint on it. Now, tell me what you think could have caused a productive and respected citizen of Streamwood to do such a thing."

Barro stood, bowed his head briefly in Perran's direction.

"Jealousy, your lordship," he said.

Perran leaned back in his chair, steepled his hands, and listened to Barro's account of the vandalism of his fabric and the perceived reason for Haivel's jealousy. He glanced once at Levron, lifted an eyebrow, to be rewarded by Levron's nod toward a beautiful woman seated next to an older man, most likely her father. So that was Trika. The source of the trouble that had escalated to vandalism. He continued to listen to Barro's tale, but he kept watching Trika as the man spoke. He could see how her eyes sparkled, how her face grew animated as Barro set forth his case against Haivel.

"And you saw Haivel throw the paint on your bolt of cloth?" Perran asked.

"Yes, your lordship."

"Was there anyone else in the shop that night?"

"No, your lordship."

"Did he say anything after ruining your fabric?"

"No, your lordship. He merely laughed and ran out of the shop."

"I see." Perran looked down at a piece of paper on the table. "You've tendered the court a receipt setting out the value of the cloth. It bears the stamp of Tabot House of Sunhame. Is this the merchant you deal with?"

"Yes, your lordship."

"And the value of the bolt of cloth is set out here at ten silver soleri. And you say it's ruined."

"It is. The paint soaked through it since it's an intricate weave."

Perran motioned Barro to sit, then turned his attention to Haivel.

"And you, Haivel." Perran motioned for the man to stand. "You've brought a claim against Barro for destruction of a shipment of paper to be used in your profession as scribe, is that correct?"

"It is, your lordship."

"Now explain to me why you think Barro would do such a thing."

Haivel shrugged. "I don't know. I can only guess it's revenge for what he thinks I did to his cloth. But I have a witness who will testify I couldn't have been to his shop that night."

"But he claims he saw you, and you laughed in his face."

"Impossible, your lordship."

"And where is this witness who can give proof you weren't at Barro's shop that night?"

For the first time, Haivel's eyes wandered. "I'm not sure."

Perran leaned back in his chair and lifted an eyebrow. "What do you mean, you're not sure?"

"He left town shortly after the incident, your lordship."

"Then why do you claim you have a witness who can assure me you weren't at Barro's shop?"

"Because it's true! I wasn't! And my witness would testify to that!"

Perran allowed a smile to touch his lips. "A witness who isn't here can't help you. Do you know where this person is?"

"No. He's another scribe who travels in the area,

serving those who can't read or write." Haivel's face reddened. "If I knew where he was, he'd be in court today."

"You didn't think to find him when you knew you were coming to court?"

"I tried, but he doesn't always take the same route."

Perran lifted another sheet of paper. "You've given this court a receipt for the paper you claim Barro ruined by slashing it with a knife."

Haivel nodded. "It's from a traveling paper merchant. I get a shipment from him whenever he passes through town."

Perran studied the receipt. "It says here the amount you paid the merchant for the paper was ten silver soleri. Is that correct?"

"Yes, your lordship. It was a large order. I have to stock paper because I'm never sure when the merchant will be passing through town again."

"You may be seated." Perran studied the two men. They returned his stare, faces set in expressions of total belief in what they recounted. But somewhere, in Haivel's recounting, he sensed a lie. He straightened. "This court will adjourn for two candlemarks while I review the cases. I want you both back here then." He looked across the room, briefly focusing his attention on Trika. "Please bear in mind that everything you've said I have taken into consideration. And I am, as you well know, an enforcer of the laws of Karse. My judgment here today is final, and your cases cannot be tried again."

Levron stood outside the inn, well aware his next duty to Perran might be one of the hardest he had ever performed. Nonetheless, any information he could find would aid Perran's decision in this case. Glancing up at the passing clouds, he made an effort to appear relaxed and calm, one more man enjoying the springtime sun.

He heard his name called, turned, and saw Trika coming his way, accompanied by her father.

"Levron," she said, her smile such that any man would immediately feel flattered to be addressed by her. "You remember my father?"

"I do. Good day to you, sir."

Trika's father wore a somewhat preoccupied expression and merely nodded.

"So, you've become assistant to the judge." She smiled again; this time the smile was more than inviting.

"Yes." Levron squared his shoulders. "A position I'm rather proud of."

"And you should be," she said, stepping close enough so he could smell the slight hint of her perfume. "I'm confused as to why Barro and Haivel are in court. Perhaps you can tell me what will happen if they're found guilty."

"That I can't. I don't make those decisions."

"Oh." She pouted prettily. "I thought you might have witnessed cases like this before."

"And why should you care?" Levron asked, keeping his voice even.

Trika lifted her chain and glanced off for a brief moment. "I don't, actually. I'm merely interested. They were both beginning to bore me."

"Trika!" This from her father, who now stared at his daughter. "That's not a kind thing to say."

"But it's true, Papa. First Haivel, then Barro." She tossed a strand of night-black hair over her shoulder. "You'd think I was the only woman in town."

Levron cleared his throat. Much as he wanted to keep his opinions hidden, the time had come to reveal them. "You haven't changed, have you, Trika?"

She appeared startled for a few heartbeats. "What do you mean by that?"

"I remember all too well how things stood when I left

Streamwood." Levron met Trika's father's eyes. "Your pardon, sir, I don't mean any disrespect." He returned his attention to Trika. "You always seemed to enjoy setting boys, and then men, at each other, simply to see how they would react. Isn't that what you've done to Barro and Haivel?"

Trika's eyes turned to black ice. "That's unfair. I thought you and I were friends!"

Friends again. Why do they think we were ever friends? "Not so I noticed. You never paid me any attention at all."

"I can see why I didn't," Trika said, her eyes narrowed now. "You're nothing more than a—"

"Trika!" This time, her father put a hand on her shoulder. "Be still!"

"I will not!" she fumed. "Why should I let Levron accuse me of—"

"Because it's true, and you know it," her father interrupted. "I've ignored your behavior far too long. You're aware of what they call you in town, aren't you?"

For a brief moment, Trika's haughty expression cracked. "Trika the Tease," she said at last, her voice gone very quiet.

Levron bowed his head in Trika's father's direction. "I think it best I take my leave," he said. "I'm fairly certain I won't be back in Streamwood for a long time, if ever, so I wish the best of everything for you both."

He turned and entered the inn, a headache beginning to pound behind his eyes. But the unfortunate meeting had been worth it . . . he now had the answer Perran wanted.

Perran couldn't deny the emotional cost of Levron's meeting with Trika. Levron had hardly spoken a word other than to recount the conversation he had shared with Trika and her father. Knowing how difficult that meeting must have been, Perran vowed, somehow, to set things right. Perran earnestly hoped a situation similar to this one would not occur in the future.

Court in session, he stared at the two men seated before his table and made a show of inspecting the receipts they had given him to prove their loss. Let them squirm a little, it certainly wouldn't do them further harm. Finally, he motioned for Barro and Haivel to stand.

"What I have here are receipts for the goods you have lost. Once again, I ask, can either of you prove the damages created by the other?"

Barro darted a quick glance at Haivel. "I saw him ruin my cloth with my own eyes."

"And I," Haivel said, "saw Barro destroy my paper."

"But neither of you has a witness. It's only your individual accusations that this is what happened."

"My cloth is ruined!" Barro exclaimed. "I *saw* Haivel dump the paint on it!"

"And *I* saw Barro destroy my paper!" Haivel growled. "Whose word weighs more here, his or mine?"

"Are you asking me a question?" Perran leaned forward in his chair. "I don't answer questions, I ask them!"

Both men seemed to shrink slightly.

"My apologies, your lordship," Haivel said quietly.

"So." Perran studied the papers again. "You, Barro, suffered a loss of ten silver soleri for the destruction of your fine bolt of cloth, caused, you say, by Haivel upending a bucket of paint on it. And you, Haivel, suffered a loss of ten silver soleri because you claim Barro took a knife to your delivery of paper. All because you're both acting out of a misguided sense of jealousy and revenge. You, Haivel, courted Trika for a considerable time, and when she started seeing Barro, you reacted."

Haivel's face turned red and he stared at his feet.

"And you, Barro," Perran continued, letting his eyes stray to where Trika and her father sat, "reacted in anger because you claim Haivel destroyed your cloth. As you said, Haivel, it's his word against yours and your word against his. Now how can I tell who's guilty and who's not? Since neither of you has a witness, and, Haivel, I'm not certain I believe your witness exists, I'm left in the unenviable position of having to decide a case that has no easy resolution."

Silence gripped the room. Perran noticed several people glancing sidelong at Trika. If those gathered to watch the trial were any example, what Levron had recounted regarding Trika's manipulations in the past seemed to be all too familiar to the citizens of Streamwood. And now he had to make a judgment. Both had suffered losses, but the reasons behind the vandalism of each man's property could be left squarely at Trika's threshold. Not that they were innocent. Perran believed each had told the truth despite Haivel's story about his witness: Barro *had* seen Haivel destroy his cloth; Haivel *had* witnessed Barro shred his delivery of paper.

Perran gathered the two receipts and set them aside.

"Now hear my judgment," he said. "By the authority granted to me by the Son of the Sun, whose rule of law emanates from Vkandis Sun Lord, I speak. Barro, I believe your recounting. Even with no witness, you have proved it more likely than not Haivel destroyed your fabric for which you paid ten silver soleri. Therefore, he will pay you that amount to recoup your loss."

Barro's face lit up and a smile touched his lips. Perran turned to Haivel, whose expression bordered on the shocked.

"And Haivel, you also have no witness, but you have proved it more likely than not Barro destroyed your paper, for which you paid ten silver soleri. Barro is ordered to pay you that amount to make you whole."

Barro's eyes widened and Haivel lifted his chin.

"And now," Perran said, "I come to the portion of this

trial that strays from the normal path I usually take. The two of you," he continued, "have behaved poorly for men of your standing in Streamwood. Now I understand, or I can *try* to understand, feelings of betrayal on your part, Haivel, and the jealousy that followed. And you, Barro, you reacted in vengeful anger at the ruination of your property. Vengeance I can also understand. However—" and here Perran stared directly at Trika who sat next to her father "—there is someone in this court who is ultimately responsible for setting these actions into motion. Trika, will you and your father stand?"

Trika's face froze into a pale mask, and her eyes darted left and right as she and her father rose.

"I find you guilty of playing petty, emotional games with these two men. Therefore, in my authority as judge, as penalty I fine you twenty-five copper soleri to be paid to Haivel and twenty-five copper soleri to be paid to Barro."

A muted gasp rippled through the room. Barro and Haivel exchanged a glance, then looked away. Trika's father glared at his daughter, who had lowered her eyes to the floor, no longer flaunting her beauty as a seductive weapon.

"And," Perran continued, "I caution you, Trika, to think how your actions can influence others. Emotions are easily manipulated in certain circumstances. Perhaps this will teach you to be more considerate of those around you. And so, by the authority vested in me, I conclude my judgment. In the name of the Son of the Sun and Vkandis Sun Lord, so shall it be!"

Levron had never felt more relieved to depart a town after a judgment. He rode next to Perran, for the first time in two days feeling unburdened by what lay in the future.

"I want to thank you again," Perran said. "I asked a

great deal of you, and I hope you understand the need. What you told me illustrated in detail how people can behave so badly. It's always a shame to see these things happen, but I'm willing to wager this won't be the last such case I'm called to judge. Only next time, you won't be so intimately involved."

"It was my duty," Levron replied, warmth flooding his heart at Perran's apology. "Yes, it was draining. Yes, I wish I didn't know the three of them. I will say this, your judgment was superb. I found it amazing to see how you dealt with Barro and Haivel. Fining Trika the fifty copper soleri to be paid half to Barro and half to Haivel meant each of them left court owing nothing to the other, and a bit better off besides."

Perran chucked. "Do you think she will have learned anything?"

Levron thought for a moment, then shook his head. "Probably not. It will take more than a fine to change her, unless her father reins her in at last. Perhaps it might happen one day when someone she truly loves spurns her." He lifted his head, took a deep breath of the fresh scents of the fields that stretched off from the roadway. "I will tell you this: I never want to return to Streamwood. If there's another case to be tried there, I beg you . . . please find a substitute."

Perran laughed and lifted the reins, urging his mount to an easy canter. Levron touched his heels to his horse and caught up, a smile touching his face warmed by the late afternoon sun.

Under the Vale

Larry Dixon

Misty and I are asked some very clever and insightful questions when we're doing Q&A sessions at conventions. One thing I invariably say is, "A Star Trek™ writer once told me, 'I have one brain to get it right, and the fans have a hundred thousand brains to find what I got wrong.'" There are fans and there are Fans, and the True Believers memorize every detail, and how it all comes together, and they make webpages, trivia games, and databases and keep track of all details. We love that. It's awesome.

We put amazing levels of worldbuilding and research go into even the most casual mentions and tertiary characters. Well, it's amazing to us anyway. We could be easy to impress. We might be weak compared to a lot of writers, especially roleplaying-game writers, but it sure feels like a ton of development. Even when something gets just a passing mention or is glimpsed in the background, there's been thought put into it. Plus, there are in-jokes, and meta-references, and braided or circular storytelling that have as much to do with stand-up joke framework (warmup, first callout, setup, gag, punchline, callback) as with screenplay or prose structure. Some person or building in the background might be important six books down the line. In one interview we laughed and said we always have four pages of notes for a two-line reference.

This essay shows a little bit of what that forethought is like. And you know what? This is our job, seven days a week, writing and drawing and researching every single day, and we still get things wrong all the time. But I promise you, we sure do our very best for you.

My specialty is the How and Why Things Happen Department. Here are some insights into the Hawkbrothers, the hertasi, and just what a Vale is—and what it's for.

About 1150 years ago from the "current" point in the Valdemar/Velgarth timeline (circa Perfect Day and Transmutation), the paired disasters known as the Cataclysm occurred. And it was a mess. A deity-level, impossible-to-fix-instantly mess. The seventy-some years before the Cataclysm were called The Mage Wars, because Velgarth's native magic fields had been harnessed like never before by cabals and individuals. In the centuries before, magic work had been at what might today be called journeyman level at best, and those who used sorcery had few, if any, mentors. Spellwork was mostly experimentation. Experimentation was often lethal. Magery wasn't a career choice for a long life. Some of these early wizards did keep notes, though, and the ones that didn't die in a flash of Mage-shaped embers passed their notes along. And so, schools of thought regarding magic and what could be done with it led to those that could eventually be called Adepts.

These Mages often became more than tyrants and more than leaders. They became strategic weapons. Alliances and one-time deals shaped the courses of tribes and nations alike. Just having the social favor of a Mage could be enough to stop a rivals' invasion of your duchy or hunting grounds. A warlord of great strategic ability could employ a Mage for tide-turning battle tactics, and the Mage would be kept safe and comfortable by the warlord all the rest of the time. Everybody—and let me stress that, everybody—who understood any sort of civilization knew that those who worked magic were to be respected.

The next turning point after Adepts came very swiftly. An Adept could train others to do parts of spellwork and then combine their subworks into a Great Work. This was first used to enrich an eroded floodplain, while the baron's men built levees to make use of the renewed soil. This historic Great Work used just under sixty journeyman-level Mages and a single Adept.

One of the journeyman Mages was a very young man named Urtho.

At this time, the "texture" of Velgarth's magic was very rough. It took a brute force approach to cause something to happen, and Great Works nearly always resulted in serious injury for two-thirds of the magic users involved, because excess energy would manifest as light and heat. Very often, spellwork simply wasn't worth the chance of losing a percentage of your Mage teams to blindness and burns. Magework was reserved solely for things that laborers, soldiers, and engineers could not replicate. And, not incidentally, wherever there was magic, something was going to explode. This was partly because no one had the slightest concept of static electricity, and magework would sometimes create a huge potential charge that would ignite materials and gasses nearby. That never helps. Other times, enchantment-prone materials would accidentally get charged up and detonate. This led to a brief and ill-advised fad of naked spellcasting, which ended not long after the first spate of full-body, smoking head and groin hair burns. Obviously comparing notes literally couldn't hurt.

A bold tradition arose, by Urtho's doing, that got Mages together in "salons" to share their information freely about spells and energies, regardless of their political leanings or ranks. It was against common law, even considered traitorous by some, but the fear of and respect for Mages were such that these salons were not once raided. Urtho was, to put it mildly, likable. Whereas so many colleagues were gruff or pained by old wounds or insufferably self-important, Urtho had kind eyes and a kind heart, to match his ability to maneuver socially. A knack for bribery didn't hurt, either.

Urtho's salons became a "movable feast" that would travel village to city, Mage school to secret cabal, and every year they became more lavish and the food much better. Mages were always wealthy. The salons advanced magical theory to a level that might have taken a century more, had they not flourished. Inevitably, these gatherings collapsed due to schism and war, but the world gained much knowledge (and fewer explosions) from them.

Urtho gazed at an oil lamp one evening and mused, "If it were a bowl of oil, touched by this fire, it would explode. But it is a lamp, and the wick is restricted, so only the wick burns. It gives just a little light and heat, and that is just what I ask of it." Urtho wrote this in one of his many notebooks, unaware that by doing so, he had just changed the history of the entire world and the spirit realms above and below it.

Urtho's great accomplishment in the years after the salons was to develop a set of "weights and measures" for magic use. It all began with that first observation from the oil lamp. His title, Mage of Silence, was because spellwork at the time put out a huge "signature" that could be detected even at long distances; but Urtho's spellwork used exactly as much power as was needed and no more. Thus, "silence," and others feared and respected the fact that Urtho could have operations going and operatives active right beside them that they simply couldn't detect. It became the bluff that saved countless lives.

Magery, like anything, has its trends and fashions. Animal husbandry enhanced by magic came into fashion, and from that came something called "uplifting." Creatures could be made stronger and swifter, yes, but also smarter. Adepts, by this time numbering in the scores and as influential as kings, became bored with being the era's equivalent of field cannon. Several put their knowledge to work on improving horse breeds, and others toward creating giant versions of small but deadly creatures like ice-drakes.

The hertasi could be described as semisentient at the time Urtho picked up where a predecessor of his, Khal Herta, had left off. The wild hertasi were mild-tempered reptiles, available in large quantity, living fairly simple lives. After Herta's experimental work, hertasi had simple structures, organized hunting and fishing, and rudimentary medicine. Several of the bands settled at Ka'venusho were former followers of Herta who adopted Urtho when Herta passed on. They brought Khal Herta's notes and all of the hertasi with them, knowing that the Kyamvir's unified tribes would easily subjugate the hertasi if any stayed in their native northern swamps.

Urtho took the approach of increasing the intelligence of hertasi social leaders, encouraging them to breed with their subordinates and then increasing the intelligence of their offspring. It created a surprisingly seamless acceptance among the hertasi, for those who were far smarter than any had been before were their own children, not strangers from an Adept's lab.

Part of Khal Herta's uplift process was instilling a mild compulsion in the hertasi to be appreciative for what they had become, and Urtho left that intact. This lives on, into the current timeline, as the unstoppable helpfulness the hertasi as a whole have. Even the grouchiest hertasi knows that they "owe" Urtho for having as good a life as they do. Interestingly, that compulsion did not carry through into the tyrill, the "bigger siblings" of the hertasi. Urtho constantly struggled with ethical questions of practicality and free will, and when the compulsion bred out of the tyrill, he simply let it go, almost as if he were making up for its presence in the hertasi.

It is also important to mention here that Urtho was but one man, but the work of uplifting a species was done by a small legion of lesser Mages working under Urtho's direction. Urtho's greatest work, the gryphons, took forty years of constant design and spellwork by nearly three hundred lower-ranked Mages, and each of them had a personal staff of helpers. Urtho's Tower had as many sublevels as it had floors, plus scores of outbuildings. Every day Urtho made the rounds of the workrooms and directed the swarms of probability sprites that tested each organ and behavior of the species. Urtho is the Great Mage who got the credit, but thousands of others supported him, including the survivors who would become the Tayledras.

Kal'enel, the goddess revered by the Hawkbrothers is, like every other Velgarthian deity, a nonphysical creature of limited abilities. When the Cataclysm was on their horizon, the deities of Velgarth could see that it was much more than they could handle. Much as a ship's crew cannot stop a storm but can choose a course and batten down the hatches, the deities that had genuine prophets knew the Cataclysm was coming and could only adjust their sails, so to speak. The most compassionate of deities made plans and worked great magics to preserve their followers. Some deities, to put it plainly, blundered, did not survive, and are only remembered in historical documents.

The Cataclysm was so horrible, even for the gods, because it consisted of one of Urtho's weapons that they knew little about and could not counter.

Indeed, to attempt to counter it would only worsen it.

As you may remember, a "spell" is the use of magical and nonmagical physics, in a structure, to produce a desired effect. A "spell" is a process, not a thing. Its nearest analogy might be the construction of a simple arch bridge, where specially shaped materials depend upon each other both to stay cohesive as a bridge shape and to perform the task of being a bridge.

Urtho's weapon was an "unspell:" a "self-sustaining disjunction," in his words, and it was not some nuclear fireball one might imagine from something named a cataclysm. To continue the bridge analogy, it caused the pieces of the bridge to cease to have a hold on each other; the friction and pressure required to maintain an arch simply broke down into thousands of fissures, and the bridge ceased to be a bridge. Catastrophically. And then the debris from the bridge caused whatever it touched to disintegrate as the bridge did, and so on.

Like most things the Mage of Silence created, it began slowly, and it initially spread from its epicenter at a pace similar to a walk. Its wave peaks were higher and closer together at its epicenters, each lengthening out until their "bow wave" reached a level of equilibrium where the arcs between magical materials were simply too far apart to sustain the effect. The edges of Lake Evendim and the Dhorisha Plains resulted from the settling of debris pushed along by the waves when they reached this exhaustion.

The disjunction, most simply put, broke down the links between energy fields that sustained long-lasting spellwork. When a spell or item's power was violently released, its "magical shrapnel" struck the next nearest one, and so forth. Therefore, the enchantment that helped a land barge float would not just collapse, it would fly apart in many thousands of "strands" that would "grasp onto" any other magical field or device in its path like chainshot. They, in turn, would lose their cohesion, and their own magical threads would fly out to latch onto the next device or Mage energy, and so forth, throwing off light, heat, and debris.

The gross effect of this during the Cataclysm was that raw strings of magic snagged onto enchantable material like, say, a good bit of hardwood or a sword with a well-made crystalline forging, and arced across them in heat and light while physically pushing them away from the disjunction's epicenter. The ground lunged upward from magic-induced liquefaction, while under the surface, crystals and other enchantment-receptive materials snatched up bits of loose raw magic and then exploded, bursting from the ground at the next wave-peak. The ground level dropped by as much as two hundred feet as the disjunction wave spread outward, due to the sudden aeration and then collapse of earth; what was left behind was not only tightly packed, but in many cases, entire acres were fused into glassine plates, such as where a magical ax or bow once lay.

Urtho's Tower itself, though, had been designed to collapse in on itself in a very specific way. Its hundreds of keystones were enchanted to project light. Most people thought of this as a mere convenience, but Urtho did this knowing that if the disjunction was ever unleashed—and odds were if things ever got that bad, it would involve the Tower—the Tower's calculated implosion would safely entomb and preserve the chambers below it. This is why the Tower's ground floor was so thick.

The southerly Ka'venusho/Dhorisha crater was wider and shallower than the Predain/Evendim crater because of the successful evacuations that took so much magical material away through Gates. The Evendim crater was far deeper. Due to the cruder, higher-powered magics used by Ma'ar and his followers compared to those near Ka'venusho, its disjunction effect was far more violent, enough so that the backlash from the expanding waves pushed up the earth behind it into what would eventually become the wracked islands at the center of Lake Evendim. The ash plume from the craters rose for weeks and spread mostly to the southwest, but over time they spread into a haze the world over, dropping global temperatures for years. The ash fallout took its toll, but ultimately it helped improve soil quality all the way to the southern seas.

Kal'enel's closest friend, Vykaendys, took on all the people who gated into the area now known as Iftel and created what was known for centuries as the Hard Border, hiding them away from the world at large. When the schism between the goddess' survivors happened, Kal'enel did what was within her power, sacrificing much and nearly disincorporating doing so. The seething, chaotic spell "strings," already mutating or stunting what plant life remained in the crater, were effectively gathered up by her by the creation of the Dhorisha Shin'a (the Plains of Sacrifice) in a Great Making, and its excess energy bled into the Pelagirs. The Pelagirs hills and forests, already home to some very strange and deadly things before the Cataclysm, became a realm of terrors. The wild magic scrambled the genetics of even the most common of animals and plants, and it soon became clear to mortal and god alike that what would come out of the Pelagirs could eradicate anyone and anything left in the world if left unchecked.

Through spirit intermediaries the Star-Eyed Goddess, in agreement with the wisest and best-educated souls of the spell-favoring clans, developed ways to draw in the wild magic and apply progressively tighter forms of order upon it. Kal'enel then faded back for several centuries, leaving only her spirit representatives to help her followers while she recovered from the Cataclysm and reached accords with the remaining deities.

The culture known as the Tayledras arose, despite staggering odds against them. This can be attributed to an early, cautious "consolidate, fortify, and methodically expand" policy centered around Hawkbrother stations.

Tayledras stations became known as Vales after they adopted the practice of using ravines or narrow valleys for their foundation. The hertasi discovered that using a ravine meant less sheer mass movement to create the lower levels, and their cave and tunnel networks could be dug in sideways after shoring up the ravine walls themselves by compressing the stone. Erosion ravines became the sites of choice since a ready water supply could be channeled as needed and easily cisterned at the lowest level of the Vale. Ravines or valleys were also chosen based upon their orientation, so that the scattered-magic refinement would more easily create ley lines in desired directions, linking Vales and future nodes to create a "skeleton" to aid future work. This is why Vales tend have an elongated, ovoid shape.

In fact, there has only ever been one Tayledras station that was perfectly spherical, its fields and tunnels extending as far below as above in a perfect circle: k'Hala, the first Vale, long abandoned with its quiescent node intact, underneath what is now Haven, the capital of Valdemar.

Tayledras Scouts are known for being tougher than nails, and for good reason. Essentially, the Pelagirs wants to kill everyone and everything. The Forest will try to kill by poison, by gas, by infection and pitfalls, clouds of deadly insects or hordes of bugs that swarm and eat you while you're asleep. Thorns scratch deep and leave toxins, deep canopy confuses direction and hides everything from giant spiders to hive-mind boring beetles. There are snakes, slime molds, decayed husks of house-sized trees serving as dens for diseased monsters, wolves, ankle-breaking vine twists, and bottomless pits, with possible packs of armored, carnivorous wyrsa to complete the joy of each mile's travel. The most experienced Scouts can cover an average of four miles through the Pelagirs on their best day. The question concerning the reordering of wild magic, especially before the Storms, shouldn't have been "that's all they've done for a thousand years?" but rather, "They made it THAT far?"

Make no mistake, establishing a Vale is a fight, and not always a winnable fight. Expeditions have been destroyed or had to fall back and try again, sometimes as many as six times before a safe perimeter could be established.

The sheer mass of growth in the Pelagirs makes a Vale site hard to pick out, but once a Scout finds a likely candidate, he faces due north and then stares at it, committing it to memory; then he thinks back along the path he took to get there. Upon returning to his home, a dyheli stag will pull the mental images from him and share them with the senior Mages and hertasi builders. Cartographers sharing these visions make notes and later consult with the Scout to confirm the route. If the site looks viable, an expedition will go there, often with as many as forty in the mixed-species party. The expedition will always include a team of hertasi stonecrafters, with their powerful magical stone-shaping tools. The party travels two days, then stops for a night or two, whereupon the hertasi examine the ground and pull up a protective stone wall (still referred to as a palisade) of bedrock pulled up into flat, tall sheets about a foot at the base and tapering up to a few inches at man-height with two exits. The excess heat from the stoneshaping is bled off into a pile of usually wet deadfall gathered while they begin, and the heat dries the wood and then combusts it for the camp's comfort fire. These palisade camps are left behind as convenient waystations.

When the new Vale site is reached, the hertasi use their instruments to map the topography and then probe into the underlying rock bed. If it is found to be of sufficient density, the very first stage of Vale groundbreaking is begun. This consists of a very large-scale version of the earlier camp palisades, drawn up through all the dirt and plant growth. One sharpened-top sheet of stone is pulled up each day, severing the root systems of the forest growth by punching upward, like a stroke by a giant ax blade. Scouts, dyheli, and hertasi reduce the downed trees into usable firewood and lumber and make a first clear patch. Sheet by sheet, these stone palisades create a wall around the eventual Vale site—a relative zone of safety to live inside. This invariably attracts creatures like wyrsa packs and anything starving and insane, which the Pelagirs never lacks.

Living, nontoxic trees within the palisade perimeter that can be cleared of dangerous parasites are left as intact as possible, to become the host trees of ekeles. Useful bushes and vines are similarly left in place, and this extends all the way down into the undergrowth of the Vale's ravine. Ideally, a Vale should begin with a ravine at least ten stories deep, with a steady-flowing stream originating from mountain runoff or natural springs.

When the incipient Vale reaches a state of defensibility and the Mages confirm that it will be an effective site for the Cleansing duties, word is carried back to their origin Vale, and hertasi and others descend upon the trailblazed site in force.

The sides of the ravine are stonecrafted into a series of ramps, switching back between platforms that support terraced gardens. The ramps are for carts assembled on site (and for the ease of any gryphons who wish to walk up or down; gryphons are fine with climbing stairs but terrible at descending them, so, modern Vales always use ramps), but most especially for the incredibly swift-running hertasi dashing around. The level resting places of each outward-facing switchback is lengthened an extra ten feet or so to make landings easier for gryphons in modern Vales, while the inner-facing ones are covered by awnings.

The first stage of making hertasi burrows begins with creating "guest apartments" alongside the ramps. These are not just a courtesy for the humans; they are also where the hertasi stonecrafters get truly intimate with the rock around them. Probe spheres and spellwork imaging "soundings" are sent in from these locations, and once the native rock is mapped and found to be worthy, the apartments are given over to the humans, and the hertasi burrow tunnelling begins nearby. The burrow tunnels go level and deep in concentric circles around where the Heartstone will eventually be placed once the Vale is "roofed" at ground level.

A sturdy wooden bridge is built across the ravine, its center pole marking where the Heartstone will eventually be. Surveying lines radiate out from the pole, and at equidistant points tripods with pulleys are set up. From these the hertasi's plumb bob drilling devices are slowly lowered. They "scoop up" earth and rock as they drop, increasing its plasticity and compressing it into the hardened sides of the shafts. Hertasi stand well back because the compression and tunnelling creates a lot of heat, which fires up out of the hole in a jet. When the plumb bob drill reaches a set depth, it is powered down and pulled back up. Then a homing crystal is lowered down into the hole after a day's cooling period and left there. Eventually between thirty and sixty shafts are made on either side of the Vale, each shaft with a homing crystal at the bottom. These crystals are the targets that the sideways tunnelling will track on. The hertasi use a specialized set of magical digging and stoneworking tools that include a "cooler," which comically looks like a spoon at the end of a polearm. The cooler sucks away the heat given off by the other tools; it is a vital tool as excavations increase in scale.

Hertasi diggers start in from the valley side and aim at the nearest homing crystal, then expand and reinforce the tunnel section once they've reached that crystal. Then the next crystal is aimed for, and so on, and eventually a circular ring tunnel is produced. This pilot tunnel is the reference ring and access for all the valleyside tunnel work that is to follow. It is from this main ring that the Vale's water distribution, Heartstone cooling system, and the radiating underground magical tuning channels are built up.

Compressed, hardened stone is scooped out as a result of the tunneling process and is in turn either reformed into marbled brick or ground into concrete. One of the first durable structures built inside the guard walls at a new Vale site is a charcoal oven. One team splits, seasons, and stacks the local wood, while a second team makes a brick kiln. Brick and concrete work better than stonepulling in many applications, like pathways, and once the Tayledras scouts and the lesser Mages have secured the area, even the original palisade is ground down to make pathways. If the Vale site has good kaolin and clay in the area, ceramic bricks are the top choice; if there is a good source of lime nearby, concrete is preferred. If a coal seam can be mined, the fly ash is saved for a particular type of structural concrete. Cement and concrete have been used for thousands of years in Velgarth; Urtho's Tower at Ka'venusho was a triumph of architecture and concrete use. Hertasi usually do the brickwork and pointing at a Vale site, but even among the Hawkbrothers there are human masons.

Depending upon the regolith of the Vale site, the upper rooms and corridors in the ravine's sides could have either a glassy or a ceramic finish, caused by the compression effect of the devices firing the earth into a hardened crust. This could be used to great effect structurally, since the compression strength could be quite high once support ribs of a foot thick or more were formed. Convenient shelving is usually built between the support ribs.

The hertasi stonepulling devices of various shapes have the property of changing stone's plasticity without creating a detrimental crystalline matrix. More accurately, stone pulling makes the stone draw like a pulled clay or molten glass into the desired shape, and then the crystalline structure that gave the stone strength does not form until the stone is "released" by the stonepuller. When stone is drawn out into its final shape, the large-area stonepuller, called the setter, aligns the crystallization inside the stone from all the previous, smaller pulls. This is why the soaring bridges and buttresses used to create rooms and floors underneath a Vale are effectively single-piece structures, since the setter fuses the subassemblies together into a contiguous form. The setter also smooths out walls, ceilings, and floors. Some of the small hills and mounds inside a Vale are actually hollow, with multiple rooms, created by stonepulling a dome and setting it, and then building a layer of soil over the dome for landscaping. Hertasi are experts at disguising structures.

The Tayledras' famed bathing pools are stonepulled creations that make use of a network of heat-regulating formed-tunnel "pipes" that circulate water from the furnaces upward to the surface and to heat-sink cisterns down the Vale's slope. Hot water is diverted to create artificial springs that bubble up to the highest level of the pools and then cascade over the sides to the progressively cooler pools. Bathing starts at the lowest, cooling levels, which is where the outright filth and dirt gets washed off; then the next higher levels are cleaner, warmer water, until the highest level is reached where the hottest water and most of the socializing can be found. The Pelagirs are brutal, and most of what sticks to a Pelagirs traveler also stinks and probably carries disease or toxins, so the hot pools are more than a hedonistic indulgence, they're vital for health and hygiene.

It is important to remember, when you consider a Vale, that it is essentially a machine that houses a small city. The Tayledras Adepts in particular are technical and procedural in how they harness and refine the Pelagirs' wild magic. This applies to their delicate spellwork as well. Subterranean workrooms are isolated from each other and put behind layers of physical shielding ranging from lead sheet to embedded crystal dust mats, so that subtle magic or "miniature" versions of Great Work spells can be laid out at low risk of interference. The floors are inscribed with diagrams and reference points, and their geometry act as an instruction set for what will happen during the course of a casting. Once the "model" is constructed, the spellwork is diagrammed, and hertasi scribes make records of every small detail, since when a Great Work is played out at full size, a "small detail" could affect an area the size of a city. These scribed accounts form a standardized reference for every Mage involved in the castings, much as architects have multiple sets of blueprints, and copies are eventually distributed to each Vale and Tayledras settlement.

Hertasi, being no strangers to magic use themselves and definitely no strangers to how Hawkbrothers do things, embed two or more of the main galleries of each Vale with the workrooms' gridwork for spell construction, just in case some Pelagirs-wide catastrophe should need to be solved by a large-scale spell that, for some awful reason, could not be done above ground.

The arched galleries themselves are more than just (to the short hertasi) vast spaces to make bigger surface-dwellers feel more welcome; they are also meant for evacuations. Every Vale has enough room in the galleries to take in a complete Vale's complement of gryphons, humans, and other species, plus their pets and Bondbirds, twice over, with sanitation and basic provisions for up to six days. Fresh air is brought in from the lowest levels inside the ravine, aided by waterwheels powered by the ravine's stream, and circulates up to the surface by convection, belt-driven fans, and the bustle of activity under the Vale.

The hertasi motto, "We Can Do This," reflects their inventive nature and their ability to define and produce solutions to problems of almost any complexity. The walls of many hallways under a Vale are covered in chalk designs, open to annotation by anyone who passes them. Lists and charts of Vale issues (sometimes including Tayledras personal relationships that need "help") line the major uprights of the galleries, constantly updated by runners or hearsay.

As a necessity of the multilayered field integrity of the upper Veil, the Vale has only two points of entry at the surface level. These entries are always in the form of two spires, curving toward each other at the top, or a full arch. Field tuning rods are set on the outermost edges of the spires, usually completely covered by greenery. The Veil is a set of shields, each adjustable, that form a dome over the Vale. The shimmer effect comes from convection heat transfer caused by the venting of the furnaces and often steam. The Veil thickness tapers from around twenty feet at the base of the dome to around five at the very peak. It is not a "hard shell" type of shield, but rather a set of "resistive" layers, permeable enough to fly through with just the feeling of encountering a sudden stiff crosswind. It can also be walked through slowly.

The Veil functions much like an air curtain you might encounter at a supermarket, and it blunts the effe even the strongest snow and ice storms, resulting in a warm rain inside the dome. Lighter rainstorms may not even penetrate the Veil at all, or might produce a pleasant mist. Unsurprisingly, the Veil is designed to absorb lightning strikes, which the Hawkbrothers believe a Heartstone attracts. It's actually the static buildup caused by the Veil itself that does it, but the Tayledras aren't quite experts in electricity; still, the frequent ionization from the lightning strikes benefits the plant life below, which is part of why Vales are so lush with greenery.

Strictly patrolled small wetlands are developed in the half-mile area around a Vale, host to rice ponds, frog and fish farms, and reed stands. Flax is grown between the wetland patches. Decorated trellises of grapevines encircle the Vale, but like many Tayledras and hertasi designs, they conceal another purpose. The control rods that maintain the shape of the Veil are in every trellis upright, and the outermost ones begin the "tuning" process upon the raw, rough magical energy drawn toward the Heartstone from the surrounding countryside. A hundred or more control stones are placed as decorations in the clearings surrounding the Vale for a quarter-mile all around; they act like a "breakwater" when there is a surge. Together, these stones and rods act as a collimator, accurately aligning and directing the rough magic the Adepts draw in from the many miles around, directly into the Heartstone.

Even a novice Mage will tell you that the biggest danger in using magic power comes from using too much of it. Limiting the amount that is drawn upon is what makes the difference between a miracle worker and a charred corpse. Uncontrolled magical power manifests as excess heat, sometimes in sheets and flares that cause clothing to combust and skin to burn. An Adept is respected not just for his skill at spellwork but for his skill at staying alive.

This brings us to the Heartstone. A Heartstone is a physical object that acts as a capacitor for huge amounts of magical energy, which the Tayledras Mages draw in through the "breakwater" stones, Veil curtain and tuning rods of the Vale. The intent is to take in the flawed, raw, random "strings" of energy, align them, and give that energy a stable place to stay. However, just like the individual "strings," by the billions, are largely unpredictable, so too can their flow into the Vale be unpredictable. Tayledras Mages work together because they can buffer each other from the surges of the rough magic through skilled use of shields. The Heartstone isn't just something that's left running and checked on once in a while.

A Heartstone is crafted on site from rock excavated during that Vale's construction. Hertasi stoneshaping tools are used to create it, and the most important part of the procedure is the month-long pulling to align the stone's inner crystalline structure to be as close to perfectly vertical as possible. Traditionally, Heartstones are sculpted as spires or obelisks, and they have a broad base that tapers beneath the visible ground level into a rounded point that seats into a socket in the top of the Vale's Great Furnace.

The Heartstone's lower point flares off the excess energy below the surface of the Vale, into the bed of the ceramic-lined beehive-shaped magic-grounding Great Furnace, which is ringed by six to eighteen lesser furnaces. Each of them has check systems both magical and physical (using series of diagonal sliding stones) to handle the shock pressures and temperatures caused by these flares. Every furnace has a system of ceramic-lined tunnels that circulate water (often heated to live steam by the check systems). These provide steady heat throughout the Vale and tunnel systems as well as sterile, fresh drinking water, and they also supply the bathing pools. Several of the furnaces are used to turn sewage to sterile ash, which is then sluiced down through the lowest level of the Vale and out into the valley. Others are used for domestic functions such as garbage removal and cooking, and at least one is always used for body disposal. The Great Furnace always has at least two heavy, adjustable accesses that are used to aid smelting, glasswork, and blacksmithing, with up to six in the largest Vales.

The smithing vents and lesser furnaces are used as inspection accessways when the Heartstone is periodically put into a resting mode, generally at the height of summer. The Great Furnace slowly cools, and Adepts, architects and hertasi go inside every furnace in turn to check and repair any structural problems, replace any damaged slider valves, and seal water tunnel cracks. This is also a time for surface-level celebrations, feasting, and rest.

You can picture a functioning Vale in its simplest form as making order out of a badly jumbled vector field (and it can be seen more complexly as a tensor field, with the control and tuning rods, stones and spells acting upon magical-string factors of stress, strain and elasticity). The area of that vector field increases, over the years, as the Adepts "reach out" farther from their Vale, until ultimately the vectors within the Vale's reach are judged adequately aligned---and the wild magic has been calmed. Time to move on. Fight monsters, survive, scout. Build another Vale. That's how it was for centuries.

The thing is, now the Hawkbrothers don't have to. They have whole new problems, though.

The Mage Storms of around 1,100 years later were ripple effects of the Cataclysm disjunction literally traveling around the planet and returning to their points of origin. The Mage Storms were not "echoed through time," as some have said. It simply took that long for the waves to travel that distance, and by then they had changed from being disjunction disruptions into more like a "strain" or "sieve" effect. You already know the story of how the Mage Storms were handled and some of the aftereffects. The Storms left "available" magic in a much different state than before. For example, gryphons, whose wingbeats filter ambient magic to be absorbed and processed by their bone linings to produce the lift for their heavy bodies to fly, now have an easier time than ever achieving flight since the ambient magic was now more evenly spread out and "particulate." Just the same, it created a "fog effect" for anything long-distance, returning magework to a very personal level rather than world-ranging. This really annoyed a lot of people who depended heavily upon long-distance spell effects, most notably the Eastern Empire, and they were already pretty cranky.

It is vital to remember that unlike many religions of Velgarth that have religious faith, the Tayledras and hertasi have absolutely zero doubt—not just that there is a goddess, but that this goddess takes an active interest in them on a personal level. There is no more crisis of faith in Tayledras life that a deity is involved in what you do than there is a crisis that water is wet or that fire is hot. Every Tayledras has a personal encounter with an aspect or representative of the goddess no less than once in their lives, and usually, much more often than that.

Tayledras have stupendously difficult lives in some regards, and while they train and strive to fend for themgelves, sometimes it just isn't enough. Spirits of ancestors and fellow Tayledras work in the goddess' service. These spirits—souls detached from physical bodies, incarnated into spirit beings—are each assigned to multiple Tayledras to watch over and help them through things they can not handle on their own. However, a direct intervention takes a lot out of them, so they'll usually depend upon affecting something small in the physical world. If a Hawkbrother is drowning in a river, they'll nudge over a weakened branch to clamber onto, rather than teleport the person to dry land. It's also important to remember that while these guardians have otherworldly insights, they are not omniscient and ideal, and they can screw up.

To be utterly blunt, at present the Goddess Kal'enel concentrates most of her attention on the Shin'a'in because the Tayledras have their magic thing way more together than their Plains brethren, and they don't usually need her help. In fact, by the time of the Storms, thanks to sixty-some extant Heartstone Vales and near-thousand Adepts, the Tayledras have collectively become the equal in power of any of the Velgarthian deities, though (fortunately?) they don't realize it.

So, after almost a millenium of continuous hard work to bring order to the wild magic of the Pelagirs, do the Hawkbrothers feel as if their efforts were wasted now that the Storms came along and scraped away what they did to tame it all? Not at all, because they know that they pretty much saved everybody. If the Tayledras had not actively pulled the wild magic into order, the dangers of the Pelagirs would have overrun the whole of the known world.

The Hawkbrothers feel kind of satisfied knowing that. The goddess is pleased.

About the Authors

Nancy Asire is the author of four novels, *Twilight's Kingdoms, Tears of Time, To Fall Like Stars,* and *Wizard Spawn. Wizard Spawn* was edited by C.J. Cherryh and became part of the *Sword of Knowledge* series. She also has written short stories for the series anthologies *Heroes in Hell* and *Merovingen Nights;* a short story for Mercedes Lackey's *Flights of Fantasy;* as well as tales for the Valdemar anthologies *Sun in Glory* and *Crossroads.* She has lived in Africa and traveled the world but now resides in Missouri with her cats and two vintage Corvairs.

Jennifer Brozek is an award winning editor and author. Winner of the 2009 Australian Shadows Award for edited publications, she has edited five anthologies, with more on the way. Author of *In a Gilded Light* and *The Little Finance Book That Could*, she has more than thirty-five published short stories and is an assistant editor for the Apex Book Company. Jennifer is also a freelance author for many RPG companies, including Margaret Weis Productions, Savage Mojo, Rogue Games, and Catalyst Game Labs. Winner of the 2010 Origins Award for Best Roleplaying Game Supplement, her contributions to RPG sourcebooks include *Dragonlance*, *Colonial Gothic*, *Shadowrun*, *Serenity*, *Savage*

Worlds, and *White Wolf SAS*. When she is not writing her heart out, she is gallivanting around the Pacific Northwest in its wonderfully mercurial weather. She is an active member of SFWA and HWA.

Brenda Cooper has published over thirty short stories in various magazines and anthologies. Her books include *The Silver Ship and the Sea* and *Reading the Wind*. She is a technology professional, a futurist, and a writer living in the Pacific Northwest with three dogs and two other humans. She blogs and tweets and all that stuff—stop by www.brenda-cooper.com and visit.

Larry Dixon is the husband of Mercedes Lackey, and a successful artist as well as science fiction writer. He and Mercedes live in Oklahoma.

Rosemary Edghill has been a frequent contributor to the Valdemar anthologies since selling her first novel in 1987, writing everything from Regency romances to SF to Alternate History to mysteries. Between writing gigs, she's held the usual selection of weird writer jobs, and can truthfully state that she once killed vampires for money. She has collaborated with Marion Zimmer Bradley (*Shadow's Gate*), Andre Norton (*Carolus Rex*), and Mercedes Lackey ("Bedlam's Bard" and the forthcoming *Shadow Grail*). In the opinion of her dogs, she spends far too much time on Wikipedia. Her virtual home can be reached from http://www.sff.net/people/eluki/ Her last name—despite the efforts of editors, reviewers, publishing houses, her webmaster, and occasionally her own fingers—is not spelled "Edgehill."

Sarah A. Hoyt was born in Portugal and lives in Colorado. In between lie a variety of jobs ranging from dishwasher to multilingual translator. Currently she lives in Colorado with her husband, two teen sons, and a small but fierce clowder of rescue cats. She writes and publishes science fiction, fantasy, historical, mystery, and romance novels under Sarah A. Hoyt, Sarah D'Almeida and Elise Hyatt.

Tanya Huff lives and writes in rural Ontario, Canada, with her spouse, Fiona Patton, nine cats, and two dogs. She served in the Naval Reserve, has a slightly used degree in Radio and Television Arts, and has now been a full time writer for nineteen years. Her most recent books include *The Truth of Valor* and *The Wild Ways*. When she isn't writing, she practices the guitar and complains about the weather.

Denise McCune has been writing since she was eleven—which was (coincidentally?) right around the time she fell in love with Valdemar. She has worked in the social networking industry for nearly a decade, and not having enough to do writing novels and short stories (her first short story sale was to Jim Baen's Universe), she decided to launch Dreamwidth, an Open Source social networking, content management, and personal publishing platform. Denise lives in Baltimore, Maryland, where her hobbies include knitting, writing, and staying up too late writing code.

Ben Ohlander is a SFWA member and has coauthored novels with David Drake and Bill Forstchen. His first publication was a 1995 short story in the anthology *Tapestries*. He has returned to the short story format to explore aspects of conflict. He is a career Army officer with service in Afghanistan and Iraq and has worked as an analyst, software developer, and technical writer. He is married and lives in Ohio with three stepsons, one daughter, two cats, and a varying number of amphibians.

Fiona Patton lives in rural Ontario with her spouse, Tanya Huff, and a pile of furry creatures. She has written seven novels for DAW, the latest being *The Shining City*, the third and final book in the Warriors of Estavia series. She has written over thirty short stories for DAW/Tekno Books anthologies. "The Watchman's Ball" is her sixth story set in Mercedes Lackey's world of Valdemar, the fourth featuring the Dann family of Haven.

Kate Paulk masquerades as a mild-mannered software quality analyst during the day and spends most of what she sardonically describes as her "abundant spare time" writing. She is a regular contributor to the Valdemar anthologies, and her first novel, *Impaler*, is available in electronic and print form. She lives in semirural Pennsylvania with her husband, two demanding cats, and a very demanding imagination.

After having been a production coordinator, proofreader, loan document researcher, and bookseller, **Dan Shull** is currently working full-tilt toward a degree in Communications, since all the cool jobs he is interested in look for that sort of thing. He was born, raised, and still lives in California, though he wouldn't mind a change of scenery now and again—especially during the summers. He has been known to engage in the hobbies of reading, role-playing games, and vigorous, meandering discussions on everything from history to physics. While this is his first published work, he has been writing off and on since his parents gave him that electric typewriter back when he was ten.

Kristin Schwengel's work has appeared in several of the previous Valdemar anthologies, among others. She and her husband live near Milwaukee, Wisconsin, with a gray-and-brown tabby cat named (what else?) Gandalf. Her work as a massage therapist leaves her just enough time to divide between writing and other pastimes.

Stephanie Shaver lives in Southern California, where she works in the games industry and enjoys soaking up the sunshine. When she isn't working or writing, she's probably cooking, camping, or herding cats. You can find her online at www.sdshaver.com.

Elizabeth A. Vaughan writes fantasy romance. Her first novel, *Warprize*, was rereleased in April 2011. The Chronicles of the Warlands continues in *WarCry*, released in May 2011. You can learn more about her books at www.eavwrites.com. At the present, she is owned by three incredibly spoiled cats and lives in the Northwest Territory, on the outskirts of the Black Swamp, along Mad Anthony's Trail on the banks of the Maumee River.

Elisabeth Waters sold her first short story in 1980 to Marion Zimmer Bradley for *The Keeper's Price*, the first of the Darkover anthologies. She then went on to sell short stories to a variety of anthologies. Her first novel, a fantasy called *Changing Fate*, was awarded the 1989 Gryphon Award. She is now finishing a sequel to it, in addition to her short story writing. She also edits the anthology series *Sword and Sorceress*. In addition to her writing, she has worked as a supernumerary with the San Francisco Opera, where she appeared in *La Gioconda, Manon Lescaut, Madama Butterfly, Khovanschina, Das Rheingold, Werther*, and *Idomeneo*.

Michael Z. Williamson and **Gail Sanders** are both veterans, though Mike is now retired from the military. For twenty years, they've run their own businesses selling historical weapons and armor, photography, and occasional prop, armorer, and consulting services for movies and TV. They work so well together that only one of them drafted this bio. You'll have to guess which one. They can be found online at SharpPointyThings.com and www.MichaelZWilliamson.com

About the Editor

Mercedes Lackey is a full-time writer and has published numerous novels and works of short fiction, including the bestselling *Heralds of Valdemar* series. She is also a professional lyricist and a licensed wild bird rehabilitator. She lives in Oklahoma with her husband and collaborator, artist Larry Dixon, and their flock of parrots.